ONE WRONG STEP

"Griffin's characters are well developed, the narrative complex, and the dialogue skillfully written in this suspenseful romance." —*Romantic Times*

"*One Wrong Step* starts with a bang and never let's up on the pace. Laura Griffin is an exceptionally talented author who has a knack for keeping her readers on the edge of their seats. The twists and turns of the story leave the LeMans racetrack in the dust." —*The Winter Haven* (FL) *News Chief*

"Enjoyable, fast-paced romantic suspense."
—Publishers Weekly Online

ONE LAST BREATH

"Laura Griffin hits all the right notes—compelling characters, unexpected twists, and a gripping story from the first gasp to the last sigh."
—Bestselling romantic suspense author Roxanne St. Claire

"Heart-stopping intrigue and red-hot love scenes. . . . *One Last Breath* rocks!" —*The Winter Haven* (FL) *News Chief*

"An action-packed tale filled with passion and revenge."
—*Romantic Times*

"Griffin's fully fleshed characters, dry humor and tight plotting make a fun read." —*Publishers Weekly*

"This tasty debut mixes suspense and snappy humor with wonderful results." —*Affaire de Coeur*

Also by Laura Griffin

LAURA GRIFFIN

Unforgivable

POCKET BOOKS
NEW YORK LONDON TORONTO SYDNEY

Pocket Books
A Division of Simon & Schuster, Inc.
1230 Avenue of the Americas
New York, NY 10020

This book is a work of fiction. Names, characters, places, and incidents either are products of the author's imagination or are used fictitiously. Any resemblance to actual events or locales or persons, living or dead, is entirely coincidental.

First Pocket Books paperback edition December 2010

POCKET BOOKS and colophon are registered trademarks of Simon & Schuster, Inc.

For information about special discounts for bulk purchases, please contact Simon & Schuster Special Sales at 1-866-506-1949 or business@simonandschuster.com.

The Simon & Schuster Speakers Bureau can bring authors to your live event. For more information or to book an event contact the Simon & Schuster Speakers Bureau at 1-866-248-3049 or visit our website at www.simonspeakers.com.

Cover design by Jae Song
Cover photo © Jeremy Woodhouse

Manufactured in the United States of America

10 9 8 7 6 5 4 3 2 1

ISBN 978-1-4391-5296-6
ISBN 978-1-4391-6324-5 (ebook)

To Abby

WHISPER OF WARNING

2010 RITA Award Winner for
Best Romantic Suspense

"A perfectly woven and tense mystery with a sweet and compelling love story." —*Romantic Times*

"Filled with intrigue, murder and toe-curling passion . . . irresistible characters and a plot thick with danger . . . a sexy and suspenseful read. . . ." —Romance Junkies

"A read you can't put down. Will and Courtney have set off electric sparks that sizzle and burn throughout this tingling love story. . . ."

—Suzanne Coleburn, The Belles & Beaux of Romance

"Action, danger, and passion . . . a compellingly gripping story."

—SingleTitles

"An exciting police procedural starring a wonderful cop and an intriguing 'femme fatale.' . . ." —Genre Go Round Reviews

THREAD OF FEAR

"Suspense and romance—right down to the last page. What more could you ask for?" —Publishers Weekly Online

"Catapults you from bone-chilling to heartwarming to too hot to handle. Laura Griffin's talent is fresh and daring."
—*The Winter Haven* (FL) *News Chief*

"A tantalizing suspense-filled thriller. Enjoy, but lock your doors." —Romance Reviews Today

ACKNOWLEDGMENTS

Thank you to the many dedicated law enforcement professionals and forensic experts who shared their knowledge with me as I wrote this book, including Manuel Reyes, Ron Peterman, D. P. Lyle, Greg Moffatt, and Kyra Stull. Any mistakes here are entirely mine.

My appreciation also goes out to the hard-working team at Pocket Books, especially Ayelet Gruenspecht, Renee Huff, and Danielle Poiesz. Also, a heartfelt thanks to my agent, Kevan Lyon, and my ever-amazing editor, Abby Zidle.

Unforgivable

CHAPTER 1

⟿

Mia Voss needed a fix. Badly.

On a normal day, she would have stood strong against the temptation. But nothing about today had been normal, starting with the fact that it was January seventh and ending with the fact that for the first time in her life she'd actually been demoted.

Her stomach clenched as she turned into the Minute-Mart parking lot and eased her white Jeep Wrangler into a space near the door. Her cheeks warmed at the still-fresh memory of standing stiffly in her boss's office, gazing down at his weasel face as he sat behind his desk, meting out criticism. At the time, she'd been stunned speechless, too shocked to defend herself. Only now—six hours too late—did all of the perfect rejoinders come tumbling into her head.

Mia jerked open the door to the convenience store and made a beeline for the freezer section. If ever a night called for Ben & Jerry's, it was tonight. For the first Thursday night in months, she wasn't stuck at the lab. For the first Thursday night in years, the only items demanding her attention were a sappy chick flick, a cozy blanket, and a pint of butterfat. Tonight was for wallowing. Mia slid open the freezer door and plucked out a tub of Super Fudge Chunk. She tucked it under her arm, then grabbed a pint of Chunky Monkey as well. As long as she was sinning, why not sin big? That motto had gotten her into trouble on more than one occasion, but she continued to follow it.

"Doc Voss."

She jumped and whirled around.

A bulky, balding man in a brown overcoat stood behind her. He crouched down to pick up the carton that had rolled across the aisle, then stood and held it out to her. "Good stuff, isn't it?"

"Uh, yeah. Thanks." She stared at him and tried to place him. He was a cop, she knew that much. But he wasn't someone she'd seen recently, and she couldn't pull a name from her memory banks.

"Not as good as mint chip, though." His droll smile made him look grandfatherly. "My wife's favorite."

She noticed his shopping basket—two pints of mint chocolate chip and a six-pack of beer.

His gaze drifted down to her fur-lined moccasins and a bushy gray eyebrow lifted. "Slumber party?"

For her quick trip to the store, Mia had tucked her satin nightshirt into jeans, pulled on a ratty cardigan, and slipped her feet into house shoes. She looked like an escapee from a mental ward, which, of course, meant that she'd bump into a cop she knew. Nothing like reinforcing that professional image. Yes, it was shaping up to be a banner career day.

Mia forced a smile. "More like movie night." She glanced at her watch and stepped toward the register. "It's about to start, actually. I'd better—"

"Don't let me keep you." He nodded. "See ya around, Doc."

Mia watched his reflection in the convex mirror as she paid for her groceries. He added a couple of frozen dinners to his basket and headed for the chips aisle.

The name hit her as she pulled out of the parking lot. Frank Hannigan. San Marcos PD. Why couldn't she have remembered it sooner?

Something hard jabbed into her neck.

"Take a left at this light."

Mia's head whipped around. Her chest convulsed. In the backseat was a man. He held a gun pointed right at her nose.

"Watch the *road*!"

She jerked her head around just in time to see the telephone pole looming in front of her. She yanked the wheel left and managed to stay on the street.

Oh my God, oh my God, oh my God. Her hands clutched the steering wheel in a death grip. Her gaze flashed to the mirror and homed in on his gun. It was big and serious-looking, and he held it rock-steady in his gloved hand.

"Turn left."

The command snapped her attention away from the weapon and back to him. Her brain numbly registered a description. Black hooded sweatshirt pulled tight around his face. Navy bandanna covering his nose and mouth. Dark sunglasses. All she could see of the man behind the disguise was a thin strip of skin between the glasses and the bandanna.

He jammed the muzzle of the pistol into her neck again. "Eyes ahead."

She forced herself to comply. Her heart pounded

wildly against her sternum. Her stomach tightened. She realized she'd stopped breathing. She focused on drawing air into her lungs and unclenched her hand from the wheel so that she could shift gears and turn left.

Where are we going? What does he want?

Her mind flooded with terrifying possibilities as she hung a left and darted her gaze around, looking for a police car, a fire truck, anything. But this was a college town, and whatever action might be going on tonight was happening much closer to campus.

How was she going to get out of this? Cold sweat beaded along her hairline. Bile rose in the back of her throat.

The engine reached a high-pitched whine. She'd forgotten to change gears. Her clammy hand slipped on the gearshift as she switched into third.

Think. She glanced around desperately, but the streets were quiet. The nearest open business was the Dairy Queen two blocks behind them.

"CenTex Bank, on your right. Pull up to the drive-through."

Mia's breath whooshed out. He wanted money. Tears of relief filled her eyes. But they quickly morphed into tears of panic when she realized that his wanting money didn't really mean anything. He could still shoot her in the head and leave her on the side of the road. She, of all people, knew the amazingly cheap price of a human life. A wad of cash. A bag of crack. A pair of sneakers.

She could be dead before the ATM even spat out the bills.

The cold, hard muzzle of the gun rubbed against her cheek. Her breath hitched, and her gaze went to the mirror. She remembered the police sketch of the Una-bomber, a man in a hooded sweatshirt and sunglasses who spent years on the FBI's Ten Most Wanted list. Mia once met the artist who had drawn that sketch. As a forensic scientist at one of the world's top crime labs, Mia had connections in every conceivable area of law enforcement—but at this moment, they were useless to her. At this moment, it was just her and this man, alone in her car, a gun pointed at her head.

Stay calm. Make a plan.

She maneuvered the Jeep up to the teller machine, nearly scraping the yellow concrete pillar on the left side of her car. Too late, she realized she'd just ruined a potential escape route.

She closed her eyes and swallowed. She thought of her mom. Whatever happened, Mia had to live through this. Her mother couldn't take another blow.

Not on January seventh.

She turned to face him with a renewed sense of determination—or maybe it was adrenaline—surging through her veins. "How much do you want?" She rolled the window down with one hand while scrounging through her purse for her wallet.

"Five thousand."

"Five *thousand*?" She turned to stare at him. She had that much, yeah. In an IRA account somewhere. Her checking account was more in the neighborhood of five hundred. But she wanted more than anything *not* to tick this guy off.

She gulped. "I think my limit is three hundred." She tried to keep her voice steady, but it was wobbling all over the place. She turned to look at him, positioning her shoulders so the camera on the ATM could get a view into her car. It probably couldn't capture him from this angle, but it might capture the gun. "I can do several transactions," she said.

The barrel rapped against her cheekbone. She would have a bruise tomorrow. If she lived that long.

She turned to the machine and, with shaking fingers, punched in her code and keyed in the amount. Three hundred was the most she could get. Could she get it twice? Had her cable bill cleared? Mia handed him the first batch of twenties and chewed her lip as she waited for the second transaction to go through.

Transaction declined.

Her blood turned to ice. Seconds ticked by as she waited for the man's response. Despite the sweat trickling down her spine, her breath formed a frosty cloud as she stared at the words flashing on the screen.

That's it, she thought. *I'm dead.*

She reached a trembling hand out and pulled the receipt from the slot.

She could make a break for it right here. Except that her doors were pinned shut by the concrete pillars on either side of her.

She could speed to the nearest well-populated area, which was a Walmart three blocks away. Could she get there before he shot her or wrestled the wheel away?

"Back on the highway." The command was laced with annoyance but not quite as much disappointment as she'd expected.

She put the Jeep in gear and returned to the highway. As she shifted, she glanced at the familiar Mardi Gras beads hanging from her rearview mirror. Somehow they steadied her. This was her car, and she was in the driver's seat. She could control this.

"How about Sun Bank?" Her voice sounded like a croak. That bank was past Walmart. Maybe she could swerve into the lot and make a run for it.

"Hang a left."

Mia's hands gripped the steering wheel. Her gaze met his in the mirror. She couldn't see his eyes, but she could read his intent—it was in his tone of voice, his body language, the perfectly steady way he held that gun.

Left on the highway meant out of town. He was going to kill her.

CHAPTER 2

∽

With every stop sign and mailbox she passed, Mia's panic swelled. Farther and farther out of town. Fewer and fewer chances to escape. But how? What could she do? Her slimy palms gripped the steering wheel as her brain groped for a plan. Her friend Alex would have had a gun in her purse. Elaina would disable the guy with a few martial arts moves. But Mia didn't own a gun—much less carry one—and she couldn't fight her way out of a paper bag.

"Right at the juncture."

Panic tightened her throat as she neared the sign. Old Mill Road. Nothing was out there but an abandoned cotton mill.

Headlights winked into the rearview mirror. She felt her breath coming in shallow gasps now. Her pulse roared in her ears. She was running out of time. She eased her foot off the gas, and the road sloped down as she neared a low-water bridge. Her gaze flicked to the mirror.

Come on, come on.

"Speed it up." The muzzle jabbed her neck again.

One Mississippi, two Mississippi—

"Faster!"

Mia jerked the wheel right, then left, causing the Jeep to skid. She slammed on the brakes, and the vehicle rabbited to a halt. She hunched low in her seat and fumbled with the door latch.

The gunshot was a thunderclap inches from her head. The sound reverberated around her as she flung the door open and landed face-first on the pavement. Her gaze snapped up as a pair of headlights blinded her.

She struggled to her feet and dashed off the road. She glanced back and saw her assailant heave himself out of the car. His glasses had fallen off, and his face was an angry scowl.

Mia turned and fled. The ground disappeared beneath her, and suddenly she was on her knees, icy water surrounding her feet and calves. She was in a ditch. She scrambled for higher ground, out of the frigid water, hunching low and trying to stay out of sight. She cast a frantic look over her shoulder as the car following them squealed to a halt. Its headlights lit up the Jeep sitting diagonally in the road.

A black silhouette moved into her view. He was coming after her! Terror spurred her. She ducked and ran deeper into the bushes.

"You there!" a voice shouted. "Freeze!"

It was the man who'd stopped to help. She didn't turn. He was yelling at her attacker.

"Drop your—"

Pop!

Then a deafening silence.

Nausea gripped her, but she kept running. Something stabbed her thigh. She tried to swat it away, then realized it was barbed wire. Near panic, she dropped to the ground and dragged herself under the fence. Her sweater snagged. The bushes rustled behind her. God, could he *see* her? Heart pounding furiously now, she jerked her arms free of the sweater and stumbled to her feet.

Pop!

Something stung her arm just above the elbow. *I'm hit!* She plowed forward through the brush, and a single thought took over: *I will* not *die tonight. Not, not, not!* She swiped the branches away and willed her rubbery legs to move faster. The ground grew steeper, harder to climb. She tripped and pressed forward until her thighs burned and her throat felt raw from the cold air.

And then in the distance, a siren. She stopped to listen. She held her breath. She crouched low and peered through the foliage at the two cars on the highway, both with headlights blazing and doors flung open. The siren grew louder.

Where was the shooter?

The Jeep's headlights went black, and she had her answer. She heard the door slam, and the engine growled to life again. Mia rose to her feet and watched, mouth agape, as her Jeep lurched forward, made a U-turn, and then—still without headlights—shot down the highway and disappeared into the night.

Mia had blood on her hands. She laced her fingers together and squeezed, trying to stop the tremors.

"You should get this stitched up."

She glanced at the paramedic beside her who was cleaning her wound. The woman had short brown hair and a no-nonsense attitude that reminded Mia of her sister.

"I have a feeling I'm going to be here a while," Mia said as yet another plainclothes detective walked up to talk to her. Detective Macon. First name Jonah, like the whale story, which was easy to remember because he was a muscle-bound giant of a man. He'd already filled half a notebook with the information she'd given him, but it looked as if he needed more.

"Ma'am." He nodded at her. "Just a few more things."

Mia took a deep breath and braced herself.

"About the Minute-Mart." He flipped through the pages of his book. "You say you arrived about nine fifty-five?"

"More or less."

"And you were there buying groceries?"

"Ice cream," she said. "I was on my way home to watch a movie."

"And Frank Hannigan entered the store as you were leaving?"

Mia's gaze darted to the knot of cops and crime-scene techs standing beside Frank's body. Her throat constricted.

Don't let me keep you. See ya around, Doc.

The guilt was like a noose around her neck. What if she'd stayed to chat for just a few minutes longer? Would it have changed anything? Would Frank Hannigan be home with his wife right now instead of sprawled across the asphalt with a hole in his chest?

"Ma'am?"

She looked at the detective. "He was there already. He must have left right after I did." She clamped her lips together to keep her teeth from chattering. She wore only the nightshirt, jeans, and wet moccasins; her sweater was tangled in a barbed-wire fence somewhere.

"Okay, but you didn't see Hannigan again until you were moving west on the highway, is that correct?"

Mia looked down at her hands. So much blood. She'd tried to stanch the flow as she'd knelt beside him in the road, desperately pressing her hands against his wound. But there had been so much of it—seeping through his shirt, his coat, oozing warm and sticky between her fingers. And that gurgling sound—

"Ma'am?"

"What?"

"You didn't see him while you were at the bank?"

"No." A fresh wave of fear washed over her as she remembered the ATM, the gun at her cheek. "Maybe he saw me on the highway when I entered or left the bank. I was, um, driving kind of erratically. You said he called nine-one-one?"

"The call came in at ten-sixteen. He told the dispatcher he'd seen you at the bank and believed you were being held at gunpoint."

Mia clenched her hands together again. Her stomach clenched, too.

"Okay, and then when the car stopped and Hannigan jumped out, you say he exchanged words with your assailant?"

"It wasn't an exchange, really. He said, 'You there!' like he was trying to get his attention, stop him from what he was doing."

Stop him from killing me.

She looked at her hands again and felt as if she was going to vomit.

"Uh-oh. Head between the knees." The paramedic pushed her head down, and Mia found herself staring at a crack in the pavement as she waited for the nausea to pass. More footsteps approached.

"How's she doing?"

Mia closed her eyes at the sound of the familiar voice. Ric Santos. She'd known he would get here eventually, but she'd hoped to be gone by then.

"We're about finished up," Macon reported.

A pair of worn Nikes and frayed jeans entered her field of vision. "Caramia?"

"What?"

He dropped into a crouch and put his hand on her knee. He'd never put his hand anywhere near her knee before, and under normal circumstances, she probably would have gone up in flames. Right now, it was all she could do not to throw up on his shoes.

"How's the arm?"

"Fine." She looked up at him. Which was a mistake. His brown-black eyes searched her face, and she could tell he knew she was lying. It hurt like a bitch. Worse than anything she'd ever experienced. And she should be grateful she wasn't lying in that road in the freezing sleet with a team of crime-scene techs surrounding her.

She sat up straight and brushed the hair from her eyes. Ric stood. Mia felt his gaze on her, even sharper than usual, as she turned to Macon. "Was there anything else? I'd really like to go home."

"This could use a few stitches," the paramedic said, applying the last in a series of butterfly bandages to the slash on her arm. "Otherwise, you're going to have a nasty scar. We can drop you off on our way back to the fire station."

Mia took a deep breath. The last place she wanted to be right now was some ER waiting room. Just the thought made her shudder. "It's fine."

The woman gave her a stern look as she put away her bandages and ointment.

"I'd make the trip," Ric said. "They'll probably give you some pain meds."

Mia flashed him a glance. She hadn't seen him in months, not since they'd worked a case together last summer. But it took only an instant for her to take in every detail about him—his lean, wide-shouldered build, his dark hair that was longer than she remembered and slightly mussed. He wore his scarred leather jacket and jeans, which told her he'd been off duty tonight. Had he been in bed when he'd gotten the call? Had he been with a woman?

She couldn't believe her thoughts had gone there, but Ric Santos had a reputation, and Mia couldn't help thinking of it every time she saw him.

"I'm fine. It's only a flesh wound." She turned to Macon. "Is that it, Detective?"

Macon's gaze went from Mia to Ric and back to Mia. "Just a few more things. We need a list of any property that was stolen with the Jeep."

"Property?"

"Credit cards, keys, cell phone," Macon said. "Anything he might use later."

Mia stared at him. A lethal criminal had not only her car but her keys, too. He could get into her house, use her credit cards. She felt sick again. A massive shiver moved through her.

"If your purse was in the car, he knows your address by now." Ric shrugged out of his jacket and held it out to her.

She eyed it warily. Was this a peace offering? His way of saying sorry for befriending her when he needed something, then dropping off the face of the earth after he'd gotten it? Ignoring his gaze, she took the jacket, slipped her arms into the warm sleeves, and turned to Macon.

"My house key is on my key chain," she said. "And then there's my purse, my wallet."

"You have someone you can call?" Ric asked. "Maybe a friend or relative you can stay with after you're done at the hospital?"

Mia looked at him.

"You need to get that arm checked out," he added, and those dark eyes dared her to challenge him.

But she knew what it took to challenge Ric, and she wasn't up for it right now. "I can call someone." She glanced at her watch. "It's getting late, but—"

"Do it," Ric said. "You can't go home tonight."

Jonah sat in the cramped back office of the Minute-Mart, trying to glean a man's identity from a blurry, poorly lit surveillance video. The good news was that an outdoor camera mounted on the southeast corner of the building had been trained on the parking lot when Mia Voss pulled up to the store. The bad news was that her assailant had entered the Jeep on the west side, thereby shielding himself—whether by luck or by intention—from the camera as he climbed into her vehicle. So despite the video footage, all they really knew at the moment was that they were looking for a white male, medium build, who might or might not be driving a stolen Jeep.

"I'm just getting a shadow," Ric said, rewinding the clip on the computer so that he could replay it for the umpteenth time.

Jonah wasn't sure what he expected to get from this, but arguing with Ric would be pointless. Ric was like a pit bull when he got focused on something, and his focus had been razor-sharp since the instant they'd rolled up to the crime scene.

Or, more specifically, since they'd rolled up to the crime scene and gotten a look at the victim sitting in the back of the ambulance.

"Something about this feels off," Ric said now.

Jonah downed another sip of tepid coffee. The manager had kept the cups full for the past two hours, but Jonah and Ric had been on a stakeout all day, and they were long past the point of caffeine helping anything.

Jonah shook off the fatigue and tried to concentrate. His partner had that intense look about him that trumped exhaustion.

"You mean because of the angle?"

"Because of the car. A two-door Jeep." Ric pressed play once again and watched the grainy image of a figure approaching the Jeep and—hidden from view—climbing in through the driver's-side door minutes before Mia exited the store. "Look at this parking lot. An Explorer, a Tahoe, even a Lexus. Every one of those vehicles has four doors, and every one of them is worth more than that Jeep."

"Maybe the drivers didn't leave them unlocked," Jonah said.

"At least two of them did. Watch the video. Hell, the Lexus guy actually left his keys inside when he ran in to buy cigarettes."

Jonah rubbed his eyes. "Maybe she pulled up and he liked what he saw, decided to go for it even if it meant the hassle of climbing into the backseat."

Ric's gaze bored into his. He didn't like this scenario, and Jonah could see why. One, it suggested that Mia was specifically targeted by the assailant. Two, it suggested that the guy hadn't planned just to drop her off with a friendly wave when he got her out to Old Mill Road.

The man had approached the Jeep from the southeast corner of the lot, which meant that he could have come from any of the businesses across from the Minute-Mart—the dry cleaner, the pet store, the doughnut shop. Not one of those places had a surveillance cam. And of course, he could have come from nowhere. Just some guy passing through town, looking for a soft target.

Ric raked his hand through his hair and leaned back in his plastic chair. "I hate this case, and it's barely three hours old."

Jonah hated it, too. Any case that involved a cop getting killed—even a retired cop—was fucking miserable. Some cops were superstitious about working such cases, as if somehow the victim's bad luck was going to rub off on them.

"Yo, you guys still here?"

Jonah craned his neck around, but the question didn't merit an answer. Vince Moore stood in the doorway. He was halfway through what was probably a day-old hot dog, and pickle relish had dribbled down his shirt.

"We found some brass at the crime scene," he said around a mouthful of food. "Two spent casings. One in the ditch, one on the shoulder. You want me to send them to Austin?"

"State lab's backed up," Ric said. "Send them to the Delphi Center."

Jonah looked at his partner. The Delphi Center was a private laboratory, which meant it was expensive. But Ric wasn't likely to get any push-back on a case like this, not with a former San Marcos police officer laid out in the morgue.

"Hey, doesn't that girl work at the Delphi Center?" The side of Moore's mouth curled up as he turned to Ric.

"Which girl?"

"From tonight. The one with the rack." Moore made a squeezing motion with his free hand.

"She's a DNA tracer," Ric said, turning his attention back to the video.

"What's the deal there? You doing her or what?"

Ric looked at him.

"I saw you two talking," Moore said. "The way she was looking at you, I figured you were—"

"I'm not." Ric tapped the mouse again and replayed the footage.

"So you lent her your jacket, but you're *not* doing her. Mind if I call her?"

"Knock yourself out."

A grin spread across Moore's face as he crumpled his hot-dog wrapper and tossed it at the trash can by Jonah's feet. He missed.

"Later, then."

When he was gone, Ric continued to stare at the computer screen, as if something new was going to happen.

"He'll do it, you know," Jonah said.

Ric looked up at him, and the muscle in the side of his jaw tightened. He glanced at the empty doorway. "How'd he know where she works, anyway?"

"Every cop in the department knows where she works," Jonah said. "She gave that seminar last year, remember? Touch DNA?"

Jonah didn't elaborate, but he could see the realization dawning. Dr. Voss had stepped up to the podium with her strawberry blonde ponytail and her crisp white lab coat, and by the end of her presentation, every man in the auditorium had undressed her with his eyes at least a dozen times.

Ric rubbed the bridge of his nose. "Shit. This is going to be a bitch of a case. I can feel it."

Jonah watched the video as Mia slid behind the wheel of her Jeep, unaware that she was about to see a cop get killed and be forced to run for her life.

"Yeah." Jonah sighed. "I can feel it, too."

Ric pulled up to the warmly lit bungalow and shook his head. He should have known. Leave it to Mia to take perfectly good instructions and throw them right out the window.

He double-checked the number as he walked up the concrete path. Four fifty-five Sugarberry Lane. The address sounded—and looked—like something out of a storybook. A giant oak tree dominated the yard. Neatly trimmed shrubs lined the sidewalk. The house itself was that quaint 1930s architecture that people with way too much time on their hands liked to restore. It had white siding, black shutters, and a wide front porch that at the moment was littered with piles of collapsed boxes.

Ric eyed the boxes as he rang the doorbell. Looked as if she'd just moved in. Or she could have moved months ago, for all he knew. He hadn't seen her since the summer. It had been four months since he'd given in to the urge to call her. Not that he'd missed her. He'd hardly given her a thought—except for a couple of times in the dead of night when he'd been driving home from work to an empty apartment.

He heard footsteps, and the light behind the peephole went dark as she peered out at him. The lock tumbled, and the door swung back.

"It's three-fifteen," she said, fisting a hand on her hip.

She'd changed from that silky pink thing into flannel pajama bottoms and a snug-fitting T-shirt. He forced himself not to stare.

"Just doing a drive-by. Your house is lit up like a stadium."

She stepped back to let him in, and he wiped his shoes on the welcome mat before stepping inside. She looked fresh from the shower and had her elbow wrapped in a clean white bandage.

"That coffee I smell?"

She tucked a damp curl behind her ear. "That depends. Is this an official visit, or are you here as my friend?"

Friend. He'd never really thought of her that way. "A little of both, I guess. How'd you get home from the hospital?"

"Sophie came to get me."

"And Sophie is . . . ?"

"You know her." She brushed past him and padded down the hall in her bare feet. Ric followed. "She works at the Delphi Center. You've seen her a thousand times."

"The receptionist," he said. "The one with the great—"

"Yes." She tossed him an annoyed look over her shoulder.

"I was going to say singing voice." He followed her into a kitchen lined with cardboard boxes. "I heard she moonlights as a nightclub singer in Austin."

Mia reached for a coffee mug, and her T-shirt rode up to reveal a strip of creamy skin.

"Sugar?"

"Black."

She poured a cup as he leaned back against her counter and crossed his arms. "I thought you were going to stay with someone until a locksmith could get here."

She passed him the coffee, then added some to her cup, which was sitting on a drop-leaf table beside a window that faced the driveway. She was stalling for time.

"I called one of those twenty-four-hour services."

"Bet that wasn't cheap."

She shrugged. "Sophie has a friend in town. I didn't want to intrude."

He watched her carefully. No boyfriend, then. Or even a friendly ex-boyfriend who would have offered her a spot on his couch. Ric could have let her crash at his place, but he didn't trust himself not to take advantage of her fragile mental state.

Although she didn't look fragile. He watched her over the rim of the coffee mug. She looked wide-awake, energized, and completely caught up in some kitchen chore that involved about a hundred little spice jars. The hostility he'd sensed from her earlier had dissipated, but years of experience with women told him it wasn't gone for good, just hiding.

"You're alphabetizing spices," he said.

"And?"

"And it's after three in the morning."

Sadness flickered across her face, and she glanced away. "I couldn't sleep."

Ric knew the feeling. Sometimes he'd come home from a crime scene completely beat and completely unable to shut it down for the night. Some scenes were like that.

A scene where he knew the victim was always like that.

"Is it your case?" she asked, and the empathy in her blue eyes made him uneasy.

"Yes."

"Were you the one to tell his wife?"

"His wife's dead."

Her eyebrows shot up. "Dead?"

"Passed away about a year ago. Cancer, I think."

Mia bit her lip, then turned around to face the sink.

He frowned at her across the kitchen as she turned on the faucet and stared at the water. "What is it?"

"Nothing, it's just—" She busied herself washing her hands. "I thought he was buying ice cream for her. I guess he was going home to an empty house. God, that's so lonely."

Interesting comment from a woman who lived alone.

She grabbed a dish towel off the counter to dab her eyes. "Sorry."

"It's okay." Ric watched her, knowing he should have waited until morning for this. She wasn't in shape to answer questions right now. But murder investigations didn't improve with age. He needed answers as soon as he could get them. He put his mug on the table, then pulled out a chair. "Sit down."

"Uh-oh." She took a deep breath and sat, and he could tell she was relieved by the distraction. "Interview time. Are you going to tape-record me?"

"I've got a pretty good memory."

He moved a wooden chair across from her and sat down. Their knees almost touched. He traced his finger over her thigh where blood had seeped through the flannel. "What's this?"

"It's nothing. I got tangled in some barbed wire when I was running."

"When was the last time you had a tetanus shot?"

She gave him a baleful look. "I work in a crime lab. I'm immunized against everything under the sun."

He leaned back in his chair and looked at her.

"So, did you have a question?" she asked. "Because I've got a serious case of the jitters, and those spices are really calling my name."

"Did the perpetrator ever ask for your PIN?"

She looked at him for a long moment. He could almost see her brain switching gears. "No."

"Do you think he saw you enter it when you were at the ATM?"

"I don't know. I keyed it in pretty fast. Why?"

"It's unusual, that's all. You'd think he'd want it for later."

"I was sort of low on cash." She cleared her throat. "My bank only let me get out three hundred, so maybe he figured I was broke."

"Are you?"

She laughed. "That's blunt."

"It's just background."

"Yes and no." She looked around. "I just spent every dime of my savings on this place, so I've got one big asset and very little cash. My grandmother would say I'm house-poor."

"It's a nice place. You just move in?"

"It's been about two months. I'm still getting organized."

Ric glanced around the half-unpacked kitchen again, seeing it in a new light. She'd added a few personal touches—the Sierra Club calendar tacked to the wall beside the fridge, the flat-screen TV, currently muted and tuned to CNN, mounted in the breakfast room. The flowered wallpaper and white lace curtains, though—definitely not Mia.

He was reminded of one of the many reasons he'd stopped calling her. This woman was nesting, big time, and Ric steered clear of women with that particular hobby.

He met her gaze. "We've been tracking your debit card for the past four hours. So far, nothing. Often after a robbery like this, the perp hits every machine in sight."

"You're assuming he has a PIN," Mia said. "And you're assuming he's stupid."

"Not stupid, necessarily, but desperate. Also, your

card has a credit-card logo on it. He could have stopped to try to buy something. Gas, beer, whatever. No hits there, either."

"I guess I should be grateful. All he wanted was my cash."

Ric watched her body language. The tension was back in her face and shoulders, and she held her arms crossed over her waist, as if talking about this made her nervous.

Or maybe it was sitting with him in her pajamas that made her nervous. Their gazes locked, and a spark of heat flashed between them. And he knew he'd nailed it. Every time he got near her, he felt this buzz of sexual awareness. He couldn't look at her without wondering what she'd be like in bed.

"You think that's all he wanted?" he asked, getting back to business. "Your three hundred dollars?"

A little furrow formed between her brows. "What, you don't?"

He could tell by her tone that she didn't believe it, either. What he needed to know was *why* she didn't believe it. What clue had she picked up on—something he might have missed—that told her there was more to this than a money grab?

She gulped and looked down at her lap. One of those corkscrew curls fell in front of her face. "I guess not. I mean, I know this sounds strange, but the money? It was almost as if it didn't matter to him. Five thousand, three hundred, he didn't really care, you know?" She rubbed the spot of blood on her pants. "And if that was all he wanted, why not just ditch me there in town and take my Jeep? Why make me drive all the way out to Old

Mill Road?" Her eyes met his, dark and somber now. "I don't think money was all he wanted. I think he wanted to kill me."

The words hung in the air as Ric watched her. He had a responsibility to two victims here: a murdered cop and a young woman who'd barely squeaked by with her life. It was time for him to shove aside his personal feelings and work the hell out of this case, because he intended to close it. Soon. Before Frank Hannigan was even cold in the ground.

He stood up. "Thanks for your cooperation. We'll be in touch."

She blinked up at him, as if not comprehending his brusque words. "That's it?"

"For now, yes. If your Jeep is recovered, we'll give you a call, obviously."

She stood up now, too, and he could almost feel the chill settling over her. "Fine. Let me get your jacket."

She walked past him into the hallway, and he followed. She veered into the bedroom wing. He waited by the front door and noticed the keypad mounted beside it. The security system looked new, and she hadn't gotten around to patching up the paint from when it had been installed.

She returned and handed him his jacket. "There might be some blood on the lining. My hands were messy when I put it on."

She looked tired standing there. And sad, too. He took the jacket from her, fully aware that he could have offered her something more tonight—comfort, at least—and that he'd disappointed her instead.

Get used to it, babe.

She glanced up, as if he'd said the words aloud. She pulled the door open and stood back.

"Set your alarm." He stepped into the cold night and glanced up and down her street before looking back at her. "And try to get some sleep."

CHAPTER 3 ·

Mia ignored the circling buzzards as Sophie pulled into the Delphi Center parking lot and found a space close to the entrance. They were early, which meant prime parking. It also meant that Mia was starting what promised to be an extraordinarily challenging day on little more than two hours of sleep.

"Looks like they've got a fresh specimen," Sophie said as they crossed the lot.

Mia didn't look. She didn't want to think about carrion birds or the fact that her workplace sat in the middle of a decomposition research center, better known as a body farm.

"You sure you're up for this?" Sophie gave her a concerned look as they hiked up the white marble stairs leading to the front lobby where Sophie had her desk.

"I couldn't stay home today. I'd go stir-crazy." Mia unbuttoned her wool coat as they passed through a pair of tall Doric columns.

"If you say so. Me? I'd call in sick and get some R and R, maybe watch a few talk shows, go get my toes done."

Mia shot her a look.

"You seem stressed. That's all I'm saying. And you should never underestimate the power of a good pedicure."

"Thanks, but I'd rather be here," Mia said.

Sophie pulled out her ID badge and swiped her way into the building. The security guard, Ralph, gave them a nod as they entered.

Mia unwound her scarf and took a moment just to stand. She loved the lobby at this time of day. The morning sun cast shimmering white beams through the glass and elongated her shadow on the pale marble floor. Everything was quiet, not many people around. Those who were spoke in hushed tones, as if in church. To many of them, this place *was* a church, a sacred cathedral dedicated to science and technology, where the guiding idea wasn't salvation but justice. Or salvation through justice, however you chose to look at it. Mia chose the latter, and she happened to know that some of her colleagues did, too. She didn't know about everyone, of course. Some people probably just came here to earn a paycheck.

Mia postponed a much-needed stop at the lobby coffee shop to swing into HR and have a word with the director of personnel. Then she purchased her sixteen ounces of caffeine and rode the elevator up to the sixth floor. The Delphi Center was an ivory tower, and DNA tracers worked at the top.

Mia strode down the glass hallway, flanked on either side by impressive views—the rolling Texas Hill Country on one side, one of the world's top DNA laboratories on the other. The short walk smoothed her nerves and made her feel right again. She could do this. She should be here. The Delphi Center had chosen her, and she had chosen it right back.

Inside her office, she slipped on her lab coat and felt instantly comforted. She booted up the laptop computer on her slate-topped worktable and reviewed the notes she'd been making yesterday afternoon when her boss had summoned her down the hall for an Important Discussion.

Case number 56–6229–12–16. Submitting officer Detective Jim Kubcek, Houston PD. The Delphi Center had been receiving a steady flow of evidence from Houston ever since its DNA lab had been shut down for grossly improper evidence handling. The scandal, uncovered by a TV reporter, had affected thousands of cases and resulted in a man being released from prison after serving years for a rape he didn't commit. Mia saw the scandal as a tragedy not only for the wrongly convicted man and the rape victim but also for the entire criminal justice system in Houston. Once a community's confidence in the system was shattered, it could take years or even decades to repair.

Mia focused her attention on the case before her. Case 56–6229–12–16 was a sexual homicide, ligature strangulation. And it had been lurking in the back of her mind during the wee hours of this morning as her restless brain played out all the might-have-been scenarios.

She picked up the phone and dialed Kubcek.

"I've run the fingernail clippings," she said, not bothering with pleasantries. Kubcek had left her daily voice mails for three weeks. The victim in this case was nineteen, and the detective had a district attorney breathing down his neck.

"Any hits?"

She heard the hope in his voice, that fervent wish that she'd called to deliver some glimmering bit of good news.

"Unfortunately, no. All of the skin cells we recovered belonged to the victim."

A pause. He didn't want to believe it. The killer had used a condom, and Kubcek had been counting on the nail clippings.

"What about the blood?"

"That was hers, too." Mia scrolled through her type-written notes, including those from the phone call she'd made to the evidence clerk downstairs. "You didn't send me the ligature, though. I was hoping to examine that extension cord."

Kubcek sighed heavily. "It's a dead end." Another pause as they both ignored his choice of words. He cleared his throat. "The security camera at her apartment shows him wearing gloves going in and going out. We examined the hell out of that cord for prints in case he took the gloves off to, I don't know, take a leak or something while he was in there with her. Came up with nothing."

"I'd still like to see it," Mia said. "Any chance you could have it shipped up, say, by tomorrow?"

"You got it already."

"I do?"

"One of you does. I sent it up to that ligature guy. Clover?"

"Don Clovis?"

"There you go. Clovis. Vic's mom helped her move into the apartment, doesn't recognize the cord. We're thinking the perp might have brought it with him, maybe had it stashed under his coat. Clovis is supposed to run it down for us, see if there's anything unusual about it."

Clovis, like so many experts at the Delphi Center, had access to a mind-boggling assortment of databases—cord, rope, fibers, tape, cigarettes, auto paint. The tracers could track down the origin of practically any forensic evidence imaginable.

"Mind if I call him and request a look?"

"Hell, I'll call him for you," Kubcek said. "You really think you might get something?"

Mia sensed someone behind her and swiveled on her stool. Her boss stood in the doorway.

"I won't know until I have a look. Ask Clovis to send it up here as soon as he's finished with it."

Harvey Snyder was the head DNA specialist at the Delphi Center. Fortunately, he preferred to leave the real work to his underlings, which meant he mostly stayed out of Mia's way. Less fortunately, he had a gold-plated résumé and some impressive connections in his field, which meant that he wouldn't be leaving his coveted post anytime soon.

"I presume you've been down to HR to inquire about your new badge." He said it as a statement, not a question, and she felt a spurt of annoyance.

Snyder stepped into her workroom and glanced around. He was one of those short, wiry guys who compensated for his size by puffing out his chest and flaunting his authority. Peering up from his desk yesterday, he'd reminded Mia of a weasel. But standing in front of her right now, he looked more like a meerkat.

"I stopped by on my way in," Mia said pleasantly.

"They said they'd have a new one ready for me by the end of the day."

She met and held his gaze. If he'd come up here to admonish her yet again for misplacing her ID badge, he was going to be disappointed. Given last night's events, she was well past the point of getting weepy-eyed over a reprimand from her boss.

"I understand you had quite an eventful evening." Now he sounded smug.

Mia sighed inwardly. She hadn't wanted anyone at work to ask about what happened, but of course, that was impossible. Her name had been kept out of the newspaper—a miracle she felt sure Ric Santos had played a part in—but law enforcement was a close-knit community that thrived on gossip. It was only a matter of time before everyone she worked with knew the identity of the unnamed "Delphi Center staffer" who was involved in yesterday's homicide.

"Are you sure it's wise for you to be here?" Snyder asked. "You're welcome to take a personal day if you're feeling less than a hundred percent. I'd hate for your work to suffer."

Yeah, right. He'd *love* for her work to suffer. It would give him an excuse to get rid of her. As it was, he had nothing on her, so he'd made an issue of her one slip-up in two years at the Delphi Center: misplacing her ID badge when she went to the gym this week. Snyder had used her "reckless disregard for security" as an excuse to take her down a peg.

"I'm perfectly fine," she said. "One hundred percent, absolutely." She replaced her eye shields, hoping he'd take the hint.

Instead, he leaned a hand on the counter. "By the way, you'll be getting a package up from Evidence soon. Three packages, actually, submitted by the San Marcos Police Department."

"Okay."

"It's a murder case. The DA called me Wednesday and specifically requested you for the analysis. I told her how backed up you've been"—as if the nationwide backlog of DNA testing was a result of Mia's ineptitude—"but she insisted. Female solidarity, I guess you would call it."

Mia gritted her teeth. He'd sat on this for two days, no doubt to show the district attorney that he wouldn't be pushed around. Forget about expediency. Forget that there were detectives somewhere waiting for these results and a victim's family to consider.

"I'll get on it right away," Mia said, hoping he'd pick up her meaning.

"Good." He nodded curtly. "See that you do."

Ric found her in the broom closet she called an office, a windowless room adjacent to the Delphi Center's enormous DNA lab. Mia claimed she liked to work there because it was dark and she often used alternative light sources, but Ric suspected that in reality she was something of a hermit.

She stood at one of her worktables, hair pulled back in a ponytail, eyes shields over her face. An overhead lamp shone down on the table as, with a latex-gloved hand, she manipulated an electrical cord. She braced her free hand against the table as she folded the cord over on itself and frowned down at it.

"Practicing your Girl Scout knots?"

She jumped back and clutched her hand to her chest. "God, don't *do* that."

"Sorry." He should have known she'd be jumpy today. "Just dropped by with your afternoon latte."

She pursed her lips and watched him. "Who let you up here?"

"Sophie." He set the coffee on her counter. "I told her I was stopping by to check on you, and she gave me a hall pass."

Her gaze dropped to the VIP visitor's badge clipped to Ric's dress shirt. He'd cleaned up finally and even managed to get a few hours of sleep. She looked as though she hadn't had a wink.

"You look tired," he said.

"Thanks a lot."

"What's that about?" He nodded at the table.

"Strangulation case. The killer wore gloves, but—" She bit her lip and rearranged the cord. "I'm thinking that if she struggled—which I assume she did, because she lost a fingernail—he would have had to hold her down." Mia mimicked the action with her free hand. "Which means that in order to tighten the ligature, he probably would have . . ." Her voice trailed off as she lifted one end of the cord and pretended to clamp it between her teeth. She stopped to examine it. "Aha, there it is. I knew it."

"What?" He stepped closer, but all he saw was a brown electrical cord. Could she see saliva on it?

"Bite marks. See?" She held the cord up, and he did— small indentions in the plastic, about three inches apart.

"You're going to get DNA off that thing?"

"That's the plan." She smiled slightly, and he could tell she was pleased with herself but didn't want to gloat. "I'll do it in a minute. After you tell me why you're really here."

Her smile faded, and he wondered what she was hoping to hear. They'd found her Jeep. They'd found her attacker. Less than twenty-four hours, and Ric had already made a collar. He wanted to tell her all of those things.

"Nothing new on your case," he said instead, and she turned away to tuck the cord back into a paper evidence bag.

He reached up and repositioned her overhead lamp so that it shone on her face. He tilted her chin up. On her right cheekbone was a faint purple bruise. "What's this?"

She didn't look him in the eye. "He tapped me with his gun."

Tapped her. Right. Goddamn it, how had he missed this? He'd seen her twice since then and hadn't noticed it at all.

"How's the arm?"

"Sore," she said. "I took some ibuprofen at lunch."

He dropped his hand and stepped back. He shoved his hands into his pockets to keep from touching her again.

"So, if there's nothing new to tell me, why the visit?"

Was it his imagination, or was there a subtext there? He hadn't dropped by her office since last summer. Evidently, she'd noticed.

"I'm here to, I quote, 'light a fire' under you guys," he said. "Rachel sent me."

Rachel was the Hays County DA in charge of prosecuting Ric's murder case. Two cases, actually. The first had been his originally. The second he'd inherited.

"I just found out this morning." She stripped off her gloves and eye shields and tossed them into a red bio-hazard bin. "Your case is next on my list."

She led him through a glass door with a double helix etched on the window. The main DNA lab was two stories high and half as long as a football field.

"They just sent up the evidence," she said over her shoulder.

He followed her past several heavy-duty fume hoods to the walk-in refrigerator, where evidence bags were lined up on a shelf. The entire opposite wall of shelves was filled with rape kits, thousands of them, all await-ing testing. Each kit fit into a box not much larger than a VHS tape, and it would take an army of Mias working around the clock for years to wade through them all. But she didn't seem daunted by the size of the job. Or if she was, she didn't show it.

She read several of the bag labels, then rattled off a case number.

"That's the one," he said. "We're thinking it's con-nected to another rape-homicide that came in last week."

She lifted three bags and took them to an empty table. Ric scanned the immaculate laboratory. Lining the walls were glass cabinets containing rows of beakers, test tubes, and other supplies he couldn't identify. On the opposite end of the room, several white-coated men peered into microscopes that probably cost more money than Ric took home in a year. The Delphi Center oper-ated on hefty fees and a private endowment, so it could afford the best of the best as far as staff and equipment.

Delphi was rumored to be every bit as good as the FBI lab at Quantico. Mia claimed it was better.

"Let's have a look." She spent a few minutes at the sink washing up, as if she was scrubbing in for surgery. Then she tore off a sheet of clean white paper from a roll at the end of the table and spread it out to create a work surface. Finally, she pulled on fresh gloves and eye shields before unsealing one of the evidence bags.

The first held the duct tape.

"Who did this?" she exclaimed, instantly zeroing in on the same problem Ric had when he'd first seen the evidence photos. Whoever had removed the binding from the victim's wrists had cut through the tape in three places.

"No idea. Could have been the crime-scene techs. Maybe the ME. Although I doubt it. He's pretty meticulous."

"You didn't attend the autopsy?" She continued to look surprised.

"Wasn't my case then. Burleson caught it. He did the crime scene, the autopsy. But then the chief tossed it over to me. Thinks it might be related to a motel murder on I-35. Woman in that case had her hands taped, too."

Mia shook her head. "Well, I hope you have pictures. This is a mess."

"We do," Ric said, but pictures weren't going to be enough if this thing went to trial. The sort of knots or bindings used by a perpetrator could reveal a lot, provided some idiot didn't recklessly saw them off the body and destroy the evidence. Photographs were okay, but they weren't as effective in court as the real thing, which was why Ric had given Burleson a ration of shit over this.

As the lead investigator, he should have kept an eye on the crime-scene techs and even the ME every step of the way to make sure the evidence stayed intact.

Mia was turning the chunks of tape over slowly with a pair of tweezers. "I should be able to get some skin cells off the adhesive side if the perp wasn't wearing gloves. But even if he was, he might have torn the tape with his teeth and deposited saliva." After a few moments, she replaced the tape in the evidence bag. "What else did you have?"

"I haven't seen the rest of it. Her shoes, I think. And her dress. I understand there was a lot of blood."

Mia resealed the bag and replaced it in the refrigerator before shifting her attention to the second bag. A new sheet of paper came out, new gloves. Mia unsealed the bag and, to Ric's surprise, pulled out a big white envelope. It was one of those waterproof bubble-wrap mailers.

Her gaze flashed to his. "Who packed this?" she asked, opening it.

"Not me."

"*Why* was this packed in plastic? It degrades biological evidence." She pulled out a royal-blue garment that was stiff with dried blood. Shaking her head, she unfolded it and spread it out on the table.

The dress was short, low-cut. The upper half was saturated with blackened bloodstains.

Mia's breath hissed out. She reached a tentative finger out and traced one of the many gashes in the fabric.

"My God," she whispered. "He must have stabbed her a hundred times."

• • •

El Patio was loud and crowded when the man's phone started vibrating on the bar. He checked the number and bit back a curse as he picked up.

The caller didn't say anything. The man waited.

Finally, a shaky sigh. "Lake View Park," the caller said. "South lot."

Unbelievable. He tossed some money onto the bar and went outside into the bitter cold.

"Are you fucking kidding me?" he demanded. "What the hell's wrong with you?"

"Come soon. This one's . . ." A nervous laugh, almost hysterical. "God, I can't believe this. Just get here, okay?"

The man stepped away from the cluster of smokers hanging out near the door. The place was packed tonight. Vehicles streamed in and out of the parking lot.

"This is the last time," he said, scanning the rows for his Buick. "I mean it. You still got that account number?"

"Just get here! We'll work that out later."

"We'll work it out now. Do you have it or not?"

"Yes."

He crossed the lot to his car and yanked open the door. "I want double this time. This is getting messy."

Shit, messy? It was a train wreck. But he was in it now, and there was no going back. The best he could hope for was to minimize the damage and get paid.

He tossed his coat inside and slid behind the wheel as the caller wrestled with the decision. There was nothing to decide. This guy was an addict—completely and totally at the mercy of his habit.

And so he went for the jugular. "Tick-tock," he said.

"All right! Come on! This is—" The caller's voice

broke, and he started weeping. *Weeping.* The sound was fucking pathetic.

"We got a deal or not?"

"Yes. I told you. Are you in your car?"

He turned the key, and the twelve-year-old sedan sputtered to life. It was about fifty thousand miles past its prime. The car, like his career plans, should have been junked years ago. He was getting too old for this shit. And he wasn't cut out for it, never had been. He needed out. Soon.

"Are you coming?" the caller asked.

He turned out of the lot and cranked the heater. It was a long drive out to Lake Buchanan.

He couldn't believe he was doing this again. He took a deep breath and focused on the money. "I'm on my way."

CHAPTER 4

Mia tipped her head back to look at the sky, grateful for the break in the bleak winter weather. It wasn't just clear, it was perfectly clear. And the sky wasn't just blue, it was a brilliant turquoise. The day was gorgeous, filled with sun and promise and possibility.

Just like the day Amy had died.

For an instant, Mia was standing beside her banana-seat bike, watching her sister pull out of the driveway in the secondhand Chevy Malibu she'd bought with life-guarding money. Mia waved, and Amy tapped the horn before driving away.

"Notice anything?"

She snapped back to the present and glanced down into the grinning, freckled face of her six-year-old nephew.

Did she notice anything?

"Umm . . . you still haven't tied your sneaker?"

"Nope." Sam's smile widened, revealing a missing incisor.

"Umm . . ." Mia crouched down to tie the shoe herself. "You got a haircut since I last saw you?"

"Nope."

"You lost another tooth?"

"Nope. Do you give up?"

Mia stood and fisted a hand on her hip. "I give up."

"I'm standing on your shadow," he said gleefully. "That means you're it."

"I thought we called time out." They'd been playing shadow tag in her yard that morning before climbing into Mia's rental car for a trip to the zoo.

"You did. But I called time in, remember? When you were getting the tickets."

Mia mussed his rust-colored hair, the same color Vivian's had been before she started dying it. "Okay, then I'm it." Mia picked up his mittened hand. "But let's call time out while we visit Cleo and Patra. We can start up again when we get home. Deal?"

"Deal."

They walked over to the chain-link fence surrounding the cat exhibit—five Bengal tigers, which for a zoo of this size was impressive. The tigers were lolling about on some rocks, enjoying the winter sun. By the bones littered around, it looked as though they'd recently devoured their usual breakfast—a deer hindquarter. Sam tugged out of her grasp and darted between strollers to kneel beside the fence.

Mia watched him with that familiar tightness in her chest. Her nephew loved animals almost as much as she loved taking him to see them. They'd been here dozens of times, but he always begged to come back, although the place wasn't even a full-fledged zoo. It was more of a rescue center, filled mostly with exotic animals people had acquired as pets before discovering it was a bad idea—pythons, monkeys, alligators. The aviary was filled with cockatoos and macaws that had decades left to live but whose owners were now in nursing homes.

"Cleo's asleep," Sam announced. "So is Patra. This is boring."

The usually playful tigers were Sam's favorite attraction. They had been rescued from a ranch not far away following a major drug bust. According to the information posted on the fence, the tigers' first owner had kept them around to impress his friends and intimidate his rivals.

"Let's go see the llamas," Mia suggested, because the cats didn't look as if they'd be stirring anytime soon. "You said you wanted to feed them this time."

They trekked along the dirt path to the petting zoo. Sam glanced up at her. "What do you think would happen if they put a person in there instead of a deer?"

"You mean in with the tigers?"

"Yeah, for feeding time."

"That's a good question," she said, which was her typical response when he caught her off guard. It seemed to be happening more and more lately, and she was waiting for the day when he'd come to visit her and the first question out of his mouth would be, "Hey, Aunt Mia, where do babies come from?"

"Do you think they'd eat him? The person?" He gazed up at her.

"I'm not sure. I guess it would depend on how hungry they were."

"I think they'd eat him," he said with confidence. "Tigers are meat eaters, like T. rexes. And people are meat."

Mia watched him as they approached the petting zoo and had the nagging feeling there was more to this conversation than tigers.

He turned to look at her. "Do you really work at a place with lots of dead people?"

She took a deep breath. Why didn't Viv get these questions? Her sister was so much better at explaining things than she was.

"Who told you that?"

"No one." He shrugged. "I heard Gram talking to Mom about it. Gram said the place where you work probably stinks to high heaven."

Some days it did. It depended on which direction the wind was blowing.

Mia cleared her throat. "Well, I work at a research laboratory." They stopped beside the animal yard, and Sam looked up at her blankly. "It's a place with all kinds of scientists. Some of us study bugs. Some of us study soil. Some of us study bones. Some of us study what happens to people and animals after they die."

"Do you have to touch them?"

"I don't, no. I'm not that kind of scientist. I study much smaller things, sometimes with a microscope. Remember the microscope I got you for your birthday last year?"

"Yeah. I lost all the slides, though. Aunt Mia, look! There's a baby one! Can I feed it?"

Mia followed his gaze and saw the baby llama wandering amid the pigs and billy goats.

"You can try," she said, glad for the distraction. She wasn't sure how much Vivian wanted her son to know about the Delphi Center, particularly the body farm. It had been controversial since its inception, and many of the property owners nearby didn't care for the vultures, the scavengers, or the macabre attention the place attracted.

Mia dug through her purse until she came up with the eight quarters needed to buy kibble from the food dispenser near the barn. She filled a large paper cup and returned to the fence.

She glanced around at the moms and kids, at the strollers parked haphazardly beside the gate. The skin on the back of her neck prickled. Her gaze skimmed over the children mingling among the goats and llamas.

"Sam?"

Her heart started to thud. Her chest tightened. She looked at the man with the little girl on his shoulders. She looked at the crying toddler cowering away from a goat. She squeezed her way through a knot of people and stepped into the barn. The smell of manure hit her. Her eyes adjusted to the dimness, and she waited for Sam to emerge from the shadows.

"Sam?"

She was answered by clucking hens and a bleating lamb. She rushed back outside and checked the animal yard again. No Sam. Her stomach did a flip. She cast a frantic look back at the tigers, but he wasn't over there, either.

"Sam!"

Panic gripped her as she did a slow three-sixty, searching the kaleidoscope of people for an orange mop of hair and a bright green coat. But she didn't see either and her blood turned to ice.

"*Sammy!*" It was loud and shrill, but still no answer.

He was gone.

• • •

Jonah propped his shoulder against the door frame as the Travis County deputy ME removed his glasses and cleaned them for what had to be the fifth time.

"And this conclusion's based on what, exactly?" Ric said, voicing the question in Jonah's head.

His partner was seated across from George Froehler in the only guest chair available in the man's cramped office. Jonah hadn't even been able to set foot in the room because of all the files and medical journals stacked in knee-high piles around the desk. No matter how many times they visited the deputy ME, the mess always came as a surprise. How could such a meticulous doctor tolerate such a cluttered workspace?

"Postmortem lividity." Froehler replaced the spectacles on his nose. "The process by which red blood cells collect in the body's lowest points after death."

"I know what lividity is." Ric obviously didn't like being talked down to as if he was some beat cop. "But I'm not getting how that means she was killed indoors. Maybe he killed her outside near the dump site, then the body ended up facedown after she got dropped off that bridge."

"It did." Froehler folded his hands in front of him. "The fall would account for the broken ribs and likely the shattered patella visible on the X-rays. My point is, despite being discovered in the facedown position near the bridge, she died on her back and was left that way for at least a few hours. The carpet fibers recovered from her hair, along with the abrasions on her shoulders and buttocks, suggest to me that your primary crime scene is indoors."

"What color are the carpet fibers?" Ric asked.

"Beige, unfortunately."

The most common color around.

"And did you see anything similar between this victim's injuries and the one from three weeks ago? The one from the motel room?"

"Aside from the fact that they both had their hands bound with duct tape and were sexually assaulted? No. In the motel-room murder, the cause of death was manual strangulation, and the assailant left behind semen. As for your more recent victim, Ashley Meyer, she was killed by blunt-force trauma to the head. *After* she sustained the forty-two knife wounds, all shallow. In other words, he didn't stab her to death, he hit her with something heavy, maybe a wrench or a tire iron, something like that. Also, her assailant used a condom, which left traces of lubricant but no semen. I believe she died indoors on a carpeted floor, then was moved from the scene and dumped off the bridge. She landed facedown, which was how the hikers discovered her." The ME checked his watch. "Any other questions, Detectives? I'm needed in the morgue."

"These fibers," Jonah said. "Did you send them to the lab?"

"Of course. They're at the Delphi Center, along with the other trace evidence in this case." He stood up and handed Ric a copy of the autopsy report.

"Thanks for your help." Ric took the report and headed for the door. "Oh, and one more thing. In the Meyer case, did you remove the duct tape from her wrists at autopsy? The tape was cut through in three different places."

Froehler stiffened. "Absolutely not. I would have used a single razor cut in order to preserve the integrity of the binding. Her hands were bagged separately when she arrived here."

Ric shot Jonah a look. Sounded as if the crime-scene techs had screwed up right under the lead detective's nose.

They made their way back down to the main floor of the Travis County Medical Examiner's Office. Hays County wasn't big enough to have its own ME, so San Marcos cops had to work with TCMEO in Austin. It was a nice facility, but the half-hour drive was a pain in the ass.

A cold gust hit them when Jonah pushed open the door.

"So, what do you think of his theory?" Ric asked, taking his keys from his pocket as they approached the unmarked police unit parked at a meter in front of the building.

"Froehler's?"

"Yeah. That the murders aren't connected."

Jonah pulled open his door with a squeak and slid into the passenger seat. "I think he's right. These two cases, I don't know, don't fit or something. The crimes seem totally different to me."

"Except for the duct tape, the timing, and the sexual assault." Ric reached behind his seat to slide the report into an accordion file that was growing fatter by the hour. He started the engine.

"Lot of rapes involve duct tape," Jonah said. "That's why the bindings are important. Perps have a certain way of doing it."

Ric flashed him a look, and Jonah knew he was telling his partner something he already knew. But he was thinking out loud here.

Ric pulled onto Sabine Street. "I get the same feeling. First crime, pretty straightforward—prostitute killed in a motel room. Maybe she tried to shake down her john or something, he got ticked off. Or maybe he didn't want to pay. Ashley Meyer was a college student, clean record. Plus, it seems like her killer was pretty amped up. The knife wounds. The blow to the head. A lot of emotion there."

"I'm getting that, too. Seems like a different MO."

Ric shook his head. "This case is gonna drag. And I really want to focus on the Hannigan shooting before that trail gets cold."

Jonah glanced at him. "You think it's a straight-up robbery that went south?"

"No."

"Yeah, me neither." Jonah hesitated, then decided to throw it out there. "How well do you know the DNA doc?"

Ric shot him a sidelong glance. "Mia?"

"Yeah."

"I know her fine. Why?"

"You notice we haven't looked at her? Not even as a long shot?"

Ric blinked at him. "You're saying Mia Voss could have offed Frank Hannigan? What are you, on crack?"

Jonah trained his gaze on the road.

"Are you fucking serious? Why would she do that?"

"I didn't say she did."

"Then what are you saying?"

"I'm saying what I said. We haven't even looked at her. We got no eyewitnesses saying what really happened on that road out there—"

"Besides Mia," Ric cut in.

"Besides her, yeah, and you haven't even teed up the possibility she might be involved. Frank was a cop. He had enemies. How do we know there wasn't some kind of setup?"

"The woman got shot. Was that part of the setup, too? And what about the surveillance video?"

"Stranger things have happened. Anyway, I'm just saying it's possible. But we haven't even looked at it, because we took everything she told us at face value. And I'm wondering, why did we do that?"

Ric's expression hardened. He didn't like Jonah bringing this up, but that was too bad. This was a murder case. A *cop* murder. And the lead investigator had allowed himself to get distracted by a nice pair of breasts. Ric wasn't approaching this with nearly his usual objectivity.

"Hey, I like her, don't get me wrong," Jonah said. "She's squeaky clean, as far as I know. But we haven't even talked about it. And it's not like you to ignore an angle."

The car got quiet. Jonah was right, and Ric knew it.

Ric's phone buzzed, and he looked grateful for the distraction as he dug it out of his pocket. Jonah stared out the window as they passed a strip of fast-food joints. He'd logged six miles that morning before coming in. Now it was after three, and he was about to eat his arm.

"Say that again? I can't understand you."

Something in Ric's tone had Jonah's head turning.

"You're going to have to talk slower. You're not making sense."

A woman's high, tinny voice came through the phone and filled the car. Jonah couldn't make out the words, but she was upset.

"All right, calm down. Which zoo?" He waited a beat, then swerved into the left-turn lane. "And who is Sam?"

Ric spotted Mia standing beside a huddle of uniformed men near the ticket booth at the zoo entrance. She wore a powder-blue ski vest and had her back to him, but he recognized her strawberry blonde ponytail. She was jabbing her finger in the air and arguing with a man about two heads taller than she was.

Only one of the uniforms was SMPD. The other three people, all dressed in khaki, looked as if they worked for the zoo. No wonder she was pissed.

"Call *now*!" she was saying as he neared the group. "What good does it do to *wait*?"

A rookie whom Ric had met only once glanced up and sent him a bail-me-out-here look.

Mia spun around. "Ric!" She rushed forward and grabbed his arm. "Your brother. In San Antonio. He's FBI, right?"

"Yeah. What—"

"Call him." Her blue eyes swam with tears as she looked up at him and clutched his arm. "We need that team. That rapid-response team. What's it called again?"

"CARD?"

"Yes. Call your brother. Call CARD. We need an AMBER Alert, *something*."

"Back up a sec." Ric pried her hands from his arm

and held them in his. They were icy cold. "What exactly happened?" He decided not to point out it might be a little early to call in the FBI's Child Abduction and Rapid Deployment Team.

"Sam is *missing*! We've looked everywhere. He's not here!" She shot an accusing look at the huddle of officials standing nearby. "Why won't someone *do* something?"

"Let's calm down, okay?" He knew instantly that it was the wrong thing to say. She jerked her hands free and glared up at him, and he rushed to cut her off. "I need a description, Mia. What is Sam wearing?"

The question seemed to focus her. She took a deep breath. "A green fleece jacket. With a hood. And blue jeans."

Ric took out his phone and dialed Jonah. Mia watched with anxious eyes as he relayed the info.

"How tall is he?" Ric asked her.

"About four feet."

"What about a hat? Gloves? Mittens?"

"Black mittens."

"And what's he wearing under the coat?"

"A red T-shirt," she said. "With a baryonyx on it."

"A who?"

"A dinosaur. From *Dawn of the Dinosaurs*. His favorite movie." Her voice broke as she said this, and she bit her lip.

Ric relayed the rest to Jonah, then clicked off.

"Was that your brother?"

"My partner," Ric said. "He's at the construction site next door. There's some equipment parked there. Does Sam like bulldozers?"

Her eyes widened. "He does." She cast a frantic look over her shoulder. "You think he might have gone—"

"Jonah's checking. Let's keep looking here, though. Where were you when you last saw him?"

"The petting zoo. I was buying food. We've searched everywhere, but—"

"Let's search again." Ric nodded at the patrol officer. "Dispatch call you?"

"Yeah."

"See if you can get another unit out here."

"They're already on the way. I'll walk the trail again."

The uniforms dispersed, and Mia briskly set off toward the petting zoo.

"He wouldn't run off like this. He just wouldn't. There's something wrong."

"Where're his parents?"

"My sister's in San Francisco on a business trip. I left her a message."

"And the dad?"

"Who the hell knows? Or cares? The guy's a shit."

Ric looked at her. He'd never heard her curse before. "There a custody situation?"

She snorted. "Yeah, my sister does everything. Sam's dad doesn't give a damn about him."

She sounded strong, but when they got to the barn, she stood beside the food dispenser, and the tears threatened to spill over.

"I just stepped over here for a *minute*. Maybe two. I fed in my quarters and filled a cup with food . . ." Her voice trailed off as she turned and searched the animal pen. There wasn't a single child in it. Maybe they'd cleared the kids out to look for Sam.

Ric tromped around the barn. He checked behind hay bales and water troughs, looked for open gates. He scanned the horizon and noticed the steel crane towering over the line of trees to the east. If Jonah was having any luck at the construction site, he'd call. Not that it would be very lucky if he did. If the boy was at that job site for this long, he'd probably either hurt himself or been hurt by someone else and left there.

"What's his favorite animal?" Ric asked.

"He likes the tigers." Mia shook her head. "We already checked there. They even put the animals inside and looked through their entire enclosure. Nothing."

Ric glanced across the trail at the reptile house, which was closed for renovations and surrounded by yellow tape. "What about snakes? Did you—"

"The zookeeper checked."

"How about the snack bar?"

Mia gazed down the trail. "We'd just had hot dogs for lunch. I promised him a hot cocoa later, but—"

Ric grabbed Mia's arm as a kid emerged from the back of the reptile house. Green jacket. Red hair. He stepped between two orange barricades and blinked up at the sun.

"*Sam!*" Mia rocketed across the trail and dropped to her knees in front of him. She yanked him against her and hugged him to her chest.

Ric tipped his head back and breathed a sigh of relief. This was why he wasn't cut out for parenting. Your whole life could go to shit in a heartbeat.

He walked over to Mia, who was checking Sam's head as if he had a fever. The kid looked fine to Ric. Maybe a little baffled by the tears streaming down Mia's cheeks.

"Are you okay? Really?" She hugged him again and again as he stood there nodding numbly. "Oh my God, Sam, you scared me to death! What were you doing in there? Are you sure you're okay?"

Another nod. "I was looking at the python. It's still in there, even though you said it was closed. There's a boa, too. And a gila monster."

"We were *very* worried about you." She shook his shoulders. "You can't just run off like that. I had no idea—" She stopped in mid-sentence and stared at him. "What's on your mouth?"

Sam looked at his feet.

"Sam? What have you been eating?"

"A Snickers bar." It was barely a whisper.

"Where did you get a Snickers bar?"

"The man gave it to me."

"What man? Who?"

"The man in the reptile house."

CHAPTER 5

M ia eased shut the door to her guest room and crept down the hall. She heard a car pull into her driveway and peeked through the blinds to see Ric getting out of his pickup. She'd known he would come. Something about the grim set of his jaw when they'd parted ways at the emergency room had told Mia he'd be back tonight.

She pulled open the front door so he wouldn't wake Sam with the bell.

"How is he?" Ric wiped his mud-caked boots before stepping inside. Whatever he'd been doing the last four hours, it had been outdoors.

"Sleeping." She closed the door behind him and locked it. "It took three bedtime stories and an epic Shel Silverstein poem, but he's finally out."

"And how are you doing?"

"Fine."

He stood in her front hallway, gazing down at her, probably trying to read whether she was lying—which she was.

She turned and walked into the kitchen. Ric's boots scuffed over the pecan plank floor as he followed her.

"You talk to your sister yet?"

"She called while we were in the ER. She spoke with the SANE nurse and the social worker. Both assured her there's no sign of sexual contact or any other kind of contact besides the man handing him the candy bar."

"Who was the sexual assault nurse?"

"Connie somebody." Mia pulled the lid off a pot of soup and stirred it with a ladle. Steam rose, and the aroma of chicken and rosemary filled the kitchen. "I have her business card. She said I could call her if anything comes up. But she really thinks we got the full story. The man didn't touch him."

"Sounds like a harmless encounter."

Mia slammed the ladle down and whirled around. "Harmless men do not lure boys into dark buildings with candy bars! How can you even say that?"

"I didn't say the guy was harmless. He probably isn't. I'm just saying Sam got lucky today."

Mia folded her arms over her chest and looked at the floor. She felt so much frustration, so much anger, and she didn't know what to do with it. She was angry at herself for turning her back on Sam. She was angry at some sick pervert for targeting him. She was angry at her sister for accusing her of being careless and self-absorbed.

"Hey." Ric stepped closer and stood there, hands on hips, until she met his gaze. "This isn't your fault."

She looked away.

"Really. You didn't make this happen."

"I didn't prevent it from happening, either, did I? Thank God I'm not a mother. I'd be a disaster."

"You'd be great."

"Yeah, right." She closed her eyes and rubbed the bridge of her nose, suddenly feeling sick again. Every time she thought of what could have happened, she got queasy. Way too many children's clothes and stuffed toys and blankets had come through her lab, all tagged with case numbers and bar codes because the items were evidence in some horrendous case.

"Come here." Ric pulled her against his chest and wrapped his arms around her. Every muscle in her body tensed. He'd never held her this way, despite all the times she'd wanted him to. His leather jacket felt cool against her cheek. His arms felt strong. He smelled like outside and man, with a faint hint of fabric softener. She curled her arms around his waist and tried to relax. This was just a friendly hug. Or maybe not. She didn't know, but it felt good.

He rested his chin on the top of her head. "Everybody screws up. That's what sucks about parenting. No matter how much you want to, you can never get it all right."

She pulled back. "*You* have a—?"

"Ava. She just turned twelve."

She stared up at his bottomless brown eyes and felt a twinge of sadness. She'd never imagined he had a child. He'd never shared that with her, and she'd never asked. God, they didn't know each other at all, did they?

She stepped back.

He leaned against the counter and watched her, and her gaze darted to his hand before she could stop herself.

"We got divorced eight years ago," he said.

Mia had a million questions, but she didn't ask any of them. Maybe she'd ask later. Or maybe not. She wasn't sure where this was going.

"Something smells good." He nodded at the stove. "What is that?"

Her Southern manners kicked in, and she got two bowls down from a cabinet. "Chicken noodle soup." She started ladling. "Sam had it for dinner."

"Is he sick?" Ric pulled out drawers until he found the silverware.

"No, I just decided to make it."

"Homemade soup. I didn't know you cooked."

"I love to cook." She scooped some extra chicken chunks into his serving, then turned to put their bowls on the table and caught him staring at her breasts. His gaze met hers, and she felt one of those sparks again.

"Cooking's like chemistry." She ferried the bowls to the table. "Only more forgiving, not as precise. Plus, it's relaxing. I cook when I'm nervous."

"And organize spices."

"That works, too." She pulled two beers from the refrigerator and used the hem of her Duke University T-shirt to twist off the tops before plunking them on the table.

"I wouldn't have pegged you for a Bud Light drinker," Ric said as they sat down.

"Why's that?"

"I don't know. You strike me as more the microbrew type."

"In other words, a beer snob?"

He shrugged.

"You don't know me very well."

"That's true."

She put her spoon down. She was tired of dancing around the issue with him. The events of the past few days had drained all of her patience. "Why'd you stop calling me?"

She'd caught him in mid-spoonful and he took his time swallowing and putting his spoon down before answering.

"I don't know."

Bullshit. They'd been on the verge of starting something last summer. Or at least, *she'd* thought so. He'd met her for coffee at the lab a bunch of times. He'd dropped by her office and her apartment on several occasions. Mia had started to let her guard down. She'd even considered taking the plunge and sleeping with him.

Considered it? Hell, she'd been dying to. From the night they'd first met at El Patio, she'd been dreaming about sleeping with him. But he never even got around to asking her on a date. His interest had been purely professional. He'd recognized her from some DNA seminar she'd given and needed her help.

Throughout the case, he'd kept finding excuses to call her and seek her out, and she'd begun to think that the intense pull she felt was mutual.

And then, suddenly, nothing. *Nada.* His case wrapped up, and so did his interest in her.

She should have been relieved. A romance with Ric Santos was the last thing she needed. It would disrupt everything. The logical part of her knew it was for the best. But the nonlogical part of her felt hurt. Her pride was wounded, especially after she'd mulled it over and realized what had happened.

She suspected it was happening again now.

"And why are you here tonight?" she asked.

He leaned back in his chair but didn't say anything.

She huffed out a breath and resumed eating. Then she pushed her bowl away. "I know why. It's the Ashley Meyer case."

His eyebrows snapped up.

"You want me to fast-track your labs for you, so you decided it's time to start buttering me up again."

"Buttering you up?" The side of his mouth twitched. He was laughing at her.

She stood up from the table and took her bowl to the sink. She turned and leaned back against the counter. He was watching her with those intense dark eyes. The amusement was gone now, but she couldn't read his expression.

"Is that what you think?" he asked.

"You're telling me you're not here on business?"

He stood and walked over to her, soup bowl in hand. His gaze locked with hers as he reached around her to put the bowl on the counter.

"*Your* business. Not the Meyer case."

"You mean the shooting?" She felt a surge of alarm. She'd been so preoccupied with Sam she hadn't thought about Frank Hannigan in hours. "What happened?"

He hesitated, as if trying to decide how much to tell her.

"Do you have a suspect?" she asked.

"No."

"Then what is it?"

"Just a hunch. Something that's been bugging me tonight. About you."

"Me?"

"Yeah. You seem to be having a rough week."

She stared at him.

"Someone kidnaps you at a convenience store. Rips off a few hundred bucks. Then he has a chance to drive away, but instead, he chases you down and tries to kill you. Next, your nephew goes missing while you're on an outing together, all in the space of two days."

"You think there's a connection?"

He didn't answer. Obviously, he did, or he wouldn't have brought it up. Mia's stomach clenched. The idea that Sam had somehow been targeted because of her . . .

"You having any trouble I should know about?" he asked.

"What do you mean?"

"Ex-boyfriends, coworkers, new neighbors who don't like you?"

She laughed. "Are you serious?"

"Yes."

She stared at him. He wasn't kidding.

"You owe anyone money?"

"No. I mean, yeah, the mortgage company, but—"

"Anyone owe you money?"

"No." Jeez. He was interrogating her as though she'd done something wrong. "Let's backtrack a minute. You think the man Sam talked to in the reptile house—"

She frowned. "Are you saying he could be the man who shot me?"

"I think we should consider the possibility."

"Why?"

"Sam's description, for one thing."

"All he could tell us was that the guy was white and had a fluorescent green SpongeBob Band-Aid on his nose. And a ball cap."

"That was a disguise, like the hood and the bandanna from the other night. When a kid talks to someone with a bright green Band-Aid on his nose, all he notices is the Band-Aid. The cartoon character. He notices that detail because his attention's been directed there. Bank robbers have been known to do the same thing. Distract someone with a phony feature like that, people focus on it at the expense of everything else."

Mia shook her head, trying to make the idea fit. "But why would someone want to hurt me through Sam?"

"That's why I'm asking. Have you had any trouble lately? Anything at work? In your personal life? Anyone following you? Any hang-up calls?"

The only trouble she'd had near the time of the shooting was that run-in with her boss. But she didn't see how Snyder could possibly be involved in this.

"There's been nothing," she said. "Nothing like that at all."

His look was intense now, and she could tell he took his theory seriously. He didn't believe these were random events.

Fear churned her stomach. What if he was right?

Ric stepped closer. He reached up and rubbed the pad of his thumb over the bruise on her cheek. Her heart started to pound, but it wasn't from fear anymore. He was going to kiss her.

Mia's throat went dry. His hand cupped her face. His heated gaze caught hers before she closed her eyes and felt his mouth press against hers. *Finally,* she thought as she went up on tiptoes and wrapped her arms around his neck.

The doorbell rang, and she jerked away.

Ric glanced at the hallway, then looked at her sharply. "You expecting someone?"

"No."

She hurried for the door, hoping whoever it was wouldn't ring again and wake up Sam.

"Check who it is," Ric said behind her.

Mia gazed through the peephole at the blond bombshell standing on her front porch. This was going to be interesting.

She pulled open the door, and Sophie stepped right in. She was dressed to kill in a black miniskirt, knee-high black boots, and a green satin shirt that dipped low in front. Her hair fell around her shoulders in a just-out-of-bed style.

"He*llo.*" She looked Ric up and down and then looked at Mia. "I was wondering whose truck that was."

"Ric, you know Sophie from the lab?"

"Nice seeing you." He nodded at Sophie and turned to Mia. "I should go." He held her gaze for a moment, and she felt her cheeks heat. He'd finally kissed her. And he looked as if he wanted to do it again.

"I'll be in touch," he said, and then slipped out.

Mia watched him walk to his truck and get behind the wheel before closing the front door and locking up again.

"I sure hope he'll be in touch," Sophie said. "And I am *so* sorry. I didn't mean to interrupt."

"You didn't. What are you doing here, though? I thought you had a gig tonight."

"I go on at eleven, but I'm having a wardrobe malfunction. Any chance you could lend me that gauzy thing you wore to Alex and Nathan's Christmas party?"

"The black blouse?"

"Yeah, the see-through one. I snagged my bracelet on this shirt, and I've got nothing else to wear tonight."

"You can borrow whatever you want. Just don't wake Sam."

Mia led her into her bedroom and straight to the minuscule 1930s-era closet. It was the least charming of the house's old-fashioned features.

"So, what's up with you and Ric Santos?" Sophie asked as Mia handed her the blouse.

"Nothing."

A perfectly shaped eyebrow lifted. "Then why were you blushing like a tomato when I showed up?"

"I wasn't."

Sophie let it go as she stood before Mia's mirror and shrugged into the shirt. Mia usually wore it over a camisole, along with black pants. Over Sophie's black lace demibra, it looked infinitely sexier.

"Kind of slutty, I know," Sophie said. "But onstage, you have to push the envelope a little, or you blend in with the crowd."

Sophie could wear a burnt-orange shirt to a UT game and still not blend in with the crowd.

"You need to make a play for that man, Mia." Sophie glanced at her in the mirror. "That dark and dangerous thing he's got going on is *very* hot."

"Why don't *you* make a play for him?"

Sophie tucked in the shirt and gave Mia a get-real look. "First off? I'm not a bitch. And second, he's, what, five-eleven? I like to wear heels. *You,* on the other hand, would be perfect for him."

Mia tried to look uninterested. "I try not to get

involved with guys I know from work. It gets compli-cated."

Yeah, she'd tried really hard tonight, hadn't she?

"Problem with that attitude is you're a workaholic. Where are you ever going to meet anyone?" Sophie fluffed her hair. "Anyway, what was he doing here? Is there a break in your case?"

Mia gave her the nutshell version of the zoo fiasco. By the end of the story, Sophie's mouth was hanging open.

"Unbelievable. You've really had a shit week, haven't you? You get reamed out by Snyder, carjacked, *shot,* and then you win the worst-babysitter award, all in the space of three days."

Sophie sounded like Ric, and the gnawing fear was back again, along with the throbbing in Mia's arm.

"But you know what they say," Sophie said cheerfully. "Bad luck comes in batches. So does good. You should probably buy a Lotto ticket. Next week will be better."

"I don't see how it could be worse."

After borrowing some slutty earrings to go with the shirt, Sophie took off for her gig, and Mia checked on Sam again. He was curled up on the twin bed in her guest room, one leg out, one leg under the covers—the same way Vivian always slept. Mia's heart squeezed as she watched him. And she forgave her sister for all of the hurtful things she'd said earlier. Vivian was a mom first and foremost, and she had every right to be fiercely protective of her son.

Mia returned to the kitchen, which was usually her favorite room in the house. But it was too quiet now, with only the faint whisper of the gas stove. She turned off the burner and cleared the beer bottles from the table.

She glanced at the window above the sink. There was a
gap between the curtains, allowing a clear view of her
to anyone lurking outside. She reached over and tugged
the panels together. She needed some real window treat-
ments, not this decorative doily crap the previous owner
had put up. The house was old-fashioned, yes, but Mia
wanted it to function like a modern home, complete with
modern security features. Maybe she was paranoid, but
she had seen far too much violence in her career to leave
her safety to chance.

What you need is a man, not a house. Her mother's
words elbowed their way into her head with their usual
tact. *What do you need with all that house when you're not
even married?*

Mia washed the soup bowls and arranged them on
the drying rack. She needed the house for herself. That
was enough. At the end of the summer—right after her
thirty-second birthday, actually—she'd come to the realization that she was tired of living in beige apartments
that smelled like other people's pets. She was tired of
storing her books in the milk crates she'd been dragging
around since college. She was tired of driving to public
parks so she could spread out a beach towel and enjoy the
sun. She was ready to own something, paint something,
plant something, and she didn't need a man in her life
to do any of those things, no matter what her mother
thought.

So she'd plopped down her savings on a two-bedroom
bungalow that she could live in all by herself, and she
was glad. Usually. On nights like tonight, though, nights
when she was restless and anxious and unnerved, she
would have welcomed a man in her home. Or better yet,

her bed. She would have welcomed a strong arm draped over her waist to make her feel safe as she drifted off to sleep. It would have been nice to have the arm—just as long as it didn't belong to Ric Santos.

Mia put away the soup and washed the ladle. Thank God Sophie had come when she did. What if she hadn't? Mia knew exactly what. She'd seen the predatory glint in Ric's eyes the second before he kissed her—like a wolf sizing up his prey. It made her blood tingle. One little kiss, and her no-men-from-work rule had gone straight out the window.

Mia felt a knot of frustration as she wiped down the counter. She should feel relieved, really. An emotional entanglement with a cop was a bad idea. An emotional entanglement with a cop who sent her his cases was beyond stupid. It could jeopardize her objectivity, the hard-earned trait that was the cornerstone of her reputation as a scientist. And in a field where juries could be swayed by a facial expression, a tone of voice, a fumbled answer under cross-examination, reputation was important. Mia's colleagues trusted her. Juries trusted her. So did lawyers on both sides of the courtroom. They trusted her because she had a sterling reputation, one that thus far had been beyond reproach, and she intended to keep it that way.

So police detectives were out. As were prosecutors, defense attorneys, and judges. What she needed was a nice doctor. Any kind would do. An orthopedist. A podiatrist. Even a dentist. People always told her she had a pretty smile.

Mia gazed at her reflection in the window above the sink and lifted her hand to her bruised cheek. What had

Ric seen in her tonight that had prompted him to kiss her? His face flashed into her mind, the corner of his mouth lifting in that cocky half-smile she'd seen only a few times. And she knew that the nice doctor she needed would bore her to tears—because she really wanted a jaded homicide detective who was attracted to her for all the wrong reasons.

CHAPTER 6

Ric capped off a shit week watching the Cowboys play a shit game against the Philadelphia Eagles.

"Christ, *I* could have made that tackle," Jonah said, staring at the TV mounted behind the bar. "Fucking cowgirls."

Jonah was in a black mood, like Ric. Maybe it was Frank's upcoming funeral. Maybe it was the stalled investigation into who killed one of their own. Maybe it was the fact that they'd spent the better part of their Sunday trying unsuccessfully to figure out who had raped and murdered two women barely out of their teens. Ric wasn't sure what it was, but he should have known that letting himself get talked into a round of beers tonight wasn't going to help.

"Heads up," Jonah said, looking over Ric's shoulder.

He turned around to see Mia step through the door and fold a coat over her arm. She wore jeans and Ugg boots and a thick white sweater that in no way accentuated her amazing body. And yet she looked hot. How was that possible?

Her gaze scanned the line of bar stools and came to rest on him.

"Shit," Ric muttered as she crossed the bar. She had that look in her eye, a look he recognized. Dr. Voss was on a mission.

She stopped beside their stools. "Detective Macon, Ric."

"It's Jonah." He sent Ric a look, then started to offer Mia his seat.

"No, don't get up." She turned to Ric. "I saw your truck outside. Could we talk for a minute?" She glanced around the crowded bar, which, as usual, was packed with off-duty cops and emergency workers. El Patio was one of the few watering holes in town that didn't cater to the college crowd. That plus the fact that it was located near the police station made it a hangout.

The bar erupted as the Eagles threw an interception. Mia watched Ric patiently, oblivious to the excitement. Not a football fan, evidently. And he could tell she wanted to talk to him in private.

"Let's go outside," he said. "They've got heaters."

"That's fine."

Jonah gave him a look. *Are you crazy? The ball's on the five-yard line.* Ric ignored him as he picked up his beer and led Mia to the patio. It was mostly smokers tonight because of the cold. He stopped at the outdoor bar to order a Bud Light while Mia claimed a picnic table that had just been vacated.

Ric slid the beer in front of her, then straddled the bench and sat down facing her. She was frowning at her phone.

"Everything okay?" he asked.

"You know Vince Moore?"

"Yeah."

"He's called twice tonight. Maybe it's something about the case."

"It's not."

"How do you know?"

"I'm the lead investigator. He's calling to ask you out. Do yourself a favor, and say no."

She watched him warily as she tucked the phone back inside her purse.

Ric sipped his beer. He needed a change of subject. "How's Sam?"

"Vivian picked him up this afternoon," she said, not really answering. Ric figured the kid was fine—it was Mia he wasn't sure of.

"Anything more on the man from the zoo?" she asked.

"No."

She bit her lip and looked away. Ric set his beer on the table and waited. A breeze kicked up, and he smelled something sweet and feminine underneath the cigarette smoke wafting over from the next table. Mia's perfume. He recognized it from months ago, although he hadn't even realized she wore perfume until just that moment.

"I want to ask you something," she said, "even though it might sound weird."

"All right."

"Do you ever dream about your cases?"

He took a second to answer. "It's happened before, I guess. Why?" He watched her, hoping she wasn't going to launch into some discussion about psychic detective work. She'd never struck him as the type to believe in all that crap, but maybe she did. He couldn't picture it, though. Mia was a scientist.

"The case you brought me—"

"From Friday," he confirmed.

"Yes, the Ashley Meyer homicide. I went into work today and looked at the evidence again."

Ric wasn't surprised she'd been at work on a Sunday. She worked the same kind of hours he did—endless. He waited for her to get to the point as she peeled the label off her beer bottle and made a little pile of scraps on the table. She started to say something, then stopped herself.

"What's on your mind, Mia?"

She looked up at him. "Did I ever tell you I got my start in Fort Worth? I spent a year at the crime lab up there right after grad school."

"I think you mentioned it once." And if she hadn't, he'd known anyway. He'd checked out her background when they'd worked together on a cold case last summer. She'd gone from Fort Worth to the state crime lab before landing her job at the Delphi Center.

"There was this case about six years ago," she said. "One of the first ones I worked all by myself. It was a sexual homicide. The victim, Laura Thorne, was nineteen. She disappeared from a party one night and was found in some nearby woods a few days later. The duct tape used to bind her hands came through our laboratory. Her clothes, too. I tested everything. Couldn't recover anything from the perpetrator, only the victim."

"Was she stabbed?" Ric asked, now seeing where this was going.

"Fifty-three times. There were slashes all over her dress."

"Piquerism," he said.

"Exactly." Mia shook her head. "Anyway, the case

made an impression on me. I still think about it a lot. Sometimes I even dream about her, and she's wearing those putrid clothes." Mia shivered, and he didn't think it was because of the weather.

"Some cases stick with you." He wasn't sure what else to say. Sometimes he'd wake up in a cold sweat thinking about a crime scene. Only there was usually some sick twist to it, such as the victim wasn't the victim but Ava. Or his mom. Or even his ex-wife. The worst part wasn't the scene but the suffocating feeling of getting there just a few minutes too late.

"I think the cases might be connected."

Ric raised his eyebrows.

"I know what you're going to say," she hurried to add. "There are a lot of stabbing victims. Duct tape is common. I know all that. But I think you should check into it."

Ric took his time answering, choosing his words carefully. Mia was the most talented DNA expert he'd ever worked with, both in the lab and on the witness stand. With a little finesse, he could get her to turn his lab work around in record time. Besides the district attorney, who liked him, Mia was probably his best contact. No, she was definitely his best contact, because she couldn't get booted out of office the way the DA could, which meant that she was with him for the long haul. And he couldn't afford to jeopardize her help by balking at her theory.

He also couldn't afford to sleep with her, no matter how much he wanted to. It would be a disaster on every front—professionally, personally. Maybe not sexually, but that didn't make up for the other two.

He thought of that kiss last night. It had been over before it started, before he'd even gotten a good taste.

"Will you check into it?" Her blue eyes looked hopeful now.

"I can take a look. Like you said, though, stabbing and duct tape are pretty common. Is there something else you noticed . . . ?" Ric let the question dangle, not wanting to ask if there was anything else that would make a rational person think these two cases might be connected.

"Isn't that enough?"

"Honestly? No. If it was an unusual kind of tape, maybe. But it looked like plain silver duct tape to me. You guys should be able to run it down, find out if that's true."

Mia sighed, frustrated. "It's just, I don't know, a feeling I get when I look at the evidence. Like the crimes *feel* the same, you know? The same kind of impulse behind them or something."

Ric just stared at her.

"Don't you ever follow your instincts?" she asked.

"Absolutely."

"That's all I'm asking you to do here."

Hell, what could it hurt? If nothing else, it would keep his best contact at the Delphi Center in his corner. "All right, I'll check into it," he told her.

She looked relieved, as if he'd lifted a weight off her shoulders.

"Thank you." She stood and collected her purse. "You have something to write on? I'll tell you the case number."

"You've got it in your head? From six years ago?"

"I told you, it made an impression on me."

Ric pulled out the notebook he kept in his jacket pocket and jotted down the number she recited. Six years ago. As cold cases went, this one was in deep freeze.

"You need to compartmentalize," he said, tucking the notebook away. "Trust me, you let yourself get emotional about this stuff, you'll drive yourself crazy."

"I compartmentalize fine," she said defensively. "And I'm not emotional, I'm just sharing a potential lead." She glanced at the door, and he knew she wanted to escape before he gave her any more advice.

"Lemme walk you out." Ric steered her back through the bar and out to the parking lot, where he spotted her subcompact pulled up beside his pickup. The white Aveo could have fit into his truck bed.

"They couldn't rent you a real car?"

She opened the driver's-side door and slid in. "It's from their Green Collection." She shot a disapproving look at his F-250. "Gets good gas mileage."

"Cheapest one they had, huh?"

"That, too."

"Your Jeep's been on the hot list for three days now. Chances aren't good we're going to recover it. You should go ahead and talk to your insurance company."

"I'm working on it."

Ric scanned the parking lot. There was a guy sitting in his SUV talking on the phone, but Ric saw the SMPD sticker on the back of his car and dismissed him as a threat.

His gaze settled again on Mia and the turtleneck sweater that covered everything up to her chin. He had the sudden urge to warm his hands under it.

"Want me to follow you home?" he asked.

"That's not necessary. I'm armed and dangerous."

"Seriously? You're packing?"

She'd told him once that she hated guns, which must

still be true, because she reached under her seat and pulled out a can of Mace that could fell a grizzly bear.

Ric whistled. "Damn, you don't fool around." He'd do a drive-by anyway, same as he'd done every night since her attack. He wasn't sure when her safety had become his personal responsibility, but he intended to keep an eye on her until they figured out who was behind Thursday's shooting.

He leaned an arm on the roof of her car and gazed down at her and suddenly wanted nothing more than to follow her home and get her out of that sweater.

"Call me if you need anything," he said.

She started the car and smiled ruefully, as if she'd read his thoughts. "How about I call you when I get those DNA results back? And guess what—you don't even have to buy me coffee this time."

CHAPTER 7

Mia navigated her way through the scrub brush, keeping a sharp eye out for body parts. Cadaver sites were supposed to be marked off with caution tape, but coyotes and other scavengers had been known to ignore the signs.

She found Kelsey Quinn on her knees beside a dead pig. Mia counted herself lucky to catch her working on animal remains instead of human. Mia pulled a pink bandanna out of her lab-coat pocket and held it over her mouth and nose, pretty sure she was the only participant in the cancer walkathon to be using the souvenir for this particular purpose.

"That's a big pig. What is it, a hundred pounds?"

Kelsey glanced up from the carcass. "One-twenty." With a gloved hand, she lifted the animal's foreleg and picked up something from beneath it with a pair of tweezers.

"Fly cases?"

Kelsey dropped the item into a glass jar, then removed the baseball cap she wore over her long auburn hair and wiped her brow with her forearm. "It's for my graduate seminar this afternoon. Postmortem interval." She replaced the cap on her head and gave Mia an up-and-down look. "Are panty hose making a comeback? Think I missed the memo."

Mia's legs felt like icicles despite the hosiery. She typically wore pants to work, but today was an exception. "I've got to be in court this afternoon."

"Bummer." Kelsey screwed the lid onto the jar. Evidently satisfied with her collection of specimens, she stood up. She looked Mia over, and her expression softened. "I heard about Thursday. How are you doing?"

"Six stitches." Mia shrugged. "It's no big deal."

"That's not what I meant."

"I know." Mia looked out at the wintry landscape. She could have told Kelsey about the fear, the jumpiness. The inability to sleep. But she didn't want to admit to anyone, maybe not even herself, how anxious she felt doing the most mundane activities now—walking down the grocery aisle, passing strangers in parking lots, taking a shower. Her irrational anxiety wasn't something she wanted to share with people from work.

Kelsey tucked the jar into a tote bag along with her tweezers, and they set off toward the building in silence. The Delphi Center occupied more than one hundred acres of rugged Texas Hill Country, a beautiful setting if you forgot the science projects littered about. Mia found them hard to forget, which was why she rarely ventured out onto the grounds.

"What brings you out here? I know it's not the fresh air."

"Dr. Heinz sent me," Mia said. "He's been examining

some duct tape for me in connection with a murder case. He said you sent him something similar a while back that was recovered up near Lake Buchanan."

"How far back?"

"Almost two years. I have the case number. Detective's name was Sandinsky."

They passed a picnic table that looked desolate beneath a barren pecan tree. Not a lot of people opting to lunch outside in this weather.

"Lake Buchanan," Kelsey repeated. "Some kids found her near the lake. Spring, I think it was."

"March." They hiked up the back steps to the building, and Mia swiped her card. "Heinz said he didn't think we ever got an ID."

"We didn't." Kelsey stepped inside and unwound a purple chenille scarf from her neck as she wiped her boots on the mat. "Remains were fully skeletonized. Disarticulated. Scattered over a quarter-mile area."

"You were part of the recovery team?"

"I was." They headed down a gently sloping corridor to the Bones Unit. Kelsey pressed her palm against a panel. The sliding doors parted, and they entered a section of the building where the temperature hovered around sixty degrees.

"We found almost everything," Kelsey continued. "Only two phalanges missing, if I remember right."

Kelsey had an amazing memory. Mia's was pretty good, but she made notes all the time. Kelsey simply absorbed things.

She stopped at a cubicle in the osteology section and deposited the jar. "She should still be here. You have time to take a look?"

"Sure."

Kelsey led her past the X-ray suite and into a spacious examining room with stainless-steel tables on either end of it. When they reached a storage area, Kelsey pressed her palm to a panel, and the door slid open.

"Most morgues are short on square footage," Kelsey said, "but we're lucky here. They modeled this room after the Smithsonian. Oodles of drawer space."

They stepped into a narrow room lined on both sides with shallow drawers, each labeled with a number. The stacks reached well over Mia's head.

"Do you need the case number?" Mia asked, but Kelsey was already making her way to the far end of the long room. She stopped in front of a waist-high drawer and checked the label before pulling it out.

"This is another way we're lucky. So many places to store bones in plastic tubs or cardboard boxes. This way, we can keep them arranged properly."

Mia stared down at the bones of a woman who had been bound with duct tape, then killed and left to rot in some wilderness.

Kelsey sighed. "I remember her." She walked over to a nearby cart and pulled a pair of latex gloves from a box. She handed a pair to Mia.

Mia studied the skeleton as she pulled on the gloves. "Her leg was broken?"

"Actually, no. That was me. I took a wedge out of the femoral shaft to get a DNA sample. One of your colleagues tested it. We entered her in the database, but as far as I know, we never got a hit."

"And you're sure it's a woman?"

Kelsey pointed to the pelvis. "The pelvic aperture

is wide and round in females, like this, but narrow for males. And it looks as though she never gave birth. Estimated age early- to mid-twenties based on the partially fused epiphyseal plates—those are the growth plates near the ends of the long bones."

So young. Mia gazed down at the bones and felt an overwhelming sense of loneliness. Her DNA profile wasn't in the Missing Persons Index, which meant her family hadn't submitted a sample. Maybe she didn't have a family. Or maybe she did, but they didn't care. The woman might be a runaway. An illegal immigrant. A homeless person who'd lost touch with her life.

Mia gazed down the endless row of drawers. "What a terrible place to end up."

"Yep."

She returned her attention to the bones, which were arranged as if the ligaments were still there to link everything.

Kelsey picked up the skull and pointed to a depressed fracture. "Blunt-force trauma. It's hard to say for sure, but based on the size, I'm guessing she was hit with a heavy tool, maybe a wrench or something similar."

Mia shuddered. "Is that why you remember her?"

Kelsey pulled a loupe from her pocket and handed it to Mia. "Actually, what stood out to me at the time were the knife marks." She pointed to the rib cage. "Twelve marks, all made with a serrated blade."

Mia peered down at the ribs and the gouges Kelsey pointed out with her gloved finger.

"Under microscopic examination, you see the striations," Kelsey said. "It's a distinctive pattern. I confirmed it with our tool-mark examiner upstairs. We concluded it was most likely a steak knife. Twelve of the wounds were deep enough to penetrate bone, but there could have been more that only penetrated the soft tissue."

Mia handed back the loupe. Their gazes met across the bones, and Mia felt that kinship she sometimes had with others who worked at the Delphi Center.

"Someone's reopening this case, aren't they?"

"I'm hoping," Mia said. "There's a similar case out of San Marcos."

"Similar how?"

"Duct tape, blunt-force trauma, piquerism."

Kelsey shook her head.

"Good news is, this latest victim was recovered not too long after death," Mia said. It always amazed her what passed for good news in her profession.

"Semen?"

"No, but we've got her clothes, her shoes. The attack was very violent. Looks like she fought hard. We've got an abundance of blood, and I'd be very surprised if the perpetrator managed to get away without leaving a DNA sample."

"Good." Kelsey snapped off her gloves. "I hope you nail him with it."

Ric watched the white roller skate of a car coast into the driveway. Mia climbed out and clutched the strap of her computer bag to her chest while the wind whipped her coat around her bare legs. He got out of his truck as she picked her way over the sidewalk in three-inch heels.

"Careful, it's slick tonight."

She whirled around, clearly surprised to see him. Her cheeks were tinged pink from the cold.

"Not the best weather for stilettos."

"These aren't stilettos. And since when are you a fashion consultant?" She looked him up and down, taking in his jeans and T-shirt, which had been through the wash about five hundred times each. He tucked his hands into the pockets of his leather jacket and stopped in front of her.

"You look hungry."

Her eyebrows tipped up. Whatever she'd been expecting him to say, that hadn't been it.

"Ever been to Klein's?" he asked.

"The grease pit just around the corner?"

"Best barbecue in three counties."

She glanced at her house, which was dark except for the porch light. "I'm supposed to work tonight."

"You work too much."

"Says someone who spent his weekend at the cop shop." The second the words were out, she looked as if she wanted them back. How had she known where he spent his weekend? She must have called the station looking for him and chatted up the receptionist. The idea of her checking up on him probably should have bugged him, but instead it made him feel good.

Another glance at the door. "I need to drop off my computer."

Ric tugged the bag off her shoulder and hiked up the steps. "What's in this thing? Bricks?"

"My laptop. And a few reference books. And about six weeks' worth of reports I need to finish."

He watched her disable the alarm. Then he stowed the bag in the hallway beside a cardboard dish box. The smell of paint thinner hit him, and he noticed the cans stacked beside the bathroom.

"Doing some redecorating?"

"Just in the bathroom," she said. "I couldn't sleep last night, so I thought I might as well. Do I have time to change?"

"Not if we want to get a table," Ric said. He liked her outfit, especially the shoes. "They get crowded by eight."

She locked up again, and they headed down the sidewalk with a chilly wind gusting around them. She shoved her hands into the pockets of her coat and inched closer.

"You going tomorrow?" She was talking about the funeral.

"Yeah, you?"

"I was planning to, but it looks like I'm going to be tied up in court all morning."

"Which case?" he asked.

"Miguel Sanchez."

"The gas-station shooting," Ric said. "SMPD worked that case. I heard it's a slam dunk. Didn't the perp drop a glove at the scene or something?"

"A hat. I recovered DNA from it, too, along with hair samples. But Russ Pickerton is running the defense."

"No kidding?" Ric had yet to meet a cop who could say the name Russ Pickerton without a string of curses tumbling out. Besides being a media whore, the guy would do anything to get a client off, including paying inconvenient witnesses to recant their stories. Or so people claimed. "How'd Mendoza manage that?" Ric asked her.

"I think he's doing it for the publicity. The whole racial-profiling angle generated some controversy. You guys pulled him over on a bum taillight or something."

"Yeah, we have a tendency to profile drivers who're breaking the law."

Mia's heel got hung up on a crack in the pavement. Ric caught her by the elbow.

"Thanks," she said.

He kept his hand on her arm and eased her closer. "Are you ready for him?"

"Who, Pickerton?" She sneered. "What do you think? The man's an eel. I can hardly stand to be in the same room with him."

"He's pretty rough on expert witnesses."

"It's not just that," she said. "He's got a mile-long list of liars for hire who will testify to damn near anything, no matter how scientifically improbable."

"I've seen him in action," Ric said. "I once watched him persuade a jury to acquit a guy based on the idea that the fingerprints on the murder weapon had been planted there by the defendant's twin brother."

"Twins don't have the same fingerprints. Not even identical twins."

"The prosecution pointed that out," Ric said. "But he had the jury so brainwashed they actually let this guy walk. I couldn't believe it."

Mia huffed out a breath. "I've got my work cut out for me tomorrow." She cast a worried look in his direction. "Any progress on the shooting?"

"We're waiting on ballistics." Ric didn't tell her the rest of what he'd learned that day.

"What about my Jeep?"

"Still no word."

The smoky scent of barbecue wafted toward them as they neared the weathered wooden building with neon beer signs blazing in the windows.

"Like I said, you should try to get a check from your insurance company. I doubt you'll get it back, at least not in one piece."

"I don't care about that. I don't think I could stand to drive it. I was thinking for the crime-scene techs."

Ric pulled the door open, and they stepped into a warm room filled with the scent of spice and hickory. He took her hand and pulled her past the empty hostess stand. Twangy country music drifted from the jukebox as they made their way through the dining room to one of the many vacant booths lining the back wall.

Ric peeled off his jacket and hung it on a hook beside their booth as Mia stood there, looking annoyed. "You said they'd be crowded."

"I'm hungry. I didn't want to wait for you to change."

She unbuttoned her black wool coat. He slid it off her shoulders, and her hair glided over his fingers as he got his first good look at what she'd worn to court: a pale blue blouse in some thin, silky fabric and a dark blue skirt that hugged her full hips. Ric felt a pang in his gut that had nothing to do with hunger.

"Sit down. You're gawking." She slid into the booth and grabbed a menu.

"Sorry."

A young waitress stopped by, and they ordered a couple of beers. When they were alone again, Mia looked down at her menu.

"You know, I don't get you," she said.

"What's that?"

She shook her head. Started to say something. Then shook her head again.

"What is it?"

"Nothing."

The waitress delivered their beers. Mia ordered rotisserie chicken while Ric went for the rib platter. When the waitress left, Ric got to the point.

"You were asking about your case. I think we might have a vehicle."

Hope flared in her eyes, and she leaned forward. "From the convenience store? What, was it parked there?"

"We found someone from the Minute-Mart who remembers a dark-colored sedan pulling up to the pet shop across the street around the time you were in the store. That whole strip center was closed down, so we're thinking it could be the shooter."

"How can you be sure of the timing?"

"We matched a credit-card transaction to a customer who was in there the same time as you and Hannigan, tracked him down for an interview. He remembers seeing you, also remembers the car."

"Why would he remember seeing me?"

"Every man in that store remembers seeing you. You were in a nightshirt."

She rolled her eyes. "I was in jeans and a sweater, too. Did he remember that?"

"There was also a dark sedan parked at the construction site adjacent to the zoo on Saturday. A security cam caught it."

She leaned back, obviously alarmed by this development. "But I thought the zoo didn't have surveillance cameras. The director told me—"

"They don't. The camera was at the construction site, mounted on the trailer they've got parked there. The construction company uses it to keep an eye on workers, keep them from sleeping on the job, stealing equipment, stuff like that. We viewed the footage yesterday, came up with a partial view of a dark-colored sedan parking at the job site about thirty minutes before you reported Sam missing. Looks like he showed up right after you did. Jonah found a gap in the fence, so he could have slipped through unnoticed."

Ric waited for the words to sink in. From the lack of color in her face, he figured they had.

"Chances are, this wasn't some garden-variety pervert hanging out at the zoo, trolling for kids." He was pointing out the obvious but needed to drive his point home.

"Did you get a look at the driver?"

"Wrong angle."

She looked away, chewed her lip.

"You notice a car like that around lately? Maybe at work or when you've been out?"

"No." Anger flickered in her eyes. "Why didn't you tell me this earlier? About this connection?"

"I'm telling you now. Anyway, it's only a possible connection. We're still running it down."

The bread arrived. They tore and buttered in silence. She was clearly upset by the link between the shooting and what happened to Sam.

Yes, it was only a possible link, but Ric believed there was something to it. This thing, whatever it was, was about Mia. It was the reason he'd spent the better part of his Saturday night tromping around a construction site, making a cast of a shoeprint and a tire track. It was the reason he'd driven by her house every night since the shooting. It was the reason he was there right now, telling a civilian confidential details about an investigation. Mia was at the center of this, and he needed to figure out why.

When their meals came, they moved on to easier topics. Mia filled him in on the unidentified remains she'd looked at that day and he agreed to check into it. She seemed hopeful about the lead, but Ric thought it was even less promising than the Fort Worth case. Unidentified bones, especially ones that had been sitting unclaimed for two years, weren't likely to offer a whole lot of warm leads.

A frigid gust slapped at them as they exited the barbecue joint. The temperature had dropped, and for a while, they walked in chilly silence.

It began to sleet. Mia shivered. Ric draped an arm around her and pulled her against him. She tensed at first, but after a few seconds, she tucked her head against his shoulder.

"So, how are those lab results coming?" he asked.

She didn't answer right away, and he remembered her theory about him buttering her up for favors. Sharp woman.

"I'm still working," she said. "I was in court all afternoon, so I'm falling behind. Sometimes it seems like all I do is testify."

"That's because you're good."

"How would you know?"

"I've watched you. You've got a way with juries. Much better than your boss. What's his name, Snyder?

Prosecutors hate putting him on the stand. That's why you get called so much."

"It is?"

"That and the freckles."

She halted in front of her house and stared up at him. "I get called to testify because of my *freckles*? Sounds like I wasted four years in graduate school."

He followed her up the sidewalk. "You look trustworthy. Like the girl next door. Juries like you." They stopped beneath the porch light. He reached up and traced a finger down her cheek. Her bruise was fading, and she'd hidden what was left under some makeup. "Being beautiful doesn't hurt, either."

She looked away and shook her head.

"What?"

She folded her arms over her chest. "I'm going to ask you something, and I want a straight answer this time. No bullshit."

A faint warning sounded in his brain, but he ignored it. "You know, you're cute when you curse."

She rolled her eyes. "See? There you go again."

"What?"

She swiped a curl out of her face and glared at him. "You're flirting with me."

"Guilty."

"Why did you stop calling me at the end of the summer? Be honest this time."

He looked away.

"Come on, Ric, out with it. You suddenly weren't attracted to me? You got bored? After all those drop-ins and phone calls, you decided you didn't like my personality?"

"Maybe I'm not in the market for a relationship."

"What makes you think I want a relationship?"

The warning in his head grew louder, and still he ignored it. "You're nesting," he said.

"Nesting."

"You're settling down. We had coffee together, what, three times? And you start looking at me like you're ready to pick out dishes or something."

Her arms fell to her sides, and her mouth dropped open. "I wanted to pick out *dishes*? Did you really just say that?"

"Yeah."

"I can pick out my own dishes! What would I need you for?"

He watched her, not sure how the hell they'd gotten to this point. And he knew that whatever microscopic chance he might have had of taking her to bed tonight had been annihilated.

"I can buy my own dishes and my own house, too, thank you very much!" Her cheeks flushed pink, only this time it was from anger, not cold. "And what is it with men, anyway? You think every woman is sitting around waiting for someone to slip a ring on her finger. Hate to break it to you, but that's a fallacy fostered by way too many overinflated egos."

"Is that right?"

"That's right! Some women just want sex, same as men."

Ric stared at her. "You're saying you just want sex?" He couldn't help himself. He started laughing.

"What's so funny?"

He shook his head, watching her, unable to control

the grinning, even though it pissed her off. "You. You're just—"

Her glare intensified.

"Forget it," he said.

"What?"

"Mia, no offense, but you're full of it. When was the last time you went out with a guy and didn't want anything out of it but sex?"

"I don't know," she said, although clearly the answer was never. "But maybe I will. Maybe I'll call Vince Moore back. I doubt he's looking to pick out dishes. And he's pretty ripped, too. It might be fun."

Ric's humor evaporated. "That guy's an asshole, Mia. Stay away from him."

His phone buzzed, and Ric checked the number. His boss. Damn it, this wouldn't be good. He turned off the ringer.

Mia shoved her key into the lock and turned to face him, blocking the door with her body just in case he thought he was getting an invitation inside.

"You need to be careful," he said as his phone vibrated, making a dull rattle against his car keys.

"I didn't ask you for dating advice."

"I'm talking about your safety," he said. "Pay attention to your surroundings. Get a security guard to walk you to your car if you need to work late. Keep your alarm on when you're at home. And if anything unusual happens, call me."

She just looked at him.

"Are you listening, Mia?"

"Be extra careful. Got it. Anything else you wanted to share?"

Another sound from his pocket, and he yanked the phone out. "Santos. Hold on." He looked at Mia. "Lock up tight tonight. And don't forget—"

"To set my alarm, I know. You'd better go, Ric. Sounds like you've got somewhere to be."

CHAPTER 8

∽

Sophie's brow furrowed with concern the second Mia stepped through the glass door. "Whoa, what happened to you?"

"What?" Mia jerked the scarf from around her neck and stuffed it into the pocket of her coat.

"You look like you just ran over a puppy. Everything okay?"

"Bad day in court." She tugged the ID badge out of her purse and clipped it to her blouse. She didn't want to talk about it right now. She didn't want to do anything besides slip into her lab coat and bury herself in work. "Any calls come through?"

"The usual. Detectives desperately seeking updates. I put them through to your voice mail. Oh, and one in particular called three times. A Detective Moore. Vince was his first name? Not sure I've met him."

"You'd remember it," Mia said. "He's cute."

"Cute as in Levi's ads or cute as in I'd look like an Amazon next to him?"

"The first one."

"Good to know." Sophie held out a stack of pink message slips, and Mia tucked them into her pocket. "And FYI, that guy Darrell's looking for you. The one from the Cave," she added, referring to the basement offices where the data technicians worked.

"Good, because I need to talk to him." What Mia really needed was to escape before Sophie could pin her down for more details. She started for the elevator bank. "Hey, if I don't see you before I leave, good luck at your gig tonight."

Mia made a dash for the elevators and squeezed into one right before the doors closed. She rode up to the sixth floor with a DNA tracer and a couple of guys from Cyber Crimes. She wondered if any of them had ever been ripped to shreds by the illustrious Russ Pickerton. Probably not.

The doors dinged open, and she stood face-to-face with Darrell. His eyes lit up.

"I was just looking for you. Where you been all day?"

"Court."

She stepped out, and he fell into pace beside her. Darrell was tall and lanky and always seemed to be eating something. This afternoon, it was a chocolate-iced doughnut, and Mia's stomach started growling.

"Got some news for you."

"What's that?" *Please let it be good news.* She needed something—anything—to salvage her terrible-horrible-no-good-very-bad day.

"You know that profile you lifted earlier this week?"

"Could you be more specific?"

"Electrical cord. Ligature strangulation case. I ran it through the database and *bing*."

In Darrell-speak, *bing* was good.

"And?"

"An offender hit." He grinned at her.

"You're kidding."

The saliva off that cord had come from someone whose profile was already stored in the database. Offender hits were rare, but Mia lived for them anyway. They were the reason she got up in the morning. They made everything worth it—the drudgery, the painstaking hours, even the Russ Pickertons of the world.

"I notified the department that submitted the sample," Darrell said, "and the detective there wants to talk to you. Kopchek, I think it was."

"Kubcek," she corrected. She was grinning now, too. "I know him." Or at least, she felt like she did. He'd been hounding her for weeks.

"He's got some follow-up questions, stuff a little out of my league. I told him I'm just the lowly data jockey— you're the DNA guru around here."

"I'll call him." She stopped in front of her office and gave Darrell a spontaneous hug, which might have been a bad idea, because when she looked up, a blush was creeping up his neck. "Thanks for letting me know."

Mia slipped into her office and shrugged out of her woolen layers. She hung everything on a hook beside the door and pulled on the crisp white lab coat that had been recently laundered and had her name embroidered on the pocket. The familiar bleach scent was comforting.

An offender hit. *Yes.*

Mia pressed her palms against the counter and closed her eyes as a feeling of relief washed over her. Some family in Houston would get answers to their questions now. And maybe someday, after the soul-rending grief subsided, they might even feel comforted by the knowledge that the person who'd taken their child from this world hadn't gotten away with it.

Mia took a deep breath. It was turning out to be a good day, despite the morning. Her work had led to a break-through, and Russ Pickerton—with all his smoke and mirrors and courtroom antics—could go screw himself.

A ring emanated from her overcoat pocket. She fished her cell phone out but didn't recognize the number on the screen.

"Hello?"

"Check your e-mail."

"I beg your pardon?" Something about the voice made the hair on the back of her neck stand up.

"Check your e-mail. And make sure you're alone."

"Who is this? Hello?"

She glanced at the phone, but the call had discon-nected. Mia's pulse quickened. This seemed like maybe an obscene call, and she wasn't sure she should power up her laptop. Instead, she tapped the in-box on her cell-phone screen and waited for her messages to pop up. Eleven new ones, one flagged urgent. No subject line. She clicked open the message, and a picture of Sam filled the screen.

Mia's stomach dropped. Sam was smiling up at the camera and standing in front of a sign: CEDAR HOLLOW ELEMENTARY SCHOOL.

The phone in her hand rang, making her jump. The device clattered to the countertop, and she grabbed it up. Same number.

"Who is this?" she demanded.

"Aunt Mia!"

"Sam!" Her heart spasmed. "Where are you?"

"Listen carefully." It was the man's voice again. Icy fear shot through her veins. "You're going to follow instructions without talking to anyone except me, you got that?"

She gripped the phone in her hand and sagged against the counter.

"Are you listening?"

"Yes." Her voice was a whisper, barely audible above the ringing in her ears. He had *Sam*.

"No cops. No lab rats. No one hears about this call, ever, or Sam gets hurt. You got me?"

"Yes." He'd said *lab rats*. Did he know she was at the Delphi Center? He must. Maybe he was watching. Maybe he was in a car with Sam right this instant, and they were sitting out in the parking lot. But how would he have gotten through the security gate? That didn't make sense—

"Write down this case number."

She snatched up a pen as the caller rattled off the digits. Then she stared with disbelief at the number she'd written. The Ashley Meyer case. Dear God, who was this? Was Sam with some violent psychopath?

"Where is that evidence?" the voice demanded.

Mia could hardly breathe. It felt as though a giant hand was closing around her throat.

"Where is it?"

"It's—I don't know." *Wrong thing to say.* "Wait, it's here. In the evidence refrigerator, right here in the lab."

"Go get it," he said. "Now, while I hold. And don't talk to anyone."

Mia's hands shook as she placed the phone atop the

file. She didn't need the case number—she knew it by heart. She knew all of her case numbers by heart. They were her *cases*. Her feet felt leaden as she crossed her workroom and pulled open the glass door etched with a double helix. He wanted her to tamper with evidence. Never in her life would she have dreamed she'd do such a thing, but she was doing it right now.

Her armpits were damp as she walked through the lab where three of her colleague stood at tables, staring into microscopes. One looked up. Two. They'd seen her. Whatever she was about to do, there were witnesses.

Mia reached for the door of the walk-in refrigerator and pulled it open. Could they see her hands trembling? The skin between her shoulder blades burned, and she felt three laser-beam gazes boring into her as she stood before the shelves lined with evidence bags and rape kits. Her movements were robotlike as she combed through the bags, checking labels. And there they were, right where she'd left them Sunday night—the bags containing Ashley Meyer's clothes, her shoes, and the duct tape used to bind her. Hardly breathing now, Mia collected everything and returned to her office, careful to avoid eye contact with her colleagues. She couldn't look at them, and she knew her distress was written plainly across her face.

The phone was waiting for her, the seconds of the call ticking away on the screen.

"I've got it." Her voice sounded raspy.

"All of it?"

"Yes. It's three bags."

"Combine it into one. Put everything under your coat and walk out."

"Where am I—"

"Keep the line open. No cops. Anyone follows you or you speak a word to anyone, Sammy is dead."

The words paralyzed her. But then their meaning sank in. She dropped the phone and sprang into action, ripping open the seal to the largest bag and stuffing the two smaller ones inside, on top of the shoes. She couldn't look at the blood-covered sandals. Ashley Meyer's sandals. Sandals that probably had her killer's blood on them, along with hers.

Sam, Sam, Sam. Please be okay. How had someone taken him from school? He had to have been at school. It wasn't even two o'clock yet, and in the photograph, he was standing right in front of the sign.

Pulse racing, Mia rode the elevator downstairs and stepped into the lobby she'd walked through only a few minutes ago. Ralph stood guard at the entrance. He gave her a nod that she returned numbly. Her gaze veered to Sophie. How would she explain her abrupt departure? Mia's mind groped for an excuse. She was feeling ill. She'd forgotten an appointment—

Sophie's head bobbed. She was on the phone, thank goodness. On impulse, Mia veered right and headed for a side exit that faced the picnic tables. Ralph's gaze met hers as she reached the door. Did he look suspicious? She imagined that he had X-ray vision and could see right through the coat folded over her arm.

Mia pushed through the door, and it whooshed shut behind her. Freezing air whipped through the skirt and blouse she'd worn to court as she set out toward the parking lot. She realized her back was sweating. And her neck, her chest, her palms. Her breath was ragged.

If she bumped into anyone she knew, they'd probably think she was having a seizure. She clutched the bundle to her stomach and walked as briskly as she could on rubbery legs. The parking lot came into view at last. She spotted her car.

Was he there, watching her? Her gaze combed the rows of vehicles, and nothing seemed out of place. But she wasn't a car person. She'd never paid much attention to who drove what around here. The Aveo was parked on the near end under a security light. In case she'd had to work late tonight, she'd been following Ric's safety advice.

At the thought of him, her chest squeezed. This was Ric's murder case, his evidence she had hidden under her coat. How would she ever explain this?

You speak a word to anyone, Sammy is dead.

Mia quickened her pace until she was almost running. Her heart hammered against her sternum, and she kept expecting someone to yell "Stop!" or "Freeze!" or "Drop the package!" But the only sound was the squawk of grackles in the nearby woods as she pulled open the door and slid behind the wheel of the rental car. She nestled the bag on the floor in back and threw her coat over it. Then she retrieved her cell and rested it in the cup holder. Should she put the phone on speaker? What if the guard stopped her and overheard something? She'd never been stopped leaving the Delphi Center, but anything could happen. Still, she put the call on speaker so she wouldn't miss some vital instruction. Her hands shook wildly. It took three stabs before she could get the car key into the ignition.

Finally, she was backing out of the space, exiting the

parking lot, following the winding road to the gate at the edge of the compound.

"How we doing?"

She flinched and glanced down at the phone. "I'm about to pass the gatehouse. Don't talk."

The gate opened even before she reached the tiny concrete building, and the guard waved her through with a friendly nod. She'd never thought about how simple it was to walk evidence right out of the lab. It was simple because people knew her. They trusted her. She trained her gaze on the road as she glided through the gate. Only after she'd entered the highway did she realize she was holding her breath.

She glanced in the rearview mirror, but the road behind her was empty.

"Okay, I'm through the gate," she said. "Now what?"

He gave her some simple directions that left her more dismayed than ever, because she had no idea where they would lead her.

"Where's Sam? I want to talk to him right now!"

"You do what you're told, he'll be fine."

"Don't you *dare* hurt him! Do you hear me? If you touch one hair on his head—"

"Shut up and drive."

Her gaze shot to the mirror again. Was he tailing her? She was on a two-lane highway and didn't see a soul.

She needed to call 911. Ric. *Someone* who could help her put a stop to this. But she didn't see a way out. A slimy knot of fear formed in her stomach as she came to the juncture in the road and made a left, as instructed. Every instinct screamed for her to change course. She had the sickening feeling that she was driving to the scene of her own death, but she didn't dare deviate from the instructions. Sam had one lifeline, and she was it.

Low, thick clouds gathered along the western horizon as she sped down the highway. At last, a weathered wooden sign came into view: PARSON'S ANIMAL FEED. She tapped the brakes and looked around desperately. The place seemed deserted. There was no one there. No one. She gazed down at the phone in her lap.

"Okay, I'm here. I'm turning." She rolled to a stop in front of a rusty gate. Clipped to it was a faded NO TRESPASSING sign. "Now what? There's a gate."

"Push it open."

Mia got out of the car and immediately stepped into a patch of mud. She tromped up to the gate and pushed it back until it was perpendicular to the fence. She looked around for something to hold it in place—a rock, a brick, anything. What if she needed to make a hasty exit with Sam? She didn't want to be trapped if the gate should swing shut. She kicked off her heels and crouched down to wedge one of them between the gate and the mud. Then she picked her way back to the Aveo in her stocking feet.

A red pickup whisked past her on the highway, and a new wave of panic hit her. This was a quiet country road. And she couldn't have looked more out of place in her business clothes, without a coat or shoes, returning to her soup-can-sized car. She looked like a woman in trouble, and for the first time in her life, she wished Texas didn't have a reputation for neighborly drivers. The last man who'd stopped to help her had ended up dead.

Mia's throat closed. She felt dizzy. Was this the same man? She didn't fully understand what this was about, but she knew the person behind it had an ice-cold heart filled with deadly intent.

Mia gunned the little car through the narrow opening and bumped over the pitted gravel road toward what had to be her destination, a dilapidated factory. The building was made of gray corrugated metal and seemed to be listing slightly to one side. On the second story, a pair of tall, paneless windows seemed to stare down at her.

Where was the caller? Where was Sam? Or was she here by herself and Sam was hidden somewhere far away? She didn't know what to hope for, so she hoped for a miracle as she pulled the Aveo up to what looked like the front entrance.

"Go around back."

She snatched the phone from her lap as her gaze flew around frantically. He could see her.

"Where are you?"

"That's not important. Go around back, and get out with the package. Be sure you have everything."

Mia steered the car around the building. At the back was a rusted Dumpster and a loading dock with a metal door. Beside the Dumpster was a brown metal cube with a gray finger of smoke curling up from it.

And she understood.

Her breath backed up in her lungs as she rolled to a stop. Her pulse pounded. She watched the curl of smoke. She bit her lip. She couldn't do this.

She pulled the evidence bag into her lap and stared down at it. How many hundreds of bags like this had she unsealed during the course of her career? How many times had she signed her name to reports and evidence receipts? How many times had she held up her hand and taken an oath to tell the truth about something that could put someone behind bars for a lifetime? What she did right now could cast a shadow over every case she'd ever touched.

"Sam's waiting."

The voice chilled her to the core. With a trembling hand, she put the phone into the cup holder. A calm settled over her. Sam was six. He was her blood. She thought of Amy, and the pain was so sharp it took her breath away.

Mia climbed out of the car. The gravel was cold and hard under her bare soles as she walked across the lot to the incinerator. The rusted metal door stood ajar, and a stripe of orange glowed. On the ground lay a pair of long metal barbecue tongs, and she knew they'd been left there for her. She picked them up and used them to pull open the metal hatch.

A pile of logs burned inside—and something else, too, judging by the acrid fumes. Her cheeks heated as she stood before the fiery pit. She said a silent prayer for Ashley. And for Sam. And for herself. And then she tossed the bag into the maw of hell.

CHAPTER 9

I'm pulling in now," Ric said as he whipped into a space in the Delphi Center parking lot.

"We're downstairs," Jonah told him. "And the night guy's expecting you."

Ric cut the engine and took a moment to yank off the tie he'd had on since the funeral. All day, he'd felt as if he was suffocating, although he doubted it was only because of the tie. Throughout the service, the burial, and the wake that followed, Ric had been acutely aware of the many gazes of other police officers and the bitter disappointment he read on their faces. Frank Hannigan had gone into the ground, and Ric was no closer to making an arrest than he had been when he'd first caught the case. Every badge at that funeral knew that with each day that ticked by, the chances of anyone ever making that arrest dwindled.

Ric tossed his tie onto the backseat on top of his suit jacket. Maybe tonight would help. This case was way short on physical evidence, and he needed to develop every piece of it he could.

He climbed the steps. The guard pushed open the

door as Ric passed through the tall Greek columns. Despite the fact that he was expected, the guard took his police ID and gave it a thorough inspection. Then he went behind the empty reception counter and entered something into the computer before pulling a visitor's badge from Sophie's desk and handing it over.

"Ballistics is on G-three." The guard jerked his head toward the elevator bank. "Right this way."

"I bet I can find it."

But the guy trudged along beside him in his rubber-soled shoes. When the elevator opened, Ric stepped inside and jabbed the button. Nothing. The guard reached in and, with a pointed look at Ric, flattened his hand on a panel before pressing the button. G-3 turned green.

Ric shook his head as the doors closed. The security here was unreal. You'd think they were cultivating anthrax or something. But what the hell did he know? Maybe they were.

When the doors parted, he faced a long gray corridor lined with cinder blocks. Following the sound of gunfire, he strode through the tunnel, noticing the downward slope. Thirty feet underground? Fifty? This building looked big from the outside, but given the subterranean levels, it was a monster.

He reached a glass window and saw Jonah on the other side, standing beside a stocky guy who was shooting a pistol into a test-firing chamber. Ric tapped on the glass and both men glanced up. Jonah opened the door and made some quick introductions.

The head of the Delphi Center's Firearms Identification Unit wore army-green tactical pants, ATAC boots, and a black golf shirt. His name was Scott Black, and Ric immediately pegged him for an operator. Former SEAL would be Ric's guess, but then, he seemed pretty chummy with Jonah, who'd done a stint in the Army. Maybe he was an ex-Ranger.

Jonah wore the same clothes he'd had on at the funeral, minus the coat and tie, and Ric noticed tiny black flecks on his white sleeves. Gun oil. That shirt was toast, but judging by the smile on Jonah's face, he couldn't have cared less.

"Check this out," his partner said. "It's an FN Five-seven. Don't see these every day."

"Good thing, too," Ric said. The gun was nicknamed the "cop killer" because of its ability to penetrate Kevlar.

Black passed the pistol to Ric. He admired the olive drab finish, the tightly checkered grip, the tactical light beneath the barrel. Ric had never seen one of these up close, but he knew a lot of SWAT guys who liked them.

"Nice," Ric said, although everyone in the room knew that was a gross understatement. He handed back the weapon.

"We were just killing time. Scott ran down that brass from the Hannigan crime scene."

"You matched the gun?"

"The shell casing." Black opened a cabinet and put the pistol away alongside an impressive array of handguns. "I ran it through IBIS."

"The ATF database?" Ric asked.

"Right. We're working on our own database, but it isn't operational yet, so we still have to go outside to get our comparisons."

"And you got a match?" Ric glanced at Jonah and saw the gleam in his eye. His partner wouldn't have called him all the way out there just to look at some cool toys.

"Take a look." Black led him across the room to a computer workstation. He tapped a mouse, and the image appeared on flat-screen monitor on the wall beside him.

"Picture on the left is from the shell casing recovered on the shoulder of Old Mill Road," Jonah said.

The screen was about twice as big as his TV at home. It showed a circular shell casing with marks from the firing pin. "That's most likely from the round that hit Hannigan."

"On the right's another image from your crime scene. This cartridge case was recovered from the ditch. Identical markings."

"Probably the round that hit Mia," Jonah said.

Ric gritted his teeth as he stared up at the screen. The idea of someone putting a bullet through that soft flesh of hers made his blood boil. A few inches to the left, and Ric could have been at two funerals today.

"Here's the third one." Black tapped a few keys, and a new image popped up, nearly identical to the other two, only this one was slightly grayer. "This was in the database. Same firing pin marks. Also, whatever weapon ejected the shell casing at your crime scene ejected this one, too. The extractor marks match."

"Where's it from?" Ric looked at Jonah and knew he wasn't going to like the answer.

"Fort Worth," Jonah said. "I put in a call right before you got here."

"What kind of case?"

"Homicide. Groundskeeper at a country club turned up with a bullet in his brain. They found him on the side of the road. Shell casing was recovered from the ditch right next to him. It's an open file. Six years old."

"Also, I took a look at the bullet collected by the ME at autopsy," Black said. "It was a little misshapen, but I ran some tests. Your murder weapon is going to be a forty-caliber Glock. Besides the rifling marks on the projectile, we've got the shells. The Glock uses a flat-tip firing pin, which leaves a distinctive mark on the primer of the casing. Most firing pins are round and leave a round dimple on the primer. You recover any candidates yet?"

"Not yet," Jonah said.

"Well, if you do, gimme a yell, and we'll do a test fire for you."

"If we get our hands on a weapon, you'll be the first to know," Ric said.

Fifteen minutes later, they exited the Delphi Center and headed for the parking lot.

"Not the first Fort Worth murder case that's come up lately," Jonah said as they tromped down the steps.

Ric glanced at his partner. He'd told him about the cold case in Fort Worth, although he'd omitted the part about Mia's dream. He hadn't wanted to make her sound flaky. Why he was protecting Jonah's opinion of her Ric had no idea.

"You think it's a coincidence?" Jonah asked.

"Don't know."

"Yeah, but what do you *think*?"

Mia's rental car was parked in the front row, beneath a security light. Ric walked over to the Aveo and touched the hood. Warm. She'd just arrived. He glanced over his shoulder at the row of windows glowing at the top of the building.

Ric looked at his partner. "I think I've never been a big believer in coincidences."

Mia's eyes blurred with tears as she stared at Sam's picture on her computer screen. Where had this come from? Who had sent it? She would have given anything for the magical ability to crawl into the photograph with Sam and see who was standing on the other side of that camera lens. Maybe Alex could tell her. She was no magician, she was the closest Mia knew, at least when it came to computers. If anyone in the lab's Cyber Crimes Unit could provide Mia with some desperately needed answers here, it was Alex Lovell. And Mia needed answers, needed them badly enough to return to the very last place she wanted to be right now, a place so flooded with unpleasant memories that just standing in the room was unnerving.

"What are you doing?"

She gasped and spun around. Ric Santos stood in her doorway, and for an instant, she thought she was imagining him.

His gazed homed in on her computer screen. Mia glanced down, panicked. Could he see the image?

"Oh, you know." She eased her body in front of the screen and forced a smile. "Just working late. More reports."

Ric's gaze lingered on her eyes, and she knew he knew that she was lying. Or at least nervous. Why hadn't she bothered to close her door? Because she'd only planned to be in there a minute, just long enough to collect her laptop and take it across the hall to show Alex, who was waiting for her right that very second.

Ric stepped closer, and Mia tensed. "Kind of late, isn't it?"

"Not really."

He glanced at her computer but didn't react. Maybe he thought it was a screen saver. She reached over casually and put the system to sleep.

"So." She turned around to face him. "What are *you* doing here? It's almost ten."

"I was down in ballistics."

"How'd you get up here?"

"Bumped into Ben in the parking lot after I noticed your car. He offered me an official escort."

Mia's brain kicked into gear. Ben was in cyber crimes, and he and Ric knew each other from the cold case they'd worked on last summer. That meant Alex wasn't alone in the computer lab, and Mia was going to have to be careful about what she said. She shot a longing glance at the door. Alex was probably waiting for her, and from her tone of voice on the phone earlier, Mia knew she had somewhere else she wanted to be. Mia did, too. Anywhere but there. She had to get rid of Ric.

"What'd you do with your coat?"

Her gaze snapped to his. Her coat? She opened her mouth to answer, but no words came out. Her coat was on the floor of her bedroom, alongside her shredded panty hose. Every stitch of clothing she'd had on today now reeked of smoke from that incinerator.

"That ski vest's not gonna cut it." Ric nodded at her

bare arms. "It's supposed to dip below twenty tonight."

He was right. In a T-shirt and jeans, she wasn't dressed for the weather. But after spending the afternoon with Vivian and Sam, she'd been in a hurry. She'd been in a *huge* hurry to drive out here and get answers to some of her questions, specifically, how had someone faked the kidnapping of a little boy when two teachers, a principal, and the boy himself claimed he'd been safely inside his school all day long?

Alex was the only person Mia knew who might be able to answer that. If Mia could just get rid of the detective standing in her office, eyeing her suspiciously.

He knows I'm guilty. The thought flashed through her brain, but she banished it. How could he know?

"You're right." She managed another smile that was so phony, her cheeks hurt. "I should have checked the weather." She tried to keep her hands steady as she folded shut her laptop and zipped it into her computer bag. She felt Ric's gaze on her as she hitched the bag onto her shoulder.

"You're headed home?"

"Actually, I am. I just have to swing by the computer lab and talk to someone for a few minutes."

He stepped closer, and his dark brows knitted. "Something wrong?"

"No. Why?" She made her eyes wide and tried to look clueless while her pulse pounded in her ears. *He knows everything. Someone saw me. He's not here for ballistics—he knows what I did.*

He reached up and brushed a lock of hair out of her face. It took every ounce of her self-control not to burst into tears. Yes, something was *very* wrong. And if he kept looking at her with those concerned eyes, she was going to break down and tell him everything.

"I'll walk you," he said, and it was all she could do not to heave a sigh of relief.

She led him out of her office. The computer lab was right down the hall, which meant only a few more seconds of dodging his questions. She remembered what her sister, the lawyer, always said—the best defense is a good offense.

She turned to look at him. "How was the funeral today?"

"Okay."

At his obvious discomfort, she pressed harder. "Any progress on Frank's case?"

"No."

And whaddaya know? The conversation fizzled.

They passed the DNA lab, where a couple of her colleagues were burning the midnight oil. One looked up from his microscope as she passed. Mark. He'd been there earlier, when she'd taken the evidence. Had he noticed her shaking? Did he look suspicious now? Her composure vanished, and her pulse started racing again.

"Mia?"

"What?" She glanced up at Ric.

"I said, how'd it go in court? Did you give Pickerton a run for his money?"

"Oh. No, not exactly."

Her court appearance felt light-years ago. In a way, it was. And in that moment, she realized that her career would be forever divided into two phases: before and after what she'd done that afternoon. That afternoon was pivotal. Irrevocable. And she'd be dealing with the fallout for the rest of her career—if she still had a career, which was highly doubtful. She felt that tightness in her chest again, that gaspy feeling, as if there wasn't enough air. What was she going to *do*?

When they reached Digital Imaging and Cyber Crimes, Alex glanced up from her computer and got up to come open the door. She eyed Ric curiously through the window.

"Want me to wait?" Ric asked. "We can grab some dinner after?"

Mia swallowed hard. He was watching her mistrustfully. He knew something was up.

She forced another smile. "How about a rain check? This could take a while."

Alex pushed open the door, and Mia slipped through without a backward glance. She couldn't handle Ric right now; he was much too observant, and she couldn't take another cross-examination.

"What was that about?" Alex asked.

"Nothing. Should we set up at your desk?" Mia glanced around the room and noticed Ben at the back, clacking away on his keyboard.

"Works for me."

In seconds, Alex had Mia's laptop open and the e-mail forwarded to herself so that she could manipulate it on her own computer.

Mia's stomach tightened as Sam's smiling face appeared larger than life on Alex's screen. Guilt swamped her. She couldn't believe her nephew was caught up in this nightmare.

"Can you trace the message?" she asked anxiously.

Alex's fingers danced over the keys, but she didn't say anything as she opened windows and read lines of text that looked to Mia like gibberish.

"This file was altered before it was sent," Alex mumbled. "Disguised, you might say. However"—*tap-tap-tap*—"there are a few things left to work with."

More clicking at the keyboard as Mia gnawed her thumbnail. Alex muttered. Mia held her breath. Finally, she couldn't stand it.

"I need to know where he got this photo," Mia said. "I need to know how this happened."

She needed to understand how someone had managed to send her this picture of Sam standing in front of his school, in front of a book-fair announcement that had been posted on the school marquee just that morning, when everyone, including Sam, said he hadn't set foot outdoors all day long.

"Gimme a minute," Alex said.

Mia took a deep breath. *Patience.* But her nerves were raw, and the adrenaline that had been rushing through her system all day was starting to take its toll.

After destroying critical evidence in an active murder investigation, Mia had rushed back to her car, only to discover that the caller had hung up. Without a word about Sam. Sick with fear and yet terrified to call the police, Mia had called her sister, launching a frantic search for Sam, who turned out to be sitting safely in his math class at Cedar Hollow Elementary. Despite the assurances of the principal, both Vivian and Mia had shown up at the school anyway to make sure there was no mistake, which there wasn't. Sam was fine. Maybe a little baffled by all the grown-ups popping their heads into his classroom but fine.

Mia had spent the next half-hour in the front seat of her sister's Volvo, spilling her guts. She'd told Viv everything, start to finish, and they'd both shed tears. But then Vivian quickly moved on to practical matters, such as what to do next. They'd come up with a plan—one for Vivian and Sam and another for Mia.

Mia's plan involved appearing to follow the caller's instructions while she figured out what the hell was going on. Her sister's plan was more complicated, but it should keep her and Sam safe.

"I think I see what happened here," Alex said, jerking her back to the present. Mia looked into her friend's chocolate-brown eyes and felt a wave of trust. Before joining the Delphi Center, Alex had managed what amounted to a civilian-run witness-protection program. She knew how to keep secrets.

"Are you listening, Mia? You look a little dazed."

"I'm listening."

"Okay, what you've got here is a picture within a picture. In other words, it's a fake."

Mia wanted to breathe a sigh of relief, but something in Alex's tone told her she couldn't. "There's a problem, isn't there?"

"In terms of Sam's safety? I'd say yes, there's a major problem." Alex pointed at Sam's face. "The image of your nephew is from an actual photograph. So is the image of the school. The doctored part is these images together. They've been overlaid. It's a pretty good job, too. If it weren't for this new software I'm test-driving, I might have missed the signs."

Mia looked at the screen. She leaned closer to study Sam's face, his posture, his clothing.

"Is it possible someone could have lifted this picture from the Internet, like from a Facebook page or something?"

"It's possible."

Mia studied his smile, zeroing in on the gap where his upper central incisor had been little more than a week ago. This was a recent shot.

"Is it possible someone changed the color of his coat? Maybe with a software program?"

"Absolutely," Alex said. "I can do it right now."

A few keystrokes, and the red zippered jacket Sam was wearing in the picture turned purple. Dread pooled in Mia's stomach as she realized how easy this had been and yet how much planning had gone into it.

"I think this picture was taken Saturday at the zoo," Mia said. "Sam was wearing green that day, but everything else is the same. He went missing for about half an hour, and it turned out that he was off with some stranger who'd offered him candy."

Alex's expression darkened. Part of her job with the Cyber Crimes Unit involved running down child predators who used the Internet as their playground, and Mia knew she'd seen some devious schemes used to target kids.

"That could work," Alex said. "Most cell-phone cams are pretty subtle, so Sam might not have been aware that he was being photographed. And that encounter could explain Sam's voice on the phone call. This guy could have recorded it."

"You're saying he got Sam to yell my name?" Mia

sat back, surprised. Sam hadn't reported anything like that to her. Neither had the social worker. Or the SANE nurse.

"Maybe he was lurking around while you and Sam were hanging out together. He could have recorded it then."

The idea made her cringe. Someone had been right there watching them, and she hadn't even realized it.

"And what about tracing this message?" Mia's temper started to kick in as she gazed at the screen. "I want to know who did this."

"I'd like to know, too. This took planning. Whoever this was not only got hold of Sam's picture but also found out where he attends school and went out there to get this shot. Someone went to a lot of trouble to scare you." Alex paused. "Any idea why someone might do that?"

Mia could tell Alex knew she wasn't getting the full story. But until Mia figured out what was happening, she couldn't afford to trust anyone besides her sister.

You speak a word to anyone, Sammy is dead.

The kidnapping might have been staged, but the threat behind it was very real. And whoever was making the threat had figured out Mia's Achilles' heel.

Alex watched her, waiting for an answer.

"I'm not sure," Mia said. "I'd probably understand all of this better if I knew where this e-mail came from. Can you find out?"

"Probably, but it's going to take some effort. This doctored photo wasn't just slapped together. Someone used a sophisticated program."

"Not a bad merge. How'd you spot it?"

Both Mia and Alex turned to see Ben standing behind them, leaning casually against one of the desks. Mia's nerves jumped. She didn't want to let yet another person in on this.

"The shadow," Alex said.

Mia's need for information overcame her apprehension. "What shadow?"

"Yeah, I'm seeing it now," Ben said. "Good eye." He leaned over and pointed to the screen. With his rimless glasses, faded jeans, and sloppy T-shirt, he could have been your average twentysomething computer geek. But after working with him on a few cases, Mia was no longer fooled by his laid-back demeanor. The man was off-the-charts smart and a virtuoso on anything with a microchip. "See this?" He pointed at Sam's face. "These shadows are sharp. This looks as if it was taken outdoors on a sunny day. The background shadows? More diffuse. Not quite as much contrast."

Mia stared at the picture. The difference was very subtle, but it was there.

"Who did this, anyway?" Ben asked. "It's really not bad."

"That's what we're trying to find out," Alex said. "Someone phonied up a picture of this child and faked a kidnapping."

Ben quirked an eyebrow. "Hope his parents didn't pay a big ransom." His gaze veered to Mia.

"We ran down the phone number earlier, but it looks like they used a spoof card," Alex said.

"You get this on e-mail?" Ben asked Mia. At her hesitation, he said, "I can tell this kid's related to you. There's a strong resemblance."

"E-mail," she told him. Her stomach tightened. She still couldn't believe this was happening.

"He used a Yahoo account," Alex said. "I haven't had a chance to trace it, but I'm guessing it's a dead end."

He nodded. "Shoot it over to me. I'll see if I can get an ID through the cell phone."

"From the e-mail?" Mia asked, puzzled.

"No, from the picture. Oh, that's good, Ben! And damn it, I wish I'd thought of it first." Alex turned to Mia, obviously energized by some brilliant idea Mia didn't understand. "If this photo was taken with a camera phone, we might be able to trace the number."

"I thought you said he used a throwaway phone?"

"To call *you*," Alex said. "But probably not to take the picture. If this guy took the picture with a cell phone, it was probably his real phone. Then he likely e-mailed it somewhere to doctor it up on a computer, using a software program. Ben's thinking we might be able to find digital tracks leading back to the phone itself. From that, he can run down an ID."

"You can do that?" Mia turned to Ben.

"I can sure as hell try."

Jonah signed the crime-scene log and ducked under the tape. He followed the muddy path, taking care not to step outside the route staked out with orange twine. A couple of guys from the sheriff's office nodded as he made his way down the soggy slope.

"Over here."

Jonah recognized Ric's voice and turned to see him silhouetted in the headlights of a crime-scene van. So much for his visit with Mia. Jonah walked over, and it took him a moment to realize that the bulky man standing beside Ric was the medical examiner. In a zip-up camo hunting suit, Froehler looked like the Michelin Man.

"Park ranger found her," Ric said.

Jonah looked at the tall portable light that had been set up near the body. Several crime-scene techs were crouched beneath it.

"Age?" Jonah asked.

"Hard to tell," Froehler said. "I'd say twenty? Maybe older? I'll have a better estimate sometime tomorrow. And I know your next question. Yes, she was beaten. Was she dead beforehand? We'll find out at autopsy."

"What do you *think* happened?" Ric asked.

"As I told the sheriff, read the report." He glanced in the direction of the body, and something in his eyes changed. "But if you want my first guess, blunt-force trauma. Someone smashed that girl's skull in. Repeatedly. But if you quote me on that, I'll flat-out deny it."

Froehler picked up his bag of gear and trudged off to his car.

"He's done already?"

"Until the autopsy," Ric said. "He got here an hour ago. We got a late invitation."

"From who?"

"The sheriff. He knows about the Meyer case, gave the chief a heads up."

They started walking toward the lake, and Jonah tried to ignore the bitter wind. The temperature had dropped again, and Froehler's hunting getup wasn't looking like such a bad idea now. Jonah scanned the area, but it was tough to see much. Only a small patch near the lake had been spotlighted.

"Same MO?" Jonah asked.

"No."

"Knife wounds? Duct tape?"

"Didn't see any."

Their boots made a slurping noise as they neared the water's edge. They stopped near a huddle of investigators in white jumpsuits.

Jonah looked at Ric. "So, why are we here?"

"See for yourself."

The bloated corpse lay facedown in the mud. Her arms were spread out on either side of her, but her ankles had been bound with rope and fastened to a cinder block. Jonah pictured someone tying her up like that and was struck by the utter coldness of it.

"Notice anything?" Ric asked him.

"Besides the hair?"

"Yeah."

The victim had long blond hair, like Ashley Meyer's, but so did a lot of women. He kept looking. One of the crime-scene guys stood up, obscuring their view, and Jonah was left with the grotesque afterimage of the swollen body.

"Well . . ." It was the first thing he'd noticed, so he tossed it out there. "She doesn't look that bad, considering."

"Considering she's been in the water? Yeah. That's what I noticed, too."

They were standing on a slope covered with mud and plants. "They just drain the lake?" Jonah asked.

"River authority opened the flood gates Sunday, lowered

it about six feet. We've had below-freezing temperatures since then. Helps narrow the timeline."

"How long's Froehler think she was underwater?"

"Wouldn't commit. But he said probably not more than a day. Two, tops."

"Santos." A deputy waved them closer, and they stepped into the halo of light.

Jonah noted the gray skin, the slimy debris tangled in the hair. A weight settled over him. Every victim he saw made him think of someone's parents. Ric looked on with a stony expression, maybe thinking about his own daughter.

"You were asking about knife wounds?"

"Yeah."

"Nothing on the torso," the deputy said.

The body-removal team rolled the victim over and onto a sheet. Jonah clenched his teeth and forced himself to look at her face, her body. His gaze stopped on her hands, which had already been bagged for transport in order to preserve whatever evidence might be trapped under her fingernails.

"What about the hands?" Ric asked, following the same train of thought. "Any cuts? Defensive wounds?"

"That's what I was going to tell you," the deputy said. "Her hands were sliced up good."

After just a few hours of sleep, Ric went in early to work on the only solid lead he had in Frank's murder investigation: a scrap of brass no bigger than a kid's thumb.

But the shell casing got him nowhere.

The Fort Worth detective who'd worked the case was dead. The case files were in storage, and it would take at least twenty-four hours to send someone into some basement closet to drag them out. And the one person who had any primary knowledge of the case—a beat cop who had been a rookie at the time—was out sick.

Ric cursed as he hung up the phone, but the sight of his partner's six-four frame charging across the bullpen lifted his hopes.

"You've got something," Ric said when Jonah stopped at his cube.

"Damn right I do."

"Tell me it's about the Hannigan case."

"The motel room murder. Maintenance guy at the motel just ID'd the last man seen entering her room from a photo lineup. We've got a suspect, and he's got a rap sheet."

Ric leaned forward as Jonah slapped a photo array onto his desk. "Which one is he?"

"David Corino, a.k.a. Spider. He's a pimp out of San Antonio."

"Spider? Where do they come up with this shit?"

"Hell if I know."

Ric studied the mug. The DOB beneath the picture put Corino's age at twenty-six, but he had the teeth and face of an old man.

"Looks like a tweaker. What's on his sheet?"

"Just what you'd expect," Jonah said. "Couple of busts for possession. Did a two-year stretch for burglary. Most recently, he got caught up in a raid on a meth lab down in Bexar County. Prosecutor gave him a pass to flip on some of his buddies."

"And he's running girls, too?"

"Looks like. And meth. Remember the victim had some onboard at the time of her death?"

Ric sat back in his chair. "Any chance we can link him to Ashley Meyer?"

"Highly unlikely," Jonah said, confirming Ric's first take. "He's got an alibi for the time of her murder."

"You already talked to him?"

"Not yet, but I made some calls. Day after Christmas, they sacked him up on those drug charges. He was a guest of the Bexar County taxpayers until two days ago, when he decided to flip."

"Takes him out of the running for the Meyer homicide," Ric said. "Even if the ME got the time of death off by a day or two, it still wouldn't work."

"So, if this guy pans out, we were right," Jonah said. "The murders aren't related."

Ric's phone rang, and he picked it up. "Santos." He listened carefully, then stood up and grabbed the jacket off the back of his chair.

"Where's the fire?"

"That was Rachel," Ric told him. "She's got Mia Voss sitting in her conference room waiting to talk to us about the Meyer investigation."

"Why can't she talk to us here?"

"I don't give a shit where she talks to us. Sounds like we've got a break in our case."

Rachel Patterson swept into the conference room wearing a pinstripe suit and a mantel of confidence befitting a prosecutor with a ninety-percent conviction rate.

"Detective Macon, glad you could make it. Where's your partner?"

"Should be right behind me. He had a call come in—"

Ric walked into the conference room and nodded

at the district attorney as he tucked his phone into the pocket beneath his gun holster. His gaze slid to Mia, and her stomach did a nervous dance.

"Good, you're here." Rachel placed a legal pad at the head of the conference table before pulling out a chair and sinking into it. "Let's all have a seat, shall we? I have to be in court in twenty minutes. Dr. Voss?" The prosecutor's ice-blue eyes settled on Mia. "You have something for us?"

Mia cleared her throat. She felt Ric's and Jonah's gazes on her as she folded her hands together on the faux-wood table. She'd spent much of the past twelve hours mentally rehearsing what she planned to say, and she was determined to do it with a steady voice.

"I'm here about the Ashley Meyer case."

The prosecutor's brows arched. Mia shifted her attention to Jonah, then Ric. An expectant silence filled the room.

Mia zeroed in on Rachel, because she couldn't stand to look at Ric.

"I'm afraid there's been a mistake. My mistake, actually."

"What sort of mistake?" Rachel asked.

"It has to do with the evidence. The physical evidence. That you all sent to the laboratory for testing." Oh, God, she was already fumbling her speech, and she'd barely started.

The prosecutor's gaze narrowed sharply. "What happened?"

Mia's pulse raced. She fought the urge to swallow. She forced herself to make eye contact with the district attorney as she said the words. "I seem to have lost it."

"Lost it?" She leaned forward on her elbows.

"Misplaced it, actually."

Rachel blinked at her, and Mia realized it was the first time she'd seen the prosecutor taken completely off guard. "Which evidence did you lose?"

"All of it."

Rachel's mouth dropped open. Silence hung in the air. The only sound was the faint trill of a phone from an office down the hall.

"We sent three separate bags."

Mia's gaze veered to Jonah, who was eyeing her hostilely with his arms folded over his enormous chest. If not for the business attire, he could have been a bouncer at a bar.

"That's correct," she said.

"How do you lose three separate bags?" he wanted to know.

"I'm not sure." Mia glanced down at her hands, clasped in front of her. Her knuckles were white. She forced herself to loosen her grip. "But they went missing earlier this week, and I've looked everywhere."

"When?" This from Ric, who was watching her steadily with those brown-black eyes.

Mia's throat went dry. "Excuse me?"

"When did it go missing? You told me you went in Sunday to have a look."

Mia nodded. She'd expected this to come up. "I did a preliminary examination of everything Sunday and jotted down some notes on which procedures I planned to use. That was in the afternoon. I thought I returned everything to the refrigerator afterward." Mia's shoulders tensed as she came to the next part. "But it could be I only *thought*

I'd returned everything, and somehow I forgot. Maybe I left it out, and it got mixed in with the trash."

"You mean it got *thrown away*?" Rachel looked appalled.

"I'm not sure. It's possible. I was tied up in court most of the day Monday, and I don't remember seeing it. Yesterday afternoon, I went in to start swabbing and testing, but I couldn't find anything." She forced herself to stop talking and allowed the silence to stretch out. *Don't say more than you have to.* Nervous blather was the downfall of many an expert witness. Rachel had taught her that. Mia found it absurdly ironic that she was using the prosecutor's own technique to deceive her.

If, in fact, she *was* deceiving her. Rachel's blue eyes were cool and calculating as she sat back in her chair.

"Any chance a coworker has it? Maybe some other scientist?" Jonah asked.

"No."

"Don't you people have controls for this sort of thing?" Rachel's tone was clipped. "How do you *misplace* critical evidence in a murder investigation? You're supposed to be a world-class forensic lab."

"We are."

"You're not!" She slapped a hand on the table, and Mia jumped. "Do you realize what this does to our case? Even if you manage to find the evidence, there's time unaccounted for. The chain of custody is ruined."

"I realize that."

"Do you realize Ashley Meyer was twenty-one?" Rachel demanded. "Do you realize she had her skull crushed by some sick pervert who also sliced her to ribbons? Do you realize the best chance we had of finding out who did that to her and bringing that person to justice was contained in the *three* bags of evidence you carelessly misplaced?"

Mia's stomach cramped. She felt her cheeks heating with every word. And when the words stopped, she felt an impossibly heavy weight settle on her shoulders.

"I realize that, yes. And I take full responsibility." Her voice wasn't steady now. Neither were her hands. She tucked them into her lap and wiped her damp palms on the tops of her thighs as she waited for more. "I also realize that time is of the essence in a case like this. I wanted to make you aware of this as soon as possible."

Rachel snorted. "Very helpful of you, thanks." Then she leaned forward and jabbed a finger at her. "This isn't over. I'll be calling your supervisor to discuss the ramifications of this."

"I understand."

Silence returned as the prosecutor shot daggers at her from across the table.

Mia made herself wait, although she wanted nothing more than to sprint from the room. She couldn't look at Ric or even Jonah. She kept her gaze on Rachel in case there were any more arrows to absorb. But she seemed to be out, at least for now. Mia rose to her feet and, with an unsteady hand, collected her jacket and purse from the back of the chair.

"I hope you realize what this means." Rachel shook her head. "I specifically requested you for this task because I knew we were dealing with a challenge here, and you have—or you *had*—an impeccable reputation. Not anymore. This incident is a disgrace to both you and your laboratory."

Mia folded her jacket over her arm and waited for more. But Rachel just sat there, glaring at her.

Mia looked at Jonah, who seemed disgusted. And once more at the prosecutor, who seemed irate.

Finally, she looked at Ric. And it was his Arctic stare she felt burning into her as she quietly left the room.

CHAPTER 10

Mia stared dazedly at the screen above the bar, still not sure how she'd ended up there. She'd gone back to work. She'd continued the charade of a normal day, all the while waiting for the anvil to drop on her head. It hadn't. Then she'd driven home and let herself into a cold, dark house.

She'd never minded living alone before, but lately, she'd been afraid of even her own shadow. Paranoia? No. Someone *had* been watching her. Someone *had* tried to hurt her. Someone *had* targeted her family. Any rational person would feel afraid.

Very few rational people would do what Mia had done about it: go out drinking with Sophie in the pathetic hopes that with the right amount of alcohol, the nightmare that had become her life would somehow go away. And *that* was how she'd gotten there, she realized. She'd ditched all rational thought and decided to numb her brain at a cheap sports bar. As ideas went, it wasn't great. But she was going with it.

"You okay?"

She felt a hand on her arm. Sophie had taken a break

from her new friendship with Vince Moore to check on her status.

"Fine."

"You seem blue tonight. And you look kind of pale." Sophie tipped her head to the side. "You're not getting that flu, are you? God, you'll be out for days."

"I'm fine. Really." Mia looked over Sophie's shoulder. The young detective was popping peanuts as he watched whatever game was on and pretended not to be listening to every word. "Do you guys want to leave?" Mia said it in a barely audible whisper. "I can get a ride home if—"

But Sophie cut her off with a slight shake of her head. She wasn't leaving with this guy. And Mia wasn't going to get stranded looking for a ride. It was the first good news of her entire day.

Sophie glanced over Mia's shoulder. "Well, look what the cat dragged in."

Mia turned around, and even that one drop of good news evaporated as Ric walked into the bar. Mia's stomach fluttered while he scanned the crowd, then settled his attention on her. She felt the urge to run, but he pinned her to her stool with that black-eyed gaze as he homed in on her like a missile.

"Hi, Ric."

He ignored Sophie's cheerful greeting and focused solely on Mia. "We need to talk."

His tone was dark, and she decided to match it with glib. "We do?"

"Not here."

She looked him up and down. He wore jeans and his black leather jacket, which told her he was off for the night and this was personal, not business. Maybe.

Mia shrugged. "It's going to have to be here. I'm in the middle of a drink."

He picked up her Bud Light and downed the last sip. Then he pulled out his wallet and tossed a twenty onto the bar.

"You're finished. Let's go."

Mia stared at him, and he clamped a hand on her arm. "Now."

The intensity in his eyes sent a hot current through her. He wasn't going to back down. There was no escape this time. She'd known they'd have it out sooner or later, but she'd hoped to be better fortified. Emotionally drained and with several drinks in her, she was at a disadvantage—which was precisely why he'd hunted her down, she felt sure.

Mia slid off the stool.

"Uh, *hello?*" Sophie's hand closed around Mia's arm. "Going someplace?"

"I need to talk to Mia." Ric spared Sophie a glance.

"I didn't ask you." Sophie turned to Mia, her eyes filled with concern. Mia could see why. Ric looked pretty ticked off right now. He looked dangerous, actually. But he wasn't a danger to Mia, and she knew she had to talk to him.

"It's okay," she told Sophie. "I'll catch a ride with Ric. See you tomorrow, all right?"

She wove her way through the crowd and out of the bar, acutely aware of Ric's hand curled possessively over her shoulder. For Vince's benefit? Mia wasn't sure. The guy seemed to have hit it off with Sophie. Maybe the message was intended for Mia.

She shrugged him off the second she got outside and

pulled on her coat. It was the sleeveless ski jacket again, but she'd brought a scarf.

Ric walked in silence beside her, his hardened gaze trained on the front row of the parking lot where he'd managed to find a space for his oversize truck.

He jerked the passenger door open without fanfare. Mia climbed in. As he went around to the driver's side, she leaned her head back against the seat and briefly closed her eyes. She could get through this. If she could handle a seasoned district attorney, she could handle a cop.

The leather seat creaked as he slid behind the wheel and started the truck. Without a word, he switched the heat to high and shifted the vent to face her.

"Where the hell's your coat? It's twenty-five degrees out."

"This goes better with jeans."

He shot her a disapproving look, then rocketed backward out of the parking space.

Mia scanned the interior of his truck. It had all the alpha-male accessories she would have expected—GPS attached to the dash, discarded baseball cap on the floor, mud-caked cowboy boots tossed in back behind the driver's seat.

She spotted a plastic CD case peeking up from the door pocket and felt a twinge of discomfort. Taylor Swift. That would definitely be Ava's.

Ric had a day's worth of stubble on his jaw and a hard, world-weary look in his eyes. She wasn't sure why the idea of him as a father should make her uneasy, but it did. She sensed that it was a part of his life he kept closed off, at least from her. And for some reason, that hurt her feelings.

Ric passed the turnoff to her street, and she glanced over warily. "Where are we going?"

"Klein's."

"I already ate."

"I didn't."

Mia gritted her teeth and looked away. This was a bad idea. She wasn't sure she could sit across a table and lie to him for an entire hour. She wasn't sure she could do it for five minutes. But evidently, she wasn't going to have a choice.

When they got there, he led her through the now-familiar foyer that smelled like hickory, but this time, she detected the scent of homemade bread, too.

And this time, he didn't hold her hand.

He walked all the way to the back of the restaurant and claimed an enormous circular booth in the corner. It could have accommodated eight people, and Mia felt relieved until he slid around and ended up right beside her, even closer than they'd been the other night. She scooted away and gave herself some space.

The waitress appeared almost instantly. Ric got good service here. Mia glanced up at the woman's flirty smile and realized he probably got good service everywhere.

Mia pulled a menu from the condiment holder in the center of the table and tried to tamp down this sudden flare of resentment toward some college girl barely out of braces.

"Get y'all started with some drinks?"

"I'll have—"

"Two Bud Lights." Ric took Mia's menu and handed it to the server. "And two rib platters, extra sauce."

Mia stared at him as the waitress dutifully wrote down the order and disappeared.

"I wanted chicken."

"No one eats chicken at a rib joint."

"I do. And I wanted a Diet Coke, too. Jeez." Mia crossed her arms and turned away. He was trying to get a rise out of her. It was some underhanded strategy to draw her out, and she wasn't going to fall for it. She'd eat a platter of freaking ribs if she had to.

Ric leaned back against the booth and rested his elbows on the back. She had a great view of his nice, firm pecs in that faded T-shirt. Oh, and the very mean-looking gun plastered to his hip. An accident? She didn't think so. He was absolutely trying to intimidate her, and she absolutely wasn't going to let him.

"Okay, Mia, let's hear it."

"Hear what?"

"What the hell's going on?" He glanced around and then nodded at her. "No cops. No prosecutor. Just you and me."

"Last time I checked, *you* were a cop."

"Is that a problem for you?" A dark brow quirked up, and she realized where he was going with this.

"Why should it be a problem? I haven't done anything wrong."

"You lied to detectives in an ongoing murder investigation."

"I didn't *lie,*" she said. "I *misplaced* evidence."

"Don't you mean you lost it?"

"Yes, I lost it."

"Which is it? Lost or misplaced?"

"I lost it."

"Bullshit." He leaned forward and nailed her with a look. Every cell in her body wanted to shrink away, but she forced herself to hold his gaze. "You didn't lose anything."

"I did."

"You didn't. You make notes to yourself about damn near everything. You organize your grocery list like the aisles in the supermarket. You alphabetize your fucking CDs in your fucking living room. Don't tell me you lost three *separate* bags of evidence."

"That's what happened."

He leaned closer. "Don't lie to me, Caramia. I don't like it."

"I'm not." Her heart was thudding in double time, and she stared at the fierceness she'd never seen on his face before. And she realized she was cowering. She'd slid down in the booth and was gazing up at him, wide-eyed and skittish, like a rabbit in the presence of a wolf.

She shifted away from him on the vinyl seat and straightened her spine. "I'm human, all right? Anyone can make mistakes and get distracted. I've had a lot on my mind."

"Yeah, like what? I want details. You're holding out on me."

"Like . . . everything. *Life.*"

He scowled. "You don't have a life. Your job is your life."

She stared at him, stunned that such a brief statement could hurt so much.

And here, all this time, she'd thought he didn't know her. He knew her entirely too well. And clearly, he didn't like what he knew.

"Two rib platters, extra sauce."

A plate the size of a hubcap appeared in front of her and she sucked in a breath. The aroma of barbecue sauce, tangy and spicy, rose from the table.

"Anything else?"

She blinked down at the food and thought of asking for a small shovel. But of course, the question was directed at Ric, not her, and he'd already dismissed the waitress with a wink.

Mia's temper festered. He was pretending to be angrier than he was. It was a ploy, as she'd first thought, to get her emotions stirred up and make her open up to him.

And she'd almost fallen for it.

She reached for the silverware beside her plate.

"Don't even think about it." He picked up one of his ribs with two hands and chomped down. Rich brown sauce decorated the tips of his fingers. He licked some from the corner of his mouth, never moving his gaze from her face.

"You make a lot of assumptions, you know." She unrolled the silverware from the napkin and smoothed it over her lap. "I mean, what? You snoop around my house a little and think you can psychoanalyze me?"

"I haven't snooped anywhere. Yet." He tugged the last bit of meat from a rib with his teeth, then set the bone aside.

"What's that supposed to mean?"

"You're lying. I don't know why yet, but I will."

She shook her head and looked down at her plate. *Platter.* As in it belonged on the buffet at a Thanksgiving dinner, right beneath the turkey.

"This is a ridiculous amount of food," she said.

"A lot of it's bone."

She sank her teeth into a rib and pulled the meat loose with as much delicacy as she could. The flavors exploded in her mouth, and she was back at her grandparents' farm on the Fourth of July. She'd always liked barbecue, but she hated eating it—ever since she was fifteen at a family picnic and her cousin had oinked at her when she had a plate of ribs in front of her, much as she did now. Mia dabbed sauce from her mouth and took a sip of beer.

For a while, they ate in silence. The ribs and homemade bread tasted amazing, and the creamy coleslaw was going to have to count as her salad for the day. She felt better with some food in her stomach. More settled, actually. And the sting of his earlier words started to fade.

Of course, it was probably the beer. Her third one of the evening, and she'd never been much of a drinker. Everything was getting fuzzy around the edges, including all of the reasons she needed to be on her guard. He probably had a lot of interrogation techniques up his sleeve, and sooner or later, one was bound to work on her.

Beside her, he seemed to have moved closer, but their place settings were just where they'd always been, so it must have been her imagination. He was watching her from beneath those thick black eyelashes. She'd always loved that feature about him. Mia's lashes were pale and gold, and she had to use mascara all the time.

Sam's face flashed into her mind. He had his mother's freckles. And Mia's, too. It was a family trait, one no one had escaped, not even Amy with her pretty dark hair.

She took a deep breath and looked over at Ric again. Thinking of her dead sister was not a good sign. She'd had too much to drink, and she should leave now.

As if tuned in to her thoughts, Ric caught the waitress's eye and signaled for another round of beers. The next thing Mia knew, he was leaning back in the booth, watching her intently as she licked barbecue sauce from her fingers. Something warm and sexual flared in his eyes, and she felt an answering pull of lust. But that didn't mean she was going to let her guard down.

"Come on, Mia." His hand found the nape of her neck, and he rubbed it lightly, making her shiver. "Talk to me. Something's going on with you."

She pushed her plate away and sat back. The rubbing continued, soft strokes down her neck with the pad of his thumb. She slid away from him, because it was the only way she could talk and keep her thoughts straight.

"What's going on is that I'm having a bad week. A bad two weeks. And I'm tired. And stressed. And human. I made a mistake, okay? Quit accusing me of lying, especially when you haven't had the guts to be upfront with me from the moment we met."

His eyebrows lifted. "How am I not upfront?"

She shook her head.

"You want upfront?" He leaned his elbow on the table and turned, creating their own private booth-within-a-booth. "I'm attracted to you. Very. I've wanted to get you in bed from the second I saw you in that lecture hall, going on and on about mitochondrial DNA or some crap. But I made myself stay away because I *like* you, all right? And I respect you—or, at least, I did until today. Too much just to use you for sex and walk away. That upfront enough for you?"

Mia stared at him, and for the first time, she knew he was being completely straight with her. Which made the middle part so much worse. He didn't respect her anymore.

She lashed back. "What makes you think I would *let* you use me? Maybe I'm not attracted to you."

He just looked at her. And his you-have-no-life comment reared its ugly head again. He thought she was desperate.

All right, she'd had enough for one evening. She couldn't do this, and she didn't have to.

She grabbed her purse off the seat and yanked out some money, which she left on the table. "I need to go."

His sigh was filled with resignation as he leaned back to dig his wallet out of his jeans. "Put your money away."

"This isn't a date." She scooted all the way around the big booth. "And I can walk myself home."

But he was right behind her on the seat and grabbed her wrist as she stood up. The warm pressure of his hand pushed her closer to the edge. She felt the beer and the stress and the emotion closing in on her and knew she was on the verge of a meltdown she couldn't have in front of him. She jerked her wrist, but his grip tightened.

"Ric, just let me go, okay?" She heard the quiver in her voice. "Please?" It was a whisper.

He searched her face for a long moment. And then he released her.

Mia got through the restaurant somehow and even

managed to make it to her street corner before the tears started leaking, making icy little tracks on her face. She dabbed the end of her scarf to her cheeks and tried to shake off the encounter. It was over. She'd done okay. She hadn't really told him anything, and she'd escaped with at least a little bit of her dignity intact.

She felt emotionally wrecked, but so what? She could deal with that. She'd protected her secret, and she'd protected Sam, which was the only thing that mattered. Whatever relationship she might have had with Ric Santos had been doomed anyway, from the very start, by his opinion of her.

He thought she had no life, and she didn't. The Delphi Center was her life. Her work was her life. Being a cog, however small, in the justice machine was her life. It was all she had, and very soon she might not even have that.

I have to leave. I should have left already. Even more than the alcohol in her system, the memories of what she'd done made her stomach turn. She'd betrayed one of the few institutions she believed in. She'd betrayed her profession. Worst of all, she'd betrayed Ashley Meyer, who deserved nothing less than the justice Mia had committed to seek out for her. Now she'd never get it. Her family would never get it. And someone who had ruthlessly torn apart so many lives would be free to do it again.

Mia wrapped her arms around herself and hurried on, as if somehow she could outrun herself and what she'd done. She turned onto her tree-lined street, and the familiar porches and driveways and yards emerged from the blur. Many of the windows had gone dark already. It must be late. She saw the abandoned skateboard on her neighbors' lawn and immediately thought of Sam.

She'd done it for Sam. Her actions might not be moral or wise or even understandable to many, but they'd been motivated by love. And she knew that no matter how wrong she'd been, no matter how selfish and impulsive, she'd do the same thing all over again if she believed Sam's life was at stake.

But there wasn't going to be a do-over. Her actions were permanent. All that remained was for her to face up to the horrible mess she'd created and hope the fallout wouldn't be as widespread as she imagined.

What she imagined was bad. For the first time in her life, she was regretting the relentless efficiency with which she'd attacked her job. Who would have thought she'd one day come to regret taking part in so many cases?

Mia swiped the last of her tears away as she reached her house. She did a quick security scan of her drive-way and shrubbery as she pulled the keys from her purse and climbed the steps to her door. Once inside, she moved quickly to silence the beeping alarm. She flipped the lock, tossed her jacket and scarf onto the bench in the foyer, and pulled off her boots. She took a deep breath.

Home again. And alone again. But it didn't feel eerie now, as it had when she'd come home from work. It felt like a relief. She'd had more than enough company tonight and wanted nothing more than to be alone with her burgeoning headache.

She padded into the kitchen and took a bottle of water from the refrigerator. Sixteen ounces and two aspirins were exactly what she needed to stave off the hangover she suspected was coming tomorrow. She twisted off the top and turned around.

Something lay on her breakfast table. She stepped closer to look—

And let out a scream.

CHAPTER 11

～

Her shriek reached him just as he'd turned his back on her house and started heading back to his truck. Ric bolted up the sidewalk and tried the door.

"Mia!"

He threw his shoulder into it, but it was locked.

"Mia, open up!"

No more screaming now, just a silence that put the fear of God in him. He sprinted around the house and up the driveway. A light was on in the kitchen, casting a yellow square on the driveway. Ric pounded on the door, then cupped his hand to the glass and peered in.

The kitchen was empty. He jerked the sleeve of his jacket over his fist and aimed a punch at the glass.

Mia walked into the room. She met his gaze through the window and moved straight for him.

His heart started beating again. She looked pale and a little shaky, but she was definitely in one very nicely shaped piece.

The door pulled back, and he stepped inside.

"What happened?"

She shook her head and glanced around.

"Mia?"

"Nothing. I just . . . I was standing here in the kitchen, and I thought I saw someone."

"Where?"

"In the driveway. I was looking through the window above the sink, and a shadow moved."

"Stay here." Ric slid his Glock from his holster and went back out to prowl around the perimeter of her house. No shadows. No footprints. No broken windows. No cigarette butts or food wrappers or signs of anyone camped in her yard, staking out the place. At the side of her garage, he found an overturned trash can. A plastic bag had been torn open and garbage strewn everywhere. Ric cleaned up the mess and secured the lid back onto the can.

When he returned to the kitchen, she was leaning against the sink and watching the back door, her arms folded tightly over her chest. He noted the pepper spray on the counter at her elbow. He rested his Glock on the counter and nudged her aside to wash his hands.

"Nobody out there," he said, reaching around her for a dish towel. "But it looks like you might have had a raccoon in your trash."

She stared at him, and he noticed the makeup smudges under her eyes. Goddamn it, she *had* been crying on her way home. Ric's gut twisted. He'd meant to coax information out of her, not make her cry.

He tossed the towel onto the counter, then pulled his phone from his pocket and started dialing.

"What are you doing?"

"Calling a patrol unit. We should have one in the area."

"You said it was a raccoon."

"It probably was. But it doesn't hurt to have someone do a loop through your neighborhood."

"No cops." She snatched the phone out of his hand and disconnected the call. "It's fine. There's nobody there."

He frowned at her as he gently unfolded her fingers from around his phone. Her hand was shaking. Her whole body was shaking. Was this a delayed reaction to getting shot the other night? He'd never seen her so uptight, but she'd probably never been under this much stress.

He put the phone on the counter and slid his hands up the backs of her elbows. His fingers stopped just shy of her bandage. She tensed. Little tremors shook her shoulders.

"Hey." He slid his hands up her neck and tilted her head back to look at her face. Her blue eyes were wide and watery and filled with so much anguish it made his chest hurt to see it, so instead he looked at her mouth. And when those pink lips parted, he leaned down and kissed them.

Ric's tongue was in her mouth. The knowledge was a five-alarm, cymbal-clanging wake-up call to every dormant nerve in her body as she stood there, pressed against her kitchen sink, being kissed by him and kissing him back. He tasted hot and spicy and fierce, and he kissed her like he was starving for her. She wrapped her arms around him and leaned into him and kissed him the same way right back. And then his hand was sliding up under her bulky sweater, curling warm around her rib cage, and clutching her against him as he pulled her up to her tiptoes and fed on her mouth some more.

She'd imagined kissing him so many times, but she'd never imagined *this*. She'd never known. She'd never dreamed he could awaken every cell in her body with only his tongue. And his lips. And his teeth and his hands and the rock-hard ridge pressing against her abdomen. His tongue tangled with hers, sweeping her mouth, tasting her, as his thumb dipped into her bra and found her nipple. His touch there was an electric shock, and she gasped, but he swallowed it. She kept kissing him, absorbing his taste and his warmth and his touch and melding herself against him and wishing he'd never stop. He murmured something, and she pulled back and looked up at him dizzily. And the reality of what was happening slapped her in the face.

No cops.

"Where'd you park your car?"

He drew back. "What?"

"Where's your truck?" She turned around. "Is it outside?"

"It's at the restaurant. Why?"

"You followed me home."

"What'd you think I would do?"

She pulled out of his arms and looked around. The green light of her burglar alarm blinked at her. That alarm had been on when she got home. And yet someone had been in her kitchen and left a message for her right there on the table. It was a wordless message but unmistakable. The purple Mardi Gras beads she'd last seen dangling from the rearview mirror of her Jeep could mean only one thing. The man who'd carjacked her had been in her house, and he wanted her to know that. He was the same man who'd threatened Sam, and he wanted her to know that, too. He was lethal. And she had no doubt he'd make good on his threat if she didn't play by his rules.

"What is it?" Ric was watching her with that intensity again.

"Nothing." She looked away, and her gaze fell on the black handgun sitting on her counter beside Ric's phone.

Ric's handgun. His service weapon. Her heart lurched as she stared at it for an endless moment.

No cops.

She glanced up at Ric, and all of the questions she'd been asking since the night of the shooting swirled through her mind. And all of the mental acrobatics she'd been doing to answer those questions suddenly ceased, because, just like that, the answer that had eluded her for so many days tumbled into place.

She understood. She'd underestimated this.

And she had to get Ric out of there, soon. Because that plan she'd made with Vivian wasn't going to work now.

That plan could easily get her killed.

She needed a new plan. And it was time to call Alex.

CHAPTER 12

∽

The storage room for the Fort Worth Police Department was a cinder-block bunker underneath the courthouse, and if the room was attached to the building's central heating system, Ric sure as hell couldn't feel it. What he could feel was a burning knot of frustration that had been with him since he'd left Mia's kitchen.

He still couldn't believe he'd kissed her. And not just kissed her—he'd damn near pulled her to the floor and yanked her clothes off right there in that kitchen. He probably would have if she hadn't slammed on the brakes. He was supposed to be investigating. What the hell was wrong with him?

Mia was wrong with him. It wasn't just his attraction to her—that was nothing new. He'd been fighting that urge, very successfully, for months now. This was something else, something more, attraction mixed with a deep-rooted protective instinct that had come out of nowhere and blindsided him. The more he tried to block it out, the more it took hold of him. He couldn't sleep for thinking about it. For thinking about *her*. He was exhausted and distracted, and that was no way to run an investigation.

Ric rubbed his bleary eyes and returned his attention to the case file in front of him. It was pitifully thin, which, given the fact that the murdered grounds-keeper had been both poor and illegal, wasn't surprising. Money was tight everywhere, and even homicide cases had to be prioritized. From the looks of it, this one hadn't been given more than about two days of a detective's time. Ric finished skimming the autopsy report and flipped to the last page of the detective's notes. The ballistics report was tucked in back, right behind a couple of crime-scene photos. The half-page report told Ric what he already knew. Carlos Garza had been killed by a forty-caliber bullet, which had probably been fired by a Glock. The shell casing had been run through IBIS, but the database didn't contain any matches.

Until now. The same weapon that had fired the bullet that killed Garza had been used to kill Frank Hannigan. Had been used to *nearly* kill Mia. Every time Ric thought about it, the burning in his gut intensified.

What was she caught up in? And why was she lying to him? She was hiding something. Ric knew it, just as surely as he knew he was about one hot look away from dragging her off to bed and stripping away everything between them—the lies, the secrets, everything. No matter what she told him, he knew that trust and sex were all part of the same package with Mia. Ric knew that if he could get her naked, he could get her trust. And that, more than anything, was what he needed right now.

Ric closed the folder and looked into the file box. It contained only two other items: an envelope holding the brass recovered from the crime scene and a paper evidence bag containing the gardener's clothes.

"Still down here, eh?"

Ric glanced up as a bulky guy with white hair stepped into the room. Ric had never met him, yet he was all too familiar. He looked like every homicide cop on the brink of retirement Ric had ever known, right down to his thinning hair and his clogged arteries.

"Brice Baker?" Ric ventured.

He leaned against the door frame and rattled his pocket change. "That's me."

"They told me you were in court today."

"Judge took a recess." Baker pulled a pack of Winstons from the pocket of his cheap navy blazer and tapped out a cigarette. "Got your phone message. What can I do you for?"

"I'm up here on a case. Carlos Garza." Ric nodded at the file. "Saw your name on the log. Looks like you checked out this jacket about six years ago?"

Baker blew out a stream of smoke, ignoring the NO SMOKING sign posted beside the door. "Groundskeeper up at the country club. Bullet to the forehead, I seem to recall."

"That's the one."

"That case is colder than a witch's tit."

"Not much in the file, either," Ric said. "Can I ask why you checked out the case file?"

"Sure can. Don't mean I'm gonna remember much." He stepped up to the table and took a look, ashing on the linoleum floor as he flipped through the pages. "Yeah, I recall it now. I'd planned to interview him. He was on my list of witnesses on another case. Checked out before I could track him down, unfortunately."

Ric's interest picked up. A list of witnesses implied a serious investigation. "What was the other case?"

"A homicide." Baker sank into the metal chair at the end of the table and took another drag.

"When?"

"Oh, 'bout six years ago." He pulled the file toward him and tapped the date on the autopsy report with a meaty finger. "Yup, just a few days before ol' Carlos bought it. This was a teenage girl. Stabbing vic. She was found in the woods near the golf course."

Ric sat forward. "Laura Thorne?"

Baker's gaze sharpened. "What have you got on it?"

"Her name came up in connection with another case I'm working." Goddamn it, Mia was right. There *was* a link. Ashley Meyer, Laura Thorne, Frank Hannigan, now this. It all tied together. Ric just didn't know how.

"You worked that case," Ric stated, although he hadn't known the detective's name until now. Jonah had given Ric a notebook full of names and numbers to follow up on while he was in Fort Worth, and he'd been planning to do it after he read the Garza file. Now the detective was sitting right in front of him.

"Messy business." Baker shook his head. "Pretty girl, too. Least she was, up until some nut job got to her. Slashed her up good, dumped her in the woods. Grounds-keeper you got there"—he nodded at the file—"he was on shift when she went missing from a party out there at the country club. Thought he might have seen something. Woods where she was found border on the golf course he tends, so I had it in my mind to interview him, see if he knew anything."

"You guys ever close the case?" Ric asked, although he knew the answer. Mia had looked into it just last week, and she was thorough.

"Nope. Sent her clothes off to the lab. Nothing useful turned up. That case file's been collecting dust for a while now."

Unbelievable. A homicide with a clear link to another unsolved homicide, and yet both cases hadn't been looked at in years.

Baker dropped his cigarette butt on the floor and crushed it out with his shoe. The shoe was polished. Baker's shirt was pressed and his hair combed neatly— probably all for his court appearance. The man might be close to retirement, but he still took pride in his job, which made Ric bite back all of the snide comments he wanted to throw out right then.

"I know what you're thinking," Baker said. "But you know how it is. Money. Case loads. Our population's 'bout doubled these last twenty years. You think the budget's kept up? Heck, no. We still got just a hand-ful of guys working a shitload of cases. We focus on the fresh ones. The ones with suspects, witnesses, physical evidence. I bet it's the same where you are."

Ric didn't say anything, which was confirmation enough. It was the same everywhere. But that didn't make it okay. Once these cases went cold, it was next to impossible to heat them up again. It took confessions, DNA hits, people like Mia who were willing to take a second pass at old, forgotten evidence using new tech-nology.

"You still have the case file?" Ric asked.

The detective nodded down the endless row of shelves lined with cardboard file boxes. "Bottom shelf. End of that row." He pushed back in his chair and stood up. "I comb through it every year or two, see if anything new jumps out."

Now it was Ric's turn to be surprised. "You do?"

"She sticks with me. Go through the crime-scene photos. You'll see what I mean."

Ric followed him down the long row of boxes, sobered by the knowledge that each one held evidence of a crime that had destroyed lives and devastated families. Baker stopped at the end and stooped down to pull out a box. He handed it to Ric, then pulled a second box from the shelf.

"Lot more than the Garza file," Ric commented as they carried the boxes back and dropped them onto the table.

"Pretty blond teenager. You know how it is." Baker pulled off the lid to his box and tossed it aside. "Turned out she was a high-class call girl. Me? I'd call that an oxymoron, but that's what the press labeled her. They got hold of some pictures from some Web site she was on and kept running them over and over on the news, so the story wouldn't go away. Even my partner got obsessed with it." Baker reached into the box and pulled out a fat accordion file. "Now, most of what you want? It's in here. The rest of this is noise mostly, stuff that never went anywhere."

But Ric was already thumbing through another folder, this one filled with newspaper articles. "What's all this?"

"Ah, just some research I did once on similar cases."

Ric glanced up at him.

"Told you, she sticks." Baker looked almost apologetic as he explained his continued interest in Laura Thorne. "Something about that girl—maybe her age, I don't know. It's a memorable case."

Ric pictured Mia sitting beside him at El Patio, peeling the label off her beer and looking uncomfortable as she told him about her haunted dreams. He thumbed through the pile of news clips. Homicides mostly. A few rapes, all of young women in Texas, Louisiana, or Oklahoma. A clipping fluttered to the floor, and Ric crouched down to retrieve it from the beneath the table. He stared at the image of a smiling young girl. "Paroled Sex Offender Suspected in Teen Stabbing Death," the headline read. Something about the girl's youthful grin made it impossible for Ric to look away.

He stood up. "Hey, they ever collar this guy?" He showed Baker the clipping.

"Nah, not enough evidence."

"Think it's related to the Laura Thorne murder?"

"My best guess is no. That was twenty years ago. And the MO was totally different. I just ran across that and kept it, I don't know why. Maybe because it was a stabbing."

Ric slipped the article back into the file, and the photo caption caught his eye. His hands froze as he read the name.

Jonah's cell phone started buzzing the second he tossed his gym bag onto the floor of his pickup. He dug it out and recognized his partner's number on the screen.

"Where are you?" Ric demanded by way of greeting.

"On my way to pick up dinner. Want me to grab you some?"

"I'm still in Fort Worth."

Shit, he should have been back hours ago. "What happened up there?" Jonah asked.

"A lot. I'll fill you in later. Listen, you talked to Mia today?"

"Nope."

Ric cursed.

"Why would I talk to her?" Jonah fired up his truck and navigated the congested parking lot filled with people still committed to their New Year's resolutions.

"I don't know. I thought maybe she'd been by the station or something. Shit."

"What's wrong?"

"I can't reach her. She's not answering her phone. I need you to go by her house."

Jonah turned into traffic and cast a longing glance at the row of neon signs lining the highway. He hadn't eaten all day, and he'd just spent an hour lifting weights.

He sighed. "Where does she live?"

Ric recited some directions, and Jonah pulled an illegal U-turn. "You want me to check if her car's there or what?"

"Let me know if she's home," Ric said. "And if anything looks funny, go in and check it out. I'll give you her alarm code."

"How do you know her alarm code?"

"I saw her enter it the other night."

Jonah filed that away along with the alarm code as Ric rattled it off. He heard the worry in his partner's voice and wasn't sure what to make of it. Ric wasn't a worrier. Protective, yeah, but he didn't sweat the small stuff.

Jonah saw the sign for Sugarberry Lane. "I'm turning on her street now," he said. "Call you in a few."

Jonah located the little white house but learned next to nothing from the first pass. Some lights were on. No car in the drive, but the door to the single-car garage was closed, so she could have parked in there. He pulled another U-turn at a stop sign and parked in front of a house across the street from Mia's where a FOR SALE sign was planted in the yard.

Jonah retrieved the pistol from his gym bag and the lock-picking tool from his glove box before climbing out of the truck. He left his keys inside. Anyone dumb enough to want a dinged pickup with nearly two hundred thousand miles on it was welcome to it. As he crossed Mia's street, he marveled at the amount of crap he was willing to put up with for his partner. But then, it was a two-way street. They had each other's back, which was more than Jonah could say for some of the guys he'd worked with over the years.

Jonah walked up the sidewalk. What was it with this girl? He didn't like Mia Voss, not since that meeting with the district attorney. He could tell when people were lying, and she'd had been lying her ass off through that entire meeting, which didn't sit well with him. It shouldn't have sat well with Ric, either, but the man was blinded by lust. Jonah half hoped he'd nail her and get it over with so he could get his head back in the game and start clearing some of their cases.

He rang the bell and waited. He peered through the windows flanking the door. He rang again. No TV on or voices that he could hear. Blinds covered the windows. He went around back. After finding the garage empty, he knocked on the door off the driveway.

Lights on in the kitchen. Drawers and a few cabinet doors hanging open. Not what he considered a good sign. Jonah knocked again, but again, no answer. He spent about ten seconds picking the lock with his slender tool before stepping inside. The alarm beeped at him, and he tapped in the code.

"Mia? Jonah Macon here. You home?"

No answer. He stood for a moment in her kitchen. All of the appliances were off. A notepad sat on the counter beside a cordless phone. It was a mess, but he didn't pick up on that weird vibe he usually got at a crime scene. No funky smells. No signs of struggle. He glanced around and ventured into the hall, where a coat closet stood open and a heap of scarves and gloves lay on the floor. Jonah turned down a hallway leading to a bedroom, a bathroom, and what looked to be the master suite, where low music emanated from a radio. He stepped into the room.

Clothes were strewn across the bed. An empty duffel bag sat on the floor, and the closet stood open, as if someone had been packing in a hurry. Jonah glanced at the clock. Nine-sixteen, and the radio was tuned to NPR. Had someone turned it on tonight, or had it gone on that morning and no one had been there to silence it? Jonah's detective instinct favored the second scenario. He glanced around some more. The top drawer of the dresser was open, and it looked as though someone had cleared out half the contents of—he stepped closer to see—the underwear drawer.

"Make *one* move, and I'll shoot."

Shit. The female voice behind him was almost as surprising as the words. He spread his hands and started to lift them above his head.

"Not *one* move! I swear I'll put a bullet in you."

Something in her tone told him she meant it. How the hell had she gotten the drop on him?

He heard steps on the carpet behind him. He smelled perfume. It was soft and musky and didn't belong to Mia Voss any more than that voice did.

"Take that gun out of your pants, and toss it onto the bed. Now."

Jonah sighed. "Lady, I'm a cop."

"Now."

Slowly, he pulled the Glock from the waistband of his sweatpants and held it up by the trigger guard. "Jonah Macon, San Marcos PD. I'm a friend of Mia's."

"Are you deaf, too?"

Jonah took a deep breath and tossed the pistol onto the bed, turning as he did to get a look at her.

She was tall and blond and wore a short black dress and high black boots that left way too much to his imagination. And she held a snub-nosed revolver aimed straight at his dick.

Her wide blue eyes didn't leave his face as she stepped to the bed and collected his pistol with her left hand. Confusion flittered across her face as she realized she didn't have a place to put it. She glanced around, then backed up a few steps on those four-inch heels and set the gun on an armchair.

"Keep your hands where I can see them."

He noticed the tremor in her fingers, which didn't

inspire much confidence as she reached into the tiny purse hanging off her shoulder and fished out a silver flip phone.

"Ma'am, would you just listen before you do that? I told you, I'm a cop."

A cop who, very unfortunately, had left his ID in his truck.

She ignored him and punched numbers on her sleek little phone. Shit, was she calling 911? This was going to be a huge pain in the ass—

"Vince? Hi, it's Sophie." Her voice shook only slightly as she held the phone to her ear. "I'm standing in Mia's house, and I've got a man here claiming to be a police officer. Jonah Bacon."

"That's *Macon*."

"Jonah Macon . . . Uh-huh. San Marcos PD, he says." Those blue eyes widened a bit. "Okay, thanks. Make it quick, would you?" She dropped the phone back into her purse and thrust the gun forward. "My friend's with the San Marcos police. He says he's never heard of you."

"What?"

"And he's coming over. Along with *several* squad cars. They'll be here any second."

"He said that?"

"Yes."

Jonah rolled his eyes. No one said "squad cars." And Moore was fucking with him, the little shit. This was probably payback for Jonah cleaning him out last month at the poker table.

Jonah weighed his options. It would take him two seconds, tops, to disarm this girl, but if by chance she got a round off, he might seriously regret not talking his way out of this. He didn't particularly feel like getting his balls shot off tonight.

"Listen, Sophie, I really *am* a cop. I'm a friend of Mia's, too. Call her up and ask her."

"What are you doing in her bedroom?" A little line formed between her brows, and he could tell she sort of believed him.

"You want to aim that thing someplace else while we talk?"

"That doesn't answer my question."

Jonah closed his eyes and counted to three mentally. "Look, my partner, Ric Santos, was worried about Mia and asked me to check in on her, all right?"

Evidently, "Ric" was the magic word, because all of the tension went out of her. She lowered her gun, and Jonah was surprised by the wave of relief he felt. He was tempted to drop to his knees and kiss her feet with gratitude. But then, that might have been because of the boots. He wasn't sure where this woman was going dressed up like that, but he was extremely tempted to follow her.

"Where'd Mia rush off to, anyway? Ric's concerned." He dropped the name in again, just for good measure.

"That's none of your business." She glanced behind him. "Neither is her panty drawer. What are you doing in here?"

Good question.

"She skip town?" he asked. "Ric's not going to like that. She's wanted for questioning in an ongoing criminal investigation."

This got him a get-real look, and she thrust out her

hip. "Mia Voss hasn't broken any laws. Unlike *you,* who seem to be trespassing."

"And what are you, her house-sitter?"

She gave him a peevish look, then stalked around him and retrieved a gray tackle box from the floor of the closet. "I'm here on an errand." She veered around him again, and he got another whiff of her perfume. Then she walked into the hall. Jonah followed, snagging his gun as he went.

"Tell your partner that Mia is fine." She pulled the front door open and stood beside it, inviting him to leave. "And if she wants to talk to him, my guess is she'll answer her phone."

Jonah stepped into the cold night air. She punched a code into the keypad near the door, then joined him on the porch. She shivered slightly. He guessed she'd left her coat in the shiny black Tahoe that was parked in front of the house now.

She turned her back on him and locked the door with a key from her purse, which was just big enough to accommodate that LadySmith revolver with the rosewood grip. Very nice.

"You got a last name, Sophie?"

"I do." She picked up the tackle box and turned to face him. "Good night, Officer Macon. Tell Ric I said hi."

"What do you mean, she's 'indisposed'?"

Ric stood at the Delphi Center reception desk as Sophie pretended to be both disinterested and professional.

"She's not available at the moment. If you'd like to leave a message—"

"I already left a message. And I need to see her. Now."

"I told you, she's—"

"Listen, Sophie, this isn't personal," he lied. "I need to interview her in connection with a homicide investigation. I'm not asking, I'm telling. Get her down here now, or get me her boss."

Sophie glared at him. Then her gaze flicked behind him, and Ric sensed the very large security guard who had been stationed at the door a few seconds earlier.

"There a problem, Ms. Barrett?"

She gave him a saccharine smile. "Not at all, Ralph. We're just fine."

Ralph backed off, and Sophie dialed something on her phone. "If you wouldn't mind waiting a moment . . . ?" She looked at Ric expectantly, and he stepped away to admire the colorless January view through the windows as she finally summoned Mia. A few minutes later, the elevator dinged, and he turned to see a scrawny guy with glasses striding toward him. King of the lab rats. Great. Ric cut a glance at Sophie, but her attention was glued to her computer screen.

"I'm Dr. Snyder, director of DNA Services for the Delphi Center. How may I help you today?"

"I need to see Mia Voss. I'm sure she's busy, but—"

"Dr. Voss is on sabbatical."

"She's *what*?"

"We encourage our scientists to take a break from their case work from time to time." A condescending smile. "We are, after all, primarily a research institution, Mr. Santos. Is there someone else who might be able to assist you?"

Ric gritted his teeth. He glanced at Sophie, who

looked to be on the phone now, although Ric hadn't heard it ring.

"How long is her sabbatical?"

"That I can't tell you."

"Can't or won't?"

"We respect our employees' privacy here, Mr. Santos. If you're interested in the details of her schedule, you'll need to contact her directly." His gaze darted down to the badge at Ric's belt. "I'm quite sure you have access to her contact information."

Ric shook his head as he left the lobby and put on his shades. Sabbatical. Un-fucking-believable.

She'd run away. Something had spooked her the other night, and it had nothing to do with a raccoon. And now she'd skipped town without so much as a phone call. Why hadn't she asked him for help?

Ric returned to his pickup and roared out of the parking lot. This was why he hated relationships. Women were flighty and unpredictable. And even the nice ones could be sneaky as hell.

Not that he and Mia had a relationship. He hardly knew her. If his trip to Fort Worth had proven anything, it was that he didn't know her at all.

And yet he had this overwhelming urge to protect her. Kind of tough to do when he had no freaking clue where she'd gone.

Did she have a weekend place somewhere? Maybe she was shacked up with a guy? He had no idea. The one thing he did know was that she'd be nowhere near her sister's house. The last place she'd ever go was somewhere that would draw unwanted attention to her nephew. Her sister probably knew where she'd gone, but

Ric had done some more snooping yesterday and learned that Sam's mother was a lawyer. Ric wasn't going to waste his time trying to wring information from a lawyer who didn't want to talk.

He came to a juncture in the road and pointed his truck toward San Marcos. Wherever she'd gone, Ric needed to find her. Almost every murder case on his desk was linked to her in some way. Mia was the key, he knew it.

And yet what did he really know about her? Even with yesterday's poking around, it didn't amount to much.

He knew she had a dead sister. Amy Voss had been raped and murdered at the tender age of seventeen. The murder had happened twenty-one years ago. January seventh, in fact—the anniversary had just passed. Mia would have been eleven at the time, practically the same age as his daughter Ava. The crime was every family's worst nightmare. It had to have been one of the defining events of Mia's life—probably *the* defining event—and she'd never mentioned it to him.

What else did he know about her? Not nearly enough, considering how wrapped up she was in his cases. He knew she was smart, top of her field. He knew she was a workaholic, same as he was. He knew she had a luscious body that she kept covered up with a lab coat most of the time, which for some reason was a major turn-on. He knew that despite the science degrees and the brainy talk, she could kiss like a . . . hell, he didn't know what it was like. It wasn't like anything. He'd barely touched her, and she'd practically combusted. There was no other word for it—all of that pent-up heat coming right at

him. He couldn't imagine what she'd be like if he ever
got her into bed.

Actually, he could. Vividly. And getting her there was
becoming one of his primary goals.

But it wasn't just sex. He needed to know she was
safe. Someone, for some reason, had threatened her, and
so she'd run. She'd run from her house, her job, everything, including him. Goddamn it, he was pissed.

He was also scared.

As a forensic scientist, Mia kicked ass. As a woman
trying to evade a killer? Different story. Mia hated guns.
She couldn't fight worth a damn. And she lacked the
ability to think like a predator.

She needed protection, and Ric would provide it,
along with a few other things she needed.

He just had to find her first.

Mia wandered down the aisle, perusing the selection of
fishing lures. Buzzbaits, Bumble Bugs, plastic worms,
spider grubs. She'd never seen such a mind-boggling
collection of fake invertebrates. She shifted the shopping basket on her arm and turned down the next
aisle, hoping it would contain some items she actually
needed.

Cereal, bread, and granola bars. She added a box of
Sugar Smacks to her basket and headed for the checkout
counter.

"Get you some bait today?"

The man behind the register was large, bearded. And
he wanted to sell her some bait. This was a bait shop,
after all—Bud's Bait Shop—and for all she knew, this
was Bud himself, ringing up her groceries.

"Actually, I'll take some lures." She reached over and snagged a package off a nearby display. This was a fishing town, and she had rented a fishing cabin. Wouldn't hurt to reinforce her cover by throwing a few supplies in with her purchase.

"You fishin' for largemouth bass?"

Oh, hell. "That's right."

"That case, can't go wrong with these."

A tattooed man in a leather Harley-Davidson jacket turned to check her out as he pulled a six-pack from one of the refrigerator cases. Something about his look made her skin crawl.

"Best top-water bait around, you ask me." Bud was still pitching his lures.

Mia smiled. "They're my boyfriend's favorite."

"Need any beer today?"

"That'll be all, thanks." She took out her wallet, careful not to flash him even a glimpse of her new fake ID as she pulled out some cash. The biker walked up behind her, and she tried not to tense her shoulders as Bud made change and bagged her groceries.

"Good luck with the spooks," he said, handing over the bag.

"Excuse me?"

"The Zara Spooks you got there. For your boyfriend."

"Oh, yes. Thanks." She avoided eye contact with anyone as she left the store. Her no-frills Toyota pickup, the one Alex had been kind enough to rent under her name instead of Mia's, was waiting right near the door. Mia tugged her ball cap down over her face as she walked the short distance. The cap, flannel shirt, jeans, and barn jacket were meant to make her blend in. They seemed to be doing the job. This town was pretty small—hardly more than a way station on the road to Canyon Lake, really—but it didn't hurt to be cautious.

She turned the ignition and noted the glowing fuel sign. An eighth of a tank. She could probably put off filling up, but the last thing she needed was to get stranded. She headed for the town's only gas station as an intolerable country song about fried chicken drifted from the speakers. Mia changed the dial, but the music selection was as limited as everything else around there. She gave up and turned it off as she coasted up to a pump. She'd pay cash. She walked up to the attendant, who was too preoccupied with the basketball game on his TV to give her more than a glance.

Mia leaned against the pickup and watched her breath form a frosty cloud as the numbers scrolled on the pump. She hugged her arms closer to her body for warmth.

The town was quiet, secluded. It was exactly what she'd been looking for when she told Alex she wanted to drop out of sight but stay somewhat close to home at the same time. Alex had come through completely. Before joining the Delphi Center, Alex had devoted her career to helping women in trouble disappear, and Mia had expected nothing less. Alex knew how to hide people, and in only a few short hours, she'd managed to throw together a cover and give Mia instructions on how to stay lost for a while. So far, everything had gone as planned.

So why did she feel antsy? Mia gazed down the long empty highway and finally put a label on the emotion that had been hounding her these past three days.

She felt lonesome.

It was silly, she knew. The whole point of being there was to be alone, as far removed from her job and her family and San Marcos as she could safely get and still carry out her plan. And yet the fact that she hadn't had a real conversation in days was starting to needle her. Her brief meet-up with Sophie at the truck stop where she'd delivered Mia's evidence kit to her didn't count. The instant Sophie had mentioned bumping into Jonah, she'd quashed Mia's interest in chitchat.

If Jonah was looking for Mia, then Ric was. And although that didn't come as a surprise, she didn't want to dwell on his interest, or she might waver from her course. And she couldn't. Not yet. She couldn't afford to reach out to Ric or anyone else, no matter how much she wanted to, until she had answers to some of her questions—namely, who was threatening her and her family. Mia intended to find out as soon as the fingerprint evidence she'd submitted the day before came back from the lab.

The nozzle clicked, and Mia removed it from the truck and replaced the gas cap. She wiped her dusty hands on the legs of her jeans and pulled the keys from her pocket. A wool glove fell out, and she stooped down to get it.

Crack!

She dropped to the pavement. She knew that sound. It was—

Crack!

Grit kicked up into her face, and she scrambled around the truck. Someone was shooting at her!

The teenager stepped out from his booth. "What the—"

"Go back inside!" she screamed, flattening herself against the back bumper of the truck. She glanced around frantically. Where had the shots had come from?

Brakes squealed, and she whirled to see a big silver grille coming straight at her. Her heart skittered as it screeched to a stop inches from her face. She lunged away, but a hand clamped around her arm. A wall of leather surrounded her. She thought of the biker guy and started kicking and screaming like a banshee.

"Mia, come *on*!" And then it was Ric's face in front of her, and she was being hauled across the pavement. He jerked open the passenger door to his truck and threw her inside, then dove in behind her. In seconds, he was behind the wheel and peeling away from the gas station, his door hanging open beside him.

"Close your door!" he yelled, yanking his shut.

Mia reached for the handle from her position on the floor. She started to crawl into the seat, but Ric shoved her head down.

"Stay low!"

She curled into a ball and squeezed her eyes shut as she tried to get her breath. It was happening. Again. Someone was shooting at her, and her heart hammered, and she couldn't breathe. Ric took a corner on what felt like two wheels, and Mia bumped against the dashboard.

Ric's expression was mean, warlike. She noticed the gun in his hand. She cowered away from it, not wanting to be anywhere near the thing if it accidentally went off.

He took another corner and looked back over his shoulder. Then he looked at her again.

"Hold this." He thrust the gun at her, butt-first. She

took it. It felt warm from his grip, and she didn't know what to do with it, so she rested it on the seat—pointed at the door—as he dug into the pocket of his jacket and pulled out his cell phone.

"Please don't call the police."

His gaze snapped to her, and his eyes narrowed.

"Please?"

For a long moment, he watched her, his expression loaded with hostility.

"Ric, the *road*."

He looked into the mirror again. His foot eased off the gas, and he looked down. "You can get up now. He's not behind us."

She returned his gun to him and pulled herself into the seat, shocked by the amount of effort it took. Her knees throbbed. They felt bruised, probably from dropping to the ground. Her palms were bleeding. She wiped them off on the legs of her jeans and brushed the hair from her eyes. She looked back over her shoulder, but the road behind them was empty. She glanced ahead. Empty that way, too.

"You sure we're not being followed?" She heard the quiver in her voice.

"That was a rifle shot. Came from the woods north of the gas station."

"So he's—"

"Probably on foot."

For minutes, they drove in silence. Mia closed her eyes and tried to get her breath back. She did, but she still felt the adrenaline pumping through her veins, making her shaky and hot and nauseated.

The truck slowed. Ric pulled over onto the shoulder

and turned to face her. Those black eyes bored into her, straight into her soul.

"Who was that?" His voice was tight with fury.

She stared at him. She opened her mouth to answer, but then Sam's face flashed through her mind and she clamped her lips shut. She couldn't tell anyone her suspicions, not even Ric. Not until she knew if she was right.

"Answer me, goddamn it!"

She swallowed. "I don't know."

He watched her for a long moment, then looked away and cursed.

"How did you find me?" she asked.

"I looked."

He took his phone from the console and started dialing.

"What are you doing?"

He cut a glance at her. "Saving your ass."

CHAPTER 13

～～

The phone call was short, clipped. Even if it had been in English instead of Spanish, Mia doubted she would have understood what was going on. After disconnecting, Ric tapped some info into his GPS and swung back onto the road, leaving a spray of gravel behind them.

"Where are we going?"

He kept his gaze on the highway.

"I've rented a house on the south rim of the lake," she said. "All my stuff's there."

"Forget your stuff."

She stared at him.

"I'm taking you to a safe house. The Bureau has one not too far from here."

"You called the *FBI*?"

"I called my brother."

"The FBI agent."

He just looked at her. He'd probably figured out by now that she didn't trust cops. Of any flavor. If there was one thing she felt certain of, it was that the man who'd carjacked her and killed Frank Hannigan and staged

Sam's kidnapping was a cop. Besides carrying a gun identical to Ric's, the man knew way too much about way too many things not to be some sort of law-enforcement insider. Current or former cop, Mia didn't know, but either way, he had connections.

She took a deep breath and stared through the windshield, resigning herself to a new fate. A safe house. With Ric. How was she going to investigate this thing with him babysitting her?

Or maybe babysitting wasn't what he had in mind. She darted a look at him. His face was hard, determined. And she could tell just from looking that it would be pointless to attempt an argument right now.

Mia opened the console and then the glove box before finding a stack of fast-food napkins. She moistened one with saliva and used it to dab away the blood on her palms.

"What about my truck?" she asked, as calmly as she could manage. Her hands were still quivering, and she felt as if she'd just downed about six espressos.

"That was yours?"

"A friend rented it for me."

He glanced at her, and she would have bet a thousand dollars that he was wondering if the friend was a man. He could continue to wonder, because she wasn't getting Alex involved, not after everything she'd done to help her.

"I'll have Rey take care of it," he said, meaning his brother.

"But how will he—"

"He'll take care of it."

And that was the end of the conversation. Mia returned her attention to her scrapes.

Soon he turned onto another narrow highway and headed west. The country was dry, rugged. The dark green cedars peppering the hillsides were the only spots of color on the wintry landscape. Ric turned south again, then west. Barbed-wire fences lined the roads. They passed through hills and canyons inhabited by livestock and the occasional ranch house. Mia tried to calm herself by looking out at the scenery, but of course, that didn't work. Nothing worked. For the second time in two weeks, someone had *shot* at her.

The truck slowed, and she saw a black dot on the horizon. It was a Chevy Suburban pulled over beside a huge oak tree. Ric eased onto the shoulder and parked behind it. A man got out and went around to the back, where he opened the tailgate and started unloading boxes.

"What's all that?" she asked.

"Provisions." Ric opened his door, and Mia reached for hers. He caught her arm. "Stay here."

He left her there with the engine running, reeling from that last little blow. He didn't want her to meet his brother. What did that mean, exactly?

The two men transferred the boxes to the bed of the pickup, and Mia watched their movements with interest. Same height, same build. Even the telltale bulge under Rey's jacket was the same, and she wondered if there were other Santos brothers and if all of them were cops. She thought Ric had mentioned something once about a sibling in the military.

When the stuff was transferred, they stood talking for a moment. Rey cast a glance her way. She wished she could read his expression behind those sunglasses, but the Santos men seemed to keep their emotions shielded.

Ric rested his hand on his brother's shoulder and said a few final words before returning to the truck. In that one stark instant, she realized that the two were close. Very. Brothers in the strongest sense of the word. She felt a flutter in her heart and a twinge of longing.

The door squeaked open, and Ric was back without a word. He pulled around the SUV and tapped the horn, and then they were back on the road, speeding toward their destination.

"How much farther?"

"Not much."

Within minutes, they pulled onto a dirt road that curved through some low hills. They reached a metal gate with a rusty chain securing it in place, and she was reminded of her trip to the abandoned factory. Ric jumped out to undo the lock. It was a combination lock, and he knew the code, courtesy of his Bureau connection, no doubt. Mia was tired of feeling useless, so she scooted behind the wheel and drove through the gate so that he could reattach the chain. Then she moved back into her seat, and he navigated the rest of the way to their destination.

Mia had never seen an FBI safe house before, never even imagined one. But even the dullest imagination could have envisioned something more impressive than the modest stone building nestled at the base of the next hill. It was less than half the size of her bungalow and flanked on either side by scraggly mesquite trees. She glimpsed a tiny shack behind it that she desperately hoped wasn't an outhouse.

"This is it?"

Ric rolled to a stop. "Yep."

They got out and started unloading gear. Rey's brother had supplied them with some basic groceries and a duffel bag that contained God only knew what. Mia carried a carton of items, and Ric heaved the duffel onto his back. She followed him to the front door, looking in all directions for any sign of human habitation nearby. But it was just hills, rocks, and scrub brush as far as she could see. Only a lazily circling hawk witnessed their arrival.

Ric used a shiny brass key to deal with the sturdy lock—the only hint she'd seen that this was anything other than a ramshackle cabin. He pushed open the door.

Mia gave him a tentative glance before venturing inside. The room was dark. It smelled of must and something else that eluded her. Pine cones? A tiny kitchen dominated one end, and Mia deposited her box on the small wooden table. She took off her cap and her jacket and dumped them on top of the box as she scanned the room. Two metal folding chairs, a sink, a range attached to a propane tank. In the fading afternoon light and with just one window above the sink, the place was almost dark.

"No electricity?"

"Nope. This place doesn't exist."

Ric dropped the duffel bag near the fireplace on the other side of the room. Then he went back out.

Mia's anxiety grew as she gave the house a more thorough inspection. No electricity, no fridge, no telephone. Aside from the table and folding chairs, the only furniture was a worn brown sofa near the fireplace. The door off the kitchen led to a rudimentary bathroom, at least.

She glanced at Ric as he ferried two more boxes, stacked one atop the other, into the house. When he went

back outside, Mia peeked behind the last unopened door,
which had to be a bedroom.

It was tiny and cold. No windows. A stripped-
down single mattress leaned against a wall. The room
looked like a closet but felt cold enough to be a walk-
in freezer.

She bit her lip and turned away. She wouldn't complain. That they were there at all was surely a favor to
Ric. And to her. She knew she should feel grateful, but
she still hadn't gotten her head around the situation.

Someone wanted to kill her. She was hiding in an FBI
safe house with a man who was extremely ticked off at her
and had the effect of making her want to throw thirty-
two years of prudent decision making out the window
whenever she got near him. And his presence was going
to make it difficult for her to accomplish the one thing
she really needed to do, which was to figure out who was
threatening her.

Panic bubbled up in her throat. Mia glanced around
at the little cabin and did what she always did when she
felt panicked. She started cleaning.

Jonah ignored the little bong party taking place on the
balcony as he mounted the metal staircase leading to
Sophie Barrett's front door. It swung open before he
reached it.

She regarded him from behind some expensive-
looking shades as she dragged a suitcase over the
threshold.

"If you're here for a panty raid, you're going to be disappointed. The interesting stuff is packed."

She paused to lock her apartment, giving Jonah a

chance to look her over. She wore a clingy sweater the color of Astroturf, tight jeans, and a pair of pointy green shoes that looked beyond painful.

"Weekend getaway?" he asked.

"Something like that." She turned to face him, hitching her purse up on her shoulder. "And I'll tell you exactly what I told Ric Santos. Leave her a message, and I'm sure she'll get back to you at her earliest convenience."

Jonah picked up the suitcase and headed for the staircase as a trio of stoned college kids watched from their deck chairs.

Sophie mumbled something he didn't catch. A few seconds later, he heard her heels clacking on the concrete behind him. "Are you always this—"

"Helpful?"

"I was going to say creepy. How'd you find out where I live? I haven't had my license updated since I moved here."

"Nice place, by the way." He waited for her at the foot of the stairs, then set off for her Tahoe. It was parked near a pool that could have used a truckload of chlorine. "You rent by the week here?"

She stopped beside her SUV and fisted her hand on her hip. "For your information . . ." She trailed off as she stood there, glaring at him. At least, it felt like a glare. Kind of hard to tell behind the glasses.

"For my information?"

"Forget it. It's none of your business. Why are you here, Detective?"

Aha. She'd been checking up on him. The other night, it was Officer Macon.

"It's about Mia."

"I told you, she's—"

"Someone tried to kill her today."

That glossy red mouth dropped open. The shades came off, and he was staring at a pair of wide blue eyes. "*What?*"

"Someone took a shot at her."

"Where is she? Is she okay? What happened?"

"She's fine," he said. "And she's in protective custody." Not officially but close enough. She was with Ric, and he was in extreme pit-bull mode.

Sophie sagged against the side of the Tahoe and blinked into space. All of the color had drained out of her face.

Damn, he'd shocked her. "You all right?"

She straightened. "No, I'm not all right. I'm totally freaked out! What is going on?"

"We're not sure. We're investigating. But I wanted to warn you."

She stared at him, and he felt bad, sort of. He hadn't meant to shake her up so much. But it was probably for the better. She needed to be careful. Everyone around Mia needed to be careful, including Ric.

Jonah filched the keys from her hand and popped the locks. He pulled open the tailgate while she recovered her composure. A black guitar case and a box of CDs occupied the cargo space. He moved them over to make room for her bag. Then he walked back to the driver's-side door.

The attitude was gone now, replaced with worry for her friend.

"What *exactly* are you all doing to protect her?" she demanded. "This is the *second* time. Can't you arrest someone?"

"We're working on it." He stood looking down at her, although he didn't have to look far. She was at least five-ten, and that was without the heels. The fact that she wore them told him a lot about her confidence.

"Stay away from Mia's place," he said. "No more house-sitting or errands over there or whatever. And don't meet up with her, either. Not until we clear this up."

"I thought you said she was with Ric?"

"She is." In Jonah's opinion, she was still a flight risk. "Just watch out, all right? Stay away from her house. You shouldn't get mixed up in this thing."

She continued to look at him, and he started to get uncomfortable. He cleared his throat. "So, where you going?"

The glasses went back on. "Houston. I'm singing tonight at the Coyote Lounge." She tipped her head to the side. "You heard of it?"

"No."

She sighed. "Well, it's this famous nightclub in Montrose. Kind of a big deal." She shrugged. "I'm a little nervous, to tell you the truth."

"I'm sure you'll do great."

She smiled slightly. "How would you know?"

"I don't, I'm just guessing."

The moment stretched out, and they stood beside her SUV. He got the strangest feeling that she wanted him to say something.

Hell, did she want him to come hear her sing? He felt tempted, if for no other reason than to get a glimpse of what she'd packed in that bag. But he knew shit about music, and he had more than enough work to do tonight.

She pulled the door open and tossed her purse inside. "I'd better get going. I need time to change before I go on."

"Careful down in Montrose." He didn't know music, but he knew crime. "That can be a rough neighborhood, especially after hours."

"Don't worry about me." She slid behind the wheel and patted her purse. "LadySmith here always keeps me company."

Ric came back with an armload of wood, and Mia glanced up from her bottle of Comet as he stacked the pieces beside the fireplace. It looked as though their sole heat would be coming from a fire.

She returned her attention to the filthy sink and scrubbed harder. When it was a slightly brighter shade of gray, she turned her efforts to the cupboards and stacked canned goods. She felt Ric's presence across the room as she went about the task, but she refused to look up. She was afraid of what she'd see in his face. He had her. And he knew it, too. Now he was waiting, drawing it out, like a wolf circling its prey.

He went outside again for more wood or kindling or who the heck knew what, and she cast a tentative glance at the fireplace.

How had this happened? She'd been logical. She'd been resourceful. She'd sought out the aid of every one of the smart, capable experts she trusted. And she'd still ended up on the run, scared for her life, and totally reliant on a cop who would probably arrest her as soon as look at her. Obstruction of justice, evidence tampering, lying to investigators—she was guilty of every last one of those crimes, and somehow Ric knew it.

Mia needed those lab results. Yesterday, she'd returned to the scene of the crime—*her* crime—with the evidence kit Sophie had brought her. She'd recovered the barbecue tongs she'd dropped in her haste to leave. Now they were at the Delphi Center being tested for prints and possibly DNA. If someone found something, then at least she'd have a lead to offer investigators when she finally came clean about what she'd done and why.

If she came clean. She knew it was the right thing to do, but she hadn't gotten up the courage yet. No matter how she handled it, her confession would probably end her career.

Mia made a neat row of canned vegetables beside the soup. Ric came through the door and kicked it shut behind him. He stacked another armload of wood, then crouched down and began arranging logs in the hearth. She heard the hiss of a match and the crackle of fire.

Mia ran out of groceries to organize. She collapsed the boxes they had come in and tucked them into a corner in case they needed them later.

"What are you doing?"

She turned around. He was leaning against the back of the sofa, watching her. His jacket was gone now, and his stance was relaxed. But the glint in his eyes told her he was waiting, biding his time, and that she couldn't lower her defenses for even an instant.

"Just cleaning up. Taking inventory." She hesitated. "How long are we going to be here?"

"That depends." He stepped closer.

"On?"

"How long it takes me to find out who's behind this."

He hooked his thumbs in his pockets. "You want to help me out with that?"

She ducked around him and went to the fireplace. The blaze had subsided. She pulled newspaper from a nearby stack and wadded it up, then kneeled down and fed it into the flames.

"I don't really know, exactly."

She heard the scuff of his boots behind her as she gazed into the fire. It was brighter now, but that was because of the paper. Everything burned hot at the beginning; it was getting it to last that was tricky.

His fingers went into her hair, and she felt the touch from the top of her scalp to the tips of her toes. Her heart started racing. She wasn't ready for this. She talked a big game, but really, she felt terrified. She wanted to cling to him and bolt out the door, all at the same time.

"Mia."

She turned to look up at him and the flames reflected in his dark eyes.

"You have to talk to me sooner or later." He lowered himself into a crouch behind her. "You know that, don't you?"

His gaze held hers. Every nerve in her body responded.

"Later," she whispered, and leaned over to kiss him.

CHAPTER 14

～

He pulled her back against him and went after her mouth. The kiss was hot, hard, like his body behind her. She twisted, trying to get a better angle, but he held her in place with a hand clamped over her shoulder and another splayed across her ribs. Finally, she gave up and just tipped her head back. He moved to her neck, and she felt him shift behind her until he was kneeling, too, and she was nestled against his thighs. His arms wound around her and pulled her tightly against his chest, so tightly she could barely breathe.

"You scared me today." His voice was low and hoarse, and he nipped at her neck. She yelped and tried to pull away, but he held her right there, firmly, as the nip became something else, something greedy. He kissed his way to the collar of her shirt and moved it aside and kissed her some more. She started to relax. With every kiss, she felt the tension seeping out of her—even as her heart sped up—until she was leaning back against his body and clutching his arms around her so he couldn't let go. He'd been chopping wood, and she smelled the outdoors on him and sweat and that sharp male scent that made her want to give her mind a break and let her hormones simply take over. She loved the heat of him, the feel of him, the possessive way he held her as his mouth played over the skin of her neck.

He tugged one of his hands free and shifted her on to his lap. She watched that big hand slide up her thigh, searing her through her jeans. She let her arms fall limp at her sides, and both of his hands rubbed over the denim, down to her knees, then back up again, making her squirm and arch. *Touch me,* she wanted to say, but then his hands glided under her shirt to cup her breasts and pull her back against him as his breath heated her skin.

"Take this off," he muttered, squeezing her breasts, making her almost too dizzy to do anything. But she started unfastening the buttons. The instant she undid the last one, he pulled the shirt from her shoulders and tossed it aside.

She was kneeling by the fire now in only her bra and jeans, and the reality of what they were about to do hit her. She felt a shot of panic. He'd said he'd been attracted to her for months, but what if the reality of being with her fell short of his expectations?

She looked over her shoulder and saw the heat glittering in his eyes. He settled a hand on her hip and traced another slowly down her spine, making every vertebra tingle. His gaze met hers. She saw the raw need in his face, and her panic went away. No one had ever looked at her like that, ever.

She turned to face him and scooted forward on her knees. His gaze drifted over her white bra and pale skin that had way too many freckles to account for the desire she saw on his face. She reached back, unhooked her bra, and let it slide down her arms, and when he groaned low in his throat, she smiled, because she knew he wasn't looking at her freckles anymore.

In one swift motion, he grabbed her by the hips and pulled her against him. Finally, she could kiss him the way she wanted to, and she hooked her arms around his neck and did, sweeping her tongue into his mouth, tasting him, and letting the unique flavor of him fill her up. His erection pressed against her through her jeans, and she rubbed against him until she got just the response she wanted. His grip tightened.

He muttered a curse, then cast about desperately for a few seconds. Mia grabbed his jacket off the sofa and tossed it behind her, then tried to lower him down with her, but he pulled back.

"This floor—"

"It's okay."

She wanted his weight on her. Now. And she didn't care what was under her, although it wasn't bad—his jacket was warm from his body heat and thick enough to give her some cushion. And he seemed to want to please her, because he stripped off his T-shirt and positioned himself between her legs, which was just where she wanted him to be.

He kissed her and touched her, and she squeezed her thighs against him.

Another curse.

"What?" She propped up herself on her elbows. "Is it your jacket?"

"No."

He unsnapped her jeans and kissed her navel, then

pulled off her shoes. He flicked a glance at her face before he slid the jeans down her legs, panties and all, and she flushed with self-awareness. His gaze didn't leave her body as he stood up to unbuckle his belt.

"Let me do that." She scrambled to her knees to help him, and his look darkened again as she hooked her fingers in his pockets and helped him get rid of his clothes. Every coherent thought went out of her head as she looked at him. Suddenly, there were butterflies in her stomach. And then he was kneeling between her knees again, his skin bronze in the light of the fire, his face a picture of male lust as his gaze trailed down her body and then back up again to her face.

He brushed her hair back from her forehead and eased her back, kissing her. She let herself get lost in it, every detail of it—the heat of the fire, the hard chill of the concrete beneath her heels, the rasp of his stubble against the plump flesh of her breasts, which he couldn't seem to get enough of. She stroked her hands over his broad shoulders, loving the feel of his muscles under her fingers.

The window rattled, and for a second, they froze.

The cabin was dark now, except for the pool of light where they lay, clutched together. She realized he'd pulled the shade behind the sink. Had he known they'd be doing this? The idea excited her.

"What was that?" she whispered.

"Wind," he said, intent on what he was doing again.

The worry faded away as he lavished so much attention on her breasts that they began to ache. He kissed and nibbled and pulled, all the while caressing her hips and thighs until she wanted to scream. And finally, he slid his hand between her legs, and the sensation was so exquisite she couldn't breathe. His touch was hot, magic. Through the haze settling over her, she saw him watching her intently from under those dark lashes. He knew what he was doing to her, and she forced herself to push his hand away so she could draw this out.

He kissed her, more urgently now. She felt him digging around for something in the pocket of his jacket and sincerely hoped it was a condom. She glimpsed the packet in his hand and closed her eyes with relief. *Please hurry.* And then he was back again, and she waited breathlessly as he shifted position and, with one powerful motion, pushed inside her. Her muscles clenched, and she made a sound.

"Am I hurting you?"

"No."

He took her at her word and pushed again, harder this time, and she closed her eyes and squeezed her legs around him. As she held on tight, he found a rhythm, a good one. A slow, sweet, delicious rhythm that fit her perfectly and made her gasp and moan and glow from the inside out. And when she thought she'd lose her mind from the full, unending *goodness* of it, he whispered a warning in her ear and increased the intensity. She opened her eyes to watch him above her, the taut muscles of his neck and shoulders telling her how much his control was costing him and how much he wanted her. His eyes drifted open, and the corner of his mouth lifted in a smile, both tender and tortured. Her heart squeezed, and she'd never felt so connected with anyone in her life. But as fast as the moment was hers, it was gone again, and she felt a sharp stab of loss before she tipped her head back and let herself come apart. She was still in a thousand little pieces when he made a fierce, final plunge and collapsed against her.

For a moment, he just lay there, his face buried in her hair as she slowly came back to herself. She was sandwiched between a hard man and a hard floor, and she felt too weak to move.

He groaned and rolled onto his back, pulling her with him. She blinked down at him, and his hands cupped her butt.

"Damn, this floor's hard." He sounded as winded as she felt. "Sure you're okay?"

"Fine." She pushed up on one palm and tried to wriggle away, but he held her by the waist.

"Where you going?"

"This isn't comfortable."

His gaze darted to her breasts. "It's very comfortable."

"But I'm—"

"Relax." He tucked her head against him. "I'll keep you warm."

Mia closed her eyes, and he did keep her warm, with his arms wrapped around her and his hands stroking her skin. She tried to relax. She tried not to think about her weight and if she was smothering him, but he seemed to like her there, and so she lay on top of him, absorbing his heat and listening to his chest as his galloping heart slowed.

She'd made it race. And knowing she'd done that caused a rush of pride. He made her feel desired, sexy. He'd always done it, not just today but ever since they'd first met, as if flannel shirts and lab coats were his idea of sex appeal. She didn't understand it.

"The couch folds out, you know."

She sighed. "Now you tell me."

"You didn't exactly give me a chance." There was amusement in his voice, and his arms tightened, as if he knew that might rile her into climbing off him.

"So I was in a hurry. Sue me. I haven't been with anyone in a long time."

She lay still, waiting for his response. Maybe she was treading into personal territory. But what was more personal than being naked on top of him?

His arms tightened again, and she felt better.

"Sorry about your jacket," she muttered.

"Are you kidding? I'm thinking of getting it bronzed."

She smiled and nestled her cheek against his chest. She liked the hair there. She liked the way he smelled. She liked his arms around her and his heartbeat against her ear. She gazed into the fire and let the flames hypnotize her. She tried not to think about another fire on another day. And she must have succeeded, because she drifted into sleep.

Something pinched her bottom, and she shot up.

"Hey!"

His attention drifted down, then back up again. "You're not going to sleep, are you?"

"No."

"Good, because we're not near finished."

Her gaze narrowed, and she stared down at him, trying to decipher what he meant. They weren't finished having sex? Talking? As usual, his face was impossible to read.

Another rattle at the window. She looked over her shoulder.

"Front moving in." Ric sat up. "I'd better go take a look around the perimeter." He gently slid her off his lap and onto his jacket as he reached for his jeans. Instantly, she felt cold.

She tucked her knees to her chest and watched him get dressed, completely unfazed by his attentive audience. And why not? His body was hard and muscled, not an ounce of fat on him. Just pure man, and she couldn't believe that a short while ago, she'd had the manliest part of him inside her.

She watched silently as he headed off to check the perimeter, whatever that meant. She went back over everything and tried to understand the subtext of what had just happened. She had to read between the lines with him, because he was amazingly tight-lipped, even for a guy. He was guarded, taciturn, which was probably hell on anyone in a relationship with him.

A relationship. Fear tightened her stomach. He'd made it clear that he didn't want one. What did that make her? Some woman he'd just screwed by a fireplace. It also made her stupid, because despite all of the things she said, he'd been right the first time. She wasn't good at casual sex. She wasn't wired that way. The one time she'd tried it had been a disaster, and she had the distinct feeling that another disaster was looming.

Mia stood up and gathered her clothes. She spent a few minutes in the bathroom washing up. When he came back from his mission, she was at the stove in her shirt and socks, heating water for cocoa.

"If you're hungry, there's soup," she said, dividing the water between two mugs. The little bits of marshmallow melted and made white swirls on top.

She turned around, and he was watching her with that predatory look again. He didn't touch her, though, just reached out and took a mug.

"There's tomato. Some chicken and rice, I think."

He looked into the cup, then put it on the table with a clunk.

"We need to talk," he said.

Mia didn't want to talk. Talking was the very last thing she wanted to do with him. This could well be their only night together, and she wanted to savor it.

Because a night was just a night. Anything more would border on Relationship Territory, and he didn't want to go there. Knowing that, she wouldn't cling to him. She couldn't, not if she wanted to maintain her self-respect. So that left her with tonight.

"Is there something you want to tell me?" He watched her, still waiting for the answers she'd promised him.

"I'm cold."

"You're *cold*?"

She took her mug of cocoa and crossed the room to the fireplace. She sank onto the sofa and folded her legs beside her.

He joined her near the fire, but he didn't sit down. Points for him for being wary. He probably figured she was going to try to distract him, which she was.

"You never explained how you found me," she said.

"I told you, I looked."

"You didn't just look. I covered my tracks. I've been using cash. And a fake ID."

He crossed his arms. "Yeah, well, you left out a few things, babe. Once I knew you were at White Oak Cabins, it took me about five minutes to find you. Next time

you want to get lost, maybe try a town with more than
three hundred people."

"How'd you know about the cabins?"

He watched her, obviously weighing how much to
say. "You left a note in your kitchen."

"I most certainly did not!"

"You left the notepad. Same thing."

She blinked at him. "You're telling me you broke into
my house and . . ." She frowned. What had he done, exactly?

"I didn't break in. And yes, I swiped your notepad
and got the phone number from the little indentations
in the paper. Basic detective work. So what? I probably
could have gotten the same info from your phone records
if I'd looked."

She pictured him standing in her kitchen, rubbing a
pencil over her notepad, figuring out where she'd gone.
And she should have been angry. He'd let himself in,
invaded her privacy. But instead, she felt blown away.
He'd searched for her and been worried about her. He'd
snatched her out of the sights of a gunman. She still
couldn't believe it.

"Truth time, Mia. Who are you running from?"

She looked away. "I don't know."

"What are you running from?"

"I don't know that, either." She said it quietly, staring into the fire. She remembered the flames swallowing up Ashley's clothes. Dread gripped her. How had she
let herself get into this mess? And what would he think
about her when he knew?

She gazed up at him, his face half-lit by firelight, his
expression hard. She wanted the expression from before
that told her she excited him and made his blood rush.

She put her mug on the floor and shifted to her knees. His gaze narrowed as she unbuttoned the top button on her shirt.

"Mia. We're not done talking."

Another button. "I know."

Something sparked in his eyes, and she didn't know whether it was anger or desire. Not that it mattered.

"Tell me something." She reached the last button and let the shirt fall open. All she really showed him was a narrow strip of skin, but it was enough. "Is this really a safe house?"

He eased closer but didn't touch her. She rose on her knees until she was only a breath away from him.

"Because if it *is,* that means we're safe, right?" She rested her index finger on the buckle of his belt and slowly traced it. "We've got all night to talk and . . . whatever else."

She leaned forward and rested her forehead on his chest. His muscles tensed beneath his T-shirt. She pressed a kiss there.

He drew in a breath and released it slowly, with control. "Mia—"

"Because I couldn't help noticing that you sort of jumped in front of a bullet earlier. For me." Those fathomless brown eyes were looking at her with so much heat she thought she'd melt. "And I never even got a chance to say thank you."

The man pulled up the long private driveway and slid his battered Buick between a souped-up Escalade and an Audi, both black. Good to see his fucking tax dollars at work. He walked across the driveway to the back door, ignoring the state trooper and the PR flack who stood on the patio having a smoke break.

He hiked the back stairs to the spacious office that sat above the four-car garage. Jeff Lane was alone, as expected, and he was on his cell phone. He had his sleeves rolled up like someone who'd had a tough day at work, but he had a relaxed smile on his face. Probably had a girl on her knees under that big desk.

Lane's smile faded as he entered the office. He strode up to the desk, pulled the phone from Lane's hand, and disconnected the call.

"I want my money." He tossed the phone onto the leather sofa behind him.

Annoyance sparked in Lane's eyes, but he managed to keep his cool. "I assume you've finished the job?"

"Change of plan. I want to get paid first. *Then* I finish the job."

Lane sighed, very put upon. He got up and crossed the room to a granite bar.

The man was relieved to see that Lane hadn't heard about the botched attempt. With a little luck, he never would.

"Scotch?"

"Whiskey."

Lane poured two and handed him a short glass with an L monogrammed on it. "I thought we agreed—"

"You're stalling," he said. "And the price just went up. I want six figures."

Lane chuckled, as if they had some private joke together. He returned to his chair and leaned back, setting the drink on the desk in front of him. "If I didn't know any better, I'd say you were getting greedy."

"This is the last time, too. Then I'm out. You have any more problems after this, call someone else."

Lane smiled. "No one's ever really out."

"I am."

He sipped his drink smugly.

"And I want my money tomorrow, or I'm out before this even gets done. I don't think you want those kinda loose ends."

Lane watched him for a few moments, as if debating his strategy. They both knew there was nothing to debate, because for once, Lane wasn't calling the shots. He was between a rock and a hard place this time, and he knew it.

"You realize, don't you, that you're all over the map with this," Lane said easily. "First, you tell me the DNA woman's a problem and we need to get rid of her. When that doesn't work out, you tell me it's okay because we need her help. Now you're saying we need to get rid of her again. Which is it?"

"We need her gone."

Lane's expression hardened. "You know, I'm beginning to think I'm being lied to. You told me she didn't see you."

"She didn't." He remembered the flash of eye contact after she jumped from the Jeep and looked back over her shoulder. The sunglasses had slipped. It had been just an instant, but he was becoming less willing to take risks. He was way too exposed.

Lane gazed into his glass and shook his head. "I'd just as soon not part with that kind of money. And I'd just as soon not have another body on my hands. Why don't you intimidate her?"

"I did."

"Then what's the problem?"

"The problem is, she's fucking a cop. It won't be long before they put their heads together and figure this out. Then you've got two problems to deal with."

"Who's the cop?"

"The same one who's in charge of the murder case."

Lane's eyebrow tipped up. "Which one?"

He gritted his teeth. "Both of them." Lane knew he wasn't happy about taking out a cop, but it had been unintentional.

He felt his composure sliding, felt the anger bubbling to the surface. Lane represented everything that was wrong with this country, and he hated the man's guts. He hated even more that he took money from him. But he kept a lid on that hate. Emotion was a weakness, and Lane was looking for any weakness he could exploit.

Better to keep this a business transaction, cold and impersonal.

He downed the whiskey in one sip, and it scalded a path down his throat. He set the glass on the desk. "One hundred grand. Tomorrow. Then I finish this for you. You wait any longer than that, the DNA woman and this detective are going to figure things out, and everything you've built over the last twenty years is going to come crashing down around your head."

"Oh, really?"

"Really." He stepped closer and lowered his voice. "And then you're going to be wearing an orange jumpsuit and missing your whores and your Jameson and wishing you'd given me every dime I asked for and more."

He towered over the desk now. It was a war of wills, and he won it because they both knew he was right.

"I'll wire it tomorrow," Lane said. "And then I want this over."

The man walked to the door, hiding his relief. Six figures. It had been a shit day, but he'd salvaged it. He turned around, with his hand on the door frame. "Hey, by the way, I saw that nice black Audi down at El Patio."

"So?"

"So, every badge in town hangs out there. Think about it."

Lane waved him off.

He opened the door to leave. This guy's ego was going to be his downfall. "I *will* get out. And next time you have a problem, I won't be around to fix it."

"Yeah?" Lane leaned back in his chair and looked amused. "Where will you be?"

"Anywhere but here."

CHAPTER 15

⁓

She came awake slowly. He watched her. Ric had gotten up earlier to stoke the fire, partly for warmth but mostly so he could look at her in the light of it. He ran his hand over the generous curve of her hip, and her eyes drifted open.

He propped himself up on an elbow. She looked from him to the fire, then back to him again.

"What time is it?" She sat up and pulled the blanket over herself.

"Six."

He held her gaze for a long moment and saw all of it come back to her, everything they'd done together, in sweet, raunchy detail. She swung her legs out of bed. At some point, they'd unfolded the couch and made it up with blankets, but it was a mess now. Ric would have been happy to mess it up some more, but she grabbed her shirt off the floor and pulled it around her. She gave him a self-conscious smile before slipping away to the bathroom.

So much for jump-starting the day.

He pulled on some clothes and went outside. The

air had a bite, which he needed pretty badly, and he did a quick survey of the perimeter before picking up the ax he'd left stuck in the stump near the tool shed. He hacked away at some oak limbs until his shirt was damp and his heart pounded. He had no idea where this pent-up energy was coming from when he'd spent most of the night not sleeping, but he needed to get rid of it.

Fireside Mia was gone, and it was back to reality. Last night had been about avoidance, and Ric was fine with that. He could think of worse ways to procrastinate. But he'd seen regret on her face just now. Embarrassment, too. And it pissed him off.

He returned to the cabin with enough wood to build a bonfire. She was standing at the sink in the light of the window, fully dressed. She'd showered already, and her damp hair was pulled back in a clip.

"I smuggled that evidence out of the crime lab and took it to an incinerator."

He stared at her back.

"It's gone."

Ric dumped the wood onto the floor and walked over to where she stood. Her gaze was fixed on something out the window, but she didn't seem to be looking at it.

"Say that again."

"You heard me." She turned to face him and looked braced for an assault.

"Sit down," he ordered.

She sank into the chair and looked at him nervously. His alarm grew with every fidget of her hands. She wasn't joking.

"Someone threatened you?" He had the insane hope

that she'd say yes, someone held a gun to her head. Why else would she do it?

"They had Sam. Or at least, they said they did, and I believed them." She looked down at her lap. "Anyway, it doesn't matter now. It's gone. All of it. I watched it burn."

Ric stared at her. Something about her calm infuriated him. She'd watched it *burn*. All that evidence. A bitter lump lodged in his throat.

He knew she'd been lying. He'd known it the second she'd started talking in Rachel's office. At the time, she'd looked miserable. Guilty. And more than a little bit afraid of him, much as she looked now.

Ric turned his back on her and muttered a curse.

"What?"

"Nothing."

"Say it to my face, whatever it is. I know you're mad at me."

" 'Mad' doesn't cover it."

"Damn it, *look* at me!"

He turned around.

"He threatened Sam! What was I supposed to do?"

"But he's okay now, right? It was some kind of scam?"

She surged to her feet, eyes blazing. "Don't you dare question me! What would you have done if someone had Ava? If someone put her voice on the phone? You would have done anything!"

He started to say something but stopped himself. She was right.

He clenched his teeth and felt the anger washing over him. She'd lied to him. That was bad enough. But worse, someone was terrorizing her, and she'd gone all this time without telling him or asking for his help—not just as a friend but as a cop. He wanted to grab her by the shoulders and shake her until every bit of information she'd been hiding from him came spilling out.

He closed his eyes and made himself get a grip. When he opened them again, she was watching him.

"Where?" he asked.

"Where did I do it?"

He nodded.

"An abandoned factory. Out on Highway 12." She shook her head. "Why does it matter? It's like I told you, there's nothing left."

"Are you all right now?"

"Not really. I'm not hurt." She shrugged. "My reputation is ruined, though." Tears filled her eyes, and she looked away. "Every case I've ever touched will probably come under fire."

Ric waited while she composed herself. Obviously, she'd been tearing herself up over this.

"No more lies, Mia. I need you to be honest now."

"I am."

"Something spooked you the other night and made you run. What was it?"

She cleared her throat and looked down. "He was in my house."

"Who?"

"The man who carjacked me and killed Frank. The person behind all this." The fear in her eyes pulled at him. "I had these Mardi Gras beads in my Jeep, hanging from my mirror. They were a souvenir from a wedding in New Orleans. When I came home from dinner with you, they were sitting on my table."

"Did you—"

"I took them to the lab already. No prints, nothing."

Another spurt of anger, but this time it was directed at himself. He'd known something was wrong that night, and he should have stayed with her, but instead, he'd let her send him away.

He watched her closely now, trying to read her mind. She wasn't much of a liar, but she was good at hiding things. And she was still doing it—he could tell.

That was going to end today. This was a murder investigation, and they were doing it his way from here on out.

He checked his watch. "All right, let's go."

"Go where?"

"Highway 12."

"But I told you—"

"Save the argument, Mia. I want a look at this crime scene."

CHAPTER 16

～◦～

M ia stood in the mud, shivering. The temperature had climbed above thirty, but a front had moved in, and a blanket of moisture had settled over everything. She hunched her shoulders against the chill as she watched Ric tromp around the site. He was in detective mode now—had been since they'd left the safe house.

"You say he was watching you?"

"I don't know. I just think he was." She shoved her hands into the pockets of her barn jacket and stepped closer. "Something he said over the phone made me think he could see my car as I pulled in."

The metal door to the incinerator stood open, and Ric shone his flashlight inside it for the third time. Nothing but ashes.

"And where did he leave the tongs?"

Mia walked over to the spot and pointed. "There. That's where I left them, too. Our fingerprint tracer lifted several good prints but said it would take a few days to run them through."

Ric muttered something.

"What?"

"You should have given it to me," he said. "I could have had our guy turn it around same day. He owes me a favor."

"I don't know your guy. I know my guy. And I trust him."

His gaze shot up. "What does that mean?"

"I think this person, whoever he is, is in law enforcement."

Ric's expression darkened. "Why's that?"

"His gun, for one. It looks just like yours."

"This is one of the most common pistols out there."

"That's because they're standard issue for so many law-enforcement agencies." Mia had researched it. "Also, he knew things. Like how the lab works, where things are stored during processing. I talked to our evidence clerk, and someone called her twice to check on the status of that evidence and find out which person in our lab was assigned to it. He claimed to be a detective."

His brow furrowed. "Who?"

"Jonah Macon."

Ric looked away and shook his head. Then he walked around to the front of the building, and Mia followed.

"I looked inside already," she said. "No cigarette butts. No soda cans. If he was in there, it looks like he cleaned up after himself."

The door stood ajar, and he pushed it open, causing a rusty squeak. He stepped inside, and again she followed.

The place was empty except for an overturned milk crate and a stack of wooden shipping pallets. The floor was dusty concrete, but there were no fresh footprints.

Light streamed through the broken second-story windows. Ric walked into the center of the room and looked around.

"What makes you think he was watching from the building?" His voice echoed through the cavernous space.

"I don't know. At the time, I just thought that's where he was. Where else would he be?"

They walked back outside. Mia looked around, but all she saw were pastures transected by the highway. There was a farmhouse about half a mile up the road, but it had pickups and a tractor out front. Not the sort of spot where you could camp out and watch someone unnoticed.

Ric surveyed the area, then walked north, toward a rise about a hundred yards away. The ground sloped up to a wire fence that bordered what looked to be the grounds of the former factory. A couple of mesquite trees swayed in the breeze, but they were too slender for anyone to hide behind. A pair of low boulders sat between them, and Ric crouched down there.

"Bingo."

She joined him beside the rocks, which were about the size of two tires. "You think he was *here*?"

"Looks like he was prone. See the grass flattened down? And these marks where he dug the toes of his boots in?" A cold look had come into Ric's eyes, one she was beginning to recognize. He took the threat to her personally, and she wasn't sure what to think of that. It didn't make her special, necessarily. He was a cop—he was protective by nature.

"This was his blind," he said. "He set up here, probably before he made the call, then waited for you to come. He probably watched every move you made through a rifle scope."

Fear rippled through her. "Why didn't he just shoot me then?"

"Why would he? You were doing exactly what he wanted. Now that it's over, though, maybe he thinks it's time to eliminate you." Ric frowned down at the rock and rubbed a finger over a black mark on it. "He smoked a cigarette here, too, while he was waiting. Stubbed it out, but I don't see the butt."

They spent a few minutes separately combing the area until Ric let out a whistle.

"Found something."

"Don't touch it." Mia pulled a small kit from her pocket and walked over. She handed him some tweezers and unfolded a paper bag, although she couldn't even see what he was looking at.

"What is it?"

"Cellophane wrapper from a pack of smokes."

Mia looked at the clear plastic. "A butt would be better for DNA."

He stood up and dropped the wrapper into the paper evidence bag. The corner of his mouth curled up. "You're making it too complicated. I bet we get a print."

Mia looked around, uncomfortable standing there, even in the presence of an armed police officer. The place felt spooky, and she pictured eyes watching her from every direction.

"The more I see of this guy, the more I think he has military training." Ric's voice was serious again.

"You don't think he's a cop?"

"Could be he's both. Anyway, if he is military, I'm guessing it's in the distant past."

"Why is that?"

He reached out and sank his fingers into her hair. It was the first time he'd touched her since they'd left the cabin.

"Because he missed, *querida*. A man on his game would have made the shot."

Mia's heart pounded. A bubble of panic rose in her throat. She smiled. It was either that or burst into tears. "Guess I'm lucky, then, huh?"

"Don't be lucky. Be smart." Ric's hand dropped away, and he looked out over the horizon. "His pride's at stake now. He won't miss again."

Jonah tossed his empty can into the trash and waited for the Red Bull to kick in. He'd been up half the night on this case, and he was starting to feel it.

"So, we've got a print at the lab from your cigarette wrapper, three matching shell casings, but no murder weapon and still nothing on the missing Jeep," Jonah said.

He and Ric were in one of the conference rooms at the station house, comparing notes on their cases. Ric seemed convinced that they were all connected, although Jonah hadn't totally bought into the theory. Shooting and stabbing were pretty different as far as MOs went. Seemed to him like two different perps.

"That's all we have on the shooter," Ric said. "At least, until that sheriff's deputy gets back to me with whatever they found yesterday at the gas station."

"If there was something to find, they probably would have found it by now."

"Our best bet is that print." Ric rubbed the bridge of his nose. "The lab is running it through AFIS. We'll see what comes back."

Jonah scarfed down the last bite of a soggy Italian sub and watched his partner. He looked tense, tired. He'd probably been up all night, too, but Jonah doubted he'd been working.

"Where'd you stash Mia?" he asked.

"Somewhere safe."

Jonah waited for more, but he didn't elaborate.

"Update me on the girl in the lake," Ric said, changing the subject. "Didn't you have a message in to that sheriff?"

"Still no ID on her. They thought they might get something off that cinder block, but so far, no word. Got some stuff on Fort Worth, though." Jonah shoved the trash away and flipped through the pages of his notepad. "I've been working on that guest list from the country-club party where Laura Thorne was last seen."

"High-class hooker at a country-club party. How come I'm not surprised?"

"First off, the term is 'escort,' according to her employer." Jonah skimmed his notes. "This woman runs a pretty big business, from the looks of it. Anyway, the victim's last scheduled date was at this pool party, which followed a men's poker tournament there at the club. Not a lot of wives invited, as you might guess. Victim's boss got a text message from her about nine P.M., saying she'd made it to the party. That was the last anyone heard from her. Her body turned up two days later in the woods off the golf course."

"And the day after that, the groundskeeper gets shot," Ric said. "Same gun used to kill Hannigan. Detective up there thinks the gardener might have witnessed something."

"So here's the interesting part. The guest list. If her boss knows who Laura's date was at that party, she's not saying."

"Any cops there?"

"Don't think so. Why?"

"Just a theory Mia has. It might be off base." Ric reached across the table. "Here, let me see. How'd you come up with this?"

Jonah slid his notes over. "Clerk at the club. Promised I'd keep his name out of it since I didn't have a warrant."

"Lotta movers and shakers," Ric said, reading the list. "Tim Connell's been all over the news. He's running for state attorney general. And Jeff Lane is the lieutenant governor. Shit, which one of these guys is using an escort service?"

"My guess is half of them."

"Holy shit. Camille Lane."

Jonah frowned. "There're no women on that list."

"No, I know. She's the lieutenant governor's wife. Her name came up already." Ric pulled a thin folder from the stack on the other end of the table.

"What's that?"

"Jane Doe case from Lake Buchanan. Some remains were found up there, never been identified. Bone expert at the Delphi Center thinks it's the same MO as Ashley Meyer—duct tape, blunt-force trauma, stabbing with a serrated knife."

"What's that got to do with Camille Lane?"

"Sheriff up there interviewed her when he was making the rounds. They have a lake house down the road from where the body was found." Ric was combing through the file now, but there wasn't much in it. "Damn, where's that guy's number?"

Jonah stared at him. "You're telling me Laura Thorne and this Jane Doe have a link to the lieutenant governor?"

Ric glanced up. "I guess I am. *Fuck.* Rachel's going to hate this." He raked a hand through his hair. "This is going nowhere. *Damn it.*"

He was right. No DA in her right mind would start investigating a political heavyweight like Jeff Lane without a boatload of evidence. Which they didn't have. They had more like a thimble, and it was all circumstantial.

Ric cursed again and stared down at the file.

"Yo, you guys hear about our boy Corino?"

He and Ric turned to see Vince Moore standing in the doorway. Jonah scowled.

"Yo, dirtbag. Thanks for backing me up the other night with Sophie Barrett. What the fuck?"

Moore grinned. "Thought you'd like that."

"She damn near shot my dick off! That girl packs heat."

"No kidding?" Moore looked intrigued, and Jonah decided to shut up about it.

"What about Corino?" Ric asked, getting them back on track.

"They picked him up yesterday, down in Bexar

County," Moore said. "Buddy of mine tells me he copped to that motel murder you're working on. Corino claims it was self-defense."

"Always is."

"Anyway, they're sending his ass up here. Rachel wants a piece of him."

Ric looked at Jonah. "That's one case cleared."

"Yeah, let's all go home."

Another detective walked by the open doorway.

"Hey, Burleson, what's up on that gas station robbery?" Moore called.

"I'm on my way over there." Burleson stepped into the room. "Any of you want in on this holdup? They got the store owner at Brackenridge Hospital. From what I got, we'll probably be looking at a homicide by nightfall. Ric, you interested?"

"I'm slammed," he said. "And I've got plans tonight."

Jonah was pretty sure he knew what Ric's plans were. He was playing bodyguard with benefits.

"I'll go with you," Moore said. "Long as we can hit a drive-through first."

"Jonah, you want in?"

"Can't do it." He traded looks with Ric. "We're on our way to go visit the DA."

Mia breathed a sigh of relief as Ric pulled into the parking lot of the FBI's San Antonio field office. Finally. She and Ric's brother had been waiting nearly twenty minutes, and she'd been getting worried.

"Well. Thank you." She turned to Rey, who had the same dark good looks as his brother, along with an aversion to small talk. "I'm sorry to interrupt your Sunday. And your Saturday, too. I really appreciate all your help."

"No problem."

What was the protocol here? Should she hug him? Shake his hand? His body language invited neither, so she rubbed her gloved hands together and smiled at him as Ric pulled up to the sidewalk. Rey reached around to open the door.

"Thanks again." She slid into the pickup, and Rey nodded. "And for my purse, too. I really appreciate it."

Ric leaned forward to peer around her. "Call you later," he told his brother.

"Later."

Ric pulled away, leaving the hulking concrete government building behind them. It was a full two minutes before he said another word.

"How'd it go?"

"Great," she said cheerfully as he turned onto the freeway that would take them back to San Marcos. "He put me in a very nice conference room with furniture that was bolted to the floor, and I read the Sunday paper twice, including the classifieds." Mia flipped the vanity mirror down and saw that her face was just as freckled and makeup-free as it had been that morning. "Funny thing, though, your brother didn't seem all that busy while I was there. If you hadn't assured me otherwise, I might think he went into the office today solely to baby-sit me."

Ric darted a glance at her, then looked back at the road. "Classifieds, huh? You looking for a job?"

Mia sighed, letting it go. "I'm expecting to get my car-insurance check later this week." All sixty-two hundred dollars of it.

She dragged her purse into her lap and rooted around for some Chapstick. Rey had recovered the purse from her rental car when he'd visited the scene of yesterday's shooting. He'd also talked to the local sheriff and then returned the Toyota that Alex had rented for her.

The list of favors Mia owed the Santos brothers was growing longer by the hour.

She glanced at Ric. "What happened today? How's the investigation coming?"

"It's coming."

She watched him, waiting for details, but his gaze was fixed on the road. "Any word from that sheriff?" she asked.

"Rey talked to him again this afternoon. No new developments."

Mia suppressed a sarcastic comment. Four hours she'd spent with the man, and he hadn't mentioned that. What was it with this family?

Ric swerved into the fast lane, and Mia stared out the window as the miles rushed by in silence. He still didn't want to let her in. She'd told him everything. All of it. And she still wasn't part of his inner circle.

Did he still distrust her? Maybe lying earlier in the DA's office had been a bad idea. Mia didn't lie well, but she hadn't known what else to do.

She hadn't known what to do yesterday, either, and so she'd trusted Ric. In every way imaginable. And now she wondered whether that had been a mistake, too.

The first sign for San Marcos came into view, and Mia summoned her courage.

"So." *Just get it out there.* "Where exactly are we going?"

He seemed ready for the question. "I'm taking you to my place."

She turned to look at him and wished more than anything that she could read his expression. Was this him letting her into his life finally? Or was this another baby-sitting arrangement, with maybe some sex thrown in to keep it interesting?

"I've got to be somewhere tonight, though." He glanced at his watch. "'Bout half an hour from now."

"I take that to mean you're dropping me off or . . . ?"

"Jonah's meeting us there. He'll hang out with you till I get back. Shouldn't be more than a few hours."

A few hours. Of waiting for Ric to show up. And once he came home, then what? Then they'd hop into bed together, and in the morning, he'd get up to go fight bad guys while she sat around his apartment, probably with some cop buddy he'd talked into babysitting for the day.

Mia looked out the window and bit her lip. God, she was such a wimp. And she was sick of feeling helpless while her life tornadoed around her.

She cleared her throat. "Could you pull over, please?"

He gave her a startled glance.

"Please?"

He checked his mirror before sailing across two lanes and taking the next exit. Mia's heart thudded as he coasted off the freeway and pulled into a Burger King parking lot. She waited for him to stop the truck, then turned to face him.

"What's going on with us, Ric?"

His eyes filled with wariness, but she steeled herself and kept going.

"A few days ago, you told me you weren't in the market for a relationship." She waited a beat. "Has something changed?"

She saw the muscle in his jaw tighten before he looked away.

"It's okay," she said, even though her insides were shredding. "You told me that from the beginning. I just wanted to, you know, make sure."

He met her gaze again, obviously hating this conversation. "Look, Mia—"

"It's fine. Let's just go." She pulled her phone from her purse and tried to keep her hands steady as she sent a text message. His eyes were on her, and she felt her cheeks get warm.

Why had she let this happen? In some tiny corner of her mind, she'd allowed herself to believe that sleeping with him would change things, would make him want what he clearly didn't. Brilliant plan. Now here she was, asking him for the very thing she'd told him she didn't need.

She finished her message and pressed Send.

"Mia, look at me."

She slid her phone into her purse and looked up, hoping her emotions weren't plain on her face.

"Everything's complicated right now. You have no idea."

"Don't explain." She held up her hand. "It's fine. Really. But I've made some other arrangements, so I can't come to your house tonight."

He muttered something in Spanish. Then he shifted

into gear again and pulled out of the lot. She didn't know what to make of it. Clearly, he was pissed.

"I need you where I can keep tabs on you," he said.

"Are you worried I'm going to take off?"

"I'm more worried about someone putting a bullet in you. Forget it. You're staying with me."

"I'm *not* staying with you." All that hurt in her chest was quickly becoming anger. "I told you, I've made other plans."

She looked out the window and tried to get her feelings under control. She didn't want a scene with him, not after last night. Last night was precious to her. She had no idea what it meant to him, but to her, it was special, and she didn't want to ruin it.

"What's the plan, Mia? Your house isn't safe, not if he's leaving you threats on your breakfast table."

She knew she shouldn't have told him about the Mardi Gras beads. He was right about her house, though. She didn't want to be alone there right now, but her emotions were too raw to want Ric there with her.

She realized he was looking at her. "What?"

"I'm not taking you home."

"You don't have to. I'm staying with a friend."

He shook his head. "You're just going to camp out at someone's place? You think Sophie's going to protect you if some thug decides to kick down the door in the middle of the night?"

She looked out the window. When she thought she could talk without sounding upset, she gave him an address on the south side of town.

"Next exit," she added as he glared at her.

But it seemed he was finished arguing, because he

silently followed the directions to the house. Mia had been there exactly once, but she remembered it well. It was a small brick one-story in a working-class neighborhood, and she prayed the garage door would be down when Ric pulled up to the curb.

No such luck.

A black pickup with oversized tires was parked in the garage. Beside it was a motorcycle.

For once, Ric's face was easy to read. "Who the hell's house is this?" he demanded.

"A friend."

"*Who?*"

"He works at the Delphi Center." Mia gathered up her purse and jacket. "This is perfect, actually. He can give me a ride to work."

"Since when are you going back to work?"

"I want my life back, all right? I'm sick of running from things. It's time I tried to salvage what's left of my career, if that's even possible. I'm not sure I can, but I know I can't do it by running away."

He glanced at the truck, and every muscle in his face hardened. "He's a friend. You want me to believe that?"

"I don't care what you believe! He offered me a place to stay. On his *couch*. And you can believe whatever you want, because I don't answer to you." She reached for the door handle, and he grabbed her arm.

"Wait."

"What?"

"Just . . . wait. Jesus." He scrubbed a hand over his face, and she could tell he was trying very hard to rein in his temper. And that little gesture pulled at her, making her wait patiently for whatever he had to say.

He took a deep breath. "Who is this guy?"

"Why does it matter?"

"Because it does."

She looked at him, not sure what was going on now. Jealousy? Hurt? Over-the-top possessiveness that had no basis in reality?

She sighed. "I can tell what you're thinking, but it's not like that."

"You have no idea what I'm thinking."

"He's a friend, okay? I've known him for years. I talked to him earlier today, and he offered to put me up. Given the circumstances, I think I'll be more comfortable here."

Ric snorted.

"God, why am I even explaining this to you? I'm too tired for this." She reached for the door again, and again he stopped her.

"All I'm asking is his name," he said with obvious effort. "I'd like to run a background check."

She looked at him for a long moment. "Scott Black," she said quietly. "He works in our ballistics lab. And you don't need to bother checking up on him, because everyone at Delphi has been thoroughly vetted."

Ric gave her a long, steady look. "I don't like this plan. I think you should take some more time off. Lie low."

"I appreciate your concern, but it's not your decision." She reached for the handle again, and this time, he didn't try to stop her. "Will you call me later, please? About the investigation? I'd like to be kept informed."

He nodded curtly.

"Thank you." She got out of his truck, amazed at how

calm she sounded as she ended one of the most emotional
weekends of her life.

"Mia."

She looked back over her shoulder.

"You can call me, too, you know. If you need anything."

"I know," she said. And the words sounded as hollow
as she felt.

CHAPTER 17

M ia awoke to the smell of frying bacon and for an instant thought she was at her grandmother's. A glimpse of the deer antlers mounted on the wall jolted her back to reality.

She was at Scott's. She'd had a fight with Ric. Well, maybe not a fight, exactly, but their passionate weekend had definitely ended on a sour note. But since it had begun on one, too, she shouldn't have been surprised.

Mia pulled off the wool blanket Scott had given her, folded it, and left it on the end of the couch. She slipped into his guest bathroom and spent a few minutes cleaning up before following the scent of bacon into the kitchen.

"Morning."

He looked up from his frying pan and gave her a sly smile.

"You slept in. Guess you needed some rest."

Mia had told him vaguely about spending the weekend with Ric, and he'd obviously drawn his own conclusions. She'd been happy to let him.

She and Scott went way back, much further than Ric probably imagined. They'd grown up in the same neighborhood, although they hadn't overlapped in school because he was five years older. He'd dated Vivian, though, and probably because of that, he'd always treated Mia like a kid sister, even after they'd crossed paths again as colleagues at the Delphi Center. Mia was relying on that kid-sister vibe now to keep this from being awkward.

"Mugs above the TV," he said, nodding at the little set on his counter where he was watching CNBC at low volume.

Mia helped herself to some coffee and looked around. It felt strange being in Scott's kitchen. She still remembered the house he'd grown up in, right down the street from her parents' place in Fort Worth. It felt weird to see him now all dressed for work, watching financial news and making breakfast in his own kitchen.

"Can I help with anything?" she asked.

"Nope."

She slumped into a chair and sipped her coffee. She felt stiff this morning. Sore. Some of it was from falling down at the gas station Saturday, but some was Ric-related.

"Fried egg?"

She glanced up, and her stomach leaped at the words. "Sure, thanks."

He slid an egg onto a plate, along with three strips of bacon. She started to add up the calories, then decided not to torture herself.

He joined her at the table and handed her some silverware. Along with khaki tactical pants, he wore a black golf shirt with the Delphi logo on it and some kind of heavy-duty military boots. The ballistics guys always looked like badasses. Most of them actually were, too.

Mia forked up a bite of eggs. "Where'd you learn to cook?"

"Breakfast I learned at the deer lease." He drizzled ketchup over his food, and she stifled a shudder. "Everything else I learned at BUD/S," he said, referring to the SEAL training he'd been through years ago.

"They teach you to cook there?"

"How to open MREs. That's about my limit in terms of cooking. You want dinner tonight, it's either eggs or carryout."

She knew this was his roundabout way of asking her how long she'd be staying. Scott had a polite streak. He opened doors for people, called women "ma'am," and would consider it rude to ask a houseguest when she planned to leave.

Mia nibbled her bacon. "Well, I might not be here tonight. If the investigation goes smoothly, I'm hoping they'll have a suspect identified and in custody soon, and everything will get back to normal."

He lifted an eyebrow. "Kind of optimistic, don't you think?"

"They're running some fingerprint evidence right now. I'm hoping that will go somewhere."

"Hoping." Scott shook his head. "I've seen the ballistics related to your case, though."

This was news to Mia.

"Sounds like this perp's been at it a while. Not sure it's going to be that easy to get enough for an arrest. What does your detective think?"

Mia doubted Ric considered himself "her" anything, but she let it slide. "He thinks they've got some good leads. But I need to be careful."

"You got any protection?"

She wrinkled her nose.

"Lemme guess. A tube of pepper spray in your night-stand, right?"

"I hate guns."

He shook his head. "You're afraid of something you don't understand. If you'd learn what to do with one, you wouldn't have to feel that way."

Mia doubted that schlepping a gun around in her purse was going to make her feel better about anything. More likely, it would send her stress level through the ceiling.

"You've got a clean record," Scott said. "Be a snap to get you a concealed-carry permit." He paused. "Or I could lend you something. Show you how to use it."

His tone told her that the offer wasn't necessarily aboveboard. He must be pretty concerned, and she felt touched.

"Thanks. But like I said, I think this will be over soon."

He looked skeptical, and she cast about for a change of subject.

"I have another favor to ask, though. I was hoping you might be able to swing by my place on the way into work. I could really use a change of clothes."

"Sabbatical's over, huh? That was short."

Calling it a sabbatical had been Snyder's idea of a PR move. After getting an earful from the DA last week, he'd needed a way to discipline Mia for "misplacing" evidence without making it look as though the lab was admitting any wrongdoing. But Mia was tired of lying to people. She'd decided she was going to own up to what she'd done, take her lumps, and get it over with. She wasn't sure what that would mean for her career, but it was time to take back control of her life.

"It wasn't really a sabbatical," she confessed.

"No kidding."

"What does that mean?"

He got up and carried his plate to the sink. "Means the rumors are flying, honey. It'll be good for you to put in an appearance, straighten a few things out."

"What are the rumors?"

"Well, let's see." The amused look on his face told her she wasn't going to like this. "There's the one that you had a falling out with Snyder and decided to quit, but the director begged you to take a sabbatical while you reconsider."

"That's not so bad."

"There's the one that you eloped to Vegas with a cop, which I'm guessing isn't true, since you spent the night under my roof 'stead of his."

"Good guess."

"There's the one that you shot Frank Hannigan."

"That *I* did?"

"And then you skipped town when SMPD figured it out."

"Oh, my Lord."

"And then there's my personal favorite." A wicked smile spread across his face.

"What?"

"I doubt you want to hear it."

"What?"

He held up his hands. "Okay, but don't Mace the messenger. I have no idea who started this. I think it has to

do with some closed-door meetings you've been having
with your boss lately."

Dread pooled in Mia's stomach. "Just tell me."

"There's a rumor you've been doing the horizontal
lambada with Snyder—"

"What?"

"—and when he dumped you for someone else, you
got pissed off and left." Scott grinned. "If it makes you
feel any better, I never bought into that. Fact, I was
ninety-nine percent sure you'd run off to Vegas."

Ric took one look at the crowd gathered in Rachel's
office and knew his case was about to get ripped away
from him.

"I knew this would happen," Jonah muttered as they
stepped into the room. "Who gave her the heads up?
You?"

"Nope." Ric had wanted to. He'd called her yesterday
afternoon and requested a meeting on the Meyer case,
but she'd put him off until this morning.

"Ric, Jonah. You know Tony Delmonico and Laranya
Singh."

Ric nodded at the two FBI agents, both in navy suits.
Standing behind them was a silver-haired Texas Ranger.
Ric didn't recognize him, and Rachel introduced him as
Bob Jessup.

"Agents Delmonico and Singh are here to brief us on
something they're working on." Rachel gestured to some
black plastic chairs that had been dragged in from a conference room. "Let's all have a seat."

Ric leaned a shoulder against the wall and waited to
hear who was running this show. The feds would be his

guess, although there was no telling with a Ranger in the room.

To Ric's surprise, Singh stepped up to the plate. "We'll get straight to the point." She made eye contact with him and Jonah. "Your investigation into the death of Ashley Meyer has caught our attention."

"How so?" Rachel asked from her desk chair, which she was using as a throne at the moment. The DA obviously had put this meeting in her office to remind everyone whose turf they were on. As if any of these people cared.

"At the moment," Singh said, "we're not at liberty to disclose all of the details."

"What are you at liberty to disclose?" Rachel's tone was carefully loaded with politeness.

"I can tell you that Ashley Meyer's phone number came up during the course of a federal investigation."

"Came up?" Jonah asked.

"A subject who has been under investigation made a call to her in the week before her death."

"Who?" Ric asked.

"At this time, we can't disclose the names of those we're investigating or even the nature of the investigations."

Ric's gaze moved over the faces. Delmonico, Singh, Jessup—two federal investigators and a Texas Ranger. It was pretty clear to him what this was about.

"If you can't disclose information, perhaps you can tell us the purpose of your visit?" Rachel's voice had taken on an edge.

"We'd like to review your case notes, interview the detectives." This from Delmonico, who acknowledged

Ric and Jonah with a nod. "We're interested to see if you've developed any suspects in the case."

Ric traded looks with Jonah.

"Let me see if I'm understanding you," Ric said to the suits. "Ashley Meyer was working for an escort service, and your guy called her. You don't really have the goods on him, though, so you need our help?"

The answer was obvious from the look on Singh's face.

"Now we hand over our case," Ric continued, "you guys make a few collars, and everyone goes home happy, right?"

Singh cleared her throat. "I think we all have the same objectives here—"

"I don't."

She tipped her head to the side. "What are you so defensive about, Detective? I would think you'd welcome new avenues for investigation."

"You would, huh? All right, why is he here?" Ric nodded at the Ranger, who had yet to open his mouth.

Everyone looked startled. Jessup straightened in his chair, clearly offended.

Singh folded her arms over her chest. "I'm not sure I understand your point."

"Neither do I." This from Rachel, who was now glaring at him. He was embarrassing her in front of the big shots she'd been trying to impress two minutes ago.

"I'll tell you my point. I'm looking at three unsolved murder cases with links to the lieutenant governor." Ric turned to the Ranger. "Last I checked, you work for the guy. I'm not interested in having every bit of information we've developed leaked to the suspect."

Singh held up a hand. "Whoa. Wait. I don't think we're ready to call Lieutenant Governor Lane a *suspect* in anything. Least of all a murder."

Delmonico shot her an impatient look, and Ric instantly knew which agent he needed to be dealing with here. "Detective Santos, you sound fairly up to speed on some of the things we're looking at here. We'd very much like to get your take on the case." He glanced at Jonah. "Yours, too."

Rachel continued to appear calm, but the flush in her cheeks gave her away. A political grenade had just landed in her lap, and she wanted Ric to disarm it. She shot him a look that said, *Whatever the hell this is, I want nothing to do with it!*

"I'd like to say something," the Ranger said, and a hush fell over the room. "I've been on the job twenty-three years. That's five governors, all different stripes. I don't give a rat's ass about the politics. Someone in the State House is guilty of a crime, they're going down."

Ric absorbed the words. He seemed sincere, but that didn't mean anything. Looking sincere while lying was the hallmark of a skilled politician, and Jessup had just said he'd spent the last two decades learning from the pros.

"Let's get back to the case," Delmonico said. "And let's be realistic. This is a federal probe. We can't share everything, but what we can share, we will. I think we can help each other."

"How about you start by helping us?" Jonah countered. "Can you confirm what Ric said? That Ashley Meyer was working for an escort service?"

"We can."

Ric looked at his partner, who knew damn well that had been nothing but a hunch.

"Firm out of Fort Worth?" Jonah added. "It's called Night Angels?"

"Her photo was on their Web site," Singh said, getting onboard. "We can confirm that a call was made to the victim from our subject's home phone. However, we still aren't at liberty to disclose who that is." A stern look at Delmonico.

"But we'd be very interested to hear your theory," Delmonico added. "You said *three* murders, right?"

"Maybe more." Ric glanced at Rachel. The DA looked to be in shock, but that was her fault for being unwilling to get her butt in on a Sunday to meet with him. He'd told her it was important, and she'd blown him off.

She leaned forward on her elbows now, and Ric knew she was engaged in some intensive wishful thinking. She and the lieutenant governor shared the same political party. This was going to be a shitstorm.

"Ric, come on," she said. "Are you really trying to tell us you think Jeff Lane might have killed three people?"

Every pair of eyes in the room settled on Ric.

"Not Lane," he said. "At least, I doubt it."

Rachel's eyebrows arched. "Then what did you mean when—"

"Someone who works for him," Ric told her. "I think he has a fixer."

CHAPTER 18

❦

Mia had been gone only a few days, but for someone who spent pretty much every waking moment at work, it was a noticeable absence. She ignored the curious looks as she walked through the lab and approached her favorite DNA tracer.

"Hey there."

Mark glanced up from his microscope, clearly surprised to see her.

"I was hoping you might have finished with that evidence from Fort Worth."

Mark recovered quickly. "Sure. Yeah. Actually, I have. You want to hear my findings?"

"Absolutely." Mia couldn't get near Ashley's case—not after "losing" the evidence—but she remained committed to nailing her killer. Her goal now was to solve a related cold case and let Ric's team connect the dots. She was counting on Mark to help her.

He tossed his gloves into a biohazard bin before picking up a file from one of the many desks that lined the sides of the lab. "You want to talk here or—"

"Let's go to my office." She led him across the lab,

grateful to be away from the interested gazes of her coworkers. Based on the reactions she'd been getting all day, she was pretty sure the rumor about her and Snyder's little love triangle had infected people's brains.

Mia left the door open after Mark entered. No sense providing more grist for the rumor mill.

"So, what did you get?" she asked.

"Well, as you're undoubtedly aware, the techniques originally used to test this evidence aren't nearly as sophisticated as what we use here."

"I understand." Mia had run the original tests herself, which Mark knew from her signature on the evidence tag. "That's why I requested the evidence again," she continued. "I was reminded of the case recently, and I knew we could do more than what was possible six years ago. We're light-years ahead of the lab up there in terms of equipment and expertise."

Just as she'd done during their first conversation, she made it sound as if all of this was routine—she'd simply remembered some evidence she'd once analyzed and asked Mark to contact the agency handling the case to suggest a reexamination using new techniques. Helping to clear cold cases was part of the Delphi Center's mission. When possible, they even ran the tests for free.

What Mia had neglected to mention, though, was that this case was personal.

She also hadn't fully explained to Mark why she'd needed him to conduct the analysis instead of doing it herself. Until Mia dispelled the cloud hanging over her reputation—if she ever did—she didn't want to jeopardize this case or any other by directly handling evidence that might one day be used at trial. Better to have someone else perform the tests, someone Mia knew and trusted and whose expertise rivaled her own.

Someone like Mark.

But now, she saw the problem with her plan. One of the traits she valued about Mark was his intelligence, which was manifesting itself right now in his steady gaze.

"Interesting to me that this case resembles that San Marcos girl you were working on. The one found in the park?"

Mia raised her eyebrows but didn't comment.

"It's been attracting a lot of interest lately. This morning, we had a call about it from the FBI."

Mia's stomach dropped. "We did?"

"Special Agent Delmonico. He called straight up to the lab, wanted to talk to the tracer in charge of the case."

"He went around Snyder."

"Apparently so." Mark looked at her for a long moment. "I told him you were on sabbatical."

Mia couldn't talk. All she could do was nod. Whatever shot she'd had of working this out with her supervisors and with Rachel was gone. The FBI was involved now. Her professional misconduct would—literally—become a federal case.

Mark seemed to sense that he'd dealt her some sort of blow. "Anyway, let me tell you what I found," he said, looking at his notes again. "First, the dress. Lots of blood there, all of it from one contributor, unfortunately: the victim. And I reexamined the duct tape. Nothing." He flipped a page in his file. "Also submitted, black thong underpants. No blood. No semen. I tested for touch DNA on the waistband—"

"Tape-lift method or scraping?"

"Both," he said. "Again, only the victim's profile. She must have removed the garment herself. Maybe he ordered her to do it, or the encounter started out consensual." He flipped another page. "No bra. No other clothing, except shoes. That's where it got interesting."

"It did?"

"Your first round of testing didn't come up with any usable blood."

"*Usable* being the key word," Mia said. She remembered the tiny blood droplet she'd found on the shoes so many years ago. Back then, because of budgets and equipment, she'd been limited to a technique that required a sample the size of a quarter, at least. Now she could get a profile from a sample the size of a pinhead.

"And?" she asked hopefully.

He peeled off his glasses. "And I came up with a second contributor. Possibly her killer."

Mia's breath whooshed out. This was what she'd hoped for.

"Now, I'm no detective," Mark said humbly, "but my thought is, he probably removed her shoes before the attack. Or she did, and the shoes were somewhere else while the stabbing occurred. They were practically clean, except for some dirt on the soles. Then maybe he picked up the shoes and dumped them with her body so they wouldn't turn up in his possession if anyone took the trouble to look. He could have been bleeding by that time."

Point by point, Mark was reciting the scenario playing out in Mia's head.

"A stabbing attack," Mia said. "That's very violent."

Amy flashed into her mind. Mia tried to keep her sister out of her thoughts while she was working, but every now and then, Amy caught her off guard. "Very violent, very intense. And she probably struggled a lot, despite her bindings."

Mark nodded. Having seen the dress, he knew the kind of emotion that had gone into Laura's murder. "Fifty-three puncture wounds," he said. "Be unusual if he didn't nick himself at least once, either pushing in the blade or pulling it out. I submitted the profile but haven't heard back yet from Darrell."

The phone on the wall rang, and Mia turned to it, surprised. Very few people had her direct line. Ric. Vivian. Panic shot through her, and she lunged for the receiver.

"Hello?"

"Hey, it's me," Sophie said. "I've got an Agent Delmonico on the line for you. He says it's urgent."

"Damn it." Mia took a deep breath and tried to steel herself. Ready or not, it was time to face the music. "Okay, put him through."

"I'll let you take that." Mark dropped the file onto her counter and nodded as he slipped out. "You'll be the first to know if we get a hit."

"Thanks," she said, as Sophie connected the call.

"Glad I caught you," the agent said. "Just this morning, someone told me you were on sabbatical."

Caught. Mia wondered if that word choice had been intentional. "What can I do for you, Mr. Delmonico?"

"I'd like to meet with you, if it's not too much trouble." His voice was friendly, but something in his tone bothered her.

"About what, exactly?"

"I've got an offer for you." He sounded as if he was smiling now. "You might say it's an offer you can't refuse."

She pulled the phone away from her ear and stared at it. Surely she'd heard wrong.

"Sorry," he said. "Bad joke. Miss Voss? You still there?"

"What is it you want, Mr. Delmonico?"

"Meet me at your house in one hour. I'll be happy to explain it."

Ric watched from one of El Patio's back corner tables as his brother entered the bar. With his short-cropped hair, overcoat, and dark suit, he looked like the quintessential fed, and Ric tried not to let that irk him.

Rey pulled off his coat and tossed it over the back of the chair. "Holy shit, Ric." He sank into the seat. "You put your foot in it this time."

Ric turned his attention to the waitress who'd just appeared. "Another Jack Daniel's. Rocks."

Rey asked for his bourbon with Coke and waited for the waitress to get all the way back to the bar before tearing in again.

"You think you could have given me a little warning? A few hours' lead time before dropping this bomb?"

"I didn't drop anything," Ric said. "You guys already had him on the radar."

"Yeah, for misusing campaign funds. For hiring hookers. But three homicides? You know what's going to happen when this hits the news?"

"How's it going to hit the news?" Ric asked, although he knew it would. Everything did, eventually. "You guys got a leak?"

Rey glowered.

"Okay, cheap shot," Ric conceded. "But I'd keep an eye on that Ranger. I don't like him on this task force. He complicates things."

"Funny, Laranya Singh said the same thing about you, and people listen to her. You're lucky to be in on this investigation. So am I."

"Why are you, anyway?"

He scowled. "My boss seems to have this idea that I can play nice with the locals, maybe rein in my hothead brother."

Rey sighed heavily as he leaned back and loosened his tie. He looked stressed, tired, and Ric felt a stab of guilt over it, because his brother had spent the better part of the weekend doing him a favor by helping Mia.

"You really stuck your neck out," Rey said. "And you know what's going to happen if you're wrong? You're going to go down in flames. Not Singh. Not Delmonico. Not the pretty district attorney. *You.*"

"You think I'm wrong?"

"I don't know yet." The waitress returned with their drinks, and Rey switched to Spanish to keep the conversation private. "What have you got on him? Besides what you shared in the meeting."

"You think I'm holding back."

"I know you're holding back. You wouldn't get in front of a room full of badges and make a statement like that based on some clerk at a country club. What else you got?"

Ric paused, choosing his words carefully. "These two prostitutes—"

"Three, if your hunch is right about the bones up at Lake Buchanan."

Ric nodded. "Right. These three cases, they've all got the same MO. Sexual homicide, with some extra kinky elements. The bondage, the piquerism. These are lust murders. Then you've got two other murders, linked to those three, but they're pretty much execution-style. And those shootings were carried out with the same gun. To me, that says we've probably got a wealthy and well-connected john. He's into pain, bondage, whatever—he gets off on some really twisted shit. And every now and then, he gets carried away, actually kills the girl, then calls in his janitor to clean up the mess."

Rey stared down into his drink, as if digesting the scenario.

"There might be another victim," Ric added.

"Who?"

"That's the thing. I don't know yet. It's a bludgeoning death from Burnet County. Girl was dumped in a lake, weighted down with a cinder block. They're still looking for an ID."

"So, what's the link?"

"Young, blond, defensive cuts on her hands. It's a pretty thin connection so far, but I'm working on it."

"Tell me about Ashley Meyer. You've got a lot more on her. What's the ME say?"

"That she was killed indoors. He found carpet fiber on the body and abrasions on her back." Ric paused. "What I'd really like to get a look at is the inside of Jeff Lane's lake house. You ever been up there?"

"No."

"Big place on Lake Buchanan. Not too far from where that skeleton was recovered."

"The lieutenant gov's lake house," Rey scoffed. "Good luck getting a warrant."

"I was hoping you guys could help with that."

"Don't hold your breath."

"I won't. Anyway, Jonah's got his own theory of the case. He thinks maybe this guy's into plain-vanilla sex, but if anyone ever realizes who he is and tries to shake him down, he calls his fixer in to get rid of her. The guy makes it look like a lust crime to draw attention to the fact that she's a hooker, barely worth anyone's time to investigate. Either way, the john's directly involved, and he's looking at murder charges."

Rey shook his head.

"What?"

"Our profiler likes the first one," Rey said.

"You guys brought in a profiler?"

"He's working long-distance. But he's seen everything we have, and he thinks we're dealing with two different perps. The hookers are sexual homicides—real ones, not staged—and the other two are hits, just like you said. Only Frank Hannigan wasn't the target. Mia was."

Ric bristled.

"I'm still not clear how she fits in, by the way," Rey said. "Why go after someone like her?"

Ric rattled his ice cubes. He'd lost a lot of sleep over that question. "I think Mia holds the key to this case, whether she knows it or not."

"You wanna explain that?"

"The things she can do with DNA. It's really amazing. And people know how good she is, especially around here."

"So she's good at her job. So what?"

"She saw the first case when she was working up in Fort Worth. Didn't have the resources to get the best tests done on that evidence."

"You're talking about Laura Thorne, the one killed out by Jeff Lane's country club?"

"That's right."

"So Mia ran the evidence . . . ?"

"Couldn't get the killer's DNA, but she remembers the case vividly. Fast-forward six years, she's at the Delphi Center, gets a similar case. Lane's fixer gets wind of it, realizes she's probably smart enough to make the leap between two totally separate cases in two totally separate jurisdictions, decides he needs to take her out. That's what he was trying to do when Frank Hannigan got in the way."

"How'd he know she was handling the case?"

"Called the lab," Ric said. "Twice. Claimed to be Jonah, too, which goes to show he's got an inside line on this investigation, because he knows which law-enforcement agency to say he works for *and* which detective to impersonate."

Ric watched his brother absorb all of this as he sipped his drink.

"By the way, Mia thinks the person who tried to kill her is a cop, or at least someone in law enforcement," Ric said. "I'm convinced he also had some military background."

Rey closed his eyes and swore.

"When he didn't kill her in the first attempt—which was staged to look like a carjacking—he figures time's been lost," Ric said. "There's a chance she might have told someone her suspicions about the cases being connected—which she did. She told me. So now he's got to worry about a DNA scientist putting it all together and also an incriminating DNA profile sitting right in the lab. So he gets her to destroy the evidence before he goes after her again. Now, even if anyone tries to connect the cases, there isn't any DNA to back it up."

"Then why's he still after her?" Rey asked. "The evidence is gone."

"I don't know." Ric swigged the last of his drink, trying to take the edge off his mood. His brother had just touched a nerve. Ric knew more about these cases and about Mia than anyone else involved. And yet he hadn't figured out why someone was still gunning for her.

"Maybe there's something else, something she doesn't realize she has yet," Ric said. "Some sort of DNA evidence or test she could do that would shed light on all of this, and he doesn't want that happening. Also, he spent some time in her car with her. Maybe he's worried about her recognizing him somehow and making an ID one day. Murder for hire's a capital offense. He gets caught, he's looking at death row."

Rey shook his head. "Or maybe he's obsessed. He missed his shot twice, now he's more determined than ever to get his payday."

Ric checked his watch. He needed to give Mia a call. He'd be damned if he'd let another night go by with her sleeping at that SEAL's house. Mia's motives might be pure, but Ric didn't trust Black for a minute. The guy was an operator, and he probably had no qualms about moving in on a vulnerable target.

Ric sure hadn't.

"Where is she now?" Rey asked.

"Who, Mia?"

Rey just looked at him. His brother had always been way too good at reading him.

"Some friend from work gave her a ride home and offered her a place to stay," Ric said. His last update was courtesy of Sophie. Ric hadn't actually talked to Mia since he'd dropped her off yesterday.

"This the SEAL I ran deep background on last night?" Rey asked.

"Yeah."

Rey lifted his eyebrows at this apparent lapse in judgment. *How the hell'd you let that happen?* his look seemed to say. As if Ric had had a choice.

Although he had. Mia had looked at him with those soulful blue eyes that practically begged him to lie to her. She'd wanted him to tell her that this thing between them was going somewhere. And he'd almost done it. All the right promises had been on the tip of his tongue, but he'd discovered he couldn't lie to her, especially not straight to her face like that.

So, instead—like an idiot—he'd practically shoved her at Black with both hands. Ric couldn't believe he'd done it. It was one of the stupidest moves he'd ever made. He deserved every bit of misery he was feeling right now and more.

"You know, the guy's clean," Rey said. As if that made it better. "It's not a bad place for her to stay, considering."

Ric looked away. His brother was trying to get a rise out of him.

"You serious about this girl or what?"

Ric didn't answer.

"Because it's been a long time since I've seen you this torqued up about something."

"I'm not torqued up."

"You look like shit, Ric. When was the last time you slept?"

He shook his head.

"Fine, keep it to yourself," Rey said. "But if you do like this girl, you're going to hate what I'm about to tell you."

CHAPTER 19

❧

Mia lay in a eucalyptus-scented bath, waiting for the tension to seep out of her muscles. After days of running, she was back in her own house, in her own bathroom, taking a soothing soak in her own claw-footed tub. She should feel Zen, relieved, finally at peace with her situation after days and days of emotional turmoil.

Instead, she felt edgy. Aromatherapy was no match for a heavy sense of foreboding and the knowledge that a team of armed federal agents was staked out across the street. There would be no relaxing tonight. She'd be lucky to catch a wink of sleep.

She turned the hot water on with her foot and tried to push the worry away. This was *her* choice, and she wouldn't second-guess herself. The FBI had offered, with Rachel's blessing, to give Mia complete immunity from any charges related to stealing and destroying evidence. In exchange, they merely wanted her cooperation—as in sit at home and wait for someone to come after her. The plan was simple yet tantalizing, so tantalizing that Mia had agreed to it without even consulting her lawyer. Vivian probably would have advised her to take the Fifth on everything and let the FBI put their own asses on the line to catch their bad guy.

And yet Mia had jumped at the deal. Why? Same reason she did almost everything: her obsession with her work. She wanted her career back, her life back. As Ric had pointed out, her career *was* her life, so it was the same thing. Her professional reputation meant everything to her, and she'd never get it back if there was a shadow hanging over her each time she signed her name to a report or got up to testify at a trial. And if it ever became public that she'd stolen and destroyed evidence? The cascade effect on all of her previous cases was unthinkable. Every defense attorney whose client had been put away with the help of her testimony would challenge the conviction.

Mia couldn't bear the thought. She needed immunity. She needed the assurance that her actions on that frigid, fateful day would never come back to haunt her. Cooperating with the FBI had been a snap decision.

And if Ric didn't like it, so what?

His words on the phone an hour ago had been cold, clipped. He'd made it clear that he thought she was making a big mistake. But it wasn't his decision. He wasn't the one who had to live with the ramifications of what she'd done. Ric was a bystander in all of this, no more a part of her life than he had been two weeks ago.

Except that he was.

She couldn't tell him that, but at least she could be honest with herself. She'd offered him something, and he'd taken it, just as she'd known he would. He was, after all, a guy. And she had no right to feel betrayed, because he'd warned her from the beginning about all of the things he didn't want that he knew she did. Even yesterday, in the midst of an uncomfortable conversation, he'd held his ground. He hadn't said a lot of things he didn't mean just to avoid hurting her feelings.

So, yes, her feelings were hurt. Ironically, she trusted him now more than ever, because he'd been honest with her about where things stood.

Mia turned off the water again and settled back to relax. She did some yoga breathing and tried to focus on something positive. But all she could think about was her meeting with Delmonico that afternoon. *He's not finished yet. He'll be back.* And then Ric's words crowded her brain: *His pride's at stake now. He won't miss again.* Both Ric and the agent seemed to think that this hired gun, whoever he was, had her on his hit list. And she'd agreed to sit there and wait for him to come after her. It went against every survival instinct she had, but she'd agreed to do it, because as long as he was out there, she would never feel confident about her safety or her family's.

Creak.

Her eyes flew open at the sound. She sat up, sloshing water over the sides of the tub.

Ric stepped into the room.

"How'd you get in?" she squeaked.

Instead of answering, he propped his shoulder against the wall and watched her. His gaze didn't leave her face, and she could tell by the glint in his eyes that he'd already looked his fill.

She pulled her knees to her chest. "What are you doing here?"

"Making sure you don't shoot me."

"You think I'd *shoot* you?"

"I penetrated your security, in case you hadn't noticed."
His gaze drifted down, then back up again. There was
something dangerous in his look now. "Didn't Black
give you one of his guns?"

She hesitated.

"Where is it?"

"My purse."

Shaking his head, he pulled his phone from the pocket
of his leather jacket and walked out.

Mia stared at the empty doorway. Then she scrambled to her feet and grabbed a towel from the rack. As
she wrapped it around herself, a tirade of angry Spanish erupted from the hallway. Mia didn't understand a
word of it, but the meaning was clear. Ric was very, very
unhappy with someone, and she guessed that whoever it
was had a federal badge.

She darted into the bedroom and put on a terry bath-
robe. The argument continued as she hurriedly pulled a
comb through her hair.

And then it stopped. Not a sound. Nothing. Mia crept
into the hallway and listened, wondering if he'd left as
suddenly as he'd come.

Her phone chimed, and she jumped. She snatched it
up from her nightstand.

"Hello?"

"It's Special Agent Delmonico. Is Ric Santos with you?"

She heard her microwave oven being opened and
shut.

"Um, yes."

A curse on the other end of the phone, followed by
some barked orders commanding someone named James
to get his ass over there.

"It's okay," Mia rushed to add. "I let him in."

A pause as the agent probably tried to understand this. Mia didn't understand it herself. She hadn't let Ric in at all, but now that he was there, she wanted to smooth things over.

"Remember the protocol, Miss Voss. All visitors must be cleared through the team leader, which means me."

"It's 'Dr.'"

"What?"

"*Dr.* Voss. Not Miss. Is there anything else?"

"Not at the moment, no."

"In that case, good night."

Mia clicked off and stuffed the phone into her pocket. She didn't like to be snippy with people, but for heaven's sake, they were supposed to be *protecting* her. That was part of the bargain. And somehow an armed man had slipped under their radar.

She found Ric sitting in her living room with a basketball game on mute. He was eating something off one of her dishes.

"I want to know how you got in here."

He took a bite, chewed, and swallowed. He swigged water from one of her glasses. "Back door," he finally said, plunking the glass down.

"You just waltzed through the back door?"

"You think I slid down the chimney?"

Mia stalked into the kitchen. She inspected her lock. Everything looked normal. She pressed some buttons on her alarm system and saw that the last entry had been eight minutes ago through the back door.

She returned to the living room. "Who gave you my alarm code?"

"You did."

She stared at him. He must have watched over her shoulder as she'd entered it the other night. She'd never thought to hide it from him.

"And the lock?"

"Locks can be picked." He polished off his food.

"What about the FBI team?"

"What about them?"

"How'd you get past them? They're supposed to be staking out my street."

He shoved his plate away. "Looks like they were sleeping on the job."

Mia refused to believe that they were sleeping. But they must have been distracted. Ric had proved his point.

She went to stand beside her sofa where he sat, watching her with an angry gleam in his eye.

"I told you this was a bad idea, didn't I? I could have just as easily been someone coming in here to kill you."

Mia stepped closer.

"And what would you have done, thrown a bar of soap at me?"

She tucked her hands into the pockets of her robe. He was right. And he'd come there to demonstrate that he was right to her and the team of agents camped out half a block away. She hoped they'd gotten the message.

"Thank you."

He scowled, and she could tell that he hadn't expected gratitude.

She sat down on the opposite end of the sofa. "You don't understand why I'm doing this, do you?"

"No."

She looked at him. "I realized something, only I realized it too late. I realized it after I'd already done what this guy wanted, after I'd already let him use me and compromise my integrity."

"You were *coerced*, Mia. That doesn't mean shit about your integrity. This whole immunity thing is pure manipulation. Ask your sister if you don't believe me."

"Just listen." She had to explain this. She needed him to understand. At some point, his opinion of her had come to matter. "I thought going along with it would keep Sam safe, and me safe, and Vivian, and whoever else. But after it was done, I realized that it wouldn't keep anyone safe at all. I did what he needed me to, and now I'm a liability. I'll never be safe until he's caught. Neither will my family, because he obviously knows that's my Achilles' heel. So if there's something I can do to help investigators bring him in, I'm going to do it."

"I can't believe you'd let them use you as bait," he said. "They don't give a damn about you. And they only care about this guy because they think they can flip him and get the goods on someone important."

Mia sighed. She couldn't make him understand, so she redirected the conversation. "What did your brother say just now?"

"Someone screwed up, but it won't happen again."

"This wasn't his idea, you know. Delmonico came up with it. You shouldn't be mad at Rey."

"He should have given me a heads up as soon as he got wind of this, when there was still time to change the plan. He didn't."

"Please let it go, Ric. I don't want you mad at your brother because of me. You two seem close."

He watched her. For the first time since she'd sat

beside him, she was acutely aware of the robe she had on and the way he was looking at her.

She scooted closer to him on the sofa. She had no idea why she did it, except that he was there, and all of the logical things she'd been telling herself about shielding her heart from him seemed irrelevant now. She wanted that intimacy back from the other night, even if she could only have it for a few hours.

"I saw the Sig in your purse." He held her gaze for a long moment. "He give you anything else?"

His voice had an edge, and he wasn't just asking about firearms. But she decided to take the question at face value.

"He lent me a shotgun. Said it's the best home-security weapon because it doesn't require much aim."

"Where is it?"

"My hall closet."

He got up and walked to the closet. She watched him take the gun out and check to see if it was loaded.

"Extra shells?"

"Box on the floor," she said. As if she'd ever need more than one. She'd had this argument with Scott that morning, but he'd insisted.

Annoyed now, Mia cleared Ric's dishes and dumped them into the sink. On the counter was a brown paper bag. She peeked inside and opened one of the foil-wrapped bundles.

He'd sneaked into her house with a bag of tamales.

When she went back into the living room, he was on her couch again, checking messages on his phone. She sat on the sofa arm and watched him.

"I brought food if you want some," he said.

"I don't like to eat right before bed."

He looked up. "You're going to bed?"

"Well, it's after eleven. Why? How long are you going to be here?"

"I'm spending the night."

She laughed at his audacity. "Oh, really? And where are you planning to sleep?"

"I'm not. I'm here to work, not play."

She jerked back, stung. Those few glib words told her exactly what he thought of their night together. Very little.

She stood up. "Good night, Ric. There's a blanket in the closet if you get cold."

The State House was dark and quiet. Light spilled into the hallway from one of the offices, and he heard low voices coming from inside.

Lane sat at his desk in the wrinkled remains of the suit he'd probably worn to some fund-raiser today. The jacket had been tossed onto the back of his chair, and the lieutenant gov and his spokeswoman were engaged in a quiet debate about something. The man stepped through the door, and Lane surged to his feet.

"Where have you *been*?"

He stood in the doorway and waited silently until Lane mumbled something to the woman. She tucked her legal pad under her arm and cast him a curious look on her way out.

When she was gone, he closed the door and crossed his arms. "Don't call me at home again. Ever."

Lane put his hands on his hips and had the nerve to look pissed. "Where the hell were you? I'm going out of my mind here."

"Taking care of business."

His eyebrows shot up. "And?"

"And it's almost taken care of."

"Almost? When will it *be* taken care of?"

"Soon."

"You said that days ago! What the hell happened?"

Ric Santos happened. Bitterness lodged in his throat as he saw him again through binoculars, slipping through Mia Voss's back door.

"I'll get it done," he said with confidence. He'd come up with a new strategy, and nothing could get in his way this time.

Lane clutched the hair at his temples and looked like a man about to lose it. "I can't fucking believe this."

Enjoying Lane's distress, he calmly walked over to a credenza lined with photographs. Probably planted by some consultant who thought they'd look good on the news.

Too bad Lane didn't get the irony. With his control over the legislature, the Lite Gov—as his security detail called him—had more power than the real one, who was mostly a figurehead. Politically, Lane was a man to fear. A powerhouse.

And right now, Lane was at *his* mercy, which made *him* the single most powerful man in the state. With one phone call, he could turn Lane's life and his family's lives and all of their political ambitions to dust.

He glanced at the man with contempt, a man some said had hopes for the White House. Squashing him now would be an act of patriotism, more so than anything he'd ever done for his country.

Problem was, by destroying Lane, he'd be destroying

himself, too. Their connection went back further than he liked to remember—back to the days when he'd still had a conscience about this shit.

Lane was watching him anxiously, as if he was going to say something to put all of his fears to rest.

He let him squirm.

Turning his back on the politician, he surveyed the wall of photographs. One showed his kid in a baseball helmet, his hands choked up on the bat. The boy was maybe eight, ten. About the age his own daughter had been when he'd first crossed the line.

He'd been thinking about that case a lot lately. Fifteen years ago, but it was still fresh in his mind. It had been a known pedophile suspected in a kid killing. Scumbag was guilty as sin, but they'd had nothing, so he'd planted the dead girl's sock in the guy's car.

One sock. That was it. Justice was done, and he slept easier knowing he'd made the world safer for his daughter.

The things people did for their kids.

"Well?" Lane demanded.

He turned around and pulled a pack of smokes from his pocket. "Well what?"

"What's the plan?"

He lit the cigarette and took a drag, then nodded at one of the pictures beside him. Lane and his wife at a college graduation ceremony.

"You know, your kid's a piece of shit," he said, and Lane's gaze narrowed. "What's your plan about *that*?" He flicked his ash on the Oriental rug. "Two DUIs out in California. A drunk-and-disorderly here in Austin. Who'd you pay off to get that to disappear?"

"Kurt is sick."

"No kidding."

"We're sending him away soon for treatment."

He shook his head. "Whatever works," he said, knowing it wouldn't. They both knew it.

There was a coffee mug on the corner of the desk, and he dropped the cigarette into it. He got up in Lane's face and poked his chest hard.

"Don't call me again."

Hatred flared in Lane's eyes, and the man realized he'd been wrong. Lane *did* get the irony. He knew exactly who had the power here.

"Get your job done, and I won't have to," Lane said tightly.

"I'll get it done." He crossed the room and reached for the doorknob. "You can count on it."

CHAPTER 20

◦∾◦

Mia found a Santos brother in her kitchen the next morning, but it wasn't the one who'd been in her dream. Rey stood at the coffee maker in a crisp white shirt and a tie. He had a gun on his hip and a BlackBerry pressed to his ear.

"I heard," he was telling someone. "But what about the barbecue tongs?"

Mia's hand froze as she reached for a mug. Rey knew about the tongs?

"All right, thanks . . . Yeah . . . Okay, will do."

He clicked off as she poured some coffee. She skipped the cream today because she needed an extra jolt.

He watched her take the first gulp, and she wondered if she looked as tired as she felt. She'd slept restlessly. Her hair had been uncooperative that morning, so she'd stuck it in a ponytail before throwing on a sweater and some faded jeans. Now she felt underdressed beside Rey's neat business attire.

"What's new on the case?" she asked.

He hesitated, probably reviewing what she'd overheard before deciding how much to tell her.

"We got some results back," he said. "From the cig-arette wrapper and the barbecue tongs collected at the incinerator."

"That's interesting, because I thought the tongs were being processed by the Delphi Center, not the FBI."

"You might have noticed that we've taken over this case. Our agents are leading the joint task force. Other law-enforcement agencies are still playing a role, but we're trying to coordinate efforts."

Mia rested her cup on the counter. "I've been involved with a lot of murder cases, but I've never seen quite this level of interest from so many agencies."

Rey watched her. He looked guarded, just like his brother.

"Are you ever planning to tell me who this mysterious suspect is? Why is everyone protecting his identity?"

"Not protecting his identity," he said. "Protecting the investigation. We don't want any leaks compromising the case we're trying to build."

An uneasy feeling settled over her. There was something very unusual about all of this, but she wasn't getting it.

"What about the tongs?" she asked.

"Prints came back to a twenty-three-year-old who has a record of check fraud."

Check fraud. Not what she'd expected.

"He also happens to have a job in the stockroom at Sloan's Hardware. The store carries tongs like that, which would explain why his prints were there."

"Any chance someone at the store might remember who bought the tongs?"

"We're looking into it. They sold nearly a hundred this year, though, so we're not optimistic."

"And the cigarette wrapper?" she asked.

"Nothing in the system. We were going on only a partial, so getting a match was iffy."

Mia watched him talk, struck once again by how much he looked like his brother. This was an older, more polished version, but their voices were similar, and so were their mannerisms. He had Ric's intensity but his was slightly better hidden.

Mia realized that she had an opportunity here—a few moments alone with someone who knew Ric better than anybody—and she'd be stupid not to take advantage of it.

"Can I ask you something?" She sipped her coffee and wasn't surprised when he simply gave her a neutral look. She set the mug down. "What happened with Ric and his wife?"

"Sandra?" He looked surprised but covered it quickly. "You should ask Ric about that."

She tipped her head to the side and gazed at him. There was a barely perceptible softness in his brown eyes that told her he knew that Ric was keeping her at arm's length.

"It was messy," he said.

Okay, three words weren't much, but they were a start. She decided to go with a hunch she'd had. She didn't know where it had come from, maybe Ric's reaction to her staying at Scott's.

"Did she cheat on him?"

Rey looked at her and took a sip of his coffee. A few heavy moments ticked by. She'd gotten a yes without him actually having to break his brother's confidence.

He set the cup aside and folded his arms over his chest. "Why don't you talk to him?"

"I'd love to, but—" She cleared her throat, feeling more pathetic than ever. "He seems to have this inability to, I don't know, open up about anything personal. With me, at least. Maybe I'm the problem."

"You're not."

From across the kitchen, her phone chimed inside her purse. She stared at Rey, trying to read the meaning behind that answer. The phone chimed again, and she walked over to dig it out of her bag. Vivian.

"How's it going over there?" Her sister's voice sounded relaxed, and Mia hoped she was enjoying her early spring break trip with Sam.

"Okay," Mia said. "How are you guys?"

"I won't use the word b-o-r-e-d. But if I have to play another game of Old Maid, I'm going to need therapy."

"I thought you guys were going to spend your time on the beach?"

"It's been raining nonstop. Listen, I'm serious. How's it really going? What's happening with the investigation?"

"Refill?" Rey held out the coffee pot.

"Thanks," she said, and he topped off her cup. "It's coming along," she told Viv. "They're exploring new leads."

"Mia."

"Yeah?"

"Is that a man in your house at seven in the morning?"

"Actually, yes." Mia walked to the back door for a small measure of privacy. "He's an FBI agent. He stopped by to brief me on the case." And to play bodyguard, but she didn't want to mention that to Vivian. Her sister was worried enough already.

"Since when is the FBI—"

"I'll have to explain later," Mia said as an enormous black pickup glided up the driveway. Scott stopped right beside the back stoop and jumped out.

Mia pulled open the door before he could knock. "I'm almost ready. Would you like some coffee?"

"Yeah, love some." Scott stepped inside and traded nods with the other alpha male standing in the room.

"What is going *on* over there?" Vivian asked.

"That's Scott. He's giving me a ride to work."

"Scott *Black*?"

"I still haven't gotten my insurance check, so he offered."

Silence on the other end as Vivian absorbed this. Mia grabbed her jacket off the kitchen chair and pulled it on. "Viv says hi," she told Scott, who was pouring joe into her sixteen-ounce travel mug.

"Tell her hi. You ready now?"

Mia grabbed her purse and did an inventory: jacket, phone, keys, purse, bodyguard. Did she have everything?

"I think so." She held the door for Rey and then Scott, who turned and blocked her way when she tried to step out.

"Conversation time's over." He nodded at her phone. "You need to pay attention now."

He was right. She kept trying to forget the whole reason all these people were there: someone wanted to hurt her.

"Hey, Viv?"

"Mia, what on *earth*—"

"I have to go now. Everything's fine, okay? I'll fill you in later."

• • •

Sophie poked her head into the office, and Mia knew she was cornered.

"You're skipping lunch again, aren't you?"

Mia sighed. "I've got a lot to catch up on."

Sophie eyed her sharply as she walked in and slung her oversize purse on the worktable. When she pulled out her red satin zipper bag, Mia knew it was hopeless.

She switched off her microscope. "You eat yet?" she asked, pulling up a stool.

"Smart Gourmet." Sophie made a face. "You?"

Mia nodded at her half-finished soft drink. "Liquid lunch."

Sophie sat down and unzipped the familiar pouch. Manicure time. Typically, they saved this activity for Friday lunch breaks, but Sophie obviously couldn't wait that long to catch up on gossip.

"Are we doing French or color?"

Mia pumped sanitizer into her hands before turning them over to Sophie. "No color for me."

Undaunted, Sophie got out her tools and lined them up on the counter. "I'll go with French. Your hands look awful. Why do you use that stuff?"

"If you saw some of the grossness I deal with, you wouldn't ask."

Sophie opened a tube of cuticle softener and dabbed a dot on each of Mia's nail beds. "So."

Here it came.

"What's up with the detective? And if you say 'nothing,' I will jab you with my nail scissors."

"We spent the weekend together."

"Ha!" Sophie's face lit up. "I knew it! How was it?" She jumped up and squeezed Mia's shoulders. "Oh my God, I bet it was *so* good! That man is sex on a platter."

She sat back down and got to work on Mia's fingernails, happy with the prospect of forthcoming juicy details.

Mia skipped most of them. "It was really . . ." she searched for a word. "Different."

Sophie pursed her lips and seemed to be considering this idea as she filed and snipped. "Different as in he wanted to wear your clothes or . . . ?"

"Definitely not that. Just . . . different. From what it's been like before. Oh, I don't know, I can't explain it."

"Please try." Sophie made a plea with her eyes.

Mia took a deep breath and groped for an analogy. "Have you ever been cliff diving?"

"No."

"Well, I used to go at this swimming hole near my grandparents. And there's always this moment when you're walking out to the edge and you can't believe you're doing it. And then you jump, and the whole way down, it's like your stomach is falling out. But then you hit the water, and it's just pure *impact*."

Sophie stared at her, and Mia felt her cheeks flush.

"Anyway, it was sort of like that. Intimidating at first. But then really good."

Sophie took out the clear polish and swiped quick strokes over each of the nails on Mia's left hand.

"So, now what happens?"

"I don't know." Mia's stomach knotted as she watched her do the other hand.

"What does he think?"

"He doesn't want a relationship. He told me that. So I guess it was a one-time thing. Here, your turn." Mia took over the manicuring responsibilities as Sophie sat watching her.

"He'll be back," Sophie predicted.

"Yeah, but back for what? He doesn't want anything serious."

"And you do?"

Mia picked up Sophie's hand and started filing her pretty long nails. "I don't know. I didn't think I did, but I do eventually, so now I'm wondering why I should let myself get down the path with someone who has commitment issues and is just going to end up hurting me." She dropped Sophie's left hand and picked up the right. Her French manicure was perfect. "You don't even need this. What am I doing here?"

Sophie pulled a bottle of ivory from her purse and plunked it on the table.

"My tips need freshening, and I needed an excuse to talk to you," Sophie said. "You've been avoiding me."

"I have not." She bent over Sophie's hand and painted perfect white crescents at the ends of each nail. She actually did have a knack for this. Something to think about if she found herself out of a job someday soon.

"Come on, Mia."

"What?"

"You haven't scratched the surface of everything that happened to you this weekend. But you know what? It's okay, because I know you can't talk about it."

Mia felt guilty. "I would if I could, but there's this investigation—"

"I understand. Which is one of the reasons I'm glad you've got Ric."

"I don't *have* Ric. Not like that."

Sophie gave her a baleful look.

"This isn't going anywhere," Mia said. "It's just something that happened."

"Trust me, I know men. I mean, come on. Cliff diving? If it was half as good for him as it was for you, it'll happen again."

Mia didn't pick up until the fourth ring.

"Are you home yet?" Ric asked her.

"Almost. Why?"

"Who's driving you?"

"Scott."

Ric gritted his teeth as he let that sink in. He had nothing on the guy, but he didn't like his arrangement with Mia, even now that it was limited to carpooling.

"Ric, what's wrong?"

"I'm running late. I'll be there in a few hours, probably around nine."

"You don't need to come. They've got plenty of people—"

"I'm coming."

"Okay," she said. "Where are you, anyway? It sounds like a carnival."

"I'm at a bowling alley."

She waited, no doubt wondering what he was doing at a bowling alley on a Tuesday night when he'd been so busy the last two weeks he'd hardly had time to sleep.

"I'm with Ava," he said. "I missed last weekend, so I'm trying to make it up to her."

"Oh."

Ric watched his daughter approach the line, her brow furrowed with concentration. The ball sailed off her hand, and she waited, waited, waited.

"Strike!" She yelped and pumped her fist. Then she strutted up to him and poked a finger at him. "Take *that*!"

"I've got to go," he told Mia.

"You don't have to come."

"I'll see you later."

He stuffed his phone into his pocket as a waitress stopped by their lane to drop off a tray of food.

Ava sat down at the table and picked up a soda. "Oh my God, I'm starving." She glanced up at him. "Who was on the phone?"

Ric sat down across from her. "Nobody."

She rolled her eyes.

"Just a friend."

One of her brows arched, and for a second, she was sixteen instead of twelve. "Male or female?"

"What?"

"Your friend. I'm guessing female, because you've got that look on your face."

"What look?"

"The look you get when you don't want to talk about something. It was a girl, wasn't it? Dad, it's *so* obvious. You might as well say it."

Ric chomped into his burger, stalling for time. He took a sip of soda. "Yes, it was a woman."

"I *knew* it."

He watched her, trying to read her reaction. She picked the bacon bits out of her chef salad and made a pile on the lid of the plastic bowl it had come in.

He frowned. "I thought you said you were starving?"

"These have, like, five grams of fat per serving."

"Why are you worried about fat grams? You're too young to be dieting." He shoved his basket of fries at her and got another eye roll.

"Dad. You sound like Grandma." She pushed the basket away. "She's always forcing food on me. I'm going to end up like Tía María. And we were talking about you."

Ric sighed. "What about me?"

Her brown eyes got serious now. "Are you, like, dating her?"

"No."

She watched him closely as she slurped her Coke. Diet Coke, he remembered now. He needed to talk to Sandra.

"Are you . . . you know?"

A little warning sounded in his head. "What?"

"You know. Does she spend the night with you and stuff?"

"None of your business. Eat your dinner."

"I'm just asking. God. You never tell me anything."

"*Gosh,* not God. And we're not having this conversation."

He picked up his soda and put it down again as Ava scowled at her food. The sparkling girl from five minutes ago had been replaced by a sullen teenager.

Shit. He was doing this wrong. Again. He could never seem to get it right with her.

He took a deep breath. "She's someone I like. We've spent some time together. It's nothing serious."

The scowl faded a little. She looked up at him from underneath long black eyelashes that had mascara on them. He still wasn't used to her with makeup.

"Is she the one from the summer?" Ava asked.

"What?"

"The woman. From the summer. You were going out with someone, and she called one night when you were taking me back to Mom's, and you told me it was no one. Is it her?"

He stared at her across the table. "How do you remember that?"

She shrugged. "I pay attention. It's not like you ever tell me stuff."

Ric leaned back in his chair and watched her pick at her salad. She looked so grown-up, and it seemed like a week ago, he was walking a loop through a tiny one-bedroom apartment, trying to get her to stop crying. She'd been a colicky baby, and Sandra had been getting by on practically no sleep—just an hour or two at a time—and whenever he was home, he tried to take the baby off her hands so she could rest.

But of course, he wasn't home much in those days, and his clumsy attempts to help weren't nearly enough. They weren't enough now, either. A weekend here. A holiday there. Dinner and bowling once in a while. Everything he'd read or heard about parenting said that consistency was important in a child's life, and he'd tried to be there for Ava consistently, ever since the divorce. But no matter what he did, the job always got in the way. He had probably been a better father before he'd made detective, when he'd had regular hours. It was a depressing thought, because he hadn't been much of a father then, either. He'd been twenty-four, practically a kid himself, struggling to support a wife and a baby and to keep his chief and every other uniform from finding out that he didn't know his ass from first base. He'd been overwhelmed. And yet he'd gotten up and gone in each day, with the crazy idea in his head that it was all temporary, that if he'd hang in there and push through, he'd somehow, someday, know what the fuck he was doing.

But here he was, eleven years later, feeling just as overwhelmed and just as clueless as he sat across from this girl who was beautiful and bright and moody and— strangest of all—his own flesh and blood.

He pushed his food away and leaned forward on his elbows. He looked her in the eye. "You think I don't tell you stuff?"

"You don't."

"Does that hurt your feelings?"

She shrugged and looked away. For an instant, she was a kid again, not the almost-teen who terrified him.

"I'm sorry, honey. I don't mean to hurt your feelings."

"It's okay. I'm used to it."

Well, shit. Was there a master list somewhere of crappy things kids could say to their parents?

"I didn't know you were curious about it."

She gave him one of her patented get-real looks. "Dad, of course I want to know if you've got a girlfriend or something. When Mom was dating Brian, she actually *asked* for my opinion before they got engaged. She wanted to make sure I was okay with it."

"No one's getting engaged," he said.

"I'm just saying. If you did get engaged, could I at least meet her first?"

"Of course," he said, and the second the words were out, he wondered how in the hell they'd gotten onto this. He needed a new topic.

But then Ava jumped up from the table, ending the conversation as abruptly as she'd begun it. "Come on, it's your turn." She grinned at him. "I'm not done beating you yet."

Ric pulled onto Sugarberry Lane and immediately spotted the surveillance vehicle. It was better than last night's but not by much. Last night's had been a cable-installation truck—inconspicuously parked on a residential street at eleven P.M. Tonight's was a late-model RV parked in a driveway three doors down from Mia's. The cover would have been slightly better if it hadn't been so obvious that the driveway in question belonged to a vacant house.

Ric circled the block, hoping he was generating at least a glimmer of interest from the agents who were supposed to be watching and taking down license plates. According to Rey, the feds felt confident that whoever was after Mia would likely case her house first before going after her. And because Ric's pickup truck might have the effect of spooking their subject, he'd been instructed to park away from the house if he planned to visit.

Ric pulled over at a park two blocks away. It was quiet, dark. No vagrants sleeping on benches or hookers selling it in cars parked around the soccer fields. Mia had bought into a nice neighborhood, and the yuppies and young families who paid taxes around there didn't put up with any crap.

Ric pulled out his cell phone and called Rey. After

last night, he suspected someone might have an eye out for him.

"How's it going tonight?"

"All quiet," Rey reported. "I talked to Singh about half an hour ago."

"She in the vehicle?"

"Yep. She's making a point to Delmonico. Those two are competitive. She thinks he dropped the ball last night."

"He did."

"Which door are you going to?"

"Back."

"I'll give them the heads up. Is Mia expecting you? She's got a twelve-gauge in there, just so you know."

"I know."

Ric ended the call and shoved his phone into his pocket before walking up the driveway of the house behind Mia's. He'd scoped out the dog situation yesterday. There weren't any, which made his life easier but also meant less warning if someone should decide to take a tour of her property. He jumped the fence, careful not to snag his jacket, and for a moment, he was back in high school, sneaking over to his girlfriend's house after her parents had gone to sleep. He smiled at the memory.

Mia's bedroom light was on. Ric used a lock pick to let himself in through the back door, disabled the alarm, and then locked everything up again. He made plenty of noise in her kitchen so she wouldn't be caught off guard.

But then he remembered her in the bath last night, her full, pink-tipped breasts rising out of the water. He thought of all that glistening skin and decided that catching her by surprise again might be a good thing.

The music coming from the bedroom lowered. "Ric?" she called.

"In the kitchen. You need anything?"

A pause.

"A beer or anything?"

"No. Thank you."

She was in polite mode again. That would make it easier to keep his head in the game but wouldn't be nearly as entertaining. She was much more fun when she let herself flirt.

He grabbed a beer from her fridge and checked the bag of tamales he'd left yesterday. She'd had a few for dinner, from the looks of it. Next time he saw his mom, he could honestly tell her that he'd shared them with a friend, which would make her happy.

He walked through the living room and checked the blinds on the windows. No gaps. He noticed the cardboard file box parked beside her front door. Jonah had dropped off the case files earlier on his way home from the station, and Ric planned to spend his night poring through everything. Somewhere in all of that paperwork, he was determined to find probable cause for a search warrant of Jeff Lane's lake house.

Jonah had told him he was wasting his time, but Ric wanted to look anyway. Deep down, he was an optimist. If he hadn't been, he would have quit the job ages ago.

Ric followed the soft tribal music down the hall to Mia's bedroom. She was probably the only person he knew who listened to NPR at night.

She sat cross-legged on her bed amid a sea of files and

papers. Her hair was twisted in a knot at the top of her head, and it was damp. He'd just missed bathtime.

He sighed and leaned against the doorframe. "Hi."

"Hi." She glanced up. She had that distracted look he'd seen on her face in the lab before.

"Work?"

"Catching up on reports." She dropped her pencil onto whatever she was reading and looked at him. "Sorry to pull you away from Ava."

"You didn't. I don't keep her out late on school nights."

She looked down. Cleared her throat. "On the phone earlier, you said you missed her last weekend." There was something wary in her eyes. "It was your weekend to have her then?"

"We trade off."

"I never realized." She shook her head. "I feel bad for taking you away from that. You could have just told me."

Ric stepped into the room and looked around. He'd been in here before, briefly, just last night. But it seemed different with Mia in it. She had on one of those T-shirts she liked to wear with pajama pants. Thick woolen socks covered her feet. She'd known he was coming over, and he doubted it was an accident that she'd picked something completely unseductive to wear.

"She spent Saturday at my mom's," he said. "They're close, so it worked out all right." Ric had picked up his daughter and returned her to Sandra's place Sunday evening, right after dropping Mia off. Maybe if he'd told her where he was going, she wouldn't have rushed over to Black's place in such a hurry.

He walked over to her dresser and rested his beer on

a glossy magazine. *Cottage Living*. On the wall nearby were several patches of paint, all different shades of red.

"Redecorating in here?"

"Thinking about it." She watched him from her bed. It was covered in a purple down comforter with lots of matching pillows. He'd never understood the thing with women and pillows.

On the wall above the dresser, where most women would have a mirror, she'd hung a series of photographs—six different shots, all bright colors and patterns. He leaned closer for a better look. Several were close-ups of butterflies. Others were too abstract to tell. There were some bright green netlooking things that could have been insect wings.

"You take these?" He turned around, and she was reading her papers again.

She glanced up. "It's a hobby."

"Insect photography?" This surprised him. He'd always thought of her as a scientist, cool and clinical all the time. He hadn't realized she had an artistic streak.

She looked up again and seemed to realize that he was waiting for an answer.

"When I was a kid, I wanted to be an entomologist. I didn't know the word, but I knew I wanted to study bugs."

He leaned back against the dresser. "When'd you change your mind?"

She shrugged. "I don't know. Middle school, I guess."

"Hit about twelve, suddenly took an interest in forensic science?"

Her gaze narrowed.

"I know about Amy," he said, and she looked down at her papers. "Why didn't you ever tell me?"

She wouldn't look at him, wouldn't answer.

"Mia?"

"Why would I tell you?" she asked, and for some reason, that ticked him off.

"I don't know, maybe because we've worked on about a dozen murder cases together? Maybe because I'm a homicide detective, and I've dealt with families like yours? Maybe because we're friends?"

Her eyes flashed up at him. "You don't know anything about my family."

"Actually, I do. Did some interesting reading while I was up in Fort Worth. One of the detectives on the Laura Thorne case had your sister's picture in the file, as a matter of fact. He'd saved a news story because the case reminded him of Laura Thorne."

She was glaring now. He'd touched a nerve with this topic.

"You were the one who pointed me to that case, Mia. And it wasn't because of some 'feeling' you got. You remembered that girl because she reminded you of your sister."

"So what?"

"So I'm just asking for some honesty, that's all. Shit. I haul my ass all the way to Fort Worth to look at a cold case based on your supposedly objective professional opinion, come to find out you're not objective at all. This is personal."

"Fine. It's personal. My entire career choice is personal. Every time I set foot in the lab, it's personal. What's wrong with that?"

"I just want you to admit it."

"Why? So you can accuse me of being emotional? Oh, wait, you already did that. So you could tell me I didn't know what I was talking about, that I was just worked up about my sister? There *is* a link between Ashley and Laura. I didn't imagine it."

Ric folded his arms over his chest as she got up from the bed.

"And anyway, why is it always my job to tell you things? To open up to you? When have you ever told me anything?"

"Like what?"

"Like *any*thing." She stepped closer and swiped a curl out of her face. "You don't ever share anything personal. You're an island. We knew each other almost six months before I even knew you had a daughter and an ex-wife. You think I might have wanted to know that?"

"Why would you want to know that?"

"Because I want to know *you*! God, why do I have to spell it out?" She sank onto the bed and looked down at her feet, as if she was trying to collect herself.

Ric stood watching her, wondering what he was supposed to say now. She wanted to know him, but he didn't want a relationship. Or at least, he hadn't. He didn't know anymore. He didn't know shit.

He stepped closer and reached out to lift her chin so that he could see her face. Her blue eyes were filled with a mix of anger and hurt, and he remembered Ava looking at him much the same way. He was 0-for-2 tonight.

She pulled back and looked down again. "I lied when

I said I just wanted sex with someone. You read me right the first time." She cleared her throat. "Actually, if you want to know the truth, I have this tendency to fall in love really easily. So unless you want to settle down and have two-point-four kids and refinish my cabinets, we should probably back away from this . . . whatever it is." She glanced up and gave him a quirky smile. "Wow, you should see your face right now."

He was completely at a loss for words.

"Don't worry, it hasn't happened yet or anything, I just wanted to warn you." She took a deep breath and squared her shoulders. "Anyway, I'm not ashamed of what I want. And I think I need to stop making compromises, or I'm never going to get it."

"What does that mean?"

She waited a beat. "I don't think you should come over anymore. I'd prefer it if you didn't."

He watched her closely, but he couldn't tell whether she was being straight with him. "You can't stay here without—"

"If someone really has to be here," she said, "I'd rather it be Jonah or one of the FBI agents."

He watched her for a few more seconds. "Is that what you want?"

"Yes."

"All right, then." He picked up his beer bottle and walked to her door, then turned to look at her. She sat on her bed, watching him, and he realized he'd never even slept in it with her. He hadn't known until that moment how much he'd wanted to.

"Tomorrow Jonah can stay with you," he said.

"Are you sure that's even necessary? I mean, why can't we all trust the surveillance team to do its job?"

"It's either him or me, Mia. You're not staying here alone."

She pulled some papers into her lap and pretended to be reading them. "All right, then, thank you. Tell Jonah I appreciate it."

CHAPTER 21

M ia made one last pass with her blue light before giving up and jotting the result down on her notepad: *No blood evident.*

The room brightened, and she glanced up to see Mark standing in the doorway between her office and the lab.

"You coming down?"

"Down where?" She pushed up her orange eye shields and rested them on top of her head.

"Evidence room. Special delivery. From what I hear, I'm gonna need a hand with this one."

Mia tucked the sneakers she'd been studying back into the evidence bag. The shoes belonged to a suspect, and the investigator who'd sent them to her wasn't going to be happy with her results. But at least she felt confident that she'd done a thorough search. She resealed the bag with tape.

"Mind if we drop this off first?"

"No problem."

They swung by the evidence refrigerator, and Mia noticed the overflowing shelves. Was it a fluke, or did her absence have something to do with the pile-up? She resolved to put in some time that weekend to help her department get caught up.

"What's coming in?" she asked Mark as they rode down in the elevator together.

"Trash dump. I hear it's a big one, too, and Snyder's got a bee in his bonnet for some reason. I've been ordered to drop everything."

After reaching the ground floor, they wound through some corridors to the intake desk, where Delphi's evidence clerk accepted deliveries from law-enforcement agencies around the country. Mia heard a familiar voice, and her footsteps slowed.

"Which case did you say this is?" She looked at Mark.

"SMPD, I think. Why?"

Before she could respond, the door to the evidence room opened, and Ric stepped out, followed by Jonah. Both detectives carried several white plastic trash bags in each hand.

"We going to need our gas masks for this one?" Mark asked.

"You might. This stuff's pretty ripe," Jonah said.

Ric glanced at Mia, but didn't say anything, and she pretended not to feel slighted.

"We collected it last night, about eleven," Jonah said. "It's been sitting in the trunk of my vehicle. I'm definitely gonna have to hit the car wash."

He and Ric carried the bags into a small, windowless room known as the Dump. It was just what the name implied: a place where people deposited large quantities of garbage, usually collected from people's curbs on trash day. The room had cinder-block walls and a drain in the middle of the floor, because it had to be hosed down and disinfected after each use.

A box of heavy-duty rubber gloves sat on a counter beside an industrial-sized sink. Ric grabbed some and passed them to Jonah. He pulled out some for himself before offering the box to Mark, who shook his head.

"Don't want to get in your way here," Mark said with a smile. "I think I'll hang back and consult."

He and Mia watched from the doorway as Ric crouched beside one of the bags and pulled out a pocket knife. He slashed through the plastic. Trash tumbled out, and everyone drew back at the stench.

Jonah kneeled down beside the mess and shook his head. "It's no wonder the suits got tied up last night." He shot a grumpy look in his partner's direction.

"This is why they pay us the big bucks," Ric muttered.

By "suits," Mia guessed Jonah meant FBI agents. Any doubt she had that this Dumpster dive pertained to the Ashley Meyer case disappeared. Mia wasn't supposed to be working this case—at least, she'd been told not to conduct any testing—but no one seemed to mind her observing, so she stayed. She'd tell Mark he'd have to get someone else to lend a hand with the actual lab tests.

If they found anything to test, which certainly wasn't a given. If the suspect was someone prominent, as Mia was beginning to believe, he probably had other people living in his household with him. Whatever DNA they found in these items could belong to a wife, a child, a maid, or a cook.

"I thought Rachel wasn't big on the surreptitious sampling," Mark said, referring to the method by which cops collected DNA samples on the sly when they either couldn't obtain a warrant or didn't want to.

"This is a special case," Ric said simply.

"You guys have an alternative?" Mark pressed. "Because some defense attorney will argue—"

"I'm gonna have to go with the Supreme Court on this one," Jonah said. "The Fourth Amendment doesn't apply to shit left out on the curb for trash pickup." He glanced at Mia. "'Scuse my language."

"No problem," Mia said. "But the Court hasn't specifically ruled on the covert collection of DNA. Some people think they have a reasonable expectation of privacy when it comes to their genetic material."

"Why?" Ric eyed her coolly. "No different from footprints or fingerprints left somewhere. If I can lift some guy's prints from the glass he uses in an interview room and compare them with the ones left at the crime scene, why can't I do the same with his DNA?"

Mia crossed her arms, defensive now. "I'm merely pointing out that this is a gray area for the courts. Until there's a ruling—"

"Whose side are you on?" Ric snapped. "We're trying to get a killer off the streets here."

"I'm not on a side. My job is to test evidence and report my findings."

"And my job is to collect the evidence. Let the lawyers argue about what's admissible. I'm trying to protect the public."

"Hey, you guys mind if we get this over with?" Jonah asked. "My breakfast isn't sitting too well just now. How about one of you experts help us out with what we're looking for?"

"Is your subject a male or a female?" Mark asked.

"Male," Ric and Jonah said in unison.

"In that case, keep an eye out for disposable razors, tissues, toothpicks, condoms—"

"This looks like the kitchen trash," Mia said, surveying the smorgasbord of food littering the floor. Ric used his knife to poke through greasy chicken bones, limp bits of broccoli, a slimy carton of Chinese food.

"Any plastic utensils?" she asked. "A drinking straw? Maybe some chopsticks?"

"Nothing I can see."

"Let's try this bag," Jonah said, then dragged it to a space across the floor before ripping it open. "Lots of papers in here. Looks like maybe from an office."

"Again, look for tissues, toothpicks, discarded gum." Mark ticked off the possible sources of DNA. "Cigarette butts, envelopes—"

"Coffee cup," Jonah announced, holding up a cardboard Starbucks cup.

"That looks like lipstick on the lid," Mia pointed out. "Is there a name written on the side?"

Jonah examined the customer name that had been scribbled by some barista. "Camille," he read aloud, then cast a look at Ric. "Think this is from the wife's office."

Ric cut open a third plastic bag, which looked a bit more promising. Tissues tumbled out, some crumpled trash, a cardboard toilet-paper roll.

"Think I got a bathroom," Ric said.

Mia stepped closer. "Any razors? Maybe a toothbrush?"

Ric lifted a piece of trash from the floor. Some sort of silver wrapper. "How about disposable contacts?" He looked up at Mia.

"Does your suspect wear them?"

"No idea." Ric picked up a small cardboard box with a prescription label on it. "Make that a yes. We got the name right here."

"There could be touch DNA on the box," Mia said. "But it would be better to have the contact itself."

"You want a *contact lens*?" Jonah shook his head. "Yeah, right. Talk about a needle in a haystack."

Ric picked up something that looked like nothing and lifted it to the light for a better view.

Jonah stopped what he was doing and looked at him. "You've got to be kidding me."

"Nope," Ric said. "I think I found our DNA sample."

Jonah passed Moore and Burleson on his way into the station. Barely eight A.M., and they both looked dead on their feet.

"You guys just clock out?"

"Been here since two," Moore said. "Vehicle versus pedestrian over on campus. Hit-and-run."

"Fatality?" Jonah asked.

"Damn near," Burleson reported. "Kid's in ICU. Probably not gonna make it past today."

"I'm toast," Moore said, and turned around as Ric exited the station house. "Hey, Ricky, how's that task-force thing coming?"

Ric made eye contact with Jonah. There was some kind of news.

"Slow," Ric answered.

Moore and Burleson didn't press, which was a good thing, because their task-force work was supposed to be kept confidential. Ric didn't talk much, though, so most people didn't realize when he was dodging questions and when he was just being himself.

Jonah lingered on the steps and tied his shoe while the other guys headed off to their cars.

"You up for a drive?" Ric pulled out his keys and flipped them into his palm.

"Sure. Where?"

"Lake Buchanan. I need to check on something."

"You want to swing by Lane's lake house?"

"This is something else. I've got a lead that might net us a search warrant."

"Long as you're driving," Jonah said. "My car still smells like a trash chute."

Forty-five minutes and one coffee stop later, they'd almost reached Marble Falls, the largest town near Lake Buchanan. Ric's idea might not pan out, but they didn't have a lot of other leads to follow until the lab results came in, so Jonah figured some legwork wouldn't hurt. Plus, he was tired of sitting around a conference room with Special Agent Singh. She was one of those theoretical types who white-boarded everything to death and never pounded the pavement.

"What do you hear from your Army buddy?" Ric asked, interrupting his thoughts. It was the first thing he had said since explaining their destination.

"The firearms guy?"

"Yeah."

"Haven't heard back yet," Jonah said, pulling his phone out to make sure he hadn't missed a message.

A friend of Jonah's was the range master at a shooting field west of town. Jonah had asked him if he knew any cops who'd come in lately for some target practice. His ranges went out to a thousand yards, and his place was popular with military guys.

"Anyway, I just called him yesterday," Jonah said. "And it's kind of a long shot, no pun intended. There are a lot of ranges around if someone wanted to brush up. Fact, if our guy is a cop, he could just be using a police range."

"Not if he's practicing three-hundred-yard shots," Ric said. FBI investigators had been out to the gas station and had concluded that Saturday's gunshots were fired from a ridge more than three hundred yards north.

"True," Jonah said, "but he might not have been practicing anything, not if his track record's any indication."

Jonah expected an argument, but Ric was too busy grinding his teeth to nubs. Jonah had known the man for years—worked some shit cases with him, too—and he'd never seen him this uptight. Ric was getting impatient for an arrest. He probably wouldn't sleep easy until they got one. Suspects they knew about were one thing, and Ric probably figured the lieutenant governor was more or less neutralized because the FBI had him under surveillance. But Lane's hired gun was a different story. Ric wanted him ID'd yesterday. He wanted him locked up and a million miles away from Mia.

"How'd it go last night?" Ric asked, as if on cue. He'd been asking for daily updates since she'd booted him off her surveillance team.

"Pretty quiet."

"How's Mia?"

Jonah rubbed the crick in his neck. "Well, her couch sucks. But she makes damn good pancakes, so I'm not complaining."

Ric cut a glance at him, and Jonah could see that he didn't appreciate the attempt to lighten things up.

"No visitors," Jonah added. "Not even any phone calls."

Ric was pissed off about that guy Black, and Jonah didn't blame him. He would have felt the same way.

"You know, you should probably work this thing out with her," Jonah said. "It'd be easier for everyone."

"How's that?"

"Well, for starters, your brother and I wouldn't be pulling these night shifts guarding her all week. It's not like she wants us there. That's pretty clear."

She'd stayed in her room all night working, except when she was in the kitchen making food. Jonah suspected she felt guilty about needing a bodyguard. The two nights he'd stayed over there, she'd offered to feed him about a dozen times.

"I bet she'll take you back if you apologize," Jonah said. "Usually works for me."

"Apologize for what?"

"Whatever you did to piss her off." Jonah looked at him. Mia seemed like the sensitive type, so he guessed it was something he'd said. "What'd you do, anyway?"

"Nothing."

Silence ensued, and Jonah watched the dreary landscape rush by. Three straight weeks of crappy weather. Today was more of the same. The temperature hovered around freezing, and every time Jonah went outside, it was either raining or sleeting or cold as shit.

"I think I might have given her the wrong idea."

Jonah glanced over, surprised. He'd figured the conversation was dead. "How's that?"

"I guess she thought I wanted a relationship with her."

"You don't?"

Ric looked at him.

"Hey, I'm just asking. She's a nice woman." Jonah started to say something about her looks, too, but changed his mind.

"This job's hell on relationships," Ric said. "Ask my ex-wife."

"Yeah, but it's not like she's going in blind. She knows plenty of cops. And she probably works as many hours as you do, if not more. She's at that lab all the time."

Ric didn't say anything, and Jonah was glad to let it drop. He wasn't one to give out advice like this. And Ric was right, to some extent. Cops weren't known for their enviable personal lives.

The Marble Falls city limits sign came into view, and Jonah started looking for the address.

"What's the street again?"

"Vista Bonita."

It took about five minutes to find the place, which didn't quite live up to its name. The store occupied the end unit of a mostly abandoned strip mall in an unscenic corner of town.

Ric got out of the car and looked at Jonah over the roof as he slammed the door. "I've got a good feeling about this place."

"Why?"

"They're the only game in town. Next-closest place is in Austin."

A cowbell rattled on the glass door as they entered the store. The reception counter was empty, but Jonah heard the unmistakable sounds of *Wheel of Fortune* drifting from the back room.

He took a moment to glance around. Carpet bolts stood on end around the room. A pegboard lined one of the walls, and bulky sample books dangled from the many hooks there. A chemical scent hung in the air, like the smell of a new car, only stronger.

"May I help you?"

Jonah turned around at the female voice. The woman was short, middle-aged, and lumpy. It looked as if she'd tried a home remedy on her mousey brown hair sometime ago, and the result was a burnt-orange color that started about an inch away from her scalp.

Jonah hung back. Ric usually tried the charm approach with women, and it was best not to crowd him.

"Ric Santos." He flashed a smile. "Pam, is it? I think we spoke on the phone."

"Oh, yes." She smiled, then cast a tentative look at Jonah. "You're the police officer?"

"We were in the area, and I thought I'd stop by to check on that installation we talked about. Out on Lake View Road?"

"The one on New Year's Day. I remember." Her smile faltered. "Like I said, though, our computer's down today. I don't know what all I can tell you besides what we already talked about. What is it you need, exactly?"

"Just wanted to get the address on that again."

Jonah would bet he'd never had it in the first place.

"Well, our computer—"

"I figure you have a record of it floating around somewhere? Maybe an invoice?" Ric nodded at the back office, where the TV blared and where someone in this outfit presumably kept a file cabinet.

"All of our records are electronic now." Pam smiled. "Ever since we went paperless."

"Maybe a purchase order?" Ric persisted. "A receipt of some sort?"

"Like I say, all that's on computer. Which is down. I could look on the schedule, though, if all you need's an address."

"That would be helpful, thanks."

She reached under the counter and pulled out a thick black binder. "I write those up myself, post them on the board each week. You said New Year's Day?"

"I think *you* said that. I believe you remembered the job because it was a holiday?"

"That's right." She flipped open the book. "We had to do a surcharge." She glanced up. "I would have let it go. It's not like we were busy or anything, but the owner's kind of a stickler, you know? So I went ahead and tacked on the twenty percent." She found the page she wanted. "Here it is. Two-twenty-six Lake View Road. January first. Our first job of the year, as a matter of fact."

Jonah inched closer and glanced at the page. The square for January first had a big X over it and an address written at the top.

The address belonged to Jeff Lane's lake house.

"That was your only job that day?" Ric asked, very low-key. The stress maniac from the drive up here was long gone, replaced by this chatty police officer with an easy smile.

"Yep," she said. "We did the whole ground floor. Berber carpet, wall to wall."

"What do the H and D mean at the bottom there?"

"Oh, that just means our haul-away service. They

wanted that, too. Most people, when they replace their carpet, they can't use the old stuff. We take it off their hands and send it to our recycling partners."

"What happens to it then?"

"It gets steam-cleaned, deodorized, the whole bit. There's a market for secondhand carpet. A lot of people don't know that, but there is. Long as it's in good condition. Not too many stains or anything."

"And what if it's stained?" Ric asked. "Say, something hard to get out, like maybe ink or blood or red wine?"

"Well, you'd be surprised what we can do about wine nowadays. Our installer can usually tell just by looking whether it's an H and R or an H and D."

"What's an H and D?"

She tapped her finger on January first, just days before Ashley Meyer was discovered facedown in a park with carpet fibers clinging to her hair.

"That's 'haul and dispose,'" Pam said. "Means we threw it away. For whatever reason, that carpet wasn't fit for recycling."

Mia passed Darrell on her way downstairs for lunch.

"Hey, glad I caught you," he said, making a U-turn back toward the elevator. "I was coming by to pass along those search results."

"What search results?"

"From the profile Mark sent over." He must have noticed her eyeing his paper bag, because he offered it to her. "Muffin? I've got extras."

"No, thanks. Tell me about your results."

He stepped onto the elevator and waited for the doors to close before telling her. Darrell handled sensitive information all day long and understood the importance of discretion.

"I ran the DNA profile lifted from that evidence that came down from Fort Worth," he said, pressing the button for G-3, where Mia was going, too.

"We're talking about the blood drop on the shoe?"

"Yeah, the one you tested. Or Mark, I should say, since you're suddenly taking a backseat on this investigation for some reason."

"I can't discuss it."

"Hey, I'm not asking. Just pointing out that your mysterious behavior hasn't gone unnoticed." He gave her a worried look. "Are you okay, by the way? Ever since your carjacking, you've been acting a little freaky."

"Freaky?"

"Maybe *anxious* is a better word." He paused. "I've been worried."

She'd been the victim of two shooting attempts, her love life was in shambles, and she had a team of investigators camped out on her street. Anxious was her middle name right now. "I'm fine." She smiled, totally faking it. "What did you find?"

"Unfortunately, I didn't get a hit."

Mia bit her lip. Laura's killer—assuming that was who dripped blood on her shoe—did not already have a DNA profile in the database. So much for an easy ID.

"I checked the Offender Index and the Forensic Index," he said. "No match with either."

Mia sighed. "I think I'll take a muffin now."

He handed one over. "Good, because you're probably not going to like my other news, either. That profile also did not match the one lifted from the contact lens Mark tested. Or did you already know that part?"

"I didn't, no."

A lump of disappointment clogged her throat. Ric's prime suspect, the owner of that contact, did not match the blood found on Laura's shoe. Which meant that the search warrant Ric so desperately wanted was even further out of his reach now. Should she break the news, or should she leave it to Mark?

She dumped the idea almost as soon as she came up with it. She'd tell Ric herself, but she definitely wasn't looking forward to the conversation.

Mia stepped out on G-3, and Darrell followed.

"Coming with me to the Cave?" he asked.

Mia glanced nervously down the corridor and heard the sound of muffled gunshots. "Actually, ballistics."

"A little lunchtime firing lesson, huh? I knew you were a secret Lara Croft."

Darrell was joking, but he'd hit it on the head. Scott had talked her into a lesson with the logic that it was pointless to lend her a handgun if she didn't even know how to hold it properly. And so, after decades as a committed gun-phobe, she was going to learn to how to shoot. Or at least, how not to shoot herself in the foot.

Darrell was staring down at her now, obviously concerned by her silence.

She summoned a smile. "Nothing that exciting, don't worry. Just down here having lunch with an old friend."

CHAPTER 22

❦

Mia sat in the front seat, nerves jangling, as Rey drove up the winding driveway toward the white plantation-style lake house. He slid into a gap between several other government sedans.

"Wait here a minute. I'll let him know I brought you."

She turned to look at him, wide-eyed. "You mean he doesn't know?"

"Not exactly."

"But I thought you said he wanted my help." Her anxiety mounted. She had enough reservations about being here without throwing Ric's displeasure into the mix.

"*We* need your help," Rey said firmly. "The task force. Ric says you're very good at what you do, that you have a knack for seeing things other people miss."

He waited for her to confirm or deny this. Instead, she glanced over her shoulder. Through the tinted back window, she surveyed the lakefront palace that made her bungalow look like a shack.

"We can't sign you in," Rey told her, "but he can come talk to you out here. Gimme a minute."

"But—"

He shoved open the door, and Mia's words were cut off by a gust of cold air.

Sighing, she wrapped her lab coat closer and pressed her knees together for warmth. She didn't even have her jacket or her purse with her, as this little field trip had been entirely unexpected. She'd been in the middle of the afternoon's second rape kit when she'd been summoned down to the lobby and literally swept away on urgent FBI business by Ric's very determined brother. Rey had hardly talked the entire drive, and all of Mia's questions had been met with evasive, one-word replies that left her exasperated.

Really, the Santos brothers could have been twins.

She rubbed her bare hands together and blew against them as she waited. And waited. After a good ten minutes, Ric emerged from the front door, talking with someone in a white Tyvek suit. One of the FBI's crime-scene techs, she guessed. Ric wore black slacks and a white shirt with the sleeves rolled up, and he had his familiar pistol and detective's shield plastered to his hip. He seemed oblivious to the cold as he spoke and pointed at the front door with sharp, jerky movements. Then he turned and stalked toward the car where Mia sat.

He yanked open the door and slid behind the wheel. "You shouldn't be here."

She laughed with disbelief. "The FBI *brought* me! You think I asked to have my work day interrupted to get dragged off to some crime scene?"

"I don't know what you think you're going to do here, besides get in the way. You can't be admitted to the house. You know that, right?"

Mia swallowed the outraged comments on the tip of her tongue. She was there in a professional capacity. At the FBI's request. This was not the time for petty arguing. When she thought she could talk calmly, she turned to face Ric, whose eyes were blazing at her.

"Someone on this task force evidently thinks I might be able to help with something. They asked me to come, so I came. I have no intention of getting in the way." She paused, and he seemed to calm down a fraction. At least, he was letting her talk. "I understand there's been some trouble executing this search warrant?" It was almost the entire extent of what Rey had told her.

Ric looked forward and rested his big hand on the steering wheel. She saw the muscles in his jaw clench.

"It's been a disaster," he said tightly. "We've been here three hours, and we've got nothing. Time's ticking. I put my head on the block to get this search warrant, and the blade's about to fall."

Mia hated his analogy, but she shoved it aside to focus on practical matters. "Why is there a time crunch? Can't you guys take as long as you need?"

"The . . . suspect"—he cut a glance at her—"and his lawyer are on a private plane right now coming back from Mexico City. They land in half an hour. As soon as they do, this is going to get very ugly, very fast."

"I know the suspect is Jeff Lane," Mia said.

He looked at her sharply.

"I saw his name on that box of contact lenses back at the lab," she added.

"Then you know how sensitive this thing is. He's got friends in high places. Even the FBI's afraid of him. We got a judge to sign off on this warrant, but so far, it's produced jack shit." Ric rubbed his forehead, looking miserable. "You got any ideas?"

Mia reached into the pocket of her coat and pulled out a small aspirin bottle. She tapped two into her palm and held them out. "Why don't you start by tackling your headache?"

His expression softened. He reached over, took the pills, and tossed them back without even a sip of water. "Thanks," he muttered, and she knew they were making progress.

"Okay, brief me from the top. What were you hoping to find here?"

He took a deep breath. "Blood. Lots of it."

"From Ashley Meyer?"

"Her, and also maybe the Jane Doe whose bones were recovered right down the road from here. And she's not a Jane Doe anymore. Did Kelsey tell you?"

"No."

"They got an ID. Natasha Sukovic. Last seen two years ago getting off work at a strip club in Austin. She had just started working for Night Angels when she went missing."

"Night Angels is the club?"

"It's an escort service. They're online, and they have girls all over the state, some even in Louisiana. Ashley Meyer worked for them, and so did Laura Thorne."

Mia listened to every word, amazed that he was letting her in on so much detail after weeks of dodging her questions. Did he finally trust her, or was he simply too tired to care?

"It gets worse," Ric said. "We might have another victim. Makayla Tomlin. You heard of her case?"

"No."

"She was dumped in a lake in Burnet County some-time earlier this month. She had defensive cuts on her hands, died of blunt-force trauma."

"Did she work for Night Angels, too?"

"Cocktail waitress. Worked at a bar off I-35. She left work one night, apparently drove herself home. Woman who shares the apartment reported her missing two days later."

Mia bit her lip. "He's getting bolder."

"If it's connected."

"All right, let's go with what we know. You have reason to believe that at least two victims might have been killed here," she said. "Why? Why not Jeff Lane's primary residence? Or maybe his car, for that matter?"

"His house in Austin has round-the-clock security, surveillance cams everywhere. We're not talking some city councilman here. This guy's second in command of the entire state. Some people think he has a shot at the White House one day, if his stars line up. Anyway, his wife lives there, and it doesn't make sense as a place to take a hooker. We ruled out a car, because Ashley's autopsy report showed carpet fiber stuck to her hair and her abrasions—residential carpet, high-end stuff. We're looking for an indoor crime scene. I got a break this morning when a local company confirmed tearing out and replacing the carpet on the entire first floor of this house on New Year's Day."

"That would be just after Ashley's death," Mia said.

"I know."

She took a deep breath. Here was where she could help.

"I assume the CSIs peeled back the new carpet?"

"They've been over everything with luminol, alternative light sources, the works."

"Nothing on the carpet pad? The concrete beneath?"

"We got zip." He met her gaze, and his eyes looked a little desperate. He must really have his butt on the line here.

"Baseboards? What about wood floors? The grain typically holds blood years and years after the fact."

"Tile or carpet throughout the house. Like I said, we've been over all of it. The place is immaculate. And just to help us out, he's got a maid who comes in every Monday, whether the place has been used or not. It's a goddamn museum in there."

"Fingerprints?"

"We're trying that, but the few we've got will probably come back to the maid, to Lane, his wife, his son, maybe even his friends or his kid's friends."

"How old is the kid?"

"Twenty-four," Ric said. "He's a grad student out in California."

"What about knives?" Mia tried. "Kelsey said the bones she examined showed signs of trauma consistent with a small serrated knife, like maybe a steak knife."

"We looked," Ric said. "Nothing. Just your typical silverware set, twenty-four place settings."

"They do dinners for twenty-four but don't have steak knives? That's pretty unusual."

"No kidding. This guy's got a four-thousand-square-foot lake house, only one sharp knife in the place, and it's an eight-inch butcher knife in the kitchen drawer, smooth blade."

"Did you—"

"We collected it anyway. Lot of good it'll do us."

"Well, just the absence of knives seems suspicious."

"I can't collar this guy for something he *doesn't* have in his possession. Any other ideas?"

Mia glanced over her shoulder at the house, wishing for a bolt of inspiration. She probably couldn't add to the expertise of the CSIs already combing the place, but Ric needed her help, and she wanted to give it.

"What about a boat?"

"Two small boats, stored down by the water. A Sunfish and a kayak. We checked."

"Clothing? Shoes?"

"Three pairs of duck boots, downstairs hall closet. His, hers, and the kid's, judging by the sizes. Crime-scene tech went over them already, couldn't find anything."

Mia shook her head. "What doesn't make sense to me is the carpet. These killings would have involved a lot of blood. It's almost impossible to hide that completely. Even if you wash everything down with bleach, it would still show up with luminol. And the bleach itself is usually a telltale sign that someone's trying to hide something. Did you try sink drains? Bathtubs? Shower tile grout?"

"Check, check, and check. Nothing." Ric rubbed the bridge of his nose. "As much as I hate to say it, I don't think we've found our crime scene. Maybe the carpet thing was a coincidence."

"Big coincidence."

He glanced at his watch and cursed.

"Bring us the butcher knife," Mia said. "Our tool

expert is a genius. He'll take it apart, maybe find something in the crevice between the handle and the blade."

Ric looked deflated, and Mia ached for him. She hated to bring up the next point, but there was no getting around it.

"Mark got the DNA results back," she said.

"Profile lifted from the shoe isn't in the database," Ric recited.

Mia waited for him to add the rest. "Did he tell you about the contact lens?"

"No." Hope flared in his eyes, then instantly faded when he read her expression.

"The DNA from the contact lens doesn't match the blood drop," she said. "So, assuming that the blood came from Laura Thorne's killer, it's not a match with Jeff Lane."

Ric squeezed his eyes shut and looked pained. "I am so fucking out of a job. How did I get so off track on this thing?"

She didn't say anything. She'd seen cases where a mountain of circumstantial evidence pointed to one person, and then DNA proved something different. The DNA won almost every time.

Unable to hold back anymore, she reached out and touched his arm. It was just a friendly touch. That's what she told herself, anyway.

"Sorry I couldn't be more help," she said. "I'll keep thinking about it and call you if I get any ideas."

Ric stared glumly out the window, oblivious to her hand on his arm and everything else, it seemed.

Mia cleared her throat. "I know now's not a great

time to ask, but how's it coming on the other front? The shooter?"

He looked at her, and his expression clouded. "We're working on it. I thought we'd have an arrest today, be able to put the squeeze on Lane for a name. Hell, I was ready to waterboard him." Ric shook his head. "That's not happening, obviously. But we're working some other leads."

He glanced up, and his expression looked cool. "Black still driving you to work?"

"Yeah. That's not the problem."

His brow furrowed. "There's a problem?"

"Vivian's vacation ends this Sunday. That's in two days. I was kind of hoping I could tell her that she and Sam were clear to come home."

Ric looked away. She didn't want to rub his nose in the fact, but this investigation was dragging, and the security precautions were getting harder and harder to keep up.

"Tell your sister to stay away." He looked her squarely in the eye. "Not much longer, I hope. But I don't feel safe about you yet. In fact, I'd feel better if you'd agree to stay with me. It would make a lot more sense."

Mia searched his face, looking for something new, some glimmer of tenderness, some indication that this was going somewhere. Once again, she didn't find it. His invitation was based on logistics.

"I don't think that's a good idea, Ric."

He watched her silently, but his face was impossible to read. He reached over and took the edge of her lab coat in his masculine fingers. Mia held her breath. He started to say something.

A rap on the window. Ric turned and pushed open the door.

"We need you out here, man," Jonah told him.

"What happened?"

"Delmonico called. The plane just landed. Sounds like the shit's about to hit the fan."

After spending his afternoon with the rest of the task force getting his ass chewed up and spit out by practically everyone above him with a badge, Jonah had thought he was done with yelling for the day.

He'd been wrong.

Mia had worked up a head full of steam and was busy unleashing it at Ric as Jonah watched silently from his place beside her front door.

"I am *not* staying with you!"

"I didn't like this arrangement before, and I like it even less now," Ric said. "Pack up. We're leaving."

"Did you hear what I said?"

"Fine, I'll do it." Ric moved for the bedroom, and she caught his arm.

"Would you just *listen* a minute? I want to be at *my* house. Mine. Why is that so difficult all of a sudden?"

Ric rested his hands on his hips and shot an impatient glance at the ceiling. "How many times do I have to say it, Mia? The task force has been 'redirected.' That means shaken up. Blown apart. As in the surveillance team has packed up and gone. What is it you don't get about that?"

"But why can't someone just guard me here, like they have been?" She shot a hopeful look at Jonah, and he glanced away. He had no desire to get dragged into this.

"Jonah's not available. Rey's not available. And I'm fresh out of favors to call in, so your luck's run out, babe. It's down to me. Got it? Now, are you going to do the packing, or am I?"

Silence settled over the room, and Jonah wasn't quite sure what to make of Mia's open-mouthed expression.

"*What* did you just say?"

"What?" Ric, like Jonah, was clueless.

"You said you're fresh out of *favors*?"

"That's right."

"Are you trying to tell me that Jonah and Rey have been staying here all week as a *favor* to you?" She shot Jonah a disbelieving look. "Jonah?"

He cleared his throat. "What's that?"

"All this time, you haven't been on the clock?" She looked at Ric, clearly horrified. "They aren't even getting paid for this?"

"What does that have to do with anything?"

"It has everything to do with everything! It was bad enough when I thought they were here as part of their job! You told me they were working. Why did you do that?"

Ric didn't answer, but he didn't need to. It was obvious why he'd done it. She never would have agreed to let them stay otherwise. She might have even—

"All this time, I could have been at Scott's!"

—gone back to the SEAL's place.

"You never told me you forced them into this as some kind of *favor*!"

The front door opened, and Sophie slipped in, although Jonah was the only one to notice. She wore black jeans, black boots, and a low-cut black shirt that made his heart stutter. In her hand was a dry-cleaning bag.

She looked at Jonah. "You can hear them on the street, you know." She eased the door shut and settled back beside him to watch. "So, what'd I miss?"

He focused his attention on the confrontation in the hallway. "Ric wants her at his place, she doesn't want to go," he said.

"Mia, I'm done arguing about this. The arrangement's changed. Get over it."

"I can't believe you lied to me. Do you know how much that pisses me off?"

"No, and I don't give a damn. Go get packed."

Sophie clucked her tongue. "He's gonna pay for that tonight."

"Unbelievable! You can't just come into my house and start telling me what to do. I live here. I'm staying here."

"What the hell is wrong with you? I had no idea you could be so fucking childish."

"*I'm* childish?"

"You're acting like a spoiled brat. Do you have any idea the effort I've put into protecting you this week? Do you know why I did that? Do you have a goddamn clue?"

Mia stared at him, not answering.

"Carlos Garza, forty-two years old. Do you even know who that is?"

She looked confused.

"Franklin Michael Hannigan, sixty-one. How about him, Mia?"

She stepped back as if she'd been slapped.

"You remember him, right?"

"What are you trying to—"

"That's two innocent people who have been in the wrong place at the wrong time who got taken out by this unidentified subject. Two. They were killed with the same gun"—he grabbed her arm and shook it—"that did *this* to you."

Mia tried to pull away, but he didn't let go.

"You think I want to find you in a ditch somewhere? Huh? Watch you get hauled away to the morgue? You think that wouldn't cut me off at the knees, Mia? You think that wouldn't ruin my fucking life?"

She stared up at him now, wide-eyed and shocked. Jonah and Sophie didn't move a muscle, didn't even breathe.

Ric dropped her arm and stepped back. He raked a hand through his hair, then glanced over his shoulder and seemed to realize he had an audience.

He turned back to Mia and took a deep breath. "Pack your things." His voice was resolute. "We're leaving in five minutes."

Mia stood paralyzed, staring at him. Finally, she murmured something and disappeared down the hall.

Evidently, Jonah could read minds, because after the scene at Mia's, he invited Sophie out for a drink. She agreed to meet him at—where else?—El Patio.

"They didn't have MGD Sixty-four, so I got you a Mich Ultra." Jonah returned to their table and set the bottle in front of her.

"That works fine, thanks."

"You know, they do have actual beer back there." He jerked his head toward the bar. "I'm happy to go back if you get tired of carbonated water."

She didn't answer the jab but instead waited for him

to sit down and get comfortable. She wasn't sure it was possible, given that the chairs at their table were so very average-size, while he was so very *not*. But the Friday night crowd had already arrived, leaving them without a lot of seating options.

"How long have you known Ric?" Sophie asked him above the noise as she took a sip.

"'Bout two years, I guess. Since I joined the force."

"Where were you before that?"

"Army," he said. "Joined up straight out of school."

Sophie looked him over. She should have guessed the military background. He kept his brown hair cut pretty short, and he had that certain way of carrying himself—not only the posture but also the confidence that went with it. Something in the plus column. He had some work to do, though, before he'd make up for all of the minuses he'd received from the incident with Mia's panty drawer. He didn't seem like a psycho-pervert, but you never knew. She'd learned years ago—when she'd first started performing, actually—to be very careful when it came to men. Even the normal-looking ones had their freakish sides.

"So, what do you think this is? With him and Mia?"

Jonah shifted in his chair, obviously not comfortable with this conversation.

"I mean, he seemed pretty intense back there. Is he always like that, or is it something special about her?"

Jonah shook his head. "You'd have to ask him that."

"Oh, come on, I'm asking you." She touched her bottle to his and made a *clink*. "You're his friend. You should know these things."

He leaned back in the chair and folded his arms over his meaty chest, and she knew she wasn't going to get anywhere with this. Oh, well. She'd tried. He was clearly one of those guys who dispensed info on a need-to-know basis, and she was just being nosy.

Anyway, Sophie could draw her own conclusions. Her EQ was extremely high, and the emotion back at that house had been off the charts. There was going to be some serious cliff diving going on at Ric's place tonight.

"How'd it go at the Coyote Lounge?" Jonah asked now.

Sophie smiled. "He changes the subject *and* shows off his elephant memory, all in one sentence. Very impressive."

He took a sip of his Budweiser and waited.

"It was great, thanks for asking. We had a good crowd."

"We?"

"Me and my band. I've got a drummer and a guitarist who back me up sometimes."

"Only sometimes?"

She shrugged. "Sometimes it's just me with my guitar. Depends on the venue, how intimate everything is."

He nodded, and she wondered whether he was genuinely interested or just making conversation.

"Do you travel a lot or mostly do stuff around here?" he asked.

"I travel some. When I can get the time, you know? My day job at the Delphi Center is pretty demanding. But I really like singing, so it's worth the effort to try to juggle both. Maybe someday I won't have to." He watched her eyes as she talked, and she got the impression that he was actually listening. That rarely happened to her, especially when she wore something with a low neckline.

"Do you like music?" she asked him.

"Honestly, I don't know much about it."

"You should come to a gig sometime. See what you think." She started to tell him that she was singing tomorrow night, but a phone buzzed under the table.

He pulled out his cell and checked the screen. "Shit." He glanced up. "Shoot. Sorry. I've got to take this. One second." He stood up and stepped toward the patio, talking to someone as he went. Within minutes, he was back inside, and she could tell by his expression that their little cocktail hour had come to an end.

She stood up and collected her black overcoat. "Work, I'm guessing?"

"Sorry about this." He helped her into her coat, and she gave him points for manners, even if he did have to leave abruptly. "It's been one of those days. They need me to come in."

"I should get home soon. I've got a big day tomorrow."

Actually, tomorrow night, but who cared? He wasn't listening anyway but checking his watch.

"Thanks for the beer." She started for the door, and he was right behind her, not quite touching her but not quite walking separately, either, as they crossed the bar.

He reached around and pushed the door open for her. A wall of cold hit them.

"Wow. Brrr." She shivered, and he zipped up his jacket. It was leather, like Ric's, only his was brown.

They started toward her SUV. "I didn't get a chance to ask you what you were doing at Mia's earlier," he said.

She shook out her keys. "Just dropping off something I borrowed. Why?"

"You remember what I told you?"

A black Audi pulled out of the lot, and she stopped to watch it.

"Sophie?"

"What?"

He was frowning at her now. "What's wrong?"

"Nothing. I just—" She stared after the car. It had a Phish bumper sticker on it, just like a black Audi she'd noticed in Houston last weekend. It had been one of the few cars left in the lot after her gig.

Jonah glanced back over his shoulder. "What is it?"

"Nothing, it's just . . . nothing. What were you saying?"

"I said, do you remember what I told you? About steering clear of Mia's? You should still do that. Until we get an arrest in this thing."

"When do you think that will be?" She stopped at her car and turned to look at him.

"Soon, I hope."

"And what does that mean, exactly? Since I don't speak cop."

"It means I'll let you know. Until then, be careful." He took her keys from her hand, then popped the locks and opened the door for her.

"Careful, meaning . . . ?"

"Meaning use your head, Sophie. Don't go to Mia's. Don't go to Ric's. Until this is over, stay away from her."

CHAPTER 23

Mia stared out the window of Ric's truck, struggling to keep her emotions in check as he drove across town. Her mind was reeling—from his words, from their fight, from the undeniable reality that after months of her imagining it, this man was finally taking her home with him.

The reality wasn't much like the fantasy.

In her fantasy version, they would have been out for a long, quiet dinner together. Over coffee or maybe drinks somewhere, he'd have given her one of his dark, seductive looks and suggested that they go back to his place, where he'd pull her into his arms the second they got inside the door.

But he hadn't said a word to her since their fight in the hallway. And the hostility inside his truck was so thick she was having trouble imagining him even touching her, much less sweeping her off to bed. The dark looks were there, but they were far more angry than seductive, and she got the distinct impression that any attraction he might have felt for her was buried under a smoldering layer of fury.

He'd blown up. He'd lost his temper. He'd done it in front of an audience, too, which he must really hate and which probably accounted for at least some of the animosity coming off him right now. She didn't know a lot about Ric—way less than she would have liked, given how she felt about him—but she knew that he was a private person. He didn't broadcast his emotions, and yet tonight they'd erupted from him in front of three people.

You think that wouldn't cut me off at the knees, Mia?

She wasn't done thinking about what that meant—what all of his words meant, including the ones that were easy to decipher. *You're acting like a spoiled brat.* Not only did he think she was oblivious to what he and Rey and Jonah had done for her, but he also thought she was oblivious to what Frank had done, a man who'd sacrificed his life to help her. For Ric to believe that she could be that callous and insensitive wounded her.

Mia's phone sounded from the depths of her purse as Ric swung into a driveway. She checked the number and turned off the ringer, then watched with surprise as Ric rolled down his window and tapped a code into a keypad. After passing through an electronic gate, he drove around a four-story stucco apartment building that backed up to some sort of greenbelt. He parked his truck and grabbed her duffel and computer bag from the backseat.

"I can get that," she said.

He shot her a glare and slung everything over his shoulder before shoving open the door.

Mia slid out of the pickup, empty handed except for her purse. He led her to a glass door, punched in another code, and held the door open as she stepped into a warm lobby with Saltillo tile floors. He walked ahead and jabbed the elevator button.

This was definitely not what she'd pictured. She stepped inside the elevator and glimpsed his reflection in the mirrored doors as they rode up to the third floor.

"Nice place," she said. "How long have you lived here?"

"Couple years."

"Lot of security."

He glanced at her in the doors just before they dinged open. "My old neighborhood was getting sketchy. I didn't feel good about Ava coming in and out of there, so I moved."

He led her down a carpeted hallway, and her stomach danced with nerves as she watched him unlock his door. Then he pushed it open, flipped on a light switch, and ushered her inside.

"It smells so clean," she blurted.

He lifted an eyebrow at her. "Were you expecting gym socks?"

"No, I just . . ." Her gaze skimmed over the shiny tile foyer, the living room sparsely furnished with a glass coffee table and a masculine black leather coach, the beige carpet lined with vacuum tracks. "I guess I didn't know you were so tidy. It looks better than my place."

"The cleaning lady came this week. I haven't had time to mess it up yet." Ric set her bags on the floor beside the door.

Mia dropped her purse next to the bags and glanced around. There was a dark corridor to her left—the bedroom, presumably—and beyond the living room a darkened kitchen. The dining area was empty, but there were

two wooden bar stools pulled up to the counter that sepa-
rated the living room from the kitchen.

She became aware of the silence. Ric was watching
her with one of those simmering looks again, one of the
hostile ones like she'd been getting in the car. She felt a
rush of insecurity, followed by a surge of annoyance.

"Don't look at me that way," she said.

"What way?"

"You're the one who insisted on this. I can just as
easily stay at a motel." *Or Scott's house.* But something
warned her not to say that, or he might go ballistic again.

His phone buzzed, saving him from a response. He
glared at her as he pulled it from the pocket of his slacks.

"Santos." His eyes stayed on her as he listened. He
turned and tossed his keys onto the table by the door.
"Yeah." He turned back to Mia. "I have to take this."
He hesitated, and something flickered across his face.
Uncertainty? Concern? "If you're hungry, I can order us
some dinner or something."

It was his way of answering the motel comment.

"I'm fine. I had a bite after work." She nodded at his
phone. "Take your call."

He took the phone into the living room, where he
switched on a lamp.

Mia looked around again, absorbing more details this
time. On the hallway table was a heap of unopened mail.
Several fliers lay on the floor and looked as though they'd
been slipped under the front door. Mia picked them up.
Pizza coupons, a notice about an upcoming visit from
a pest-control company. She tucked the fliers under the
stack of mail.

Ric stood at the bar now. He had his sleeves rolled

up and one hand braced against the bar as he spoke to someone in low tones. In the yellow lamplight, the lines of his face were sharp, and she could see the tension there as he talked. Was it his brother? Jonah? She didn't know everything that had happened tonight, but apparently, the investigation was in disarray. She got the sense that Ric and Jonah were being set up to take the fall if the case fell apart, which seemed increasingly likely. The DNA results that afternoon might have been the final nail in the coffin.

Mia scooped up her duffel. She felt nervous, jittery. Her instinct was to organize something or maybe cook, but she couldn't do that now. The very last thing she wanted to do was show up at this man's home for the first time and start acting like his mother.

She forced herself to move from her spot and cautiously began exploring. The first door on the right was a bathroom, where she saw a pink toothbrush in a cup beside the sink. She peeked into the room across the hall and flipped on the light. An entire wall was papered with posters of teenage boys, which confirmed her guess about the owner of the toothbrush. A turquoise bedspread covered the twin bed. Beside it was a desk that seemed to have been converted to a makeup table. Mia's gaze scanned the row of lipsticks and nail polishes before she turned off the light and continued down the hallway.

The master suite looked much more like Ric. Kingsize bed, black bedspread, a dresser topped with loose change, deodorant, a box of bullets. On the corner was a framed photograph of Ric and a beautiful young girl in a green soccer uniform. He had his arm hooked playfully around her neck as they both smiled out at the camera.

The girl had smooth olive skin and thick black lashes and looked so much like her father that Mia's heart turned over. Her gaze went back to Ric, who appeared more relaxed and happy than she'd ever seen him. *Look how much he loves her,* she thought, and felt a pang of yearning.

She turned away from the picture and surveyed the rest of the room. In the corner was a weight bench and a stack of impossible-looking disks and barbells. She walked over and ran her fingertips over the cool metal bar. She pictured him lying back on the bench, straining as he pressed up the weight. A memory of their night together came back to her, and her legs went weak.

She sank onto the bench and closed her eyes. Okay, honesty time. She could no longer lie to herself about what she felt for this man. She was in love with him. Not a crush, not infatuation—as she'd felt so often in the past—this was love.

But what did he feel?

You think that wouldn't ruin my fucking life?

If something happened to her, it would ruin his life. He'd said that. But did he mean that as a cop—as in if he couldn't protect her, he'd feel like a failure professionally? Or did he mean it as a man—if something happened to her, it would take away his chance to be happy?

She had so little to go on with him. But she did have her instincts. And her instincts told her that this man wasn't going to be at all like what she'd pictured when she'd pictured being in love. This man wasn't going to give her wine and roses and pretty words. He was a cop, and his hardened, streetwise attitude affected everything he did. He didn't use words much, and when he did, they weren't often pretty. And he sure as hell didn't walk around with his heart on his sleeve.

But she loved him anyway. And she thought that maybe, just maybe, it was possible that he loved her, too. All of that hostility could have more to do with him not knowing what to do about his feelings than about him not having feelings.

Mia took a deep breath and gathered up her courage. Before she could change her mind, she strode into his bathroom and stripped off her clothes. She folded them neatly and left them on the counter beside the sink. Then she turned on the water, and when it was scalding, she stepped under the spray. She tipped her head back and let it wash over her, clearing away all of her doubts and confusion. She might not know what he wanted, but she knew what *she* wanted, and damned if she wasn't going to try to get it.

Ric inventoried his refrigerator as his brother filled him in on the latest developments in the case. In a nutshell, everything was screwed. Lane's lawyer was screaming witch hunt and threatening lawsuits. The only good news was that the press hadn't got wind of the story— a circumstance Ric figured would last about another five minutes—so both sides had an interest in keeping a lid on things. But everyone on the task force was running for cover, and Ric, as Rey had predicted, was being offered up as a scapegoat for today's fiasco.

"What are you going to do?" his brother asked as Ric grabbed a couple of beers and took them into the living room.

"I'm going to work the case, like always."

"This isn't like always. This isn't anything like always."

"Yeah, no shit." Ric sank onto the sofa and twisted off the bottle caps. "But what do you want me to do? I can't just manufacture evidence against the guy. I'm going to have to keep digging." He lifted the beer to his lips and paused. Pipes hummed at the back of the apartment, and a vision of Mia in his bathtub flashed through his head.

"You know, you could be off base on this thing," Rey said. "Maybe Jessup's right."

"How's that?"

"Maybe we should be looking at someone else."

Ric set down his beer. His brother had a point. Ric's cop intuition had told him repeatedly that Lane was their man, but the physical evidence didn't lie. Still, he might just be missing something. Ric figured he had about one more day to salvage the case, or his reputation as a homicide detective was trashed.

"Give me twenty-four hours," he said.

"What happens in twenty-four hours?"

Ric had no idea, but he needed more time. "I've got a couple of leads left. Just don't let them pull the plug yet, okay?"

"Yeah, sure. Like it's my call. I'm just an agent. You want any favors, you should be working on Singh, but I hear you fucked that one up from the first day."

"She still doesn't like me, huh?"

"She thinks you're a loose cannon. Plus, she's political, and she wants to cover her ass. Just a heads up, I wouldn't be surprised if you and your partner get kicked from the task force by tomorrow morning."

"Stall them. I need another day."

"What are these leads, anyway? This is no time to hide the ball."

Mia walked into the foyer and crouched down beside her purse. Her hair hung in messy wet curls around her shoulders, and he watched her dig around for something. Her feet were bare. Her legs were bare. And she wore a gray hooded sweatshirt that looked familiar.

"Ric?" Rey said.

"What?"

"What's this evidence?"

"Mia's working on it," he improvised, watching her rummage through her purse. "I should know more tomorrow."

"You need to get real with this thing. He's the goddamn lieutenant governor. We either have to put up or shut up, and if we don't do it soon, heads are gonna roll. Starting with yours."

Mia twisted her hair into a clip and crossed the living room to the kitchen. He caught her attention and held out a beer for her. She paused and looked at him.

"Ric, are you listening to a damn thing I'm saying?" Rey's voice came distantly through the phone.

"No."

She walked over and stood in front of him, all warm and damp and sweet-smelling. All of the blood rushed out of his head. She took the beer and watched him as she brought it to her lips.

"Later, bro." He clicked off and tossed the phone away. For a few seconds, they stared at each other, and she looked as if she was sizing up an opponent.

"You took a bath."

"A shower." She leaned over to set the bottle down, and his sweatshirt rode up on her.

That tight, strangled feeling he'd been battling all week was back again, and all he could think about was having her. He wanted to drag her to the floor and pound himself into her. And then he wanted to haul her into bed with him and do it again. And again, until he finally got this choking lust out of his system.

He wrapped his hands around the backs of her thighs and pulled her closer, watching her face to see if she'd resist. She didn't, and he slid his hands up and found all that smooth, bare skin beneath his sweatshirt. He leaned his forehead against her stomach and cursed softly.

"Something wrong?" she asked.

He took her perfect hips in his hands and squeezed. God, he'd missed her. He kissed her through the sweatshirt. Then her fingers slid into his hair, and he felt it in every cell of his body. He looked up at her, and there it was again. The look.

A little knife twisted in his chest. He didn't want to hurt her. Never in his life had he been so determined not to hurt someone, but he couldn't stay away. He couldn't leave her alone. He'd tried to be cool and distant, but it hadn't worked at all. He burned hotter for her than ever, and knowing what she would be like, warm and pliant underneath him, just made everything worse.

"What is it?" she whispered.

"It's just . . . this." Her skin was hot silk under his fingers, and all he could think about was making her come. He filled his hands with her lush, beautiful breasts and watched her eyes glaze over. "Do you know how much I've wanted to touch you?"

"It's okay," she whispered. "You can show me."

• • •

His eyes locked on hers as he slid the zipper of the sweat-shirt down and pulled her against him. The stubble on his chin rasped against her breast, and she felt a hot jolt of lust. She held his head against her and sighed as he pulled her into his lap. He pushed and tugged at the sweatshirt until it disappeared and she was sitting on his thigh without a stitch of clothing, while he was completely dressed right down to his sidearm.

"Get this off." She pulled on his belt.

He tipped her back onto the cool leather and jumped to his feet. She smiled at his rush to undo his belt. Seconds later, it, along with his gun and badge, had been tossed onto the coffee table. He started to lower himself over her, then cursed and jerked a pair of handcuffs from his pocket and tossed them to the floor.

She laughed. "In a hurry?"

He planted his knee between hers and leaned forward to kiss her, stroking his hands over her arms as his mouth moved from her lips to her chin to her rib cage, completely bypassing her breasts, and she realized what he was up to.

She sat up. "Ric, wait!"

He shot her a glance. "No." And then made a dive for her navel, and she squirmed beneath him, but he held her firmly by the hips as he kissed her. And kissed her. And kissed her some more, until she saw stars behind her eyelids, and her entire world was reduced to a tiny blissful pinpoint. She was dimly aware that she should object to this, that she didn't want to be in this heavenly place all by herself, and she took his head in her hands and moved her leg to force him up.

"Please." She gasped. "Please, come here."

He came back to her and kissed her thoroughly, and she was so gone for him that she wanted to weep. She felt his heat through his clothes and started jerking at the buttons of his shirt. He sat back to help her, then stripped the shirt off and threw it onto the floor. She glided her hands beneath his undershirt so she could feel the muscles there. His skin was warm, the roughness of his hair achingly familiar. He pulled the T-shirt over his head and tossed it away, and then he was back again, and she kissed him and smoothed her hands over his strong back.

I missed you so much, she wanted to say, but instead, she just touched him, reveling in his wonderful heat and the weight of him and the way his muscles bunched under her hands. She pressed her hips against him and knew how much he'd missed her, too, even if he'd never say it. But in a way, he *was* saying it with his long, deep kisses. With his low moans of approval. With the urgent way he clutched her to him, as if he couldn't get enough.

He sat back, breathless, and stared down at her and she reached up and cupped her hand against his sandpapery cheek.

"What?" she whispered.

He kicked off his shoes and shed the rest of his clothes as she watched him, her pulse thrumming with anticipation. His gaze never left her, and her skin burned from it and felt feverish and much too tight. Finally, he kneeled between her legs again and kissed her breasts and her neck and then her face, and she felt the heavy weight of him pressing against her thigh. Then his breath was hot against her ear.

"You okay with this?" he asked.

She brought his mouth to hers and kissed him. He shifted over her as she braced herself.

"Mia?" He pushed up on one arm and looked down at her. She nodded.

He shifted her hips, and she felt the brutal force of him pushing inside her. He closed his eyes and made a low groan in his chest. He drew back and did it again. She pulled him as close as she could, and tears sprang into her eyes, because she was finally as close to him as she'd wanted to be. He moved above her, powerfully, forcefully, setting that perfect pace again, as if by instinct. As if he knew her, all of her, right down to the very beat of her pulse. His neck corded with tension. She brought his head down and kissed him roughly, with the same reckless abandon she was feeling with every thrust of his hips. She clawed at him, clutched at him, struggling for control as he pushed her and pushed her and pushed her into a place where there was nothing but the two of them, joined, and in a blinding flash, she knew she didn't need control at all. She didn't want it. She threw herself into the white-hot flame and let herself go.

Seconds or maybe minutes later, she lay boneless beneath him, her pulse still humming in her ears. He propped his weight on his elbows and stared down at her. His forehead was slick with sweat, and she wanted to reach up and touch his face, but she doubted she could move. His gaze was serious, and he seemed to be asking her something, but she didn't know what it was. And then she realized.

"I'm on the pill," she whispered.

"I know."

He shifted her onto her side, and she gasped as her

skin unglued itself from the leather, like a giant Band-Aid being ripped off. Then he wedged himself between her and the back of the couch and pulled her snugly against him. His hand reached over and settled on her breast.

She closed her eyes and let contentment wash over her as their heart rates returned to normal and his thumb stroked her nipple. Then his hand glided over her stomach and found her hip.

"I love this." He stroked his palm over the curve of it.

Her impossibly wide hips? She turned to look at him over her shoulder as if he was crazy.

"You do?"

He made a sound in his throat, kind of like a growl, and gripped her skin. Then his hand slid around to her rump and squeezed. "Yep. Every inch of you."

Her already flushed cheeks warmed, and she turned away and settled her head on his biceps as she tried to think of something to say. *Actually, I've been working half my life to get rid of those particular inches.* But she wasn't about to lie there against his perfectly toned body and start pointing out her flaws.

She closed her eyes and let herself drift, not thinking about anything beyond the contentment spreading through her and her heightened awareness of her own body. The minutes flowed by as he lazily stroked her. She heard footsteps in the hallway. A dog outside. The distant snort of someone's Harley tearing out of the parking lot. How quickly she'd forgotten what it was like to live right on top of people.

He kissed her beneath her ear, and it was so gentle that her heart melted a little.

"Mia?"

"Hmm." She held her breath, waiting for whatever he might say.

"I'm starving."

She turned to look at him as he got up from the couch and went into the bedroom. When he returned a few minutes later in a pair of jeans, she was shrugging back into his sweatshirt. It was fuzzy on the inside, and she loved the feel of it against her newly sensitized skin. She stopped by the bathroom to freshen up and then walked into the kitchen.

"You want some dinner?" He was already rooting around in the refrigerator, and she took a moment to look at him in the brighter light. In only blue jeans and with a day's worth of beard darkening his jaw, he looked amazingly sexy. She couldn't believe he found her so attractive—attractive enough to make love to her so fiercely that it left them both sweaty.

Of course, maybe he made love to all women that way. The idea put a sour taste in her mouth.

He switched on his stove and started melting a pat of butter in a pan, and her eyebrows tipped up as she surveyed the ingredients lined up on his counter.

"Grilled cheese?"

"Ham, cheese, and jalapeño. You'll like it."

"I'm really not hungry, thanks."

Thirsty, though. She opened his fridge and peered inside. Beer and condiments dominated the scene. Out of curiosity, she peeked into the freezer. Pizza, TV dinners.

"Ben and Jerry's?" Not only did he not strike her as the decadent ice cream type, but she never in a million years would have picked him for New York Super Fudge

Chunk. He worked on his sandwich as she pulled out the carton. Behind it was a tub of Chunky Monkey, and Mia froze, staring at it. A little lump rose in her throat.

"How did you know?"

He shrugged. "I can read a police report."

She looked at him, stunned. He'd bought her favorite ice cream knowing he would ultimately get her there, in the middle of his kitchen, looking for a postcoital snack. She didn't know whether to be blown away by his arrogance or deeply moved that he'd been so thoughtful. Her brain jumped at the second choice, and her eyes suddenly blurred with tears.

His brow furrowed. "Don't tell me you're crying over ice cream."

She turned her back on him and took the Super Fudge Chunk to the other side of the kitchen, where she started opening drawers. She went through three junk drawers before finding the silverware.

He eased up behind her and wrapped his arms around her waist. "See?" He muttered against her neck, then kissed it. "I'm not always a jerk."

She gave a watery laugh and turned around. "Who said you're a jerk?"

He cupped her face in his hand and gazed down at her. "I blew up earlier." His hand trailed down and lingered at her elbow, right below where her line of stitches was healing. "I hope I didn't hurt you."

"You didn't."

He set the ice cream aside and pulled her against his chest. His heart was back to normal now, and it thudded strongly against her ear.

"I'm having a crap day," he said against the top of her head. "Or I was. Until a minute ago."

She squeezed her arms tighter. "Is there anything I can do?"

Laughing softly, he pulled back from her, and she didn't miss the gleam in his eye. "Uh, yeah."

Her cheeks flushed. She turned her attention to the ice cream, pulling the top off and digging in with her spoon. Someone had already made a dent.

"Looks like you've got mice living in your freezer," she said around a rich bite of chocolate.

He switched off the stove, then leaned back against the counter and chomped into the sandwich, not bothering with a plate.

"Tell me about your crap day," she said, scooping up another velvety bite. Even more than the ice cream, she was savoring just being with him at the tail end of an evening and hearing about work. She'd never had that kind of companionship, and it felt good.

"Investigation's a mess. Basically, our search warrant netted us zip, not even any good prints. Just Lane's family and his housekeeper."

"Does that mean you're backing off him as a suspect?"

"I'm not, but everyone else is." He turned to retrieve a beer from the fridge and opened it bare handed before tossing the cap onto the counter. "Everyone with anything in the way of survival instincts." He took a swig.

She got a flutter in her stomach watching him move and talk and drink in only his faded jeans. This seemed so natural to her. Couldn't he see it?

"Maybe you should look out for your job a little."

"My priority is this case." His look darkened. "It's keeping me up nights. And in my gut, I know I'm not that far off. I can't be." His shook his head. "I'm just missing something."

The silence settled between them as he polished off his sandwich and she picked at the ice cream. One thing she did know about Ric, he was a good detective. She'd seen him in action many times. If he was that certain that he was onto something, she believed he was right. And she admired his courage in going after one of the most powerful politicians in the state the same way he would have gone after some low-life drug dealer who'd killed off a rival, even if said rival was just as much of a low-life. He worked the cases for every victim, every time, whether the victim was a prostitute or a teenage gangster or a little old church lady.

Mia zeroed in on a hunk of white chocolate, determined not to find any more reasons to be in love with Ric tonight.

"There's something else."

She was startled by the ominous look he gave her. He had his arms folded over his chest now, and that simmering thing was back. She swallowed a cold bite.

"What?"

"It's been eating at me all day. All week." He stepped forward and planted himself in front of her, settling his hands on his hips. She felt a stir of apprehension.

"It's Black."

"What?"

"Your friend. Black." He rubbed the back of his neck and looked down. "I'm so jealous of the guy I can't—" He glanced up and frowned. "Why are you smiling?"

She licked the ice cream from her spoon and shook her head. "That's such a male reaction. He gives me a ride to work. I'm not standing in his kitchen half-naked, eating his ice cream at eleven at night."

He gazed at her, the side of his jaw still twitching. "Why did he call you? Earlier in the car? You didn't answer, but it was him, wasn't it?"

"Yes."

She saw the question in his eyes.

"It wasn't a booty call, if that's what you're wondering. Jeez."

That had been exactly what he was wondering, she could tell. Mia took a deep breath and reached for patience. This was coming from his experience with his ex-wife, and they were going to have to get past this hang-up.

"He's been helping me. Giving me transportation. Lending me his pistol and teaching me some basics."

Ric took the ice cream carton from her hands and put it on the counter. "Ask me. Not him." He stepped closer and settled his hands at her waist.

"Okay." She tipped her head to the side. "In that case, I need something."

He waited.

"He's supposed to pick me up tomorrow to go look at used cars. I finally got my insurance check."

"I can help you look at cars." His gaze went to her mouth, and she seriously doubted that he was thinking about cars.

She licked ice cream from her lip, and she *knew* car shopping was the furthest thing from his mind. "I don't need your help picking out a car. I need a ride to the dealership."

Suddenly, his hands tightened around her waist. He lifted her onto the counter, and she gasped at the cool tile under her bare butt.

"I can do that." He slid his hands under her sweatshirt and held her hips again, then leaned in and started kissing her neck.

She closed her eyes and let herself feel him—the warm pull of his mouth, the pressure of his palms stroking her thighs. He eased her legs apart and pulled her forward until she was almost slipping off the counter, but he caught her against him.

"Ric?" She leaned back to look at him. His shoulders tensed under her hands, and she knew he was expecting her to bring up something he didn't want to talk about right now.

"Do you think it's possible that someday : . ." She stretched the question out and watched him brace himself. "Is there even a slight possibility that you and I might, at some point, do this in a bed?"

Relief washed over his face, and she tried not to let it hurt her feelings.

The side of his mouth curled up. "I can definitely make that happen."

CHAPTER 24

～～

Ric's bed turned out to be a very, very good place, and he left her in it early the next morning, with a brief kiss and a promise to come back around lunchtime to take her car shopping. It was more like early afternoon by the time he got free. From his expression when he picked her up, she knew it had been a rough morning. But rather than drop her off and go back to work, he insisted on sticking around for the negotiations and actually ended up helping her by playing the role of the skeptical, car-savvy boyfriend while a man in a bad suit tried to separate her from her money.

Now Mia whipped her beautiful new Jeep—new to her, at least—into a parking space as close to the lab entrance as she could manage. Aside from being royal blue instead of white, the Jeep was remarkably like the one she'd had before, and it had cost her every penny of her insurance check and then some. Still, she was elated to have transportation again and couldn't wipe the grin off her face, even as she made a mad dash through the freezing drizzle to the Delphi Center entrance. She key-carded her way into the building and stood for a moment, shivering and dripping on the marble floor.

Ralph eyed her from across the lobby with disapproval.

"Hi." She smiled at the armed guard whose presence there had helped her convince Ric that the lab, with its many layers of security, was a safer place for her to spend the afternoon than either of their homes.

"Wet out there," she said brightly, although Ralph had never been much of a talker. She combed her fingers through her damp hair and tried another smile. "I saw Kelsey Quinn's car outside. She downstairs, do you know?"

A silent nod sent Mia on a detour to the Bones Unit before heading up to the DNA lab, where she intended to spend the remainder of her afternoon catching up on the evidence that had stacked up that week.

She found Kelsey at a stainless-steel table, bent over a charred pile of bones.

"Fire victim?" Mia asked.

Kelsey looked at her curiously. "What are you doing here? I heard you were under some kind of house arrest."

Mia laughed. "Who told you that?"

"You're the hot topic around here these days." Kelsey put down her forceps and reached for a can of diet soda sitting on the counter behind her. "What brings you down here? Not that I'm not happy to see you. I'm getting ready to send you a tooth for DNA analysis." She nodded at the blackened remains. "We need a positive ID on this burn victim."

"Homicide?"

"Probably, judging by the bullet hole in his temple. Most suicides don't set the house on fire around them before they pull the trigger." She leaned back against the counter, seeming ready for a break. "So, what's up?"

"I wanted to thank you for identifying the Jane Doe from Lake Buchanan. I thought she'd been forgotten."

Kelsey shrugged as if it was no big deal, but Mia knew better. Kelsey took seriously her duty to bring closure to victims' families whenever possible.

"I rattled a few cages, that's all. Turned up a couple of missing persons whose families had never sent in a DNA sample for ID purposes. One of those panned out."

Mia nodded. "Was she young, like you thought?"

"Twenty-two," Kelsey said, and there was sadness in her voice. "She'd been working as an escort only a few months when her mother lost track of her. Mark used mitochondrial DNA to make the ID."

Mitochondrial DNA came in handy because it was much more plentiful within the cell, meaning that it could be recovered more easily than nuclear DNA. It could be found in bone and hair, too, and Kelsey resorted to it frequently to identify remains that lacked soft tissue. Unlike nuclear DNA, mtDNA was inherited only from the mother's side. It passed unchanged down the maternal line, so sons and daughters had the same mtDNA as their mothers, maternal grandmothers, maternal great-grandmothers, and so on. In missing-persons cases, maternal relatives were often called on to provide samples to help ID remains.

"You went above and beyond," Mia said. "You didn't have to do all that."

"Mark did most of the work. I just made the phone calls, tracked down the sample."

"Well, thank you. And Ric thanks you, too. I know you've helped their case."

Kelsey got a glint in her eye. "How is Ric, anyway?"

She must have read the look on Mia's face, because she smiled knowingly.

"He's fine," Mia said. "Good, in fact." Nerves flitted in her stomach. Maybe she was being stupidly optimistic. But it felt different this time, and she deeply hoped that she wasn't about to get her heart crushed.

Mia needed to go before Kelsey asked her any more insightful questions. "Anyway, just wanted to say thanks." She checked her watch. "I'd better hit it before the afternoon gets away from me."

"Don't work too hard."

"Same to you."

The words were empty on both of their parts, and Mia was already drumming up more to-dos for herself as she headed back to the DNA lab. Kelsey had sparked an idea, and Mia wouldn't be able to focus on anything else until she checked into it.

She veered away from the elevator and headed for the evidence room, where a clerk was supposed to be posted until five that evening. She inquired about the garbage bags that had been brought in earlier in the week. The sour expression on the woman's face told Mia that they were still kicking around, probably more fragrant than ever. She led Mia to a separate cool storage room lined with plastic trash bags. Even the brisk temperature didn't keep the fumes from nearly knocking her over the instant the door was open.

"All of this is scheduled to be hauled off next Tuesday," the clerk said. She stayed as far away from the door as she could while Mia took a brave step inside. "If you need anything from here, better get it now."

Mia poked through the bags and examined labels until she found the batch Ric and Jonah had brought in. They had collected everything they needed from it— about half a dozen items that had been analyzed by Mark already.

Mia spent a good twenty minutes sifting through garbage before she found what she wanted. Her thighs burned from crouching, and she was nearly faint from the stench as she lifted a cardboard coffee cup in her latex-gloved hand. She examined the lipstick mark. She examined the name scrawled on the side with black wax pencil.

"Well, now, Camille, let's see if you can tell me what your son's been up to."

Ric cursed his partner as he sailed through another yellow stoplight. Why didn't he pick up? He waited through a couple of rings, then got kicked to voice mail and hit redial.

Something was about to break. Ric could feel it. Or maybe it was him—*he* was about to break. Fifteen years on the job, and he'd finally hit his limit of stress, setbacks, and political bullshit.

"Macon here."

"You wanna answer your phone once in a while? Shit, I've left two messages. What happened at the firing range?"

"I haven't gone yet."

Ric gritted his teeth. "I thought you were heading over there at two."

"Got sidetracked on something for Singh. Anyway, I'm on my way now. I'll let you know. You get anything more on that brass?" Jonah asked. Rey had some other database up his sleeve, and he'd promised to see if they could get any more hits off the shell casings recovered from the shooting scenes.

Ric had woken up that morning much more concerned about the unidentified shooter than about the lieutenant governor. The shooter was a direct threat to Mia. Lane wasn't. But after spending the entire day checking and rechecking every lead they had on that front, Ric was being forced to shift focus.

"Nothing new from Rey," he told Jonah now. "I'll let you know. I'm up at Lake Buchanan, trying to shake something loose."

"You going back to the house?"

"Got an interview with the carpet installer." As Ric said it, he spotted the sign for the roadside café where he was supposed to meet the kid, nineteen-year-old Clayton Sands. "I want to find out what that carpet looked like when they ripped it out. Hell, maybe I can even get my hands on it."

"Call me if you do."

"Lean hard on that buddy of yours," Ric ordered. "I turned those case files inside out, and I can't get any new leads on that shooter."

They clicked off as Ric pulled into the lot of the café. It was filled with pickups, and he hoped one of them belonged to Sands. It did. Ric spotted him right away— the only solo guy anywhere near nineteen, camped out at a table and nervously rearranging condiments. His T-shirt and jeans were covered in paint spatters. The woman at the carpet store had told Ric he moonlighted for a house-painting company on the weekends.

"Clayton Sands?"

"That's me."

Ric flashed his creds and sat down. "I've got a few questions for you about a job you did a couple of weeks back."

"Ask away," he said, but his casual attitude didn't mesh with his fidgeting hands. The kid was drinking a soda. If he'd been old enough, Ric might have bought him a beer to loosen him up. Instead, he cut to the chase, rattling off the address and all of the details he remembered from his interview back at the carpet store.

"Yeah, I remember it." He made a lean-to out of sugar packets. "Got paid time and a half because of the holiday. New Year's Day."

"That's right."

"Missed half the bowl games but made some good coin, so, you know, can't really complain."

"And do you remember what happened to the carpet?"

"The old stuff?"

"Yeah, the carpet you ripped out."

He nodded, focused intently on his construction project. "Took it straight to the dump soon as we finished."

"What was wrong with it?"

"What, the carpet?"

Shit, this kid needed to get his nose out of the paint. "Yes, the carpet."

He shook his head. "Nothing worth salvaging. Maid that let us in said someone broke a case of red wine on it."

"A whole case?"

"That's what she said. Twelve bottles. Red wine everywhere."

Ric tried to imagine how someone could shatter twelve wine bottles, all in a box, on a carpeted surface. If you dropped them from the ceiling, maybe.

Kid cleared his throat. "We wouldn't have salvaged it anyways. We had specific instructions not to take it for recycling."

"Whose instructions?"

"The maid's." The kid's gaze met Ric's, and there was something there. Ric's skin prickled. Goddamn it, he knew he'd been right about this case.

"And you're sure this was wine?" he asked the kid. "Not something else, like maybe blood?"

"I know my carpet stains. That was wine." He looked down at his hands, rearranging the packets in rows now.

"Did you see anything else while you were in the house that looked to you like blood?"

"Nope." No eye contact. "Not at the house."

Ric waited. Finally, the kid looked up, and he saw the conflict in his eyes. Whose identity was he protecting here?

He glanced down and started over on the lean-to. "Guest house was a mess, though."

Ric leaned forward. "What guest house? You're talking about the same property?"

"One driveway over." He looked up through his shaggy bangs. "Just next door, right down by the lake."

"And this job was when?"

"December thirty-first. Day before New Year's."

December, not January. No wonder he hadn't seen it on the calendar back at the carpet store.

The kid's hands were outright shaking now with

whatever information he was holding in. But Ric waited him out. He wanted to talk, he just needed time.

"Anyways, this guest house was pretty small. Maybe five hundred fifty square feet? Not nearly as nice as the main house next door." The sugar packets were in motion again. "There was all this brown paint everywhere, too."

"Brown paint." Ric leaned back in his chair. "You're sure about that?"

"Yep. It was paint, all right, same color as the deck outside. All over the place, like somebody spilled a whole gallon. No way we could recycle that carpet. It went straight to the dump, too. Maid's orders."

Had someone dumped paint on that carpet to disguise the bloodstains?

"This maid," Ric said. "She happen to give you a tip or anything? For following these orders?"

A minuscule nod.

"Okay, what else, Clayton? Besides the brown paint."

The lean-to collapsed. He laced his fingers together and looked down at them, then up. "Got rid of the carpet pad, too. Whole thing was soaked with blood."

CHAPTER 25

❧

"K urt Lane," Ric said the instant Jonah picked up.
    "What? Where are you?"
    "I'm driving like a bat outta hell back to Lane's lake
house. His son's our man."
    "You're talking about the grad student? Out in Cali-
fornia?"
    "He's not in California." Ric took a curve in the high-
way going double the speed limit. "He's been living in
his parents' guest cottage right here on the goddamn
lake. I can't fucking believe it. We even checked him
out, remember? Got a cell-phone dump two weeks ago.
Everything was up in Oakland."
    "But he wasn't there? Shit, how did—"
    "Maybe someone has his phone. How the hell do I
know? Anyway, I need you out here ASAP," Ric said. "I
spent the last two hours getting a search warrant for this
guest cottage. Had to go to the freaking judge's *house* and
drag him away from the ball game, and now I'm on my
way to meet a CSI team—"
    "Hold up. I've got news."
    Ric tensed at the words. He'd been so caught up with

the warrant he'd hardly thought about the firing range.

"Just left the range. My buddy showed me the sign-in logs dating two months back. About half a dozen cops that he knows of, could be more. I took down all the names."

"And?" Ric gripped the steering wheel.

"One stands out. Burleson was out here last weekend doing some long-range shooting."

"Todd Burleson?"

"One and the same. He's ex-Army, turns out, so he and my buddy know each other some from talking shop whenever he comes by. I didn't know this before, but Burleson was in Desert Storm a good ways back, before he was on the job. And get this—he got his start as a uniform up in Fort Worth, where he first made detective."

Ric's skin went cold. He knew what was coming.

"I called up there," Jonah said. "Got hold of his former partner. You're not going to believe this."

"Guy named Baker?"

Pause. "How did you know?"

"God*damn* it. I met him." Ric remembered his words about the Laura Thorne murder. "He said his partner was obsessed with the Thorne case."

"Exactly. Which makes me think Burleson maybe got assigned to it on purpose, so he could derail the investigation and protect Lane."

"That'd be pretty hard to pull off," Ric said. "More likely, he caught the case legitimately, then Lane got to him and paid him off to protect his son and keep his name off the suspect list." The bitterness was like a rock in Ric's throat as he said the words.

"However it went down, Burleson was out here last Sunday, worked on five- and six-hundred-yard shots all afternoon."

Sunday afternoon, the day after he tried to kill Mia.

Ric slammed on the brakes and pulled a U-turn. He narrowly missed an SUV that was barreling down the highway and a horn blared behind him as he stomped on the gas.

"Listen, Ric, I know what you're thinking, and before you do anything—"

"I'm going to fucking bash his skull in."

"Calm down."

"Calm *down*? Are you out of your mind? He tried to kill Mia *twice*! He murdered a cop!" Ric glanced at the clock on his dashboard. "Meet me halfway. I'll hand off this warrant, and you can meet everyone over there."

"Ric, listen to me before you do anything. I checked the schedule. He's not on today. I went by his house, too, and he's not there, either. So before you go off half-cocked, we need to think about this. If we tip him off, no telling what he'll do."

Ric's gut burned with rage. The highway stretched before him in a haze of red.

"Man, think about what you're doing."

Ric thought for about half a second. That's how long it took him to realize that going after Burleson with a tire iron wasn't what he needed to do right now, no matter how much he wanted to.

"Meet me at the Highway 71 and Bass Road juncture," Ric said. "This warrant's all yours."

"And what about you?"

"I'm going to get Mia."

• • •

Mia checked her phone as she stepped off the elevator. Ric.

"I'm glad you called! I'm running late, but I might have a breakthrough, so—"

"Where are you?"

Something in his voice made her feet stop. "Just leaving the lab. Why?"

"Stay there."

"What?"

"I'm coming to get you."

"But—"

"We know who the shooter is, Mia, and you were right. He's a cop. Goddamn SMPD. You know Todd Burleson?"

She stood there, shocked, in the middle of the dimly lit lobby. *SMPD?*

"Has he ever talked to you? Approached you?"

"No. I don't know." She shook her head. "Wait, *who* did you say again?"

"Todd Burleson. He's a homicide dick. Caught the Meyer case before the chief tossed it over to me."

"I don't know any Burleson." Mia tried to conjure a face.

"I'm sending you a picture. Check your phone, okay?"

Mia looked anxiously around the lobby. Sophie's desk was empty. The coffee shop was empty. All of the corridors she could see were empty. She looked out the windows, where daylight was disappearing behind the tree line.

"Because he's a cop," Ric went on, "he could probably badge his way past the gate."

She felt the first stirrings of fear. "You think he's coming *here*?"

"I don't know what he's doing. He's not answering the phone or his door. He's freakin' AWOL, Mia. Are you inside?"

"I'm in the lobby. I just—"

"Get away from the glass. Go into an office. Not your office. Call the security guard, and tell him to come wait with you, and I'll be there in twenty minutes. Twenty-five at the most, okay?"

Her chest constricted as she stepped toward the elevator bank.

"Okay, Mia?"

"Ric, do you really think—"

"I don't know. It's probably nothing, but until we pick him up, I'm not taking any chances. Call me if anything weird happens, anything at all, okay?"

"All right," she said, trying to sound brave. She ducked behind one of the tall Doric columns and leaned her back against the cool marble. She took a deep breath.

"I'm coming fast, Mia. I'll be there soon."

"Be careful. The roads are icy."

"I will."

They disconnected, and Mia stood motionless as the silence enveloped her. A trickle of fear slipped down her spine, and she realized that something very weird was already happening.

She was in the lobby, and she didn't see Ralph.

CHAPTER 26

From the minute he set foot in the room, Jonah knew they'd found their crime scene. Even without the tip from the carpet installer, the place had a particular smell about it—new carpet, yeah, but something else, too.

"Look, but don't touch," one of the crime-scene techs warned, walking around Jonah to kneel in the corner of the room. He took out a utility knife and started peeling back a corner of carpet.

Like the CSI, Jonah wore a Tyvek suit and shoe coverings to keep from tracking debris either in or out. He wore latex gloves, too, but didn't plan to touch anything until the place had been thoroughly photographed and dusted for prints. Jonah was there as a pair of eyes only, at least for now.

The photographer continued snapping away with her camera as Jonah tried to get a feel for the place. It had all the features of what might have been a college apartment: efficiency kitchen, combination living and sleeping area, faded futon slouched in front of a TV hooked up to a gaming system.

"Hey, you smell that?" Jonah asked, turning to look at the CSI.

"What, the carpet?"

"Yeah, but I'm getting some other funk, too."

The guy sniffed the air. "Think you're right. Good nose."

Jonah scanned the room for investigative possibilities. Should he start with the unmade bed? The papers littering the breakfast table? The closet overflowing with dirty laundry? He walked over to the TV and surveyed the tall stack of video games. He eyed the joystick with disgust. This jerk off had an extreme case of Failure to Launch.

"Damn, what a hovel."

He turned and saw a Tyvek-clad woman standing in the doorway—the FBI's computer expert, Beth Something-or-other. She wrinkled her nose at the mess and went straight for the laptop on the coffee table. Kurt Lane was considered a flight risk, so the task force was after any information that might indicate his whereabouts. E-mail was a good place to start.

"Let me know what you get on that system," Jonah said, stepping into the bathroom for a look. Nothing on the sink. A can of beer sat on the back of the john. Jonah poked his head behind the moldy shower curtain and scanned the tile grout for anything suspicious. Nope.

His phone buzzed, and he pulled it from his pocket.

"What was Burleson practicing with Sunday?" Ric demanded without preamble.

"Remington 7600."

"Does it have a night scope?"

"Don't know. Why?" Jonah glanced through the

frosted-glass window and saw that daylight was fading fast.

"Mia's at the lab. I'm on my way, but she just called, and she can't find the security guard."

"You think he's out there?" "He" meaning Burleson.

"I've got no idea," Ric said, but the edge in his voice told Jonah that was exactly what he thought.

"Guard's probably taking a piss break or maybe making his rounds or something," Jonah said.

"Mia's been there for hours. If he set up waiting for her out by the parking lot, he's bound to figure he's missed his shot by now. It's almost dark."

"And you think . . . ?" Jonah didn't even want to finish the sentence.

"I think the guard's missing and so is Burleson. I think he's about to make this up close and personal."

Mia sat at Kelsey's desk, clenching her hands as she waited for Ric to call. Where was he? Maybe the roads were icy and he'd taken it slow, as she'd asked him to. But she didn't really believe that, not after hearing the alarm in his voice. He thought she was in danger. Right now. And as the minutes ticked by, she was starting to believe him.

Her phone chimed, and she jerked it to her ear. "Ric?"

"You find Ralph yet?"

"I looked around some more, but I didn't see him."

"Is there a control room somewhere? Maybe where he monitors security cams or something?"

"I don't know. I mean, there probably is, but I've never seen it."

"Okay. Anyone else there?"

She took a deep breath. "Not that I can tell. Kelsey left hours ago, and the evidence clerk clocks out at five on weekends. There were only three cars in the lot when I pulled in."

"Where are you?"

"The Bones Unit." Mia's gaze rested on the skull-and-crossbones coffee mug she'd given Kelsey last year for her birthday.

"Did you lock the door?"

"Yes."

"Double-check for me."

Heart pounding now, Mia got up and tried the door to the room where Kelsey and her colleagues kept cubicles.

"It's secure," she said. "Are you almost here?"

"I'm probably ten minutes away."

Silence stretched out, and Mia bit her lip. "Ric, this feels wrong to me. Ralph never leaves his post."

"Maybe he's making rounds."

Mia thought about that. She didn't know the guard's routine, but she'd never seen him anywhere besides the lobby.

"Should I call the police, maybe?" Mia had almost done it a minute ago.

"I already did, as a precaution. But I'll probably get there before they do." He paused. "Do you have your gun?"

A little bubble of hysteria rose in her throat. "What gun?"

"The pistol Black lent you."

"It's at home. I don't have a permit." Not that she would have felt comfortable carrying it even if she had—although having a pistol in her hand might go a long way toward calming her nerves right about now. "Maybe I should go down to the ballistics lab, see if I can find something."

"Is it locked?"

"Probably, but my key card might work."

"Good thinking. Be careful, and I'll call you when I get there."

Cautiously, Mia left the Bones Unit and headed for the elevator. The corridor was dim and silent. What had happened to Ralph? And was she really alone in the building with someone who wanted to kill her? As she rode the elevator down, she took a deep breath and closed her eyes, reaching for that inner reservoir of calm. Ric would arrive any minute. This was nothing. The police knew who they were looking for now, so it was just a matter of arresting him. Maybe she'd even be called to ID him in a lineup. Mia pictured herself behind mirrored glass, surveying a row of suspects, all wearing bandannas and ball caps like the man who'd carjacked her. Then she pictured the same line of men, all with Band-Aids over their noses, and it was Sam standing behind the glass and pointing a pudgy little finger at one of them.

God, she wanted this to be over. She wanted her life back, the same as it had been before, only with Ric in it.

The elevator dinged open. Her footsteps echoed through the long corridor as she made her way to ballistics, where only yesterday Scott had given her a firearms lesson. The office was locked, as Ric had predicted. Mia tried her palm print and her key card, to no avail. She cupped her hand against the window and peered inside. The entire section was dark except for the blue glow of somebody's screen saver.

She glanced up and down the corridor. A chill settled over her and she zipped her jacket. Never in her life had she felt so alone and vulnerable.

It's nothing, she told herself. *Ric's on his way.* Besides, even if someone *was* looking for her, how would he ever find her way down there in the bowels of the laboratory? The Delphi Center was enormous, and he'd have no reason to look in this precise spot unless he had a crystal ball.

Mia leaned back against the wall, slid to the floor, and hugged her knees to her chest. This was as good a place as any to wait for Ric's call. She looked down the corridor, and a glowing red light caught her attention. It belonged to a camera mounted up on the ceiling. Ric's words came back to her as the lens stared down at her like a giant eyeball. *Is there a control room somewhere? Maybe where he monitors security cams or something?*

Mia's throat went dry. She heard a faint rumbling noise at the other end of the hallway.

The elevator dinged.

CHAPTER 27

Jonah hovered over the crime-scene tech as he swabbed a tiny brown dot on the baseboard.

"Blood?"

"We'll know soon. Could be more of that paint, but . . ."

"But?" Jonah prompted.

"I think it's blood. Based on the spatter pattern."

"Well, looky here."

Jonah shifted his attention to the computer examiner, who was busy pecking away on Kurt Lane's laptop.

"This guy likes the rough stuff," she said. "Listen to these sites: Houseofpain.com, Hurts So Good, Beauty and the Beast. Ick." She made a face. "I'm pretty sure I don't want to see that one. The Coyote Lounge."

Jonah walked to the coffee table and peered over her shoulder. "You said the Coyote Lounge?"

"Yep. That one looks like a nightclub, though."

Jonah skimmed the list of sites in Lane's browsing history and went back to the most recent one.

"Gil's Garage," he said. "Isn't that a nightclub in Austin?"

"I think so."

"Click on it," he said.

"Are you sure you—"

"Do it."

She clicked on the link, and a Web site for the night-club filled the screen. Jonah homed in on the words "Onstage Saturday" right above a publicity photo of a beautiful blonde. His stomach plummeted.

"Holy shit."

Sophie put the finishing touches on her lipstick and sur-veyed the result in her rearview mirror. Her makeup looked good tonight. So did her hair, if only it would stay that way. She gave it one last fluff before grabbing the umbrella off the seat beside her, shoving open the door, and stepping down from the Tahoe.

Right into a puddle.

"Damn it," she hissed.

She'd worn boots tonight, luckily, but they weren't exactly Timberlands, and she could already feel cold water seeping between her toes as she walked around to the tailgate and gathered up her CDs.

"Need a hand?"

She jumped and whirled around. A man in a baseball cap stepped out from between two cars and smiled at her.

"I'm fine, actually." She hitched her purse up on her shoulder and tried to balance the umbrella over her head as she pulled the box of CDs from the cargo space.

"That everything?" He put his hand on the door and nodded inside.

"Oh, uh—" She looked nervously around the park-ing lot. It was early, so the place was still fairly empty. "I think so."

He closed the door, then smiled again as he carefully took the box of CDs from her arms. Her instinct was to cling to it, but she didn't want to seem rude, and she also wasn't eager to drop the umbrella shielding her hair from ruin.

Raindrops dampened the shoulders of his tweed sport coat. He smiled again, and her wariness melted. He had a clean-cut look about him and an expensive watch.

"Thanks," she said. "We can go inside through the back here. I'm performing tonight, so I've kind of got VIP access." She led him past a loading dock that smelled like vomit, which underscored what "VIP" meant there at Gil's Garage. The place was a dive.

"Is this all your music?"

"Yep." She smiled again as they neared the door. "I go on at nine. Hope you'll stay for the show." *And buy a few CDs.*

He veered left, toward the corner of the building.

"Oh, it's okay. We can go in back here. It's actually unlocked, so——" She stopped as he kept going toward a row of cars.

"Just need to get something out of my car."

She watched him uneasily. Surely he wasn't going to take off with all of her CDs? She started after him. "You know, I can take it from here. It's really no problem."

The taillights blinked on a black car, and the trunk popped open. He dropped the box inside. She opened her mouth to protest, and her gaze landed on the bumper sticker.

Understanding dawned. She took a step back, and he lunged toward her.

• • •

Ric pulled right up to the sidewalk and sprinted up the steps to the lab entrance with his gun drawn. The door was locked, as expected, and Ric practically vibrated with impatience as he waited for the guard from the gatehouse to pull his cruiser up and join him at the door.

"Tried Ralph on the radio just now," the man said, lumbering up the stairs. "He didn't answer."

"Is that unusual?"

The guard looked grim. "Ralph always answers." He finally reached the door and swiped his ID card to open it. "I notified my supervisor, and he's on his way over. You're to wait in the lobby until he gets here, and he'll accompany you to locate Dr. Voss."

"Not happening." Ric plucked the ID card from the guard's hand and took off for the elevator.

"Hey! You can't roam around without an escort!"

"Guess you'll have to shoot me," Ric tossed back as he got into the elevator. He swiped the card against the security panel and jabbed the button for the ballistics floor, which—to his relief—lit up green. As the doors slid shut, he heard the guard yelling at someone over the phone.

The doors opened, and Ric ran down the hallway, but he didn't see Mia. The ballistics lab was shut down. He used the guard's ID card to open the door.

"Mia?"

Silence answered him, and his heart rate took another leap. Where had she gone? And why wasn't she answering her phone? He called her for the third time in five minutes as he sprinted back down the hallway. The other side of the floor contained the database room, according to the sign posted near the elevator. Ric checked inside but, again, nothing.

Panic tightened his chest as he rode the elevator back up to the lobby. Was she hiding somewhere? Maybe she'd turned her phone off so no one would hear her. She had to be hiding. The alternative terrified him.

The doors parted, and he rushed back to the lobby. He needed that control room. Checking the security cams would be faster than combing each floor. But where the hell was it? He searched Sophie's desk, hoping maybe she had a map or something to guide visitors.

Ric heard a commotion down the hallway and ran toward it. Light spilled out from an open door, and he recognized the security guard's agitated voice.

Inside the room, a desk faced a giant video screen that had been divided into squares. The control room.

"We need an ambulance!" the guard barked into his phone as he kneeled beside Ralph. The big man was bound and gagged with duct tape and sported a baseball-size bump on the back of his head. Ric dropped to his knees and ripped the tape off his mouth as the other guard worked on the bindings with a pair of scissors.

"Where's Mia Voss?"

Ralph wheezed and coughed and shook his head. Ric pounded him on the back, and his attention went to the video screen. It was a five-by-five matrix of ever-changing camera images, displaying feed from all over the compound. The words "Perimeter Breach" blinked under one of the squares. The view above showed the razor-wire-topped fence that surrounded the compound.

An alarm sounded. More words flashed on the other side of the matrix: "Unauthorized Exit Southwest Door." Ric watched the screen as a shadow disappeared through a doorway.

Mia.

He turned to the guards. "Southwest door! Where is that?"

"Just past"—Ralph coughed again—"the evidence room."

Ric jumped to his feet and looked one last time at the grainy video image.

A man in a ski mask stepped into view. Ric's world tilted as the man yanked open the door and darted out after Mia.

CHAPTER 28

Jonah kept a heavy foot on the pedal as Ric's brother talked with the task force from the passenger seat.

He cursed under his breath, and Jonah shot him a look.

"What? What is it?"

"Nightclub manager," Rey said. "Delmonico talked to him. There's a black Tahoe in the parking lot, but Sophie Barrett hasn't shown up yet."

The slimy ball in the pit of Jonah's stomach expanded. "Any black Audis seen entering or leaving the area?"

Rey relayed the question, then glanced over. "No. We've got an APB out, though."

Jonah tried to stay focused, but his imagination kept getting away from him. The moment he'd seen Sophie's picture, he'd known she was in serious trouble, and learning that their prime murder suspect drove a black Audi only confirmed it. That car had been at El Patio the other night when Jonah had walked Sophie to her SUV. And judging by the look on her face, it was a car she'd seen before, one that made her nervous. Damn it, why hadn't he pressed her about it then? He hadn't wanted to

come off as pushy and overbearing, and now look what
had happened.

"I don't like this game plan," he told Rey when he got
off the phone. "What are we going to find at this club?
He took her someplace else. Our focus should be on figuring out where that is."

"Maybe we can drum up a witness who saw something."

"Like what? A woman being forced into a car?" He
pounded the steering wheel with his fist. "That doesn't
tell us shit about where she is now! This is a waste of
time!"

Rey looked at him. "You involved with this girl?"

Jonah took a deep breath. "No." *Fuck.* "Try Singh
again. See if they've spotted him out near the lake house.
He's got to be taking her there. That's his MO."

"Yeah, well, his little hideaway's not going to work
tonight."

Rey got on the phone again and learned that Lane's
vehicle had not been spotted in the vicinity of the lake
house, despite the lookout they'd posted at both ends of
the road.

Not that that meant anything.

"Who's posted on the eastern side?" Jonah asked. If
he was taking her from the nightclub to his lake house,
he'd be coming from that direction.

Rey asked the question, then gave Jonah a name.

"That guy? Shit, isn't he the one who missed Ric
sneaking into Mia's earlier this week? Our best chance to
intercept this guy is probably blown to hell!"

Rey disconnected again, and the car went silent
except for the swish of the wiper blades. Sweat beaded

on Jonah's brow. His hands felt clammy. He envisioned Ashley Meyer's autopsy photos and felt sick.

"It's good, you know, that we've disrupted his plan," Rey said. "If Ric hadn't found his cave, she'd probably already be back there with him."

Jonah shot him a look.

Rey checked his watch, his face grave. "And it's only been an hour. She might still be okay."

Jonah trained his gaze on the road as he sped toward the last place Sophie was known to have been. Rey was trying to be hopeful, and Jonah wanted more than anything to believe him. But the cop part of his brain kept getting in the way.

"Any minute," Jonah said tightly, "Lane's going to realize his game is up, if he hasn't already. Then he'll turn tail and run, like the dog that he is." He glanced at Rey. "The last thing he's going to want at that point is a woman slowing him down."

Mia tripped through the brush, desperately trying to figure out where she was. She'd exited on the south side of the building—she knew that much. But a mental picture of the grounds wouldn't form, because she'd always made an effort not to think about what surrounded the laboratory. Maggot-infested corpses. Decaying animals. Pits filled with half-buried skeletons. Mia's fear mounted with every step, and the only thing propelling her forward was the certainty that she couldn't go back. She was being followed.

She squinted at the darkness, trying to make out the varying degrees of black. Sensing an obstacle ahead— maybe a tree?—she veered left and kept her hands in front of her as she continued into the blackness. Where was Ric? How would he find her? And if he didn't find her, how was she going to evade the ski-mask guy, who was armed to the teeth? Mia had watched him, quaking with fear, from the window of the stairwell nearest the ballistics lab. He had some sort of rifle strapped to his back and a pistol gripped in his hand, and he might as well have carried a scythe, too, because to her he was the Angel of Death. Soul-freezing terror had sent her scuttling up the stairwell and racing for the nearest fire exit.

Which had sounded an alarm, no doubt pointing him right to her.

Mia paused to listen now. The alarm had ceased. Rain pitter-pattered around her, and wind rustled through nearby branches. The noise covered her movements, but it was impossible to see. What if she crashed right into him? The thought petrified her. But the alternative—standing there and waiting for him to find her—was even more frightening.

She forced her feet forward. The cell phone tucked deep within her pocket had vibrated three times now. Ric was looking for her. Could she risk the noise and light that using her phone would create? Maybe she could huddle at the base of a tree and text him something. *SOS!* But he knew that already. And how could he come to her rescue if she didn't even know where she was?

Mia pressed forward and willed her brain to work. She had to think her way out of this. She struggled for calm as she catalogued her assets. She had no gun. She had a phone but couldn't risk using it until she found some sort of cover. She had a tube of Mace clutched in her hand, which was better than nothing but no match for a bullet. Her greatest asset was that she was familiar with the landscape, and her assailant probably wasn't. On the verge of hysteria now, Mia tried to conjure a map of what lay south of the building. There was a winding path leading past cordoned-off burial sites. She pictured Kelsey and her teams of students filing out there to document their experiments.

The teaching pavilion. She suddenly remembered the open-air classroom where students would sit at picnic tables, sheltered from the blazing summer sun as they discussed cases. It was an outdoor facility, but there were restrooms there and a drinking fountain. If she could lock herself inside one of those bathrooms and make a call to Ric—

Her toe caught on something hard. She flung her hands out and fell head-first into a void.

Ric raced through the blackness, tracking the man who was tracking Mia. He was going by sound mostly, with an occasional flash from his penlight to keep him on course.

Hang on, Mia, I'm coming.

He pictured her running for her life out there in the freezing dark. The thought that someone might get to her before he did and snuff the life from her eyes chilled Ric straight to his bones. He couldn't let it happen. He *wouldn't* let it happen. He'd do anything to get her out of harm's way.

Get low, Mia. Get still somewhere and hide.

She had to be terrified by now, reduced to raw animal instincts. But instincts were good, especially given her lack of training. Instincts might be her best chance for survival.

Ric said a prayer to himself—something from his childhood, something he hadn't said in ages and hardly remembered—as he plunged through the dark.

If she'd only stop moving, her pursuer would have to stop to get his bearings. He might even break out a flashlight, and Ric would be on him in a heartbeat.

Ric halted in his tracks. The rustling continued, but the noise was no longer man-made, just a light wind through the trees. He eased forward, waiting for the slightest mechanical sound that would give away the gunman.

Mia sprawled on her stomach, struggling to get her breath back. Blood filled her mouth. She'd bitten her tongue. She sucked in air, and along with it came a sickly odor. She pushed up on her palms and registered the lumps beneath her frozen fingers.

It couldn't be. She hadn't . . . ?

Dear God, she had. Revulsion flooded through her as every one of her senses confirmed that she'd fallen into a grave. She scrambled to her knees and clawed out of the pit, only to realize that she was hyperventilating. She clamped her mouth shut, but the silence came too late. She heard him now, advanced toward her through the brush, and the confidence in his footsteps told her that he understood their roles. He was the hunter. She was the prey. And he intended to finish her off as he would a wounded doe. She scrounged frantically for her Mace, but it was lost amid the dampened leaves and rotting limbs.

A flashlight beam pierced the darkness. It swung left, then right, searching for her. She scampered backward out of the pit and away from the hunter. The light swept over her face.

Mia screamed to wake the dead.

Everything came at once: a flash of light, a panicked scream, a slight shift in the shadows. Ric raised his gun and fired, purely on instinct. Something howled in agony, and the flashlight hit the ground.

"Mia, get down!"

To his side, movement. Ric dropped to a knee, pivoted, and raised his gun again. He got a shot off just as a bullet zinged so close it made his ears ring. Her attacker was wounded, not dead. Ric lunged sideways, crashing into something hard. A tree. He yelled out, trying to draw attention away from Mia. Another shot rang out, this one hitting the tree trunk just inches from his head.

Mia snatched up the flashlight and pointed it toward the noise. The beam landed on a patch of mud where the rifle had fallen.

The rifle!

She realized she'd betrayed her location the same instant another shot sounded. Swaying with fear, she switched off the flashlight. This was crazy! Everyone shooting in the dark! Mia dropped to her knees and groped around until her hands found the rifle butt. She picked it up and looked around in a panic. Now what? She couldn't see to aim it.

A sudden *oomph,* followed by a *thud.* Then grunts and snarls, like a pair of wolves wrestling on the ground. Mia tucked the rifle under her arm and fumbled for the flashlight. She aimed it at the noise, illuminating the man in black—Burleson—fighting viciously for control of a gun. Ric was beneath him, a knee pinned to his chest, his own pistol out of reach at his feet. The gun pointed up, toward the sky, but Burleson was locked in a mortal struggle to point it down toward Ric's head. The ski mask was gone now. Mia shone the light straight in the man's eyes, hoping to break his concentration, but he didn't blink.

"Mia . . . gun," Ric ground out.

She lifted the rifle, and the flashlight beam wobbled.

"Stop right there, or I'll shoot!" The threat sounded pitifully weak, which it was, because the thought of firing a bullet so close to Ric's head made her dizzy. Instead, she set the flashlight on the ground so she could see by the glow, then rushed to Burleson's side and, with all her might, jabbed the rifle butt at his head. Pain reverberated up her arms. He slumped sideways, and Ric leaped on top of him. In an instant, Ric had him flipped onto his stomach, with a knee in his back and a pistol jammed into his neck.

Blood oozed from the man's temple. He'd gone limp.

"Oh my God," she croaked. "Did I kill him?"

"No." Ric held the gun at his neck, chest heaving, and in the glow of the flashlight, she saw the battle raging in his eyes.

"Ric, don't do it."

But he wasn't listening.

With shaking hands, she lowered the rifle to the ground and stepped toward him. "It's over, Ric. You can't just execute him."

He groaned painfully, still at war with himself. She watched his chest heave, his jaw clench, the beads of sweat slide down his temples. And in a flash, she saw all of her dreams for a future together being destroyed by a single unchecked impulse.

She put her hand on his shoulder. "Ric," she whispered. "I'm okay. It's over."

Something flickered in his eyes. He reached a hand around and dug a pair of cuffs from his back pocket. He wrenched the two arms backward, eliciting a moan from the man beneath him as he slapped on the cuffs.

Ric got to his feet and stared down at him. If she'd ever wondered what pure hatred looked like, it was right there in front of her, etched on Ric's face. He still held the gun in his hand, and Mia took his sleeve and tugged him away as the sound of sirens drifted toward them over the treetops. The sound grew louder and louder as she stood there watching him.

He turned to face her and seemed to be seeing her for the first time. He tucked the gun into the back of his jeans and cupped her face in his hands. His thumbs stroked her cheeks, and he stared down at her with so much intensity she couldn't speak.

"Are you all right?"

She nodded.

"You sure?"

She nodded again. And then she buried her head against his chest and held on tight.

"We got a call from our spotter at the airport," Rey said. "Kurt Lane just climbed aboard his dad's plane."

"Which airport? Where?"

"Marble Falls. It's a private runway out near the golf course." He exchanged some more info over the phone with Singh. "They're sending a team over there, ETA four minutes."

Jonah floored it, hoping against hope that they weren't too late.

"Did the spotter see—"

"He's traveling alone."

Jonah flinched at the words. "Who is this spotter?"

"We put an agent there two days ago. Family's got access to a private plane, so we've been treating everyone like a flight risk."

Rey navigated, and the twelve minutes it took to reach the airport felt like an eternity. Jonah ignored the "Authorized Vehicles Only" signs and drove straight onto the tarmac, where a SWAT team was standing in the sleet, surrounding a small Cessna. Jonah pulled over next to an unmarked unit and jumped out.

Rey jogged over to Delmonico, who was on the sidelines watching the takedown. Maybe it was a hostage situation, with the pilot caught in the middle.

Jonah scanned the area, hungry for any sign of Sophie. On the other side of the chain-link fence surrounding the tarmac was a lot filled with pickups, SUVs, and several nice sports cars but no black Audi. How had Lane gotten there?

And then he saw it. Parked at the very far end of the lot was a black sedan. He didn't realize he'd started running until he was halfway across the lot with his gun in his hand. He halted just feet from the car, and dread gripped him as he read the bumper sticker. This was the vehicle. Everything he knew about crime-scene protocol went out the window as he yanked open the door. Not even locked. His gut tightened as he looked inside. A roll of duct tape sat in the cup holder. On the backseat was a heavy-duty Maglite and a woman's purse, the contents strewn across the floor.

His gaze landed on the trunk-release button beside the driver's seat. He popped the trunk and rushed to the back of the car.

"Oh, Jesus."

She was curled in a fetal position, her hair matted with dried blood. Jonah reached inside, and his knees nearly buckled when his fingertips met with warm skin. He couldn't find a pulse for the life of him, but she was warm.

"Jonah?"

He looked over his shoulder as Rey hustled over.

"Call an ambulance! Now!"

He scooped her into his arms and lowered her to the ground, looking for any more signs of life.

"Sophie, talk to me. Come on!"

Her wrists were bound, her ankles, too. He bent over to start CPR, and her eyelids fluttered. She looked up groggily before her eyes drifted shut again.

"You're safe now. We got you."

She blinked up at him. "Jonah?" Her voice was raspy, almost a whisper, but it sounded like music.

"I'm right here."

She turned her head right, then left. She pushed against him and tried to sit up. "Where the hell am I?"

CHAPTER 29

～～

It was nearly four A.M. by the time Ric pulled into Mia's driveway. She looked dazed from fatigue. Hours of briefings and debriefings and never-ending questions had left her totally whipped, pushed way beyond any normal point of exhaustion. She needed food and sleep, but all Ric could think about—all he'd been able to think about for the past six hours—was how long he had to wait to get his hands on her.

Ric cut the engine and went around to her door. She slid out of the truck, and he caught her arm as she swayed on her feet.

"You okay?"

In the faint glow of the porch light, he could see that she hadn't registered the question.

"Time for bed," he said, wrapping an arm around her waist.

She leaned against him as they mounted the three wooden stairs to her door, and he took her purse and rummaged for keys. He came across her phone, and the smudge of blood on it smacked him with so much force he took a step back. Her blood. Hers. She'd bitten a hole in her tongue falling into that pit, and just thinking of the man who'd stalked her there and almost killed her made it hard for Ric to breathe.

Mia closed her eyes now and slumped against the door frame as he took out her keys.

"The silver one," she mumbled.

He unlocked the door, pulled her against him, and got her inside. He disabled the alarm and forced himself to think practically. She needed food. She probably wanted a hot bath or at least a shower. And then she'd need about twelve hours of sleep before she'd be functional enough to handle anything even resembling what was on his mind right now.

He closed the door and locked it, and she fell back against it with a sigh. "Finally," she murmured, closing her eyes.

Ric couldn't stop himself. He kissed her. Hard. He pressed her right up against the door and took her mouth with absolutely no finesse, no gentleness, not even caring enough to stop when he tasted blood on her tongue and knew that he'd hurt her. He dug his hands in her hair and squeezed it in his fists, and she made a sound in her throat, and he knew what he was doing, and still he couldn't stop himself. He couldn't do a goddamn thing but pin her against that door and kiss the hell out of her until she squirmed and moaned and he was crazy with want. He knew the very last thing he should do right then was to treat her this way, but he still couldn't stop. He had to touch her and taste her and feel the warmth of her struggling against him and know that she was alive. She made another noise, and finally, *finally,* he forced himself to pull back, but she wouldn't let him.

She wouldn't let him.

Her fingernails dug into his scalp as she pulled his head back down and kissed him just as fiercely as he was kissing her, and he thought he might burst from the joy of it. Then one of her hands disappeared, and he felt it down at his waist, fumbling with his belt, and he wanted to fall to his knees and cry from relief. She knew. Somehow she knew exactly what he needed right then, and she was telling him with her tongue and her teeth and her hands that it was exactly what she needed, too.

The low thump of rap music penetrated the wall beside Sophie's head as she lay on the sofa and stared at the television. They'd started early today. Yesterday, actually. She was pretty sure every one of the guys who lived on either side of her had ditched class all day, because they'd been drunk since before noon. Earlier that evening, she'd heard them wrestling a keg up the stairs, so she knew she was in for a long night.

And if one more wasted idiot hummed a basketball against the wall beside her head, she was going to call the cops.

A hot tear trickled down her cheek, and she wiped it away angrily. What the hell was wrong with her? She didn't know. She wasn't sure when she'd become such an intolerant bitch, but she was seconds away from reaching for the phone.

Um, yeah, this is Sophie Barrett—you know, the girl from the news? I willingly rented a cheap apartment about half a mile from campus, and there seem to be a lot of drunken students living around me. Can someone do something about that? No? Okay, just checking.

Sophie sighed. Friday night. Going on night six alone in her apartment. She watched listlessly as some British special-forces guy mashed beetles and locusts into a patty and ate it for breakfast. On the table in front of her, her phone vibrated for the nth time that day, and for the nth time, she ignored it.

Thum-bump.

She shot off the couch and charged across the room. She didn't have to put up with this. She paid rent here! She had a freaking *job* like a freaking *adult*, and she didn't have to take this shit from anyone, especially not a bunch of spoiled, do-nothing frat boys! She yanked the door open—

And nearly crashed into a giant.

"Hi."

Jonah Macon stood on her doorstep. He wore a brown leather jacket and jeans. No badge—he looked off duty—but still the sight of him panicked her.

"Can I come in?"

His green eyes were solemn, and she hadn't seen them since before that night. *That night.* The only night that mattered anymore. The only night she could think of.

Actually, she had seen them. Jonah's eyes. She just didn't remember clearly, because she'd been so out of it. And then so many other detectives and agents and investigators had come and gone that she'd lost track. Everything had blurred together.

He shifted on his feet and looked uncomfortable and she realized that she hadn't said anything.

"You want to come in?" she asked.

"Is that all right?"

A series of whoops went up from the apartment next door, and he turned to glare.

"Are those guys bothering you?" he asked. "You want, I can go knock some skulls."

"No, it's fine. Come in." She stepped back to let him in and for the first time thought of her appearance. She'd been wearing the same pajamas since Tuesday, which was about how long it had been since she'd had a shower. She put a hand to her tangled hair but somehow couldn't bring herself to care.

Jonah stood beside her sofa, glancing around. A collection of soft-drink cans and pizza boxes littered the coffee table. She tried to remember if she'd eaten anything that day that wasn't junk.

"So." He coughed into his hand. "How's it going?"

"Fine. How's it going with you?"

He looked at her, and there was a spark of understanding between them as they both realized how ridiculous they sounded. Suddenly, she had no energy for pleasantries. She walked over to the couch and sank down beside her chenille nap blanket.

"Sit down," she said.

He glanced around, searching for a spot, and moved a stack of catalogues off her armchair. He sat on the edge of the chair, legs apart, and leaned forward on his elbows.

"I hear you haven't been at work."

Tears sprang into her eyes, and she looked away.

"Are you quitting or just taking some time off?"

She looked at her lap. She picked at a loose thread on the blanket, and the dull thud of bass from her neighbor's stereo surrounded them. She wanted to answer him, but making something up was beyond her.

"How's the head?"

"It's better." She lifted her hand to the bruise there.

The swelling had gone down, but it still felt tender to the touch. He'd hit her with a Maglite. One of those heavy ones. He hit all of them with a Maglite, but usually, he waited until after he'd raped and tortured them.

Her phone vibrated on the table again, and Jonah frowned down at it as the caller ID appeared.

"KVUE News?" He looked at her. "They're still calling you?"

She stared at the phone as the call went to voice mail. She looked at his face and didn't answer. She didn't really want to talk about how the press had been hounding her. She didn't really want to talk about anything. Mainly, she wanted to go to sleep.

"Listen, Sophie." He cleared his throat. "I was wondering—"

"I saw on the news that Jeff Lane hired some hot-shot defense lawyer, and his son's going to get off. Is that true?" Her voice quivered with anger, and she hardly recognized it.

Jonah looked at her. He seemed to be weighing what to say. If he gave her some bullshit answer, she was going to kick him out of there right now.

"He hired an attorney, yes. But as for getting off, I'd say that's pretty impossible."

She stared into his eyes, wanting to believe him, wishing she could. But she didn't trust anyone anymore. She wondered why she ever had.

"We've put together a mountain of evidence," he continued. "Physical evidence. Irrefutable. I don't think he's going anywhere for a very long time. He and his dad and Burleson are all looking at murder charges."

She'd seen that on the news, but it seemed truer now

coming from his lips. Sophie relaxed a little. She looked at her lap again and picked at the blanket.

She felt his gaze on her, but she didn't look up. She should be thanking him right now for saving her life. And she would. She intended to. But she couldn't string the words together at the moment. She didn't know what to say.

He was watching her with concern. God, she must look horrible. She didn't even want to imagine it. He was probably sorry he'd come over.

Why *had* he come over?

She tipped her head to the side and looked at him. "You were wondering something?" She took a deep breath. "Sorry, I interrupted you. I've been kind of . . . scattered lately."

"I was wondering if you had plans tonight."

She stared at him.

"Because if you don't, I wanted to see if you would go out with me."

She kept staring. Then her gazed dropped to her stained, wrinkled, stinky pajamas, and she started laughing. Uncontrollably. She bent forward, clutching her stomach, and laughed until her muscles ached and tears seeped from her eyes.

"You're asking me on a date? Are you serious?"

He smiled slightly.

"Um, no, I have no plans tonight." She dabbed at her eyes. "In case you couldn't tell by my fabulous appearance." She managed to sober up, because he didn't seem to think his question was nearly as funny as she did. "I've been feeling a little antisocial, I guess you'd say. Why? What did you have in mind?"

"I thought we'd go the Gruene Hall and hear some live music. Do you like Patty Griffin?"

Her mouth dropped open.

"The singer?" he clarified.

"I know who Patty Griffin is. God, she's a poet. She's amazing! But we couldn't possibly get tickets—"

"I've got some." He patted his pocket.

"You *have* tickets. Right now?"

"I thought, you know, now's the time. To get back out there."

She stared at him, suddenly understanding what he was trying to do, what he was trying to give her.

He cleared his throat again. "I figure if you let it go too long, it'll be hard for you, you know, down the road, to do the things you like to do, so—" He glanced up at her, and for the millionth time that week, she felt her emotions start to overwhelm her.

She reached over and squeezed his hand. "Thank you," she whispered, and it was the most inadequate thing she'd ever said to anybody, but it was the best she could do.

Maybe he sensed the tears coming, because he glanced at his watch and looked uncomfortable. "Anyway, if you want to go, we should probably get moving, so . . ."

"I definitely want to go." She stood up and smiled. "Give me a minute to change."

Mia stepped off the elevator into the sun-drenched lobby and was surprised to see Sophie standing at the reception desk.

"When did you get here?"

She turned around and smiled as she tucked her purse

into a drawer. "Just a minute ago. Had some catching up to do before Monday."

Mia looked her over for any signs that she was rushing this return to work. She still had a nasty bruise on her temple, but she looked worlds better than she had when Mia dropped in on her two days ago.

"Your bruise is coming along," Mia said with a grimace. "It's an interesting shade of green."

"You should see it without makeup." Sophie glanced around the lobby, and her gaze paused on the new security guard who was subbing for Ralph. "Hey, you have time to come with me to the break room? I could use a caffeine boost."

"Sure," Mia said, not eager to get home. Her exciting plans for that Saturday afternoon included grocery shopping and about four loads of laundry.

Mia eyed the bruise again as they headed down the corridor. "You sure you're ready to be back? You could probably get a little more time off if you need it."

"I'm ready," she said firmly. "If I spend one more day on my couch, I'm going to go nuts."

"I know what you mean." Mia had tried to take Monday off, but she'd ended up driving in after lunch, because she couldn't stand to stay at home when there was nothing wrong with her. Ric hadn't been happy with her decision, but he hadn't pressed.

They reached the break room, and Sophie fed quarters into a vending machine. "So, tell me some news. I feel as if I've been living under a rock. How are you? How's Ric?"

"He's fine." Mia forced a smile, but Sophie instantly saw through it.

"Uh-oh. What's wrong?" Her soft drink clunked down. She retrieved it from the slot, and they sat down at one of the lunch tables.

"It's just, I don't know." Mia shrugged. "I feel like something's missing between us. Like he's holding back."

"Is it the sex? Maybe he's afraid you're kind of fragile after everything that happened."

It definitely wasn't the sex. If anything, he'd been having trouble keeping his hands off her for the past week. Every night, he had come over to her house straight from work, and he'd barely walked in the door before they'd started taking each other's clothes off.

"I guess *that's* not the problem."

Mia glanced up. "Huh?"

"From the look on your face, I can see that sex is not the sticking point. What is it, then?"

"I guess, I don't know, I just wish he'd *talk* to me. Tell me things. I haven't told him I love him yet, but it's getting harder and harder to keep in, and I know it's going to come bursting out of me at some point, because I'm terrible at hiding my feelings."

Sophie smiled gently. "You're in love?"

Mia blew out a sigh. "Yes, and it sucks! Why didn't anyone ever tell me this? I'm a wreck. I can hardly sleep at night, because I'm lying there with his arms around me and realizing that I'm getting way too attached, and he hasn't really committed to anything."

"What is it you want him to commit to?" Sophie asked reasonably. "It's a little early for a marriage proposal, isn't it?"

"Yes. No. I don't know." She shook her head. "I just want something. We're spending all of this time together, and he hasn't even brought over his shaving kit. He's got a toothbrush on my sink. That's it. I'm ready to spend my life with him and bear his children, and he's at the toothbrush stage."

Sophie watched her thoughtfully. "Why don't you talk to him about your feelings?"

"Because he doesn't *talk*! That's the problem. I don't know about his daughter or his family or why his first marriage broke up. I don't know anything."

Sophie got a guilty look on her face.

"What is it?" Mia demanded. "You know something. Tell me."

She cleared her throat. "Well, I heard a rumor about his ex."

"Why didn't you tell me?"

"I figured you knew about her." She looked apologetic. "Sorry, I didn't know it was a big mystery, or I would have said something."

"What is it?"

"Well, this is from Vince. We were talking that night, after you and Ric left the bar? And he mentioned that Ric's wife cheated on him. And not only that, but it was with another cop."

Mia's heart sank. "That's awful." She felt a spurt of anger. "God, how could she do that to him?"

"I don't know."

And then Mia's anger was replaced by frustration. Why hadn't he ever told her that? Was he embarrassed? He must have felt so betrayed. She wished she'd heard this from him, not through the grapevine.

"You seem pretty stressed out about this," Sophie said. "Why don't you talk to him tonight? Clear some of this up."

"I'm not seeing him tonight. It's his weekend with his daughter." She hadn't seen him since Friday morning, when he'd kissed her good-bye at her door and promised to call Sunday night. She'd smiled and watched him go, hoping that he hadn't been able to read on her face how much those few words had hurt her feelings.

Sophie started to say something, but Mia's phone chimed. She took it from her purse.

"Speak of the devil," she muttered, and then answered it. "Hi."

"Hey, you free for lunch?" Ric asked.

"Um, yeah." She checked her watch. "I thought you were tied up all weekend."

"Ava's busy, so I've got a few hours. Meet me in the parking lot. I'm just pulling in."

"How'd you know I'd be here?"

"Lucky guess."

Two minutes later, Mia slid into his pickup and stowed her purse on the floor. He took her arm and dragged her over the console until she was sprawled across his lap. He kissed her hungrily.

When he stopped, she smiled up at him. "Wow, what was that for?"

"Missed you last night."

She settled back into her seat as he backed out of the space.

"Okay if we leave your Jeep?" he asked. "I can bring you back after lunch."

"Sure." She pulled on the seat belt and felt her stress melting away. The sun was bright. The sky was clear. And instead of spending a beautiful afternoon doing laundry, she had a few stolen hours with Ric.

She turned to look at him as they made their way to the highway. They'd spent only one night apart out of the last seven, and she'd missed him much more than she should have.

He glanced at her. "Don't look at me like that if you expect to get lunch."

"Like what?"

"Like you want to come sit in my lap again."

"Not happening. I'm too hungry. Where are we going?"

"To a park." She thought he looked wary now instead of happy. "You okay with sandwiches?"

"Sure."

"Turkey and cheese?"

"Sounds great." She saw a deli bag in the backseat. He'd already been to the store.

"How was work this morning?"

"Fine," she said. "Oh, I was going to call you. We got those results back from Camille Lane's coffee cup."

He gave her a blank look.

"I never told you this, did I? It all happened last Saturday, right before everything else. It totally slipped my mind."

"You sound excited," he said. "Tell me what Camille Lane's coffee cup has to do with anything."

"Mitochondrial DNA. It's passed down through the mother's side."

His eyebrows tipped up.

"I'll spare you the details, but basically, we can show that the blood droplet found on Laura Thorne's shoe is from someone maternally related to Camille Lane. In other words, Kurt Lane fits, but his father doesn't."

"You can tell that?"

"Yes. And I know you already got him to submit a blood sample, but this gives you a sneak preview of what it's going to prove. Odds are very good that it's going to be Kurt Lane's DNA on that shoe."

"Nice work," he said, but he didn't look quite as excited as she'd expected. He looked distracted. Feeling uneasy now, she turned and watched the scenery fly by as they neared San Marcos. They reached one of the parks on the banks of the river, but instead of turning there as she'd expected, he kept driving until they reached a smaller park near the center of town. He pulled into a crowded parking lot and found a space.

Ric grabbed the deli bag, and they got out. Mia stood for a moment, closing her eyes as the sun warmed her cheeks. She stripped off her jacket and tossed it into the pickup. For the first time in weeks, it was warm enough for just a sweater. She felt like her soul was thawing.

The park was packed—families picnicking, kids playing soccer, a few flying kites. A trio of teenage boys darted by, throwing a Frisbee, and Ric picked up her hand and tugged her out of the way.

"Come here." He pulled her under the shade of a giant oak tree and dropped the deli sack onto the grass there.

It was too close to the parking lot to make a good picnic spot, and she looked at him curiously.

He let go of her hand. The grave expression on his face sent a chill through her heart.

"I have something to tell you." He looked at the ground and seemed to be choosing his words.

Mia's throat tightened. Had he brought her there to break up with her?

He met her gaze. "The last few weeks have been pretty tough. The week before this was actually—" He looked down again and rubbed his hand over the back of his neck. "Well, it was miserable. You were spending all that time with Black. You wouldn't talk to me. One of the hardest things I've ever done was drop you off at that guy's house."

She started to say something, but he held up his hand.

"Let me finish." He cleared his throat, and she forced herself to wait. "I was worried about you. The investigation was upside-down. And I was practically climbing the walls with jealousy."

Mia's heart pounded. He picked up her hand, and the impossibly tight knot in her chest loosened.

"But none of that was anything compared with how I felt Saturday, when I was driving out there and I knew someone wanted to hurt you. And when I was looking for you in the dark and I heard you scream, I felt—" He paused. "It was like someone had yanked my heart out, because you needed me and I was too late."

Tears filled her eyes as she looked at him. She laughed suddenly.

"What?"

"Nothing. It's just—" She rubbed her nose, which was running now thanks to what he'd said. "For a man who doesn't say much, you're doing pretty well."

"I am?"

"Yes. Keep going." She swiped the tears off her cheeks.

"Well, that's about it. I wanted you to know. And as soon as you're done crying, there's someone I want you to meet."

Mia froze. "We're not here for a picnic?"

"We are. But then I thought we'd catch Ava's soccer game."

"Right now?" She glanced around, panicked. "Is she here? Oh my gosh! Why didn't you tell me?"

"I'm telling you now. She's over there practicing with her team."

"Ric, I'm a mess! Look at me! What is she going to think?"

He smiled. "She's going to think you're great, like I do." He lifted her hand to his lips and kissed her knuckles. "And she's going to love you, because she loves me, and she knows you make me happy."

"How does she know that?"

"Because I told her."

Mia smiled up at him and gave up holding back the words. "I love you," she said, and her heart lifted, because he didn't look wary anymore. Or even surprised.

"I love you, too." He cupped her face in his hands. "And I want us to be together. I'm not much on painting and cabinets, but I can do other things for you. I think I can make you happy, Mia."

She went up on her toes and kissed him. "You already make me happy."

Turn the page
for a sneak peek at

SNAPPED

the next heart-stopping
Tracers novel
from
2010 RITA Award–winning author

Laura Griffin

Coming soon from Pocket Star Books

Parking on campus was a bitch and so was Sophie. Or at least, she was in a bitchy mood. She was hot, hungry, and doomed to spend the better part of her lunch hour waiting in line at the registrar's office.

But then she spotted it—a gleaming, perfect, gorgeously empty parking space not fifty feet in front of her. The green flag indicating time still left on the parking meter was the cherry on top of her lunchtime sundae.

"Thank you," she sighed, as she rolled past the spot, shifted into reverse and flipped her turn indicator. She started to ease back when an old-model VW zipped up behind her.

"Hey!" Sophie pounded her horn as the Bug driver whipped into her spot while pretending not to see her.

"*Un*believable!" Sophie jabbed at the window button and leaned over to yell at him. "Yo, Fahrvergnügen! That's *my* spot!"

She might as well have been invisible.

A horn blared behind her and she glanced around. Now she was holding up traffic. She shifted into drive and muttered curses as she scoured the busy streets for another scrap of real estate large enough to accommodate her Tahoe. Of course, there wasn't one. She glanced at her watch. Damn it, she was going to be late getting back to work, and she'd long since used up her tardy passes. With a final curse, she pulled into an overpriced parking garage three blocks downhill from her destination. After squeezing into a spot, she jumped out and dashed for the exit, pressing numbers on her cell phone as she went.

"Mia? Hey, it's me." She stepped onto the sidewalk and blinked up at the blindingly bright sunlight.

"What's up, Soph? I've got my hands full."

"Shoot, forget it then." Sophie caught a heel on the pavement as her crappy luck continued.

"What?"

"I'm at the university," Sophie said. "I was going to ask you to cover the phones for a few minutes if I'm not back by one."

"I'll get down there if I can, but—"

"Don't worry, I'll get Diane to cover it." Diane was the assistant evidence clerk at the Delphi Center where Sophie worked, but she wasn't exactly known for her cheery disposition. "She owes me a favor, anyway. We're still on for margaritas with Kelsey, right? Six o'clock?"

"El Patio," Mia confirmed. "See you there."

Sophie dropped the phone in her bag and continued uphill. The sun blazed down. Her blouse grew damp. Her tortured feet reminded her of the folly of buying

Victoria's Secret sandals on clearance from a catalog and expecting them to fit. After waiting for a break in traffic, she darted across the street and felt the heat coming up off the asphalt in waves. Jeez, it was *hot*. Thank goodness she was signing up for a night course. At last, she reached the grassy quadrangle and enjoyed a few patches of shade as she neared the registrar's office. Students streamed up and down the sidewalks, talking with friends and reading text messages. Sophie gazed wistfully at their cut-off shorts and tank tops. Once upon a time she, too, had lived in grunge wear. She didn't miss the clothes so much as that time in her life when she'd had nothing more to do than go to keg parties and cut class to hang out with her boyfriend. Now both those pursuits seemed worse than trivial— they seemed wasteful. How could such a few short years make such a difference in her outlook?

The admin building came into view, and Sophie marveled at the irony. Here she was plunking down her hard-earned money to attend a class she would have happily ditched just a few years ago. The perfect revenge for her "I told you so" parents. Only they'd never get the chance to say that because she had no intention of telling them she was back in school. This was her private mission, and if she failed to accomplish it, no one would ever have to know she'd tried.

Sophie navigated the busy sidewalks, longing for a pair of Birkenstocks instead of heels. She glanced again at her watch and *knew,* without a doubt, she was going to be late.

Crack.

She halted in her tracks.

People shrieked behind her, and she whirled around. Her gaze landed on someone sprawled across the sidewalk. A man. Sophie stared in shock at the jacket, the tie, the bloody pulp that should have been his head.

Crack.

Someone's shooting! The words screamed through her brain, and she scanned her surroundings. She was in an open field. She was a target.

More shrieks as she bolted for the trees. A staccato of bullets. Clumps of grass burst up at her; she fell back, landing hard on her butt. Before her eyes, a woman collapsed to the ground, clutching her throat. A child in pigtails howled. Crab-walking backward, Sophie glanced around frantically. What was happening? Where was it coming from? Screams echoed around her as people ducked and dove for cover.

I'm a target.

She rolled to her knees and lunged for the nearest solid object—a cement block at the base of a statue. She crouched behind it, gasping for breath, every nerve in her body zinging with terror.

Where is he?

More gunfire. More screaming. Sophie cupped her hands over her head and tried to make herself small.

"She *lent* it to you? That's the best you got?" Detective Allison Doyle scowled down at the pimply-faced perpetrator and waited. It didn't take long.

"She didn't say it *exactly*."

"What did she say, exactly?"

"Well, it was more like understood, you know?" The kid slouched against the door to his dorm room. "Like I could use it as long as I wanted, so long as I returned it."

"I see." Allison nodded over his shoulder, looking at the array of loot spread out on his single bed: four iPods, two BlackBerries, and an iPad not even out of the box—which constituted the reason for her little visit to this room that smelled like gym socks and God knew what else.

"What about the iPods?" Allison asked. "You borrow them, too?"

A girl burst into the hallway. "Someone's shooting! Oh my God, people are *dead*!"

Allison yanked out her Glock and rushed down the hall. "Who's shooting? Where?"

"The quad! Someone's *killing people*!"

"Go into your rooms and lock your doors. Now! Stay away from the windows."

Allison raced across the lobby and pushed through the glass door. The heat hit her like the air from a blow dryer. She took an instant to orient herself, then took off for the university quadrangle just as her radio crackled to life.

"Attention all units! Active shooters on campus! South quadrangle!" The usually calm dispatcher sounded shrill, and Allison felt the first twinge of panic. "Reports of casualties. All units respond!"

Allison jerked the radio from her belt. "Doyle responding." *Jesus Christ.* "Where is the shooter? Over."

For a moment, silence. Then a distant wail of sirens on the other side of town. Allison sprinted across University Avenue and did a double take. Cars were stopped in the middle of the road, doors flung open. The engines were running, but the cars were empty.

"Shooter's location is unknown," the dispatcher said. "I repeat, unknown."

Jonah Macon stared at the dilapidated house, where absolutely nothing had happened for the past seven hours. He hated surveillance work, and not just the boredom of it. His six-foot-four-inch frame wasn't designed to be crammed into the back of a van for days on end.

"If I drink another cup of this coffee, my piss is gonna turn black."

He shot Sean Byrne a look of disgust.

"Nice image," Jonah's partner quipped, tossing his empty Styrofoam cup into the trash bin he'd made earlier from an empty Krispy Kreme box. Ric Santos had volunteered to bring breakfast this morning, and the doughnut shop was just around the corner from his girlfriend's place.

So now here they all were—bored, caffeinated, and jacked-up on sugar that needed to be burned off. Jonah leaned back in his seat and popped his knuckles as he stared at the video monitor.

"Seriously, how late can he sleep?" Sean asked. "I'm about to bust in there and drag his skinny ass out here myself."

"Movement at the door," Jonah said, and everyone snapped to attention.

A man stepped onto the porch, finally breaking the monotony. Jonah's team had been there since before dawn, waiting for their subject to kiss his girlfriend good-bye and lead them to the crib where they were ninety-nine percent sure their murder suspect was holed up. Sure enough, they watched on the screen as their subject got some good-bye tongue action before tromping down the rickety front porch steps.

"Think he's stepping out for a paper?" Sean asked.

"I'm not sure he can read." Ric eased out of the bucket seat in back and slid behind the wheel while Jonah reached for his radio to give the team down the block a heads-up.

The phone at Jonah's hip buzzed. Then Ric's phone buzzed. Then a snippet of rap music emanated from Sean's pocket.

Everyone exchanged a grim look as they took out their phones. Jonah answered first.

"Macon."

"Get to campus, ASAP! Where's the SWAT van?"

"Perkin has it," Jonah told his lieutenant. "He's at a training op—"

"Someone's shooting people all over the quad! Get over there and suit up. Grab everyone you can."

Jonah braced himself against the side of the van as Ric peeled away from the curb. From the look on his partner's face, Jonah knew he was getting similar instructions.

"What's your setup?" Lieutenant Reynolds demanded.

Jonah was already leaning over the backseat to do a quick inventory of the cargo space. "Two shotguns, a rifle, and a couple of flash bangs." His pulse started to pound. "How many shooters?"

"We don't know."

"What kind of weapon?"

"We don't know that either. We don't know shit! All I got is a bunch of hysterical nine-one-one calls, someone's gunning down people on the lawn. Some kid just got shot off his bike. ETA?"

Jonah glanced through the tinted windows as a blur of storefronts raced past. "Two minutes, tops."

"Okay, then you're it, Macon. I'm fifteen minutes out. You guys got any Kevlar?"

"Three vests and a flak jacket."

"Take all of it. And call me when you get there."

Crack.

Another burst of cement on the nearby sidewalk. Sophie huddled tighter and looked back at the howling little girl.

"Get *down*!" Sophie shouted.

From the pavement, an arm reached up and tugged weakly at the girl's shorts. The arm was attached to a hugely pregnant woman who was lying in an ever-expanding pool of her own blood.

Dear Lord. Someone had to get them out of here, but there was no one. The campus that had been crawling with students just moments ago was now a ghost town. Sophie darted her gaze around. Where was the shooter? Had he entered a building? Sophie eased up slowly and peered around the base of the bronze statue.

Crack.

An agonized scream behind her. Sophie recoiled. She peeked beneath her quivering elbow and saw a man to her right. He was hunched at the base of a flagpole, clutching his ankle with a bloody hand.

Sophie's gaze was drawn to the corpse behind her, now baking on the hot sidewalk. At the edge of the grass, another man lay sprawled across the ground, a backpack beside him. A student. Her heart jackhammered against her rib cage.

The crying intensified. Sophie glanced at the child again, and she was hunched over her mother, sobbing uncontrollably. She had to be two, maybe three years old. The woman twisted onto her side, probably trying to shield the girl with her body. They were behind a large oak tree, thank goodness. But if the child moved too much—

Crack.

Glass shattered on a building nearby.

Crack. Crack. Crack. One by one, the second-story windows exploded, and she thought of those shooting games at carnivals where the targets were little yellow ducks.

Sirens grew louder as Sophie scoured the rooflines for any sort of movement or muzzle flash. She went from building to building all around the quadrangle, searching the red-tile roofs and the highest row of windows.

Her gaze came to rest on the white limestone monolith that sat atop the hill, overlooking the entire campus like a giant Sphinx.

And suddenly she knew. The gunman was on top of the library.

And from there he could see everything.